RETURN TO BETHEL SPRINGS

Written By

OWEN WILKIE

ACKNOWLEDGMENTS

It doesn't take a village to write a book, but it helps to have others around to assist in the project.

First, I want to thank my wife, Beverly, a retired schoolteacher. Her encouragement and suggestions were invaluable in the creation of this book.

Next, I want to thank my children for their assistance. Matt Wilkie, a minister who leads compassion teams around the world through Convoy of Hope, helped get this book into print. Debbie Wells, a children's pastor, gave me helpful critiques and ideas.

Two other people had a big part. Dr. Laynah Rogers, professor emeritus at Evangel University, gave me additional ideas and helped in the editing. Nathan Reighard, a colleague of mine at the national office of the Assemblies of God, designed the cover and formatted the book for publication. Thanks to all of them.

Thanks especially to the Lord Jesus Christ for salvation and for every good gift in my life, including His inspiration in putting together this novel that I trust will honor Him.

DEDICATION

This book is dedicated to our pastors and church workers. Thanks for all the time, effort, and energy you put into helping lead people into the kingdom of God.

RAYMOND HOUSE
PUBLISHERS

By the same author:
Another Mt. Moriah
available on Amazon.com and Owenwilkie.com

CHAPTER 1

The white-haired man pulled his late model Ford sedan into an open parking space, put the car in park, and took out the keys. With a slight smile he turned to the passenger seat and opened his mouth to speak. Then he frowned, shook his head, cleared his throat and got out of the car, pocketing his keys, not bothering to lock the doors.

Bethel Springs, Missouri. Back to many pleasant memories. Good times. Happy times. Yet, back to one frightening event that he relived in his mind almost every day.

The town square had changed considerably since he had left in such a hurry nearly fifty years ago. There were fewer trees, more grass and more playground equipment. The stone library making up the center of the square was gone, replaced by a swimming pool full of laughing, shouting children cooling off on this hot, sultry June day in the Ozarks. Some of the buildings surrounding the streets across from the square were still standing, but a few had been replaced by newer, more modern structures.

Dressed in gray slacks with a light blue short-sleeve shirt, he began walking along the sidewalk that bordered the town square. His shoulders drooped a little with age and his clear blue eyes were partially hidden behind a pair of steel-framed glasses, but his quick steps and warm smile combined with an almost full head of snow-white hair made him appear younger than his seventy-one years.

A mother with her baby in a stroller came toward him. Fifty years ago she would have smiled and said, "Hi, Pastor Paul. How are you today?" and paused to chat for a few moments. But today she barely glanced his way as she passed.

At the southwest corner of the square he came upon a metal bench in the shade of a towering oak tree. Sitting down he pulled out his cell phone and scrolled down to a name which he tapped. "Trey," he said when he heard a familiar voice at the other end. "I'm here. In Bethel Springs. In the town square. It's changed a lot. Feels strange being back. Nostalgic in some ways, good in some ways, scary in other ways. I'll find a hotel or motel and stay here for however long it takes. I hope I can find your answer."

"Glad you made it, Grandpa."

The white-haired man smiled, picturing his 21-year old grandson probably speaking to him from his dorm room at Fuller Theological Seminary in Pasadena, California, or maybe at the seminary bookstore where he worked part-time.

Called Trey since birth because he was named Paul Andrew Whitfield the third. A shade over six feet tall, slim, wavy blond hair, engaging smile—good-looking according to his female admirers. A lot like he himself had looked, he reflected, when he came to Bethel Springs at the same age. "Any news yet?" the voice over the phone asked.

The white-haired man shook his head. "I just got here. Hopefully, I can find out soon. But the fire was 47 years ago. Who would remember it now?"

"As you know, Grandpa," the voice on the phone continued, "after I wanted to ask Rachel to marry me, like a respectful future son-in-law, I asked her dad first. He approved and said I had his blessing." Trey paused and gave an embarrassed laugh. "Rachel told me her dad was pleased to have me as his son-in-law. Said I was a 'gem of a fellow'."

Then Trey paused again. "But, like I also told you, when he found out who my grandfather was—you—he went ballistic. He said he would never let his daughter marry the grandson of the arsonist who had burned down his father's church. You could tell he was still angry, even after all these years. He quoted that bit in the Bible about punishing the children for the sins of their fathers to the third and fourth generation." Trey cleared his throat. "I told him every way I could think of that even though some people blamed you, no one ever had any proof. It was all rumor, of course. Not true. There was no way you would have burned down anything, certainly not a church."

"And," Paul Whitfield senior looked around him to make sure no one was near enough to hear him talk and continued the conversation, "you volunteered me to return to Bethel Springs and find the person who burned down the other church in town, or at least prove I hadn't done it so you can get married." He gave a short laugh. "I'm here. I will try. I do believe in miracles, but this a stretch."

"You need to really try," Trey pleaded. "When Rachel's mom found out who you were, she said right then and there that Rachel couldn't marry me. With her mother it's all about image. Her family's. Rachel's. When I told them you would return to Bethel Springs to try and find out who the real arsonist was, her dad said he would give us until a week before the wedding. That's in less than three weeks. We are supposed to get married a month from yesterday.

"He said if you can't prove your innocence by then, he's canceling the wedding. He figured that would give the out-of-town people time to change their plans about coming. A tough guy when he wants to be.

"Rachel's always been an obedient daughter so is having a tough time with this. She's on my side and unhappy with her parents. We discussed eloping and getting it over with, but then we both agreed that's a bad way to start a marriage. I love Rachel but like you and Dad have said over and over, you marry a family. It would be tough to have in-laws that would forever be upset with me because I had married their only daughter over their objections."

Trey pleaded again, "Please do what you can to get to the bottom of what really happened. Please find the person who did it to get you—and me—off the hook. I love Rachel and don't want to lose her."

"I will try, son," the senior Paul said. "I will really try. And I'll pray and ask God's direction."

"By the way, how are you doing without Grandma?"

"I eat out mostly. But I have learned how to make a mean plate of beans and cornbread. I'm working on biscuits and gravy. Salads not so much. But she should be back in time for your wedding and before I lose too much weight."

"Sounds good. Love you, Grandpa."

"Love you, too. Talk to you later." With a sigh, he put his cell phone back in his pocket.

Reaching into his brown leather portfolio, he took out a worn spiral notebook with a blue cover. Adjusting his glasses he opened the notebook and turned to the first page filled with his well-worn handwritten journal. As he began reading his mind returned to fifty years ago.

1955   **CHAPTER 2**

Paul Whitfield arrived on a steamy June day in nineteen fifty-five. He arrived in two ways. The drive from Springfield, Missouri, to the church he came to pastor in Bethel Springs took just over two hours in his wheezy black nineteen thirty-nine De Soto.

But it really took fourteen years to get here. Ever since that memorial service for his chaplain father, he had vowed to the Lord and to his mother to follow his father into the ministry to preach the gospel, to lead people to faith in Christ, to help change people's lives. Today he fulfilled that vow. He was now in the ministry. A pastor, Pastor Whitfield. Or should he have his flock call him Pastor Paul? Or just Pastor? Or just Paul as he was used to being called?

His drive to Bethel Springs had proved uneventful, except for the unusually hot weather for this time of year. Even with his windows rolled down and his car fan on high, perspiration rolled down Paul's face as he drove by farms, woods, and an occasional country store on winding two-lane Highway 13. Then the houses suddenly bunched closer together, and he rounded a curve and came to a white sign with black letters reading "Bethel Springs, population 512."

He passed stores and other larger buildings with signs out in front: "Harvey's Grocery Store, "Sally's Diner," and "Elven's Auto Shop." He passed people walking on the sidewalk. Cars were parked on both sides of the narrow streets. A typical Midwest town, he told himself. But it was now his town. He would win Bethel Springs for Jesus, or at least a good portion of the population. He hoped. He dreamed.

The church had been without a pastor for five months. They had tried to hire an experienced pastor. When none would come, the church contacted Zion Bible College to see whether they had any graduating students who would be interested in pastoring their church. They were willing to try a new pastor for a year.

Following the directions on the sheet of paper from Professor McFee, he turned left one block past the town square on Cedar Street, went one more block and there it stood on the right side of the paved street with a sidewalk out in front, in the long row of wooden buildings.

The church wasn't much, he decided as he parked the car, got out, and stood on the sidewalk staring at the building. It was something called by many a storefront church. A faded brown wooden door stood in the center with large windows on either side. A stenciled sign in white letters painted on the left window read, "Community Chapel." Looking up, he saw a large upstairs window where Fred Pittman, the head deacon, told him by telephone, he would live.

Several cars drove slowly by and a few people passed with curious stares, some with friendly smiles and hellos. He returned the greetings, wondering if they were parishioners or soon would be.

Excitement filled him, then ambivalence. That was a word Paul Whitfield learned his first year at Bible school and that is how he now felt. He couldn't remember ever feeling so excited. Or so scared. The deep seated doubts he had about himself bubbled up. Just because he had a Bible school degree, did that qualify him to be a pastor? Could he handle being a spiritual shepherd to people? Could he handle the pressure, the problems, the people? Well, he would try. He took a deep breath and said a silent prayer. With the Lord's help he could do it. He would do it. He would be a success.

Bethel Springs. This was his first time in town. But the name sounded good. A biblical name. Bethel meant "house of God," according to his Bible school notes. It was in Bethel where Jacob had his dream of a stairway reaching to heaven where the Lord told him that all people of the earth would be blessed through his descendants. He hoped he could hear the voice of the Lord giving him promises of a fulfilling future as well. Although, he also remembered studying that Bethel in future years became the center of some kind of sinful behavior; he couldn't recall what it was. He would have to check again.

But, he was here now. This was his town, his place of ministry. He expected to find kind, homey, friendly folks. A good town to live in. Now that he was here he hoped he was right.

Frieda Thornton was to meet him at two o'clock. Since he was fifteen minutes early, he walked up and down the block on both sides of the street, looking over his new neighborhood. Five buildings lined his side of the block. On the corner to his right stood Stan's Hardware. His storefront church was next. To his left was Dolly's Clothing Boutique. The next building had a sign out front, "Featherstone Shoes." Then, Paul wrinkled his nose. On the corner, just three buildings down, the black and white sign on the door read "Zeb's Bar and Grill." To the right of the words was a drawing of a glass of foamy beer. To the left of the words was a drawing of a scantily clad woman. "So close to a church," Paul heard himself saying out loud.

Suddenly the church door swung open with a bang. A rather large lady of about 60 in a shapeless blue dress with her gray hair tied up in a bun stood facing him. "Pastor? Pastor Paul Whitfield?" The tone of her shrill voice sounded more like a command than a question.

Hurrying back to the church from a quarter of a block away he gave the woman what he hoped was a friendly smile. "Yes. That's me." Hearing someone actually call him pastor for the first time sent a thrill up his spine. Frieda Thornton, surely one of the pillars of the church. "Glad to meet you, Sister Thornton." He extended his hand, and she returned his handshake.

The woman's hand felt limp and damp. "Frieda. Everyone calls me Frieda. I don't go for this 'sister' business." Frieda spoke louder than necessary to her one person audience, as if a turned up volume implied authority.

"Frieda it is." Paul kept the smile plastered on his face as he released Frieda's hand and unconsciously wiped it on his tan corduroy slacks as he followed her into the building. "Thank you for coming to show me around. I really appreciate it."

"Well, someone had to. Fred Pittman, the head deacon, I guess you would call him, had to work, so he asked me to come. Hope you do better than the last preacher. He chickened out and skipped town."

"I heard there were some problems." Paul tried to remain neutral, remembering all that Professor McFee had told him.

"At least you don't have a family with kids that might get their legs broke. You married?"

"No, ma'am."

"Either married or not married is okay by me. But just behave yourself with these country girls. They aren't like the city girls you are used to. You need to treat them with respect, you hear." Through the open door, Paul realized her words were clearly audible to the young couple just walking by.

Paul nodded. "Yes, ma'am," he answered gravely, revising his opinion about Frieda, wondering if she was one of the troublemakers Dr. McFee had told him hovered about in some churches.

Frieda started down the aisle, her shoes making a pronounced thump on the wooden floor. "Let me show you around for a short spell."

Paul closed the door and started to follow when Frieda said sharply, "We leave the door open in the summer to stir the breeze through the church."

Paul nodded and obediently reopened the door. He could see why. Or feel why. The expression "hot as an oven" came to him as he felt perspiration appear on his body. Breathing was difficult. Didn't the church have better ventilation? Then he noticed two fans on the other end of the building in front of the platform facing in his direction. When turned on they would, no doubt, help.

Following her down the hall he noticed four single light bulbs illuminated the room, hanging down from what was probably a ten-foot white ceiling. He judged the building to be about thirty feet wide and sixty feet deep. He counted ten benches on both sides of the hall with an aisle down the middle.

A wooden platform about eight feet square and about six inches off the floor stood at the far end. A simple wooden pulpit graced the front of the platform with two folding chairs against the back wall next to the door that led outside to what he later found was the alley behind the church. A black upright piano sat against the right wall with a folding chair for a piano bench. An oil furnace stood on the left side of the back door with a stovepipe curving into the back wall.

"This is it. Probably wasn't what you all expected." Frieda's tone of voice indicated she didn't think it was much either. Paul, comparing this to the stained glass, carpeted church in Springfield he had attended for many years with his mother, silently agreed. Yet, this was his church, at least for a year. And it looked beautiful in many ways—at least to him. Tomorrow, Sunday, the pews would be filled with people—his congregation. He would preach to them and they would respond. It was the start of a great life.

His reflecting was cut short by Frieda. "Used to be about full," continued Frieda, "until Pastor Charlie got too prickly in his preaching and they ran him out of town. Now, not that many come."

Two windows behind the platform stood open, and Paul felt a brief stirring of breeze against his hot skin as he approached. The sweat by now was sticking to his clothing in the oppressive heat of the building, much hotter than the temperature on his drive.

"A lot of potential here," responded Paul looking away from Frieda, pulling out a quote he remembered Professor McFee saying on several occasions. The first pangs of uncertainty hit him. Could he really do something here? Could he build up the congregation? Or would the pressure get to him and he be forced to leave too? Would the church die on him and close down as he knew sometimes happens?

"That's all there is downstairs." Frieda cut into his thoughts. "Let's go upstairs." She led him up the wooden steps located on the left side of the room near the back door with a two-by-four wooden hand railing. Paul followed Frieda, realizing he was about to see his new home.

"You should have enough room up here, seeing you're alone and without a family," commented Frieda when she reached the top.

Paul surveyed the second floor of the building. One big open space, as was the first floor, except for a small room with a closed door on the left side against the front wall, which must be the bathroom. A small sink and counter stood on the right wall at the front of the room with two small cupboards above the sink. A two-burner electric stove sat to the left of the sink. Pushing open the door of the bathroom, he noted the sink, toilet, and small shower stall. "Church folks use the bathroom during the service, so you best keep it clean," Frieda instructed him, her voice filling the empty space. "Try and keep the kitchen part clean. And don't fry bacon or anything else that smells on Sundays or Wednesday nights. The odor will make the folks hungry."

Toward the back of the room facing the alley they came to the living space. "The last pastor left some furniture," Frieda commented as Paul noted a double bed with a brass frame, a dresser and a closet. She pointed to a large window in the center of the back wall. "Cooler up here," noted Frieda. "You're above the street and higher than many of the buildings around here, so if you open both front and back windows you get more breeze." She stood in the middle of the large room, her hands on her hips facing Paul. "Well, what do you think?"

Was her mouth curved in a smirk or a smile? Paul wondered. He thought of his home he had just left this morning. His mother's cooking, their carpeted home with wallpaper on the walls and a lawn in front with a fenced-in backyard.

"This is great, Frieda. I will do just fine." The frozen smile was back in place. Raising his chin, he looked beyond Frieda. "The Lord and I. We will do just fine."

After Frieda left he sat on the bed with a worn, stained mattress and mopped his forehead with the back of his hand as he vividly remembered the conversation in Donald McFee's office. The college was housed in a dozen wooden barracks of a former army hospital on a main street going through Springfield. Professor McFee had his office in an old operating room. Rumor had it that the wall-to-wall linoleum covered splatters of blood on the wooden floor. McFee had called him in after class one day and Paul sat in the upright wooden chair across from his metal desk with a degree of apprehension. He was to graduate in two weeks and hoped nothing would hold it up.

"Ever heard of Bethel Springs?"

Paul nodded. "I think I have. Isn't that somewhere south of here?"

"Yes, about two hours drive from here. Several miles south of Branson."

"There's a church in that small town looking for a pastor. The last pastor by the name of Charlie Meredith was doing pretty good for a couple of years. The church was running about fifty, sixty, sometimes more. Then he faced some opposition with some of the people in town. I'm not quite sure what it was. Soon after that his eight-year-old son got hit by a car while riding his bicycle and got a broken leg and other injuries. Charlie thought someone was out to get him. He and his family left town shortly after that. After their departure, which was about five months ago, attendance really dropped. But there's potential. Every church has potential with the right pastor. You can build it back up." Dr. McFee paused and looked Paul in the eye. "The church is a little gun shy of pastors, as you can imagine. But they said they would take a pastor on a trial basis for a year. Interested?"

"Maybe. Let me pray about it. Can I let you know tomorrow?"

"Sure. I wouldn't expect you to do anything less." Professor McFee cleared his throat and leaned back in his chair. "Paul, as with all students, I have had a chance to observe you during the three years you have attended here. You are a good student, good grades and you've stayed out of trouble for the most part. You have a good foundation in biblical knowledge. You are a good preacher. I could say that about most of the ministerial students here. But you have two attributes that you have going for you that I believe will enhance your ministry.

"First, you are constant. You don't quit. I have noticed when you start on a project, you see it through. I'm sure you remember the six a.m. prayer meetings you started in your dorm your second year. At first, only one or two or sometimes no one came. But you kept at it. Today, that's one of the most well attended and dynamic events of the week for several of the students. And you and other students started Sunday schools in Battlefield, Mountain Grove and Nixa. I understand you have leaders in place for these Sunday schools to carry on after you are gone. Wouldn't surprise me if they don't become full-fledged churches soon.

"Second, I've observed you love people. You show a deep compassion for them. You look at each person as a valuable treasure. Along with that, you are an encourager to everyone you come in contact with. Your roommate, George Bates, one of the students in my Prison Epistles class, has told me several times how you have encouraged him and helped him with his lack of self esteem. You befriended Tatum Washington, the only Negro in school. You have been an encouragement to Thad Baker who stutters, and with Peter Johnson who gets around in a wheelchair. Everyone to you is your friend, and you see potential in each one. If you keep this up, you will be a success in the ministry or whatever you do in life.

CHAPTER 3

Twenty minutes after Frieda left, Paul stood in the middle of the second floor of the church, his new home, having brought up two suitcases, a duffel bag with towels, washcloths, bedding, his record player, a cardboard box half filled with 78 rpm records, his guitar, accordion, trumpet, and three other cardboard boxes of books and assorted items his mother said he needed to set up house. He regretted he didn't have enough room to bring his chess sets from around the world, his favorite mementos from his father.

Still shaken by the visit from one of his flock, he surveyed the scene. "Lord, I need an encouraging word from you," he said out loud. "Like now."

He waited a moment as if expecting a heavenly voice to boom down words of support and inspiration. When none came, he continued out loud, "What am I doing here? Alone in this rundown storefront building of this little itty bitty church, following a pastor who ran away from his responsibilities. Is this really where you want me?"

Still no answer came. The flies kept on buzzing in and out of the window facing the street. *I need to get screens,* he told himself. The sound of a car driving by on the street below and voices of people on the sidewalk made him feel lonely. Perspiration dripped off the end of his nose and ran down his forehead into his eyes. He remembered Mr. Pember, his fourth grade Sunday school teacher, telling the class that God made eyebrows to keep the sweat from getting into our eyes. It didn't work very well this time, he concluded, as he rummaged through his boxes, found a washcloth, soaked it in cold water from the sink in the kitchen area, and ran it across his face.

A decidedly musty smell complemented the flies and heat. He pushed open the rear window at the back of his apartment and immediately the breeze flowing through the building helped dissipate the odor and some of the heat. The view behind his apartment was depressing: just the weather-beaten back of buildings across the alley. Blue sky above the structures was the only scenery he saw.

Then he made his way toward the window in the front of his home and looked at the street below. Saturday afternoon on a hot summer day with not much going on. Then his eyes swept past the downtown area, and he noticed a small hill to the northwest that rose above the town. On top of the hill among the trees he could barely see a large, stone building with a wooden steeple. There's the other church in town, he realized. Beside it stood a house, also made of stone, probably the parsonage.

An almost overwhelming feeling of jealousy touched his heart. *Why couldn't I have been elected to that church?* he asked himself somewhat bitterly as he gazed at the view.

At the young age of seven, when his father died, he determined to follow in his father's footsteps and become a Navy chaplain. Black was the day when at age eighteen, a doctor told him that because of a heart murmur he would never be allowed in the Navy nor any other military unit.

For weeks he grieved over his dilemma and asked his mother why God had allowed his dreams of ministering as a military chaplain to be shattered in this way. Then Pastor Watson called him aside one Sunday night after church. "You want to be a chaplain, but you can't be. Did you ever consider becoming a pastor? Or evangelist? Or missionary? Or Bible school teacher? You wouldn't be ministering only to sailors. You would be ministering to people of all types, probably including sailors. God loves them all just as much. After all, the world is the mission field.

"Just a few years ago, many people were missionaries in China, Japan, India, and other nations. The war made some of them leave and go elsewhere to places where they could travel with relative safety. Some went to South America, Central America, even the United States. I have a friend, Reverend Stanley Jacobson, who had to flee China. He is now a missionary among the Yakima Indians in Washington State and happy as a clam."

About two o'clock the next morning, after spending a restless night in bed, Paul finally gave in to what he felt was the Lord's direction. "Okay, Lord," he said out loud as he stared at the dark ceiling above him in the bedroom where he had lived since he was a small boy. "I'll go where you want me to go. I'll be what you want me to be. If it's not on a ship sailing around the world, I'll be happy—or try to be—even if it's next door. Or wherever."

Now here he was, not quite next door, but pretty close. He stared out the window at the church on the hill, then back down to the quiet, steamy street below.

"Lord, help me be the best pastor I can be here," he prayed "for as long as you want me to stay here. Help this to be the start of a long, successful ministry career."

The heat, the flies, the loneliness finally got to him. He had noticed a library on his drive in. Along with his ministerial books, he enjoyed reading fiction. His favorite author was Zane Grey. He had several of this western writer's books at home but didn't have room to bring any fiction on this trip. Maybe the library would have some.

Combing his hair again and wiping the perspiration from his face, he looked himself over in the mirror. His deep blue eyes topped by his ivy league cut blond hair stared back at him. More than one fellow student had told him he looked like Billy Graham, that famous young evangelist who had just returned from England. Changing into a pair of brown dungaree pants and a beige Dacron shirt, he made his way down the stairs, out the front door, and walked the few blocks to the city square.

The Bethel Springs Library stood in the center of the town square, a stern gray stone building with a red sloping roof. Paul climbed the stone steps and made his way inside the rather small structure lined with rows of shelves stacked with books. Straight in front of him seated at the desk that read "Information" sat the most beautiful girl he had ever seen. Golden hair adorned her head like a halo. Her porcelain clear skin with a Michelangelo-like sculptured face reminded him of a Hollywood movie star. His heart stopped beating and he had a hard time breathing. Then she looked up at him and smiled. Her warm smile with her dazzling white teeth and the deepest blue-violet eyes he had ever seen lit up the whole room. "Good morning, may I help you?"

He glided toward her desk, unable to speak.

He looked at her name plate which read "Patsy Lundquist," so she couldn't be a movie star, at least not one he had ever heard about.

"May I help you?" she asked again, the smile still in place.

"I'm sorry." Paul cleared his throat. "I thought you looked like someone I know, or sort of know. But I see by your name, you're not."

Patsy Lundquist stood and extended her hand. "I don't believe we've met. Are you new in town?"

Paul, seldom at a loss for words, reaching for her hand, just stared at her for what seemed an eternity. Why was someone so beautiful working in a library at Bethel Springs? She should be on stage, in the movies, or at least in some fashion magazine.

The timbre of her voice was pleasing, not too high pitched or too low, just right.

"Y-y-yes, I-I-I am new in town," he finally stuttered. Her liquid velvety eyes with shiny green flecks mesmerized him, and he couldn't think straight. Couldn't even think at all. To get his mind back in focus, he looked away from her and looked down at her nameplate instead. He said, "My name is Patsy Lundquist."

"Now, that's a coincidence." Her laugh reminded him of the ringing of chimes. "That's my name too."

Good grief. Had he just said what he thought he had said? Paul could feel his face burning and knew it must be beat red. What a way for a pastor to make a debut. Or anybody, for that matter. "I-I-I'm sorry." He closed his eyes to keep his mind from spinning. When he opened them, he concentrated on looking beyond the top of her head to avoid looking at her eyes. Actually, my name is Paul Whitfield. I'm the new pastor at Community Chapel. I was just reading your name plate. Sorry about that."

"Oh, really? Nice to meet you."

He suddenly realized he was still holding her hand. Warm, soft, long, shiny red nails—he held it for too long. No ring on the third finger of her left hand, or any rings on any fingers, he observed. She didn't pull it away, and actually smiled again as she became aware of his admiring gaze. Later he couldn't determine if it was a tolerating smile or an accepting smile.

Finally she let go of his hand and sat back down. "I get that reaction from new people sometimes." She laughed again. "I think people expect librarians to be little old ladies with their hair in a bun and glasses on the end of their nose. Sorry I don't fit the stereotype. But, anyway, welcome. How long you been in town?"

Paul looked at his watch. "Two hours."

He grinned, suddenly feeling more relaxed. He breathed normally for the first time since he'd been in the library. Maybe Bethel Springs wouldn't be so bad after all. In fact, he might even learn to enjoy this town.

"Well, I hope you like it here. But you came to look at books." She smoothed out her yellow pleated dress and cleared her throat. "May I help you find something?" Her voice became businesslike, quiet, so as if not to bother others, even though they were the only people in the building. Paul wasn't sure if that was a brushoff or just her way of getting back to doing her job.

"Yes, as a matter of fact. I..." and he paused. He had started to tell her he wanted to check out a couple of Zane Grey books. But, he was a pastor. Did he want her first impression of him to be that he liked to read cowboy books? "Where's your religious section?" he asked instead.

"We follow the Dewey Decimal System, so that would put the religious books in the 200 section." She pointed a slim hand with her perfect red nails to a row of shelves behind her.

"Thank you." Reluctantly, Paul turned and made his way toward the books she had pointed to, walking by the fiction section. He recognized books by Zane Grey, Owen Wister and other western authors. Gritting his teeth he passed by them to the religion section. He usually loved reading religious books. But not today. He wanted to relax and escape for a few minutes tonight back into a world of make believe.

Instead, after examining some of the books, he picked Andrew Murray's book *Abide in Christ*, and a small book by someone called Brother Lawrence titled *The Practice of the Presence of God*.

After Paul filled out a library card she said, "These will be due back in three weeks." Then she smiled her heart-melting smile again. "I'm sure I'll see you again."

"Yes, I'm sure.

"You know," he continued, not willing to leave so soon, "do you realize the important job you have? This is a small town a couple hours away from a city of any size. I bet most kids, and even most adults, don't often get away and see much of the rest of the world. But in a library, with all these books…" he swept his arm around the room. "I remember the first time my mother took me to a library in Springfield. I must have been five or six. I got to choose three books. One of the books contained short stories from different countries. When my mother read me that book, it opened up new horizons for me. I realized then that reading was entertaining and fun and that I could learn at the same time; I could travel with my books around the world and be anywhere at anytime in history. I never looked back." He smiled at Patsy as he tapped the books he was holding. "I've been an avid reader ever since and have learned so much from books. And you, with this great job of yours, have the awesome privilege and great opportunity to get into the hands of the children and even adults here in Bethel Springs all these wonderful books in your library full of information and fun and adventure that can open up new worlds for them."

As Patsy watched Paul walk out the door, she smiled to herself. She knew she was attractive and was accustomed to having an affect on young men, and men of all ages, although most not reacting as foolishly as Paul. As a cheerleader since junior high and high school, she was the prettiest girl in school. Both her junior and senior years, she was chosen as prom queen. It didn't hurt that her dad was the richest man in Bethel Springs with his shoe factories in the South and Midwest. With all this going on for her she was able to get her pick of boyfriends from the most popular and handsome boys in school.

Secretly she liked the attention and always tried to look her best, especially after she got her job as librarian at the public library last year. She had always considered her attractiveness as her main asset in life and thought of her position in the library as mostly just a job to earn money. Yet Paul had just brought up a dimension she had never considered. She reflected last week how Peggy Dunbar, a young girl whose father owned the local dairy, brought back a book she had checked out on animals and excitedly told Patsy all she had learned about her daddy's cows. And Larry Amundson, a junior high boy who lived down the street from her, had checked out a book on magic several weeks ago. Then last week he came in and showed her several magic tricks he had learned. Maybe her job was of value, as Paul had said. She sat up a little straighter in her chair and smiled as Penny Jackson walked through the door with her two children, followed by Sandra Smith with four children. They had come just in time to watch the Mickey Mouse Club on the television she had set up in a side room.

Paul didn't go straight home. Walking back to the church he dropped off his books, climbed into his De Soto, and took off down the street he didn't care where; he just wanted to drive somewhere away from Bethel Springs for awhile to clear his head.

He didn't realize where he was going until he climbed a small hill and passed the familiar stone church he had seen from his window. Up close, the stone building was larger and more imposing than he had thought as he looked at it from his apartment far below. It was tall with a peaked roof of cedar shingles and a white steeple pointing to the sky with a cross on top. Three huge stained glass windows on each side of the building displayed colorful images of Jesus and various saints he couldn't identify. The hand-carved front door featured baby Jesus, Mary and Joseph in a manger scene, all with halos about their heads. Above the door was another hand-carved wooden sign that read: "Blessed all who enter here."

"Hope Fellowship Church," he read out loud, looking at a large white sign on the lawn in front of the church. "Pastor David Gannon." Then a schedule of services was listed.

The lawn was perfectly groomed with trimmed shrubs on both sides of the church with a smooth graveled driveway and parking lot in front. To the left of the church stood the two-story parsonage made of identical stones— larger than his pastor's parsonage in Springfield.

Paul drove by slowly. Three cars sat in the driveway of the church and two by the house.

Without stopping he turned around in the parking lot and drove back down the hill, made his way out of town, wound through forests, farmland with houses and barns and silos dotting the countryside, thinking and praying and asking God to use him and give him the right attitude about his work here.

Three hours later he returned, parked in front of the church, and made his way into the hot, musty hall. A new smell hit him: the delicious aroma of fried chicken. Just inside the front door someone had left in a paper sack a plate filled with three pieces of fried chicken, a bowl of grits, and an apple. Inside the sack a scrawled note read: "When finished leave the plate on the back steps of the church." The note was unsigned. Beside the sack was a gallon of fresh milk in a glass bottle with about an inch of rich cream on top.

Having forgotten to buy any groceries, he gratefully took the food upstairs and ate the whole meal plus drank a glass of milk. Opening his small refrigerator he put the rest of the milk away, cleaned up his trash, deposited it to the trash can in the alley behind the church, dutifully leaving the washed plate outside the back door.

Back upstairs in his new home he lay on his bed to relax. Alone. He wasn't used to being alone. At home he always had his mother. In college, he had his roommate plus other friends. Here he was alone. Really alone.

He looked at his watch. Nearing bed time, he took out his notes to review for his sermons the next day. He had decided to preach a new message on Sunday morning about the name of the town. In the evening service he would preach a message he had given in homiletics class in Bible school since he already had it almost memorized.

After going through his notes he got out his journal, recorded the events of the day, turned out the lights, and tried to go to sleep as he contemplated what the next day would hold, his first Sunday as a pastor.

1955   CHAPTER 4

Flies buzzing around his ears woke Paul at six-thirty on his first Sunday in Bethel Springs on that June day in nineteen fifty-five.

Covering his head with his pillow he tried to go back to sleep. But, with his stomach tied up in knots, mentally going through his sermons, he had been awake half the night wondering how his first Sunday would turn out. He envisioned several scenarios—not all of them good. He was awake and realized he would stay that way.

Five minutes later he threw off the covers, jumped in the shower, then carefully put on his dark blue rayon suit, white shirt with a button down collar and black, narrow tie. He examined himself in the cracked mirror in the bathroom. Too young and too scared looking, he told himself as he slowly shook his head. How would the congregation react to a single young preacher barely out of Bible school and obviously a novice when it came to preaching and every other pastoral church duty?

"But, you called me here," he reminded the Lord out loud. "And through You I can do all things. Even pastor this church." I hope, he added silently.

With a nod to himself in the mirror, he removed his coat and tie since he was already starting to perspire in the morning heat.

Going downstairs to the hall he opened the front and back doors for ventilation. Placing the songbooks along the benches, he silently prayed for the people who would come: his congregation. Assuming someone would come.

When he was finished he looked at his watch. Seven-thirty. Sunday school started at nine forty-five. Remembering he hadn't purchased any food yet, he decided to walk the two blocks to the restaurant he had seen earlier.

Only two people passed him on the almost silent streets at that time on Sunday morning. A breeze gently blew across his face, already warm and muggy, portending the coming heat on its way. He hoped the restaurant was open and was relieved to see the lights on and people inside. A white sign at the top of the building read: "Martha's Café."

He opened the door located at the center of the building and stepped inside. There were about a dozen square tables in the restaurant with white cloth tablecloths and four chairs around each table. Four large windows facing the street were already open in an effort to stir up a breeze in preparation for the coming heat. Two large fans sitting on metal stands on either side of the room circulated cooling air around the room. Several framed pictures of scenic places in the Ozarks hung on the pale yellow walls. A pair of black louvered café doors led into the kitchen on the left side of the room, with a white door on the right side marked "Restroom."

Sitting down at the table in the far left corner nearest the street, he surveyed the diner. On the other side of the room he saw an older man dressed in farmer-type overalls with his wife in a flowered dress. At the table beside them sat a young couple with an infant in a high chair dressed as if they were ready for church. Near the door a group of four men dressed in suits and ties were eating two tables from Paul.

"Welcome to Martha's Café," came a cheery voice. Turning toward the speaker, he saw a young woman with a red and white checkered apron over her knee-length blue uniform.

Handing him a worn menu she continued, "My name is Laura. Glad to have you eating with us this morning. Just passing through or new in town?"

Paul glanced up at the waitress. She was tall, slim, probably in her early twenties with a head full of dark wavy hair tied back in a pony tail, an attractive face behind her dimpled, wide smile.

"New," he replied. "Just moved in yesterday."

"Welcome to our small town. Hope you like it. Want to start off with coffee, or tea, or water?"

"Coffee will be fine." He glanced at the menu. "I see you have eggs, hash browns and toast. I think I'll take that."

Paul's eyes followed her as she walked back toward the kitchen through the louvered doors, wondering if all the girls in Bethel Springs were as attractive as the first two he had met. She glanced back at him just before she entered the kitchen and their eyes met for a few moments.

Embarrassed, Paul looked back down to his menu.

When the waitress returned with his food, Paul decided to continue the practice he and other students had started while in Bible school. He looked up at her. "Just before I pray silently thanking the Lord for the food as I always do, I usually ask the waitress if she would like prayer for a need she may have." He smiled up at her, noticing her perfect white teeth, flawless complexion and flexes of gold in her large brown eyes. "Is there anything you would like me to pray about?"

Paul was always fascinated by the responses he had gotten. Some waitresses had turned away without answering, others had told him no, while others had gratefully shared a need in their lives. Laura stared at Paul for so long he thought she wasn't going to answer. Finally she said, "My mother. I'm afraid she's getting sick. She won't admit it or go to a doctor. But she's losing weight and has had a bad cough for some time."

"What's her name?"

"Mildred."

"Thank you. I'll pray silently for Mildred right now and every time I think of her for at least the next week or two."

While Paul was eating the four men in suits and ties got up to leave. The oldest man, probably in his fifties with a diamond pinkie ring on his left hand approached Paul. "Didn't mean to eavesdrop, but heard you are new in town, son. George Hackett. I'm a real estate salesman." He extended his right hand. "If you are looking for a house to buy or rent, or any building, give me a call." Paul shook his hand and accepted the offered business card. "My boy, Norman," he said indicating the young man beside him, "and Jake and Carl." All three men shook Paul's hand.

"What brings you to our fair city?" continued the older man in a friendly voice.

Paul pointed down the street. "I'm the new pastor of the Community Chapel a couple blocks from here."

"Oh." George Hackett raised his eyebrows and extended that word out for several syllables. "You take the place of that Meredith character?"

Paul's toast stuck in his throat. He cleared his throat and nodded.

George Hackett's smile disappeared and his demeanor hardened. "Well, let me tell you something." George Hackett lowered his voice and leaned down toward Paul. "Your former pastor was up to no good. He got to meddling in other people's affairs that were none of his business. It got so hot for him he had to leave town." He wagged his finger in Paul's face. "I suggest you work in your church and don't go sticking your Bible-thumping fingers into someone else's business. Or you may get them cut off." He stood back and stared at Paul for a moment as if contemplating adding more to his tirade. Then he glanced around the room and noticed everyone had stopped talking and was watching him. Taking a deep breath, he smoothed his hair. "Anyway," he said in a louder voice, "nice to meet you, Reverend. Please consider my offer. Enjoy your stay in Bethel Springs." Then he plastered a smile on his face, adjusted his tie and walked out, the other three men following.

Paul sat in his booth staring after them, too shocked to come up with a response, even in his mind.

Immediately after the men left the building and disappeared out of sight, Laura brought the coffee pot over to Paul and filled his cup. Quietly she said, "Those are not good guys."

Paul looked up at her. "Sounds like it."

She briefly sat in the seat across from him and carefully sat the coffee pot on the table. "I think you are a nice person and I would hate to see happen to you what happened to Pastor Charlie Meredith."

Back at church, badly shaken, he tried to put George Hackett's warning out of his mind as he went over his sermon notes again. He then rearranged the songbooks, stood on the platform behind the wooden podium and practiced the first part of his message.

A few minutes after nine a familiar gray Plymouth pulled up to the curb in front of the church. Hurrying outside Paul greeted the visitors who had driven from Springfield to attend his church on his first day as pastor. Kate Fuller, his neighbor whom he had known since childhood, now a Bible school student at Zion Bible School, got out. Paul noticed with approval how attractive and how much like a church worker she looked in her brown pleated nylon skirt and white blouse, every strand of her auburn soft curls in place.

"Good morning," she said, closing her car door and coming up to Paul giving him a quick hug. "So, this is your church and you're the pastor. Isn't this wonderful?" Her eyes mirrored the excitement of her words which gave him a warm feeling.

Then the passenger door opened and another young woman got out, about the same age as Kate, dressed in a stylish burgundy dress with matching shoes. Paul turned toward her in surprise. Immediately he recognized her as Mary Brunner, classmate of Kate's at the Bible school. He remembered she was the daughter of missionaries to Argentina, last year's class president, always on the honor roll. Not only was she one of the most popular students on campus, but ever since he had gotten to know her, Paul had been impressed with her spiritual maturity. If anyone he knew personified Jesus in the flesh it was her.

"Paul, you remember Mary, don't you? When I told her I was coming here this Sunday for your debut as pastor, she asked if she could come along and keep me company since this is quite a drive from Springfield."

Mary came up to Paul and extended her hand in greeting. "Nice to see you again, Paul. I'm glad the Lord has given you this wonderful opportunity to pastor this lovely church."

Paul returned the handshake, a little surprised that Mary had come. Taller than Kate, slender, with red hair cascading down to her shoulders, she looked elegant and distinguished in her plain black dress with a white collar, a strand of pearls around her neck.

They followed Paul into the church. "Rustic," Kate commented. "But room for maybe seventy-five people. A lot of potential here. Paint the room a lighter color, add a few Bible paintings and Scripture passages on the walls, and you will have an attractive church."

"I can already feel the presence of the Lord here," added Mary. She touched each bench as she walked down the aisle. "Lord," she said out loud with her eyes open, "I pray that very soon you will fill these benches with people, and fill each one of them with your love and the power of God in their lives."

Kate turned to face Paul, a wistful look on her face. "I wish I could come every Sunday and help you with this church right away. But, like I told you, I'm doing an internship to get credit for a class at Bible school and am committed to being the children's leader at that little Baptist church down the street from the school. But, come January, I plan to start coming every Sunday to help in whatever way I can."

Paul nodded. "I know you will be a big help when you can come."

By nine-forty-five, Paul counted fifteen people seated in the benches when Sister Patricia, who had introduced herself to Paul as the Sunday school superintendent, got behind the pulpit, opened the service in prayer, and led in three children's choruses. During the singing a few more people came in and sat down. Sister Patricia closed the opening exercise with prayer.

Then she dismissed the smaller boys and girls to children's church, leading them upstairs to Paul's apartment. The adults all moved to the right side near the front. James Harmon, a local elementary schoolteacher, moved the pulpit to the floor in front of that row of pews. Taking out his Bible and quarterly he began teaching the lesson.

At ten fifty-five the children noisily returned back down the stairs, and James hastily concluded the lesson with prayer, transferring the pulpit back to its original spot on the platform.

When everyone was settled, acting more confident than he felt, Paul stood before the congregation—his congregation. "Welcome to God's house this morning," he said with as big a smile as he could muster. As you can see, I'm the new pastor here. My name is Paul Whitfield. You can call me 'Brother Paul,' 'Pastor Paul,' or 'Paul.' Just don't call me late for dinner," he quipped and noticed only Kate and Mary chuckled at his joke.

Fred Pittman led in the song service and took up the offering. Then Paul rose to preach. Again he smiled. His homiletics teacher told him if you look confident, you will feel more confident. Breathing a silent prayer for help he started in.

"The name of your town—our town—Bethel Springs intrigued me," he began. "Before I came I did some research and discovered the town was founded by four Quaker families coming out west to seek a new life and start a new community. They had already settled on the name 'Bethel' which means 'house of God' in the biblical language. Then they came upon your two artesian wells north of town, and they decided to call their new town Bethel Springs, planning on making this a Christian community.

"Most of you have probably heard many stories of how the town got settled. They built their homes, barns and a church. They farmed and hunted.

One of the men, Jeremiah Lundquist, was a cobbler. He started making shoes as a sideline to his farming. Soon it became a full-time job as the town grew. During the Civil War he made boots for the soldiers." Paul chuckled. "I hear for either the North or South, he didn't care which side, as long as they had the money. His business grew. His sons and descendants continued making shoes. That's why we have the Lundquist Shoe Factory over on Highway 13 and in several other states in the South and Midwest.

"I'm sure most of you know the story in the Bible of Jacob when he fled from his family because he had deceived Esau out of his birthright. In Genesis twenty-eight, we read how he had a dream of a stairway reaching from earth to heaven with God's angels going up and down the ladder. Then God spoke to Jacob and told him he would have many descendants that would bless the earth. We know one of his descendants was Jesus Christ. When Jacob woke from his dream he changed the name of the city from Luz to Bethel, or 'house of God,' as we just mentioned.

"He set up an altar at that place and vowed that he would serve God if God would be with him on his journey and allow him to safely return home.

"We next read about Bethel in Genesis chapter thirty-five. He now has a family. He has made peace with his brother Esau whom he had deceived. As he approaches Bethel he tells his household to get rid of their foreign gods and to purify themselves. Then he acknowledges that God had helped him during his time of trouble, and he builds an altar there to worship God. God blesses him and changes his name from Jacob, which means 'deceiver,' to Israel, which means 'he struggled with God,' since he had wrestled with an angel."

Paul read the passages in the Bible he was describing to make a few more points. As he talked he looked out over his sparse congregation. Scattered around on the benches were a few people, most he had just met this morning. He didn't really know what they needed or expected from him as their pastor. But he would try to minister to them. He hoped he had gotten his facts right and was glad none of his college professors were there to critique his message.

Putting those thoughts aside, he closed his Bible and looked up from his notes. "Like Jacob," he concluded, "some of us may have sinned against God or wronged someone. Maybe we have idols in our lives that we are worshipping above our worship to God. But we are here in Bethel Springs, in the house of God. If we repent and put away whatever else we may be worshipping, God is here to forgive us and help us and bless us."

Emily Miller came to the piano and played, "There's room at the cross for you" while he gave the invitation for people to come forward to give their hearts to the Lord or for prayer for any need.

After waiting during two verses of the song with no one responding to the altar call, he asked James Harmon to close in prayer.

As James prayed, Paul made his way to the back of the church so he could shake hands and be there as his flock walked out. Everyone was friendly, shaking his hand as they left. Most told him what a good sermon he had preached and welcomed him as their pastor. Last to leave was a lanky teenage boy who hung back until everyone had left. "You don't fool me none," he told Paul on his way out, looking him in the eyes. "I bet you're just like the last preacher. Take our money and run when the goin' gets tough." Before Paul could reply, he hurried out the door and joined his family.

Kate quickly moved to his side. "Why did he say that?" she questioned.

Paul wiped the sweat from his brow with the back of his hand. "Dr. McFee said the last pastor had some problems and then left town without telling anyone."

"You won't be like that. I know that." She touched his arm. "Don't worry about it. I thought you did a wonderful job in your first service. You're off to a great start. Other than this one boy, the people seem to like you. There were not a lot out this morning, but there's potential in this church and town. I doubt if anyone else thinks you will be like the last pastor."

"We'll soon find out." Paul took off his jacket, loosened his tie and stared at the pulpit for just an instant. *Was the boy right?* he asked himself. *Was he just like the last pastor? Would he fail too and run if the going got tough? And leave more bad feelings in the minds of people toward his church and Christianity?*

Shaking off his thought, he stood. "Anyone for lunch? I haven't had a chance to buy any food yet, so let's go to Martha's Café a couple blocks away. I went there for breakfast and they have good food."

"Sounds wonderful," replied Kate, then smiled. "After we eat let's go to the Safeway store I noticed on the way into town. I didn't put any money in the offering this morning. Thought I would save it to buy some groceries for the new pastor."

Laura Taylor had just gotten off her lunch break and had gone back to work in the diner when she noticed the tall, blond young man whom she had served at breakfast returning. This time he brought two young women with him. The shorter, plain one with dull clothes sat beside him. The prettier girl sat across from them. She saw the young man say something to the woman beside him who smiled at him and touched his shoulder in an intimate way.

Laura swallowed. Was that a stab of jealousy she felt? Ridiculous. She didn't even know the young man's name or anything about him, other than he was a pastor and the best looking guy that had ever come into the diner—at least for a long time. And he had offered to pray for her. She closed her eyes for an instant and shook her head to clear her mind. *Forget about him and do your job, she told herself.*

Grabbing three menus she approached them. "Hi, welcome back," she said looking at Paul with her best smile. "I see you brought friends with you this time."

Paul returned her smile. "Yes, I did. Laura, this is my friend, Kate. She lives in Springfield. We were neighbors and she came to be at our church this morning." He pointed across the table. "She brought her friend Mary. They both attend the same Bible school in Springfield I just graduated from.

"Nice to meet you." Laura placed the menus in front of them. "Can I get you some coffee or tea or water?"

That night, ten people showed up for the seven o'clock service. Paul preached on John 10:10, how Jesus came that we might have a more abundant life as we serve Him. They had to close the front door halfway through the service because of the laughter and other loud noises drifted from Zeb's Bar and Grill down the street.

Kate and Mary left the church at eight-thirty and started their two-hour trek back to Springfield.

Mary waited until they were out of town and into the dark countryside before she spoke up. "Now that Paul is pastor, do you think he'll ask you to marry him?"

Kate looked away from the dark road to her friend for an instant. "Don't count on it, yet. Paul and I have been neighbors and known each other for several years. I know my parents and Paul's mom expect that one day we'll get married. The friends we hang around with also assume we'll get married. And," she paused, "we might. I like Paul and know he likes me. Paul is twenty-one. I'm twenty. We are both the right age. I think I would like that someday. "She sighed. "Maybe after I graduate next year, but I don't want to rush him."

"Did you notice how that waitress looked at him every time she came to our table?"

"I did notice that. I also noticed how Paul seemed to perk up when she was around."

"You need to keep in touch with Paul personally, not just through letters," suggested Mary. "Maybe set up some special kids' meetings like a vacation Bible school or something like that."

"Good idea. I'll think about that."

They drove on in silence for several miles, then Kate spoke up. "How about you? Any guys you are interested in?"

Mary smiled in the darkness. "Growing up in a different culture it's taken me awhile to adjust to the American way of life, including all this dating scene. They don't do it the same way where I was raised. But I'm starting to come around, finally. There are a couple of guys that have caught my eye. But I believe the Lord has called me back to the mission field. I feel I should only date men who also have a call for missions, or at least for the ministry. So I'm waiting for that special young man for the Lord to send that way. Maybe," she twirled her fingers through her hair and paused. "I don't know, but maybe I've found him. I just don't know if he's interested in me."

After the service and after everyone had left, Paul closed and locked the front door of the church, turned off the lights and fans in the hall, and went up to his bedroom.

Opening a bottle of Coca-Cola from the groceries Kate had bought that afternoon and making himself a baloney and mayonnaise sandwich, he sat on his bed and stared out the window at the lights still on from the church on the hill. The day hadn't turned out too badly in his little church, he reflected. He thought his preaching was fair. The people seemed to respond, at least most of them.

He needed to learn their names. In his mind he reviewed where everyone sat. The Pittmans sat on the second row on the left side. Fred and Nadine were near retirement age. Fred was the treasurer and worked at the pharmacy. Their son Samuel and his wife Betty sat beside them with their children scattered around the church. They had four children. Josie was twelve and he couldn't remember the other children's names.

Frieda Thornton, the woman who had showed him around the church yesterday, attended both services and gave the longest testimony.

Millers. John the father, Emily the mother. Middle aged. Jimmy, the outspoken teenager who had inferred that he was no better than the last pastor. Jenny and Jack, the other children.

Before he could think of anyone else, his thoughts turned to Laura the waitress. Almost as tall as he was. Attractive, feminine. Her face showed strength and character, or so he thought. But what did he know about people's character just from their looks?

And Patsy. Beautiful, gorgeous Patsy. The most beautiful girl he had ever seen. His heart beat faster thinking of her. Yet, what did he know about her? Maybe someday he could find out more. Or maybe not. He didn't even know if either girl was a Christian.

But, as a single pastor in a small town, if he showed an interest in any girl, it would spread all over town faster than a wildfire. What would that do to his reputation as a single pastor?

Besides, there was Kate. Wasn't he going to marry her? That thought warmed his heart. Kind, good-hearted Kate. His friend, his playmate growing up, soon to be his wife.

He had to forget Laura and Patsy and every other girl he would meet in Bethel Springs, even Mary Brunner, whom he had had a crush on for a short time his second year in Bible school.

With that matter resolved, to the sound of music from the bar up the street coming through his window, he drifted off to sleep.

PRESENT DAY   # CHAPTER 5

The white-haired man closed the notebook and smiled to himself. Yes, his first day was interesting. The first several days were interesting. He could still remember many of the events during those eventful three years he lived here during the middle nineteen fifties. He had done a good job as pastor, he felt, until that one incident that forced him to leave.

He glanced at his watch and saw it was still early enough to visit his old church, if the building still existed. Getting back in his car he drove the two blocks to his old church and was a little surprised to see that all the old buildings on the block were still there. A black and white sign over his former church read "Fred's Flea Mart." The old hardware store to the west of the old church was vacant with a "For Rent" sign in the picture window. To the east of the church, the clothing store was now a used bookstore. A pawn shop had taken the place of the shoe store. He smiled briefly as memories flooded back of Zeb's Bar and Grill on the corner that was now a Starbucks coffee shop.

Since only two cars were parked on that side of the street, he easily pulled up right in front of his old church. The wooden door had been replaced by a bright red metal door. The picture windows on either side of the door displayed old long-play records, various pieces of kitchenware and a life size cutout of Elvis Presley in his white jump suit.

Feeling nostalgic, he stepped through the door that opened with a ding. A small wooden counter stood on his right with a computer, screen and printer. A wrinkled older man in jeans with a gray and black flannel shirt, sat in a chair behind the counter reading a Louis L'Amour book. He nodded to Paul, gave a brief greeting, and went back to his book.

As Paul glanced around he saw an aisle way stretched the length of the room ending at the back door leading to the alley. Small booths lined both sides. As Paul walked past the booths toward the back, he saw merchandise like one sees in every flea market: old records, video tapes, books, knickknacks, furniture and other assorted items. He approached the stairs. They were now padded with green carpet. A modern railing made of stained wood with round slats every few inches had replaced the two by four.

Making his way up the stairs, he saw the bathroom was in the same spot. Booths filled the front half of the upstairs. An unpainted wall of Sheetrock with a wide door blocked off the back half, no doubt for storage.

Paul stood for a moment at the top of the stairs, savoring the cool air conditioned air and remembering the heat and humidity he had to endure when he lived here. No other customers were there. He looked around at the spot where his kitchen stood, his bookcase, his bed and dresser. He smiled briefly, then felt a lump in his throat as the memories flooded back. Many good memories, great memories. He walked to the window and looked out to the hill where the old stone church had stood. He had seen the church burning from this spot, an event that ended his ministry in this town and left a black stain beside his name forever.

With a heavy sigh he made his way back down the stairs and went to the back of the building where the pulpit had stood. He smiled again. Many good messages preached here, at least he had thought so at the time. God had moved. People had come to Christ. Lives had been changed. He had done some good here, he told himself. If…he shook his head. If he had not been accused of starting the fire, would he still be here in Bethel Springs as pastor? Or, if he had kept his convictions to himself and not spoken out about the evil and evildoers, would the fire even have happened? Would he this year be celebrating his fiftieth year of ministry in this town? What a celebration that would have been! But, he shook his head again. The front door dinged, and a man and woman with two young children came through the door, the children running down the aisle toward him talking loudly to each other.

With another shake of his head, his hands in his pockets, his head down, he made his way up the aisle and out the door.

Stepping out of his old church he looked up at the blue, cloudless sky and thanked the Lord for life, health, strength and for all his blessings, trying to shake the melancholy feeling that had come over him.

Wondering about another building that held memories he drove up the street and around the corner to where Martha's Café used to be. He couldn't believe his eyes to see it still there. New paint job, new sign, but the same building.

With a smile at the memories the old restaurant brought he looked at his watch. Too early yet for lunch. But then maybe he didn't want to eat here, at least not yet. Returning to the town square with a can of Root Beer he had purchased from a vending machine in his old church, he sat on a park bench and opened up his journal again. It wasn't too many days into his ministry at Bethel Springs that he found out what he was up against.

1955

CHAPTER 6

At 6:05 a.m. Paul rolled over in bed and looked at the calendar he had thumbtacked to his wall yesterday. Monday, June twenty, nineteen fifty-five.

What was a pastor to do on Monday? Wasn't that the traditional pastor's day off? But, having worked just one day, should he be taking the day off? Whatever the case, what should he do today?

After shaving and taking a shower, he fixed himself a bowl of oatmeal and a piece of toast from the food Kate had purchased for him. After breakfast, he decided as a newcomer he needed to meet his neighbors, the businesses on his side of the street. But, first, he wanted to deposit for safekeeping in a bank the three hundred and twenty dollars in cash he had taken from his bank in Springfield, and the ten dollars and thirty-nine cent offering he had received in the offering last night. While going to the library yesterday, he had noticed an impressive brick building on the square with "Bethel Springs First National Bank" imbedded in the brick above the door in white lettering.

Putting on a pair of gray corduroys and a blue nylon shirt, he took the money, folded it, put it in his pocket and walked to the bank. The warm breeze and sun overhead on an almost cloudless day foretold of another hot day.

Making his way into the bank he looked around at the gray tile floor with a high white ceiling. To his right he saw two tables with chairs around them. Farther down were three desks with men sitting behind each one. He approached one of the two teller windows on his left. A young woman greeted him with a smile. "May I help you, sir?"

"Yes, I would like to open an account here, if I may."

"Certainly." Young, Paul decided. Not over twenty. Yet business-like and friendly. Dark, curly hair, a short-sleeve white blouse with blue Capri pants. She disappeared through a door into a room behind her and emerged a few moments later with a folder of papers. She pointed to a table. "Please sit over there and fill out the paperwork and bring it back. New in town?" she added with a smile.

"Yes." Paul smiled back. "I'm the new pastor at Community Chapel. I wanted to open a personal checking account."

Taking the papers and the pen she handed him, he went over to a table and began filling out the paperwork.

He was halfway through when a man emerged from an office down the hall and approached Paul. "Good morning," he said, extending a hand with a smile. "My name is Milton Passmore, bank president. My daughter Sarah, your teller, said you are the new pastor at Community Chapel.

"Yes." Paul stood and shook hands.

"Splendid. Welcome to Bethel Springs. We trust you enjoy your stay here."

He was short, stout with thinning dark hair. Paul inspected the man in his dark suit and blue tie, wondering if he was sincere, or just voicing the rhetoric he gave everyone.

"It's too bad about your predecessor, Charlie Meredith," continued the bank president. "He had his checking account here, too. A wonderful man. Great family. Too bad about his boy."

Paul nodded, not sure how to respond.

"The church still banks here, of course. Your treasurer, Fred Pittman, brings in the offerings every Monday like clockwork. However, I've noticed the last few months the offerings are down.

"But," Milton Passmore smiled, "enough about business. You came to Bethel Springs at the right time. We are at the cusp of real growth in our little town. The city fathers have plans to build a hotel, bath houses and an opera house that will bring in tourists. That will add more work for the residents in our community which will bring in more people for your church and the other church in town." Milton Passmore was rubbing his hands together as he talked, as if anticipating the additional income it would bring to his bank.

Paul talked to the bank president about the town for several more minutes. Then he finished filling out his papers and opened his account, gratefully leaving his cash in the safekeeping of the bank and taking home some temporary checks.

His next stop was to Stan's Hardware Store, the business on the corner to the immediate right of the church. With identical picture windows as on the front of his church, he walked through the front door and found himself in a building about the size of his hall. Shelves lined the left wall with a section for power tools and another for hand tools. In front of him and down the aisles were bins with nuts and bolts and other hardware. Along the right wall were rakes, shovels and other farming tools. In the corner to his right were several choices of push mowers and gas lawn mowers. At the back of the store he spotted a man and woman talking, sitting behind a desk. The man got up, adjusted his black framed glasses, and approached Paul. "Good morning," he called out. He swept his hands across the store. "Feel free to look around. Let me know if you have any questions."

"I didn't come to buy any hardware, just came to introduce myself." Paul approached the salesman and held out his hand. "My name is Paul Whitfield, new pastor of the church next door."

"Oh. Hello. Nice to meet you." He gripped Paul's hand with a firm handshake. "Stan. Stan Manning." He pointed to the back of the store. "Judy, my wife." He leaned back against a bin of door knobs and latches. "I was friends with Charlie, the previous pastor. Nice guy. A little outspoken, but I liked him. Sorry to see him leave. Hope you can do better than he did and stay longer."

"Thank you." Paul took an instant liking to this young man. He was probably around thirty, dressed in jeans and a short-sleeve blue Dacron shirt, medium height, slim, a plain face with a small mouth and slightly crooked nose. His outstanding feature was his red hair worn in a short crew cut.

"You live above the church like Charlie and his family did?"

Paul nodded and leaned against the bin opposite the store owner.

"Gets noisy at night, doesn't it?" Stan Manning laughed and ran his hand through his hair. I've been here at night a few times. The crowd and music at Zeb's can get loud at times. Best stay away from that bunch," he warned.

"Thanks. I'll keep that in mind. By the way, I just opened up a checking account at the bank. Met the president, Milton Passmore. He mentioned something about building a hotel and bath house and opera house. What's all that about?"

"Did he also say they were planning to build a casino with gambling and who knows what all?"

Paul shook his head. "He didn't mention that. I thought gambling was illegal."

"It is, but there's a petition going around town to vote on legalizing gambling. We will vote on that in November if they can get enough signatures to get it on the ballot."

"How do you feel about it?"

Stan shrugged. "Bad for our town. We are doing just fine as we are. Bring in outside gamblers, and we will have no end of trouble."

By this time Stan's wife Judy had walked up. She was obviously pregnant, pretty with long dark hair in curls, at least two inches taller than her husband. "Stan doesn't like it," she said with a short laugh. "Thinks it will make our town sinful. Me," she paused and ran her fingers behind her ears to catch any stray hairs, "I think this town is boring and needs a little excitement. Besides, we are barely making it with this store. And, we will soon have another mouth to feed." She patted her stomach. "We will need the extra money all these businesses and new customers will bring."

Stan raised his hands in surrender. "That's our town in a nutshell: some on one side and some on the other. Anyway," he reached out and shook Paul's hand again. "Welcome to Bethel Springs. Holler if we can help in any way."

Paul left the store, walked by the church and went into "Dolly's Clothing Boutique," the store to the left of the church. Racks of women's clothing almost barred his way as he made his way into the building. He noticed children's and men's clothing were toward the back of the store.

"May I help you?" An older woman came out of a curtained room off to the left. In her sixties, Paul decided. Prim, proper, stylish and friendly. Paul introduced himself and said he wanted to meet his neighbors. "Wonderful to meet you," she told him in a cultured voice, extending a limp hand. "My name is Dolly Knight. Your previous pastor's wife Anna shopped here quite a bit for herself and her family. A delightful family. Too bad about little Johnny," she added. "I was sorry to see them go."

Just then a mother with two children walked in. Paul continued to look around the store and decided he would shop here when he needed more clothes.

A bell sounded as he opened the door to "Featherstone Shoes," the business to the left of the clothing store, two buildings down from his church, next to Zeb's Bar and Grill. Boxes of boots and shoes of all sizes lay in shelves in the middle of the store and along the sides. To his left was a large display of Lundquist shoes. Next to that were several shelves of Red Ryder shoes. A man was stacking boxes of shoes on a shelf against the left wall. When he heard the bell, he turned.

"Hello," he called. Putting down the box of shoes he came toward Paul. Tall, husky, with the features of an Indian, he wore his black hair in a single pig tail that dropped halfway down his back. In a red plaid shirt and pair of gray overalls, he looked more like a farmer than a shoe salesman.

"You must be new here," he said by way of introduction in his deep voice. "At least I haven't seen you here before. Name's Bull Featherstone." He reached out a huge hand and shook Paul's hand with a surprisingly light touch.

"Yes, I am new. My name is Paul Whitfield." He pointed to his right. I'm the new pastor at Community Chapel, two doors down."

"Oh." The salesman raised his eyebrows. He looked at Paul, examining him from his head to his feet. "You look like a fine, young man," he said finally. "I hope you're not like the other pastor," he added shaking his head. "Didn't like him."

After the friendliness from the people in the other stores he was a little taken back by the directness of this imposing salesman.

"Didn't like him," the Native American repeated when Paul didn't reply. "When he came in to buy shoes for his family, or just to visit, he always tried to convert me. He didn't believe that our Great Spirit was the same as his white God." He stared at Paul, his brown eyes boring into his. "What do you believe? Am I a sinner bound for hell because I worship the Great Spirit and not your white God?"

Paul stared back, not knowing how to answer. He dropped his eyes and looked around the store, trying to think of what to say. "You know," he said finally, "to be honest, I have never thought about that theological point. I don't know that much about your religion. But I do know that God looks at our heart. He's our judge and not me. You know," he added remembering what other preachers had said, "I'm in sales, not in management." Paul pointed up. "That's His call, not mine."

Bull Featherstone put his head back and laughed. "That's a good way to avoid answering the question." He slapped Paul on the back so hard that he had to catch himself to keep from falling forward. "You keep your preaching inside your church and out of my store. I'll keep worshipping the Great Spirit, and you, your white God and we will get along just fine."

Zeb's Bar and Grill on the corner was closed, but Paul decided he wouldn't have gone in anyway.

Back at the church Paul swept the hall and put the songbooks back in place. He cleaned his apartment. When noon came, he decided that since this was his day off, he wouldn't cook and walked in the afternoon heat to Martha's Café.

He sat again in Laura's section, seeing she was already there waiting on other customers. She came to his table holding a coffee pot. "Coffee?" she asked, her dimpled smile in place showing her flawless white teeth.

"Sure." Paul scooted his cup toward her.

"Do you need a menu?"

Paul nodded toward the chalkboard leaning on the counter with today's special: vegetable soup and ham sandwich. "I'll take that." With a nod and another smile she disappeared back into the kitchen.

While waiting for his food he looked around the diner which was about half full. Mostly farmers, he decided as he examined their clothing. Some merchants, those wearing white shirts and ties. Two or three of them glanced his way and smiled. He returned the smile and wondered if any of them would begin attending Community Chapel in the near future. Who among the people here should he try to befriend first?

A few minutes later when Laura brought his lunch she got ketchup from another table and sat it down across from him. "Can I talk to you for a minute?" she asked quietly looking over at Paul, a tentative smile on her face.

"Sure." Paul smiled back. He got a whiff of her perfume. Lilac. Was that the kind his mother used? He liked the fragrance.

"It's none of my business." Laura looked down at the bottle of ketchup for a moment, then slid in the seat across the table from Paul. "But you seem like a nice young man. I could hardly sleep last night thinking about you and

George Hackett, that man you met yesterday. If you want," she added with a tentative smile, "I get off work at three o'clock. If you meet me here I would be glad to tell you a little more about him. I would hate to see you run out of town like Pastor Charlie was."

Somewhat puzzled by the offer, yet anxious to get more acquainted with this intriguing waitress, he nodded in agreement. "I'll be here at three," he promised.

"Wait for me by the back door," she said softly, then stood and disappeared into the kitchen.

After lunch, restless and wondering what Laura was going to tell him, Paul didn't go back to the church but walked toward the city square, his hands in his pockets, greeting everyone he passed with a smile and a "hello," realizing he needed to start getting acquainted with people in town.

He suddenly found himself walking toward the library. He reminded himself he was here for the long haul (at least he hoped he was) and needed to take care of himself as well as his church. He figured now that Patsy had seen him check out scholarly religious books, she wouldn't think it improper to check out a little fiction.

As he approached the town square he asked himself if he had come to check out some Zane Grey books or to see Patsy? Or both?

Squaring his shoulders and smoothing his hair with his hands he walked up the stone steps, opened the door and stepped into the library and was met with the breeze from two fans circulating the warming air coming in from the open windows.

"Good afternoon, Pastor Paul," the honey-filled voice said. As Patsy walked toward her desk with an armload of books, her brilliant smile was in place as was every strand of her blond hair, accented by her sleeveless yellow blouse and matching plaid skirt. "What can I do for you today?"

"Just Paul," he said self-consciously at her use of the title. "I'm not in church."

Patsy's melodious laugh rang through the library. "Paul it is."

"Just want to browse," he said, smiling back at her.

Returning to where the religious books were, he decided on *Preaching from the Prophets* by Kyle M. Yates and *The Acts of the Apostles* by G. Campbell Morgan. Then he picked up three Zane Grey books he hadn't read for the past year or two: *The Drift Fence*, *The Lone Star Ranger* and *The Desert of Wheat*.

While Patsy was checking out his books, the library door opened and a young man in a white smock and black trousers sauntered into the library. "Good afternoon, Patsy," he said as he approached Patsy's desk.

She looked up to him with a smile. "Good afternoon to you, Michael. May

I help you?"

The young man produced a white paper sack he had been holding behind him and offered it to Patsy. "Had a couple minutes off from the pharmacy so I went to Perry's Bakery. Bought a raspberry jelly-filled donut and thought you might like one too."

"Thank you." Patsy took the sack and looked in. "I'll eat it during my break." She placed the sack into a drawer, smiled at him again and turned to Paul, "Michael, I'd like you to meet the new preacher at the little church downtown. Paul…" she glanced at his library card. "Paul Whitfield. Paul, meet Michael Champion."

"Hello." Paul stretched out his right hand. "Good to meet you, Michael. Nice town you have. Glad to be here."

"Thank you. Welcome to Bethel Springs." Michael returned the handshake. The young man was about his age, shorter, yet with the build of an athlete. Paul sensed a determination in the firm handshake and the clear eyes that looked directly into his.

Michael looked at his watch and turned back to Patsy. "Gotta get back to work. See you soon." With a wave of his hand he hurried out the door.

Patsy waited until he left, then spoke up. "Michael is from Bethel Springs. I've known him most of my life. We were friends in school. Then he went off to college in Kansas City where he met a girl. They got engaged and had set a wedding date. Then he or she broke it off, depending on whose version you hear."

"He came back home after his graduation, just a few weeks ago." She gave an embarrassed laugh. "Now I guess he wants to start going out with me. A few days ago he asked me out on a date."

After a pause when she didn't reveal as to whether or not she had accepted the invitation, Paul finally said, "He seems like a nice young man,"

"Oh, he's nice. And rich," she added with another melodious laugh. "His dad owns the pharmacy in town plus several other pharmacies around the area."

After leaving his books at the church and donning his Cardinals baseball cap to keep the sun off his head and face, Paul headed back outside, deciding to walk around town and see what was there.

After an hour of going up and down the streets of the small town, and saying a short prayer for the businesses and homes he passed, he decided to rest his legs and splurge with the few dollars he had and purchase a sundae at Champion's Drug Store. He was rather surprised to see Michael behind the counter, dressed in his white smock. Over a loudspeaker *Blue Moon of Kentucky* was playing. He recognized the voice of Elvis Presley, a new singer he had heard on his car radio a few times.

"Pastor Paul," he said jovially. "Nice to see you again so soon. Read those books you checked out already?" and he laughed at his own joke.

Paul smiled. "Just Paul. Not quite. After I left the library I just walked around town to get acquainted." He sat on a stool facing the counter. "You have a nice town here. I think I'll like it. I'll have a hot fudge sundae. Large, please."

"Ever heard of McDonald's restaurants?" asked Michael as he was preparing the ice cream dish.

"No."

"They started in California. Two brothers, Mac and Dick McDonald. It's a restaurant, but not like other restaurants. You can get your food almost instantly. They only sell hamburgers, cheeseburgers, French fries and shakes. Not much of a menu, but you don't have to wait. People like the instant service part and are starting to like hamburgers more. They started in one restaurant in California and have branched out. Just started a McDonald's in Chicago."

"Sounds interesting. You planning to start a restaurant like that too?"

"Yes, I do. And, I have added onto their idea." Michael's face lit up as he spoke. "Dad has loaned me the money. I'm planning to start a restaurant here in Bethel Springs. I'll call it 'Champ Burgers' or 'Burger Champs' or something like that. We'll sell hamburgers, cheeseburgers and milkshakes too. But I'll add chicken sandwiches. Maybe later fish sandwiches. Should go over big. If it does well here, I'll open one in Springfield. Then, maybe in Kansas City or St. Louis. Get in on the bottom floor of something that may be big.

"My five-year plan is to go nationwide. Dad has already bought several acres of land on what will eventually be the shores on Table Rock Lake once they get the dam finished. I will build a mansion there, become rich, retire at forty and travel the world.

"And," he added with a wink, "Patsy is a part of that plan. I've loved her since I was little. I almost made a mistake in Kansas City but came to my senses just in time. Now I'm trying to win her back and to make it big so I can take care of her and to make her proud of me."

Michael kept talking about Patsy and hamburgers until another shopper entered the pharmacy that he went to wait on.

CHAPTER 7

Back at church Paul worked briefly on his Bible study for Wednesday night and sermons for Sunday, had lunch, swept the floor of the hall and cleaned his apartment, all the time nervously looking at his watch waiting for three o'clock.

At five to three Paul locked the church, got in his car, and drove to the back door of Martha's Café.

Promptly at three Laura stepped out of the restaurant, having changed out of her uniform into a yellow dress with white trim, her dark hair in a ponytail with bangs down her forehead. She carried a bulky sack that she sat on her lap. She smiled briefly at Paul. "Just drive out of here," she said quickly. "I don't want anyone to see us. Angel, Holly and Martha are already wondering why you keep coming in and sitting in my section."

Paul smiled. "Are they jealous?"

"I don't know. They just like to gossip."

"Maybe I should sit somewhere else next time I come in," Paul suggested with a smile.

"Oh, that's not necessary. I like you coming in." She gave a short laugh. "Anyway, turn left here and drive out of town. I know a place where we can talk. I realize you have that girlfriend you brought in on Sunday. She seems nice. So I hope you don't think I'm trying to make this into a date. I'm not, but I just want to talk in private. And, knowing you are probably hungry, I brought two bacon, lettuce and tomato sandwiches, half of a boysenberry pie and two bottles of Pepsi. I hope you like them."

"Sounds delicious." Paul looked over at Laura who was looking at him with an anxious look on her face as if hoping to please him. "Thank you."

They drove on in silence for several minutes until Laura pointed to a side road off to the right. "Turn here. There's a huge oak tree off to the side of the road that gives a lot of shade. I saw this place the other day and thought it would be a good spot for a picnic."

Paul turned down the road about a hundred yards, then pulled off to the side where she indicated. It was a quiet spot with trees as far as Paul could see in all directions. Nothing marred the solitude except for an old shack a quarter of a mile away they could barely see through the trees. They got out and walked to a fallen log that lay under the oak tree that created a welcoming shady spot. A soft breeze cooled the afternoon.

Laura took a tablecloth and laid it on the ground, then took out the food and placed it on the cloth, along with plates, forks, knives and several paper napkins. She took another tablecloth and spread it on the ground beside the food. Taking a sandwich out of its paper wrapping she put in on a plate. "Here," she said, handing it to Paul. "You can sit on the tablecloth, or over on the log, or stand." She smiled. "And here's a Pepsi I can open for you any time you want."

"Thank you." Paul took the plate, admiring the quiet confidence and maturity he saw in Laura. She took a sandwich and sat across from him on the tablecloth, crossing her legs and modestly pulling her skirt over her knees. "I guess this is like a meal," she added, "so let's pray." With that she bowed her head and said a simple prayer over the meal and their conversation.

"George Hackett is a wicked man," she began, setting the plate beside her before even taking a bite. "He was born and raised here. Several years ago he went off to Chicago, then Las Vegas, and I don't know where all. About three years ago he came back married to, I think, his third wife, Bernice. He brought with him his son Norman, daughter Katie and some goons he picked up along the way.

"He said that the two springs in town have healing minerals, which others have said too, but haven't really done anything about it. Hackett wants to build bath houses so people can come and receive healing from arthritis and other ailments from the mineral water. He wants to model our town after Dawson Springs, Kentucky. At the beginning of this century Dawson Springs became big time when they exploited their mineral water. They built bath houses, a huge hotel, and brought in celebrities to perform at the hotel from Hollywood and other places. They built a railroad into town, made the place famous, and raked in a lot of money for the bath house owners, hotel owners and other merchants.

"But, Hackett wants to do one better here. He wants to bring in gambling. In fact, he has already started. He opened Hackett House a year or so ago out on the Mill Road. Gambling, bootleg liquor and who knows what all."

"I thought gambling was illegal."

"It is. But he gets away with it somehow. Hackett wants to have a vote on gambling on the November ballot to make it legal in our county. If it passes, and Hackett and others like him do all they want, it will mean big bucks for most everyone in town, including our restaurant. The bath houses would be okay. But imagine the change in our town and the great number of people who would visit our town if we had not only bath houses but gambling casinos and opera houses with shows put on by movie stars. Add to that bars, booze and who knows what else.

"Paul," Laura moved closer to him and briefly put her hand on his knee. "Bethel Springs is a small, conservative Midwest town. Most of us are church goers. Most are good people. Few people are rich, but most are getting by and happy and peaceful. It's a safe place to live and raise children. But if you bring in gambling, poof! That will bring in unsavory characters like the mafia and others. Crime will increase. Some of our good citizens will no doubt become addicted to gambling and lose everything. Marriage and families will break up. Our town will never be the same again."

Laura paused and picked up her sandwich and took a bite, looking off into the distance as if trying to collect her next thoughts. After a moment she put down her sandwich, wiped her mouth with a napkin, and looked back at Paul.

"I liked Pastor Charlie and his wife Anna and their two kids. They came into the restaurant quite a bit, just like you do. Although," she smiled, "they didn't always sit in my section.

"But," she continued, turning serious, "I think he was a good pastor...a good man. I didn't go to his church. I attend a little Pentecostal church in Cape Fair. But I heard a lot of talk and have friends who went there. He tried to stand up to George Hackett. He preached about the evils of gambling. He told the people to stay away from Hackett House and not to sign the petition or vote to legalize gambling. He did whatever he could to try to tell people the right way to live and not to follow anyone who wants to do evil."

"Because of his outspokenness he was threatened?"

"That's right." Laura took the two bottles of Pepsi, opened them with a bottle opener, and handed one to Paul. Taking a drink, she sat the beverage back down. "I don't know what all the threats were, but Pastor Charlie and his family were brave about it for a long time and hung in there. He kept preaching the gospel and talking about the evils of what Hackett and others were doing."

She took another bite of her sandwich before continuing. "This went on for about a year. Then five months ago Pastor Charlie's son, little eight-year-old Johnny, got knocked off his bicycle by a hit and run driver. He broke his leg and got cut up some. No one found who did it. At least no one fessed up. And that did it. The next week, without a word to anyone, he was gone. He got scared and gave up the fight. I heard he moved down to Arkansas somewhere with relatives."

Paul finished his sandwich and picked up a piece of the boysenberry pie. "Why would Hackett care about what a preacher in a little church says?"

"Paul," Laura leaned toward him again. "There's a civil war going on in our town. On one side are several of the merchants and influential people in town who attended his church back then. Two councilmen, George Waterman and Philip Peck, went to his church and were outspoken about Hackett and his doings. Angela Shell, the editor at the newspaper, attended his church and began writing editorials against gambling. This gave others the courage to speak out against it. Grandma Peak used to lead a Saturday night prayer meeting at his church until she passed away last year. About a dozen people came, sometimes less, sometimes more.

"On the other side is Mayor Tom Peterson who is all for voting in gambling, as are about half the merchants in town. After all, it will mean the town will grow. The merchants will make more money. As I said, more tax money, more big bucks for them, probably some given under the table.

"From the gossip I heard in the restaurant it seemed that our side was getting the upper hand. People were building up their courage and speaking out about the evils of gambling and all that goes with it. Then, when little Johnny got hurt and Pastor Charlie and his family left town with their tail between their legs, it scared everyone else. Many people left his church, your church now. Hardly anyone talks about it anymore above a whisper, and Hackett and his cronies seem to have the upper hand."

"How about the other church in town, Hope Community Church?"

Laura shook her head and wrinkled her nose. "Not much help there. Most of the other half of the townspeople on Hackett's side attend church there. Besides, from what I hear, Pastor Gannon and the church are so liberal and soft on sin the devil himself would feel welcome there."

Paul laughed. "Where did you hear that from? Is that original, or did you hear it from someone else?"

Laura smiled and relaxed a little. "I won't take credit for it. I overheard someone at Martha's say that."

They sat in silence for several minutes as they finished their meal.

"Let's go for a walk in the woods," suggested Laura as they placed the remains of the food on the tablecloth. "I see a trail. Let's see where that takes us."

"Was it Hackett himself who threatened the pastor or was it his cronies? Or someone else?" Paul asked as he began following her away from the road into the woods.

Overhead, the trees blocked out the sun in most places bringing welcoming shade. A squirrel ran down a tree ahead of them, looked at them, froze for an instant, then scurried up another tree. Through the branches Paul spotted a hawk gliding through the sky. He became aware of the crunching of their shoes against the underbrush in the silence around them as they followed a path through the woods for about a quarter mile where the grass had been worn down and came to a clearing facing a small lake. The reflection of the trees in the placid water on the other side of the lake reminded Paul of the picture on a postcard.

"I don't know the details about who or when. But I do know he was threatened several times. I think they caused other problems for him too."

"So what do you think I should do?" queried Paul, "Should I stick to preaching the gospel and ignore Hackett and his gang? Or should I speak out and possibly get threatened too?"

Laura turned around and looked at Paul. "I don't know. That's between you and God. I supposed you can just preach the gospel, stay out of the conflict, and hope that the Lord will change enough lives so people will vote down gambling. Or, you can be like the prophets who preach against evil and trust in the Lord to see you through whatever Hackett tries to throw at you. But," she cautioned, "he won against the previous pastor of your church. I'm sure that has given him the boldness to think he can take care of you, too, if you try to cross him."

Laura sat by a fallen log and Paul sat beside her as they gazed at the water.

"I just wanted to let you know what you are getting into," Laura said after a long pause. "I don't know what you should do. But I want you to know I'll be praying for you." She paused, then added with a smile, "Please keep coming into Martha's and sitting in my area. It gives the other girls something to talk about."

After silently contemplating the quiet scene before them, filled with their own thoughts, they returned to their picnic area and began packing away the items they had brought when they were suddenly interrupted by the sound of something crashing through the woods. "What's going on here? Get off my property."

Paul and Laura stopped what they were doing and turned in the direction of the gruff voice to see an elderly man with a long white beard holding a shotgun pointed at them. Immediately into Paul's mind popped the potpourri of stories he had heard about backwoods characters and what they did to strangers.

"I'm so sorry." Paul raised his hands and extended them toward the old man in a friendly manner. "We were just here having a picnic. I didn't realize you owned the property. We'll leave immediately."

The man was wearing a straw hat with a pony tail of white hair sticking out behind it. His short-sleeve dirty blue shirt was almost covered by a pair of bib overalls. He appeared to be in his seventies or maybe eighties with a face full of whiskers and several missing teeth.

"Clean up your mess first," the old man growled, "or ol' Betsy here," he shook his gun, "will make you wish you had."

"We sure will," Paul replied hurriedly. He picked up the picnic basket to take it to the car when a wave of sympathy swept over him. This old man probably lived alone. He no doubt was lonely. He probably faced physical problems and an unknown future. He was maybe hungry and living in poverty.

"Sir, we still have some boysenberry pie left." Paul reached into the picnic basket and took out a large piece of the pie wrapped in wax paper. "Would you like this in payment for having trespassed on your land?"

"Get off my property," the old man said again, almost in a shout. "Just get out of here."

"Please." Paul held out the food, not moving. "Please take it. It's the least we can do."

"Well," the old man lowered his gun. "Haven't had dinner yet. I guess I could use it."

Paul put the food in a paper sack and handed it to him. "My name is Paul. This is Laura. What's your name?"

"Rocky," growled the man. "Now git." He took the food from Paul, then ambled away back through the woods toward his cabin.

"You need to visit him," suggested Laura as they continued cleaning. "I bet he's really a harmless, lonesome old man. Maybe take him some food. I bet he hasn't had a home cooked meal in a long time. Or come by the restaurant and I can prepare something for him."

Back in the car, with all the picnic items safely in the trunk, Paul opened the car door for Laura. "Tell me about yourself." Paul asked as they started driving back to Bethel Springs.

"Not much to tell. I was born and raised here. My father left Mom and me and disappeared when I was twelve. I guess he couldn't stand being poor and working so hard or something. I never figured out why. I started working at Martha's when I was sixteen to save money to go to college. This fall, in just a few weeks, I'll soon be starting my last year at Burge School of Nursing in Springfield. I will just come home on weekends. Hopefully, by this time next year, I'll be an RN and working at some hospital somewhere."

"Any brothers or sisters?"

"No, just Mom and me. As I told you, she doesn't seem to be feeling well and hasn't for quite a while. But she won't see a doctor. I'm worried about her." She turned to Paul. "Tell me about yourself."

Paul smiled and briefly looked over at Laura, admiring her soft brown eyes and dimpled smile. He felt comfortable with her. It gave him a warm feeling to think that someone as attractive as Laura would pay attention to him. However, a warning bell went off in his head. *Don't get involved with local girls*, it told him.

Forcing himself back to reality, he continued. "Not much to tell either. Raised in Springfield most of my life. My dad was a chaplain in the Navy.

He was stationed on the Battleship West Virginia during the attack on Pearl Harbor on December seventh, nineteen forty-one. He was one of the sixty-six people trapped on board when the ship was sunk by enemy torpedoes."

Laura lay her hand on Paul's shoulder. "I'm so sorry. I'm sure that was rough on you and your mom."

"Yes. I was only seven. I have no brothers or sisters. Just me and mom. But we've made it okay. She works as a bank teller in Springfield. I decided to be a Navy chaplain like my dad, but the military wouldn't take me because of a heart murmur. So," he shrugged, "I became a pastor instead."

"Would you rather be a chaplain?"

"As one of my professors in Bible school said, 'The world is the mission field.' I'm happy as pastor here. Although," he gave a dry laugh, "you have certainly made pastoring in this town more interesting by your comments here today. I came to Bethel Springs," he added after a lengthy pause, "because I believed God had placed me here. Since He did, I know He will give me the wisdom and courage to do whatever I'm supposed to do to combat the evil that has sprung up in this town."

Laura looked over at him, keeping her hand gently on his shoulder. "I hope and pray you can help overcome the evil and the evildoers that are trying to destroy our town."

Back in his apartment, alone in the big, empty building, alone with his thoughts, alone with his imagination of what could happen to him if he stuck it out here and faced this challenge, he wasn't so sure. Did he have the wisdom and courage he needed? Could he be a good pastor in a normal town and church, much less pastoring in a town that seemed like he was back in the wild west?

He walked back downstairs to the hall. Pacing up and down the center aisle he tried to pray and ask God for direction. He walked to the front of the hall and knelt down at the backless bench they used as an altar and prayed. He stood and raised his hands in prayer. He stood behind the pulpit and prayed. "Where are you, God?" he asked. "What shall I do?"

He remembered Joe Taylor, a year ahead of him at Zion Bible School. He had taken a church in Branson even before he graduated. It was growing so big Pastor Joe was looking for an assistant. He considered: *I can go there, become an assistant pastor, and learn all about pastoring from a real pastor for a couple of years. That will prepare me better when I go to pastor again.*

Thinking this may be his answer, in spite of what he told Laura, Paul finally went back upstairs and went to bed.

Paul had just drifted off to sleep that night when he heard men begin to argue down the street in front of the bar. He ignored it for several minutes, but when it continued, he, at first, decided to close the windows to try and shut out the noise but then decided to have a look. By this time, since he had gotten the screens on the windows, he took off the screen from his front window and looked out. Under the street light on the corner, he could see two men in the center with a ring of men surrounding them. He only heard bits and pieces of their conversation, but the way their fists were up and they were facing each other, he knew a fight was coming.

Then from inside the bar out walked a huge man. Taller than any other man in the group with wide shoulders and long black hair, he fearlessly forced his way through the crowd to the two men. "Gus, Duke," Paul heard him shout, "knock it off." He grabbed one man by his right arm. The man cried out in pain. "Gus, you go home. Sleep it off." He pointed to the other man. "You leave his wife alone, you hear! You go home, too, and stay away from each other. Everyone else," he let the man's arm go and turned in a circle looking at the other men. "Either come back in and finish your drinks or go home, too. No more fighting here tonight."

The two men staggered down the street in opposite directions, and the other men slowly walked back into the bar.

Paul closed the window and put back the screen. *Those men need Jesus,* Paul told himself in a flash of discernment, *and they are just down the corner from our church that can tell them were to find real happiness, not just the momentary buzz of a glass of liquor.*

The next evening at six o'clock when Zeb's Bar and Grill opened, Paul was standing in front of the bar with a handful of tracts he had stored at his church. They were titled, *How to Find Real Happiness.* As men walked in he smiled, greeted them, and handed them a tract. Most of the men accepted the paper with some stuffing them in their pockets, and others throwing them on the sidewalk after they had glanced at them and saw what they were. Paul simply picked up those tracts and reused them.

At six fifteen the door opened and the huge man Paul had seen from his window the night before walked out. "What you doing?" he demanded, looking at Paul.

Paul suddenly realized he should have expected this. Reacting quickly Paul stuck out his right hand and smiled. "Hello, sir. Paul Whitfield, pastor from down the street. Just out here passing out some tracts."

He ignored Paul's outstretched hand. He looked bigger close up, probably six foot four or five inches. Three hundred pounds at least, most of it muscle.

His long hair and scraggly beard gave him the appearance of a bear. A strong, big, mean bear.

"Zeb's my name. Zeb Stone. I own this joint. Have for ten years. I'm telling you, leave my patrons alone. They are doing just fine without you and your fancy church and you chicken pastors."

He narrowed his eyes and looked directly into Paul's eyes. "I was in the Army, fought in Guadalcanal and other islands. Took care of my enemies one way or another. Lots of them." The huge man laughed, showing a missing front tooth. "Still do. So you best keep to yourself and don't become my enemy." With that he turned from Paul and went back into the bar, slamming the door after him.

Realizing he needed to change his tactics, Paul walked back down the street and back into the church, replacing the tracts on the book rack.

1955 CHAPTER 8

On Monday, Paul decided to drive up the hill to Hope Fellowship Church and finally meet Pastor Gannon. He had dreaded this occasion, knowing he would feel intimidated by this young, handsome, established, successful pastor. He knew courtesy demanded he meet him at some point. In spite of what he had heard, Paul felt it important to let the townspeople know both churches were partnering together to spread the gospel and minister to this community and fight this battle with George Hackett and his cronies and all sinfulness in a unified way. At least he hoped that would be the case.

Carefully dressing in his best gray slacks, short-sleeve white shirt and freshly-polished black loafers, he got in his DeSoto he had parked in the alley behind the church and started on his way. Checking his odometer as he drove the winding road on West Hill he made a mental note that his church was two point eight miles from Hope Fellowship.

Parking in the first stall in the graveled parking lot, Paul got out and self-consciously made his way to the main entrance of the church, facing the parking lot, on the north side of the church. Opening one of the wide wooden doors, he stepped into the foyer that was almost half the size of the entire hall of his church. To the right were men's and women's restrooms. To the left was a large room with chairs and toys, obviously the nursery.

The foyer had a table with an open guest book and a pen beside it. Various tracts and booklets were displayed in a rack attached to the wall above the table. Paul choose two brochures and put them in his shirt pocket.

Opening the door into the large sanctuary, Paul saw two sections of brown padded pews with an aisle down the middle. He counted twenty pews on each side of the sanctuary. The floor was covered with deep blue carpet. Light brown wood paneling lined the walls, covering the rock walls. His attention was drawn to the high sloping roof held in place by wooden beams that curved up from the floor and joined in the middle.

A choir loft with perhaps thirty seats filled the back of the platform with a grand piano on the left side and an organ on the other side. A large ornate pulpit stood in the center of the platform. A door on the back of the platform on the right side opened as Paul stood in the entrance to the sanctuary. A man of about thirty with a mound of jet black hair piled on his head called out, "May I help you?"

Paul raised his hand in greeting as he walked down the aisle. "Good morning, Reverend. Glad you are in. My name is Paul Whitfield. I'm the new pastor at the Community Chapel. Thought I would drop in and introduce myself."

"David Gannon, pastor." He waited for Paul to approach him and climb the platform before he stretched out his hand in greeting. "Nice to meet you. I've heard a bit about you. Follow me." He led the way back through the door beside the platform into a spacious office with a window overlooking the driveway and his house. "I just put on a pot of coffee, and I have an extra cup for visitors."

Without asking Paul if he wanted coffee he poured a cup, handed it to him, and motioned him to a black leather couch against the wall facing the desk. Sitting behind the desk and crossing his arms, the pastor surveyed Paul for a few moments before speaking. "Welcome to Bethel Springs. How do you like our town so far?" His voice was deep, his enunciation precise, speaking as he would if he were preaching, Paul decided, as he looked back at Pastor Gannon. He was tall, slim, with penetrating brown eyes, dignified in his dark suit and blue tie.

"I like it fine." Paul quickly surveyed the plush office, noting the Royal typewriter on the pastor's desk and the bookshelves covering one wall, filled with study books. The desk was huge, made of solid oak.

"Is this your first pastorate?"

"Yes, I just graduated from Zion Bible College in Springfield last month. I've wanted to be in the ministry most of my life. I helped lead the youth in my church in Springfield and preached a few times in the main service. My dad was a chaplain in the military. I am following in his footsteps as a preacher."

"Is he still in the military? Or retired?"

"He's in heaven. He was aboard the U.S.S. West Virginia during the attack on Pearl Harbor. He's buried in the Springfield National Cemetery."

"Sorry to hear that." The pastor uncrossed his arms and steepled his fingers. "I know that was tough. Is tough. He could be helping you out in your church here if he were still around. I'm sure he would be proud of you. So," he folded his hands and placed them on the desk, "what brings you to this small town in the Ozarks to pastor that little storefront church?"

"When I was nearing graduation one of my professors said there was an opening here and invited me to come."

"Are you aware the previous pastor, Charles Meredith, left town in a hurry? Some say he was run out of town because he was meddling into other people's business."

"I heard he left town because he was threatened by certain people, and they took it out on his son."

"Yes, that's the rumor that is going around town, although nothing can be proven since the hit-and-run driver was never caught."

"I heard a man by the name of George Hackett is trying to bring gambling and who knows what all to this town. Maybe, if both of our churches get together, we can put him out of business and keep this town and county free of gambling."

Pastor Gannon gave Paul a superior smile. "That sounds like a great idea—a noble cause—something churches should fight for." He took a sip of his coffee and sat the cup down and stared over Paul's head. "But is that what we really want? Our town has been about the same size for the past hundred years. Besides the Lundquist Shoe Factory and the chicken processing plant, there are few places to find employment here. Young people are leaving and going into bigger cities because they can't find work here. Hackett has big plans to grow the town, bring in new jobs, and attract tourists who have a lot of money."

"But, the gambling." Paul forgot to drink his coffee. "We don't want that in our town, do we? That would bring in all kinds of unsavory characters, probably make gambling addicts out of some of the townspeople, plus break up marriages and ruin families. I hear there is already gambling at Hackett House that I'm sure is causing problems already."

"Any time a town grows and gets new businesses you might get some bad eggs. But that shouldn't be much of a problem." Pastor Gannon leaned in toward Paul. "Just look at it this way. New people in town mean new prospects for our churches. I hear your church has really gone down in size lately. Wouldn't you like new people coming to your church? More money in the coffers would raise your salary. I know I could use a few more people and their tithe in my church."

Paul remembered Laura's comment that many of the people on the side of wanting to legalize gambling attended Gannon's church, and he realized he was probably not going to get any cooperation from this pastor. At least he had tried. Moving to Branson seemed more attractive all the time.

Paul dropped the topic. Trying to build some sort of rapport with Pastor Gannon he asked him about his background, his family and other topics he thought the pastor would be interested in discussing. After several minutes of this almost meaningless dialogue Paul rose to go, leaving his coffee untouched. "Thank you for taking time to talk to me," he said.

"Anytime." Pastor Gannon also rose. "You know," he added almost as an afterthought, "we are in the middle of the twentieth century, and we have to reach the modern man with the modern gospel, not some antiquated fire and brimstone fundamentalist preaching like the former pastor from your church used to preach." He smiled condescendingly. "If you take on George Hackett, and if you preach fire and brimstone and that everybody's a sinner and going to hell, I give you six months, and you'll be moving to Arkansas with Charles

Meredith or someplace else." He stood and shook Paul's hand. "So good luck. You're going to need it."

Without responding to his comment Paul walked out of the office door, shutting it behind him. He was anxious to walk down the aisle and get outside in the fresh air and sunshine. Then he stopped as an overpowering anger engulfed him. Righteous indignation he would call it later.

Turning around, he opened the office door again just as David Gannon was sitting down in his leather cushioned chair behind his huge desk. The pastor looked up in surprise.

"I was just thinking," started Paul, then swallowed and took a deep breath, trying to keep his temper in check. "You just passed judgment on the fundamentalist preaching that talks about the wages of sin and hell as being old-fashioned. Yet, that's the lifestyle the early settlers of this town followed, and, in fact, the whole country. This nation was founded on the belief that every word of the Bible was true and needed to be followed. That's the same gospel we need to preach today, not some watered down version that makes everyone feel good with no accounting for their sins." Paul suddenly remembered a comment one of his Bible professors made. "The apostle Paul's prediction is coming true, apparently. He said in Second Timothy that in the last days people will gather around them teachers with itching ears that will preach fables to make the listeners feel good. Paul advised preachers to not fall to that temptation."

He cleared his throat again and took another deep breath as he looked at the pastor leaning back in his big chair, his arms folded across his chest, a bemused expression on his face. "I've heard of churches like this. Hopefully your church is not one of them. Have a wonderful day." He tried to smile as he started backing toward the door.

David Gannon raised his hands as if to stop Paul. "Before you go," he said, "I've heard you have likened Bethel Springs to the Bethel in the Bible. Did you read the part in the Bible where a certain prophet came in to try and clean up the sin in Bethel and straighten everyone out? If you're not careful you might end up the same way he did. Thank you for coming." With that he gestured toward the door. Paul took the hint and walked out of the pastor's office, closing the door behind him.

Hurrying back down the aisle Paul revisited in his mind the various passages he had studied in the Bible about Bethel. He would have to look them over again. Before going outside he stopped, tried to relax, said a silent, unintelligible prayer, then opened the big front door and stepped out into the warmth of the sunshine.

As Paul left the church and was making his way toward his car he saw a young, attractive woman in a pink dress, her long dark hair held in place by two gold combs leaving the parsonage and going toward the church. A small boy in short pants and a Roy Rogers T-shirt walked beside her, stopping every few steps to pick up a rock and throw it. "Hello," she called when she saw Paul, changing course and coming toward him with a welcoming smile. "I don't recognize you. New in town?"

"Yes." Paul paused as they approached. "My name is Paul Whitfield, new pastor at Community Chapel."

"Oh, welcome. Nice to meet you. I'm Helen, Pastor Gannon's wife. This is our five-year-old son, Jacob. She approached Paul and gave him a firm handshake. Unlike the tone of voice he had just heard from her husband, Helen appeared friendly and inquisitive. They talked for several minutes while Jacob continued to throw rocks, one narrowly missing Paul's car. Paul told her a little about his background. Helen told him she had been raised in Little Rock, Arkansas, daughter of a Baptist pastor. She and her husband had been married for seven years. This was their second pastorate, their first having been a small church near Little Rock.

As Paul was leaving Helen said she would talk to her husband about inviting him over for dinner sometime where they could get better acquainted.

Back at church he looked in his Bible until he found the story in First Kings chapter thirteen, about the man of God who came to Bethel. He did his best to confront King Jeroboam about his sin and clean up the town. But on his way out of town, the man of God sinned and was eaten by a lion.

Paul sat the Bible down and paced up and down the center aisle of the hall praying and thinking. "Lord," he said out loud, "what is going on? I believed you called me into the ministry. I believed you called me to this church. But am I like the man of God that came to Bethel? Will I make a mistake and sin like he did and be eaten by a proverbial lion or have some other catastrophe happen to me? Again, Lord," he added in a conversational tone, " is all that's been going on an indication from You that I should stay on and fight this battle, or are you telling me it's time to go visit Joe Taylor in Branson?"

1955 CHAPTER 9

Eight adults showed up for Bible study on Wednesday night. Not quite sure yet what he should be teaching his congregation Paul used some notes he had taken from his Corinthians class at Bible school and taught a lesson on First Corinthians, chapter one.

The next morning as Paul was fixing pancakes, eggs and bacon for breakfast, looking forward to some time off again to reflect on how he should deal with this problem in his town, he heard a knock on the church door.

Turning off the stove he hurried downstairs and opened the door. Betty Pittman stood before him, wringing her hands in distress. "Pastor Paul," she pleaded, tears running down her face, "may I talk with you?"

"Sure." Paul opened the door and let her in. "I don't have a church office, but we can talk here on the benches, if you like. Would you like me to get you some coffee? Just made some upstairs."

"No, no." Betty sat on the nearest bench. Smoothing her red and yellow floral print dress, she kept her head down as she talked, looking at the hardwood floor. "I know you're new here and not good at this pastoring thing yet, but I need to talk to someone. I borrowed a neighbor's car and she is watching the kids so I can't stay long."

"I'm here to listen and do whatever I can do," Paul replied, feeling an instant compassion for this young woman from his church.

"Ever heard of Hackett House?" For the first time Betty looked up at Paul.

He frowned, then adjusted his facial expression when he realized the woman was looking at him. He had heard of the evils of Hackett House. Now, he was apparently going to hear more about this detested place. "Yes, I have had heard some talk of it," he said vaguely, fearful of what was coming next.

"I don't know what you've heard, but it's a sin hole if I ever saw one. It's about three or four miles west of town on Mill Road. A huge house, almost a mansion, built by old man Hackett many years ago. After he died his son George moved in. He went through three wives, don't know if he's married now or not. I think his son and daughter live with him. Every Friday and Saturday nights the place is packed with men. Gambling, pool playing and more. They bring in blue movies from Springfield. Rumors are that sometimes girls even show up to entertain the men. That's where my Sam goes sometimes, more and more lately. He doesn't earn much at Elven's Auto Shop where he fixes cars. What he does make he's starting to gamble away at that sin hole. He tells me he's going night fishing or out to a restaurant with his buddy, Andy, or something. But he comes back smelling like a still."

She paused, looked down at her dress again that she continued smoothing out. "And our money's gone, or most of it. Pastor Paul, we have four little kids. They need food, shoes, clothes. Our house is a dump. We may have to move." She looked up at Paul. "What can I do?"

Paul stared at the young woman. She couldn't be much over thirty, he decided. Still had a youthful face with the start of bags under her eyes. Dressed in nicer clothes with her hair combed, she would have been attractive had it not been for the tears and hopeless look. He remembered Sam: balding, a round stomach, quiet and withdrawn, at least in church. Four kids: three girls and one boy. He couldn't remember their names or ages.

"How long has this been going on?" asked Paul, silently praying for wisdom and trying to recall what he had learned in psychology class about how to deal with these problems.

"I don't know. A year, maybe two. Hard to tell since he has always gone out at night occasionally with his buddies ever since we've been married."

"How many men show up at Hackett House? Any wives go with their husbands?"

"Course not," Betty scoffed. "Wives not invited. I don't know how many go there. I've never gone by there since Sam has the car, and he wouldn't let me drive at night, even when he is home. But from what I hear quite a few."

Paul gently reached out and grasped Betty's shaking hands. "Let's pray about it right now. I will pray about it some more after you leave. I know the Lord is able to turn this into a miracle in His way and His time. And, if the Lord leads, I'll talk to Sam. If what you say is true, he's certainly not being the Christian husband and father he should be."

"Oh, it's true all right. Not only Sam." Betty gripped Paul hands as if her life depended on it, looking at him in the eyes. "You best look at a couple of your other upstanding church members and see where they go on weekends."

After prayer Betty left. Paul went back upstairs to his kitchen and finished making pancakes.

Paul finished his breakfast, then came back down and stood before the altar. "Is this your answer?" he asked the Lord conversationally, his eyes open, looking up at the white Sheetrock ceiling. "Did You send me here to stay in this town and attack this evil that has invaded this community and my church? God, what do you want me to do about it?"

He stood before the altar praying for several minutes, then walked up and down the aisle of the church as he continued in prayer, waiting on the Lord for some kind of direction. He went over to the bench and laid hands on the spot where Sam and Betty and their family sat and continued praying.

After praying about an hour he decided to get another opinion. Combing his hair and putting on a clean nylon shirt he walked to the library. "Hello, Paul." Patsy's voice was cheery as usual, her dazzling smile appeared to show she was happy to see him. "In here for more Zane Grey or more Andrew Murray?"

"Neither." Paul looked around at the book lined room and didn't see anybody sitting at the tables or examining books on the shelves. "Can I talk to you for a minute?"

"Sure." Patsy's smile wavered slightly. She pointed to a folding chair across from her desk. "Have a seat. I just made coffee. Want some?"

"No thanks." Paul sat in the chair. "I need some information. You working at the library, I'm sure you hear a lot."

Patsy nodded, the smile still in place. "If you want gossip, I hear plenty, especially from young mothers who bring in their kids."

"What can you tell me about Hackett House and George Hackett wanting to bring gambling to Bethel Springs? I hear half the town wants gambling and half the town doesn't. I also heard the last pastor of my church was run out of town because he tried to stand up to George Hackett and his cronies."

Just then the door opened and a young woman came in with two small boys that ran down the room toward Patsy.

"Nate, Peter." Patsy stood and walked toward the boys giving them a hug. "Rose," she turned toward the woman. "Nice to see you again." She pointed toward Paul. "Rose, this is Paul Whitfield, new pastor at the little church downtown. Paul, this is Rose Stokes."

Paul stood and shook hands with the woman. "You have a beautiful town here," Paul said to make conversation. "I came here to get some information about the town from your librarian," he added, hoping the woman wouldn't think he was there just to visit Patsy.

Each boy grabbed one of Patsy's hands and pulled her toward the children's section. While Patsy was with the boys Paul continued talking to the woman. "Tell me about your town," he asked her. "What should I know about Bethel Springs to help in my ministry to this community?" The woman was in her early thirties, Paul decided. Her dark hair hung loose, down to her shoulders. Her brown faded dress sagged down around her shoulders like it was a size too big. Her scuffed brown shoes and large pink purse with a torn seam told Paul much of what he needed to know about her.

"Well," the woman paused and looked toward her children who were busy taking books out of the shelves with Patsy trying her best to corral them. "I was born and raised here," she began, avoiding looking at Paul. "Been a good town so far. I went to school here. I married Tom a few years back. He's a farmer. We live on a farm beyond Valley Drive."

"What do you raise on your farm?"

"We raise hogs mostly. Some beef. Some hay. Have a pretty big garden where we raise most of our vegetables."

"How's the farming business these days?"

Rose shrugged. "No worse than most years. Except now my Tom spends most of it at Hackett House, so there's not much left for me and the boys."

Just then Patsy returned with the boys clutching books. "Mommy, can we get these books?" they asked in unison.

"They each chose three books," Patsy added. "It's okay with me if they check them out. They will be due back in three weeks."

She turned to Paul and said quietly, "Why don't you come back at five when I close up? We'll talk then."

Paul returned to the church, had lunch, worked on his sermons for Sunday, and restlessly waited until five o'clock.

Promptly at five, as he was walking up the steps to the library, Patsy opened the door with her purse over her shoulder. Locking the door she turned to Paul. "Had dinner yet?"

"No."

"Good." She pointed to a late model pink Cadillac convertible sitting at the curb. "Can I take you to dinner?"

Paul nodded and got in the passenger seat beside Patsy. Not a bad start, Paul told himself as they started out of town. *Going out to dinner with the two most beautiful girls in town. And I've only been in town a few days.*

"Ever been to the Riverview Restaurant?"

Paul shook his head.

"It's one of my favorite places." They drove on in silence for a few minutes. The houses got fewer and fewer until there was mostly just woods around them. The top was down and the breeze felt good as it ruffled Paul's hair and blew against his face. Patsy had wrapped a yellow scarf around her head to keep her hair in place. White clouds lazily chased each other across the blue sky. Paul took a deep breath, enjoying the freshness of the country air. It felt good to be alive on this beautiful summer day in the Ozarks.

"Do you go to church anywhere?" Paul asked after several minutes of small talk, trying to get a feel of Patsy's spiritual life.

"I go to the Hope Fellowship church. My parents and I have gone there all my life."

Paul felt a chill go down his spine as he remembered what Laura had said about the church. "I'm curious," responded Paul, trying to understand her views about Christianity without seeming to be offensive or intrusive, "what's the church's view on the Bible, salvation, sin and heaven?"

Patsy looked over briefly at Paul and laughed. "Is this some sort of test you're giving me?"

Paul returned the laugh. "Just asking. I met your pastor and his family. They seem like nice people." He hoped his comment wasn't a lie.

"Yes they are. I like Helen, the pastor's wife. She comes into the library some with little Jacob to listen to my stories and sometimes to watch the Mickey Mouse Club. He's a cute little kid. Pastor Gannon is a good preacher. He uses the Bible some, but preaches out of books mostly." She turned back to Paul for a moment. "I'm sure he's not the fire and brimstone preacher like I imagine you are."

"I wouldn't classify myself in that way. I like to emphasis more the love of God and the salvation He offers. However, since the Bible does teach about the wages of sin, we also include that teaching." He looked over at Patsy. "You might want to drop by some Sunday to find out."

"I might do that some time."

They climbed a gradual hill and finally emerged into another community set on a ridge. Patsy drove down a graveled road passing several hotels and restaurants and pulled up in front of a white frame building with a flashing neon sign reading "Riverview Restaurant."

The building appeared to be an old gas station. The pumps were gone, but there was still the overhanging roof and the concrete foundation where the pumps had been. With no formal parking lot, Patsy eased into a space between an ancient black Ford truck and a newer green Hudson.

Walking under the roof they entered the front door to the noise of voices, the clattering of dishes and the odor of fried food. On the left a woman stood before a cash register on a counter. To his right Paul saw tables mostly filled with customers. An older woman dressed in a bright calico dress with a bonnet smiled at them. "Hello, Patsy. Two?" she asked.

"Yes, by the window please."

"Certainly." The hostess grabbed two menus and took them back through a hallway into another large room and showed them to a table. The restaurant stood on the edge of a bluff overlooking the White River about fifty feet below them. Remembering his etiquette, Paul stood at the back of Patsy's chair and helped her scoot her chair up to the table before sitting down himself across from her. He looked out the window at the beautiful display of God's creation: the sparkling river below, the rolling wooded hills of green trees and fields stretching out to the horizon, white clouds in the west getting brushed pink by the setting sun.

Paul's attention was brought back to Patsy when she said: "Before we talk about George Hackett, can I talk to you about something else?" She picked up a menu and looked at it briefly. "My brother, Lamar, I don't think you've met him yet. He's lost. I think you can help him."

Paul looked up from his menu. "Lost?" Have you told the authorities? Anybody out looking for him?"

"No, I don't mean lost in that way. He's probably home now. He's a nice guy. He's been to college one year at Southwest Missouri State College in Springfield. Dad is trying to groom him for the family business. But he's told me several times he hates college. He hates the family business. He hates people. Or at least hates working with people. He's a loner. He's told me if he had his choice he would be a hermit in the hills, living by himself. Just him with his two dogs."

"How do you think I can help him?"

"Just talk to him. Make friends with him. He never had many friends in school or anywhere else. I don't think he has a real friend now. He confides in me some, but even the two of us have been getting more and more distant. Mom still gets along with him, but Dad is losing patience. Thinks he's lazy."

"How is he doing spiritually? Does he go to church with you? Show any interest in spiritual things? Talk about the Bible or his relationship with Christ?"

Patsy shook her head. "He quit going to church when he was in high school. He doesn't read his Bible or pray as far as I know."

Paul nodded. "Sure, I would be happy to talk with him. See what I can do. No promises, though. Whatever he chooses to do will be up to him."

"Thank you. I'll tell him you would like to meet him. Maybe the three of us can come back here for dinner where you can get acquainted with him."

Just then the waitress came and they placed their order. Patsy ordered a lobster tail with a baked potato and salad. Paul, not knowing what half the items on the menu were, to be safe, ordered a T-bone steak, mashed potatoes and green beans.

"So tell me about George Hackett," Paul asked quietly after the waitress had left, so the other diners wouldn't overhear their conversation. "I hear he runs the Hackett House where there is gambling and who knows what else, and that he is wanting to legalize gambling so he can build casinos, hotels, bath houses and bring more money into the town."

"That's true. He's trying to get a measure on the ballot for people in the county to vote on in November. He claims if gambling becomes legal the town will grow and prosper like never before."

"How do you feel about it?"

"Dad likes the idea. He thinks it will help his shoe business and the whole town. Other merchants like the idea too. But me," she shook her head, "I don't like it. I see wives and mothers come into the library. More and more of them complain about their husbands losing money at Hackett House and spending too much time there. If they build casinos I'm afraid more and more men will get involved in gambling. Women too."

"So what should we do to stop it?"

Patsy looked over at Paul for several moments before replying, then looked out the window. They both watched as an eagle about a hundred feet away majestically glided by above the trees, catching the wind in its wings. Several ducks took off on the river below in front of a motor boat making its way upstream, leaving a V-shaped wake in its path. Finally she spoke: "Nothing." She reached across the table and placed her hand on Paul's hand. "I'm getting to like you. I know what happened to your last pastor and his family. I hear gossip. If you get involved in trying to stop George Hackett and his crew, I fear what will happen to you." She took her hand away. "You are an outsider and don't really know what's going on or know the people here. I suggest you just preach to your congregation the love of God or whatever you preach and let it go at that. Let the town fight its own battles."

The waitress brought their food and Paul dropped the subject.

An hour later they left the restaurant. Darkness had settled over the Ozarks. A breeze cooled the evening. Leaving the top down on her Cadillac, Patsy started the car. "Do you mind if I show you a beautiful spot overlooking Bethel Springs and the valley?"

"Sure." Paul nodded in the darkness as Patsy drove another few miles with the cooling night air whipping past them and parked the car just off the road onto a wide graveled shoulder on a bluff overlooking the valley. The landscape, partially lit by the half-moon and overhead blanket of stars, stretched before them, dotted by stationary lights and a few lights moving slowly on darkened roadways.

"The main reason I brought you here," she said, "was to give you a lay of the land, in case you haven't been here before. As you can see, directly in front of us in the cluster of lights, is Bethel Springs. The town square with the library in the middle with the two lights in front, is almost directly in the center of town. Your little church is in the row of lights a little to the left. Way to the left, or east, you can barely see the outline of Valley Drive with just a few lights along the road. That's mostly where the poorer people live. A chicken processing plant where some of them work is farther down. To the right, or west of town, on that small hill, surrounded by lights pointing to it, is Hope Fellowship Church, where I attend. To the right of that is Highway 13. Ahead, in the distance on the road that you can't see, is Lundquist Shoe Factory, Dad's main factory. Branching off Highway 13 and going farther west is Mill Road with Hackett House down a few miles." She continued describing landmarks in and around the town.

When she finished, she turned her car around and steered back on the road. "Just so you know," she commented with a laugh, poking him playfully in the ribs, "if you are ever interested, this is where guys like to take their dates. It's called Lovers' Lookout. I came here once on a date with a boyfriend I had in high school. But only once, so far." She turned to him and said again, "Only once so far, but that can change."

Then she turned serious. "I'm afraid if you try to fight Hackett, I doubt that you'll be here long enough to bring a girl up here."

1955 CHAPTER 10

All day Saturday as Paul prepared for his sermons for Sunday his mind went over and over his conversations with Betty, Rose, Laura and Patsy.

After dinner and cleaning the kitchen, Paul went out for a walk in the deepening dusk. After circling the square he returned home, went back in the building, got his car keys and locked the church door. Finally, making up his mind, he drove toward Mill Road.

"God," he prayed out loud. "I don't know if it was your voice or not, but something told me to check out Hackett House tonight and see what's up. I hope it was You."

Not sure where Hackett House was located, Paul drove west on Mill Road past occasional homes dotting the farmland. Then, ahead on the left, he saw a larger-than-average house. Driving slowly by he saw stone lions guarding both sides of a long gravel driveway bordered by shrubs and an immaculate lawn. Beyond the driveway and lawn, maybe a hundred feet off the road, stood a two-story brick house with four white pillars holding up the roof over a large porch. Every light in the house seemed to be on. Behind the house on both sides, Paul thought he could see the reflections of parked cars. Must be Hackett House, he decided.

He pulled the car off the side of the road about a quarter of a mile beyond the house. "Lord," he breathed, "should I check this out? Or go back home and not get tangled up in this?"

Not hearing an answer from the Lord, he finally got out of the car and made his way through the darkness to the driveway between the two lions. Staying behind the shrubs as much as he could, he cautiously approached the house, hoping no one was on the lookout for intruders. If what the women said was true, he imagined how it would look if the new preacher in town was seen at Hackett House.

A faint sound of music came to his ears as he approached. It was *Rock Around the Clock*, a song he had heard on the radio a couple of times by Bill Haley and His Comets. Suddenly the driveway was lit up behind him as a car approached. Crouching behind a shrub, hoping he couldn't be seen, he watched as the car passed, occupied by two men in the front seat and one in the back. He observed the men get out and disappear behind the back of the house.

Creeping further toward the house he noticed the shades or curtains were drawn on all the windows. No one could peek in and see what was going on. He counted at least twenty cars parked behind the house, probably far off the road, so people passing by couldn't see whose cars were there.

Making his way to the end of the driveway he crouched behind the last shrub before the house wondering what to do next. Should he walk up to the house and try to go in? If he did, what would he do once he got inside? Should he see if Sam Pittman was there and confront him and tell him to go home? Or, should he leave now while no one had seen him, return home, and plan his next move?

"Hey, buddy, what you doing?" a voice behind him called out.

Startled, Paul looked up into the face of a young man about his age, vaguely familiar in the darkness. Then he remembered Martha's Café and the four men. Norman. Norman Hackett, the son. His father, George, was the owner of Hackett House. Crouched in the darkness as he was, Norman looked tall and big and strong, way beyond what Paul decided he could take on in a fair fight.

What general was it that said it was sometimes prudent to retreat so you could fight another day? Paul realized his only advantage was speed. Without replying, he jumped to his feet and ran as fast as he could toward the road.

With a grunt of surprise, Norman Hackett followed. Hearing pounding footsteps behind him, Paul turned around and noticed his pursuer was keeping up with him, even gaining a little. Maybe he didn't have the advantage of speed, after all. The only alternative that came to Paul was to try a stunt he and his friends had done on each other as kids. Without warning he knelt down, covering his head and neck with his hands.

With a grunt of surprise he felt the feet of the guard slam against his back, the rest of his body flying over him and landing with a thud on the graveled driveway in front of him. Noticing his pursuer was wearing loafers, as another spur-of-the moment action, he jerked off one of Norman's shoes and threw it as far as he could behind him.

Resuming his running, he looked back and noticed with satisfaction that even though Norman had finally gotten to his feet and was limping along after him, he was losing ground. When Paul reached the end of the driveway he sped toward his car, taking the keys out of his pocket as he ran. He jumped in his car, locked the door, and started the engine just as the guard ran up. Ignoring the pounding on his window and yelling, Paul put his car in gear and sped off into the night. Looking into the rearview mirror he saw the guard standing with his hands on his hips staring at him.

Back in his bedroom above the church, Paul shook his head as he got ready for bed. "What an idiot," he said out loud as he fixed himself a cup of Ovaltine. He wondered: *Did Norman recognize me? Will he come after me and break into the church and beat me up tonight? Or tomorrow? Or tell the whole town the new pastor in town showed up at the Hackett House?*

1955   CHAPTER 11

All during Sunday school the next day, the morning service, and church at Sunday night, Paul nervously kept his eye on the front door, expecting any time that one or more of Hackett's men, or George Hackett himself, would barge into the service to accuse him of trespassing on their property the night before.

But the services went off as normal with no disruptions.

Monday, July fourth, dawned bright and clear and beautiful. A few white, cotton clouds slowly drifted by on the azure sky for a perfect Independence Day. Thomas Spradley had told Paul the town had a parade starting at four o'clock, followed by a picnic on the town square with music, speeches and fireworks when it got dark. "The parade goes right by the church," Spradley told him.

His wife, Patricia, added, "Why don't you join us for the picnic? None of our kids are with us so it's just us. I can fix some extra fried chicken and potato salad. Bring a folding chair from church, if you want, and eat with us. We generally spread out our blanket and set up our chairs in the northwest corner of the square, by the tall oak tree." Paul agreed to meet them there.

He spent the morning cleaning and reorganizing his upstairs living space, especially the bathroom that was used by everyone in the church.

As four o'clock approached, Paul noticed from his upstairs window people lining up on both sides of the street outside.

Putting on his St. Louis Cardinals baseball cap to shield his head from the hot sun, he made his way outside to stand with the other spectators. Since the parade hadn't started yet he decided to walk to Martha's Café to get a cold soda pop while he waited.

Sitting at a table in Laura's section, she soon came out of the kitchen with her usual dimpled smile. "Why aren't you out waiting for the parade?" she asked. "We are officially closed. We always close on the fourth when the parade starts. I just haven't locked the doors yet. You're the only customer. Everyone else is outside getting ready to watch the parade."

"Sorry." Paul rose to go. "Just wanted a Coke or something cold while waiting for the parade to start."

"No, sit down." She touched his shoulder. "I'll get you one. On me."

She returned a minute later with an open Coke bottle she poured in a glass filled with ice. "This should help quench your thirst on this hot day."

"Thanks." With a grateful smile he looked into her soft brown eyes. "You going to see the parade?"

"Wouldn't miss it, Pastor Paul." She sat in the booth across from him.

"Thought any more about what we talked about? Still planning to stay?"

"Yes I did think about it, prayed about it, and talked to others about it. I have considered moving to another church, so they could get a mature pastor in here that would know better how to handle this situation. Or, I could trust in the Lord and see what I can do. I don't know how much good that would be. I may get tarred and feathered and run out of town on a rail if I stay. I haven't made up my mind completely yet, but I believe the Lord wants me to stay."

Laura touched Paul's hand holding the soda with her finger. "Paul, in one way, I hope you stay and get involved. The town needs someone like you. In another way, I'm scared for you if you decide to stay. But I will be praying, and I know the Lord will help you make the right decision."

Paul felt genuinely touched. He took both her hands in his hands across the table. "Thanks for your encouragement and for caring."

The front door slammed. "What have we here?" a raspy voice called out loudly. Laura jerked her hands away and put them on her lap. Paul looked up to see a young man about his age swaggering toward them, sporting black leather boots, tight blue jeans with a huge monogramed belt buckle, a black leather jacket over a white T-shirt with a black skull and crossbones symbol on the front. He placed a smoking cigarette back in his mouth as he leaned back and ran both hands through his duck tail haircut.

"Ready to paint the town red, hon?" he called out to Laura.

"Oh, Claude." Laura sounded exasperated as she glanced guiltily at Paul. "You were supposed to meet me outside in a few minutes. I need to lock up first." She nodded to Paul. "Claude, this is Paul, a customer and the new pastor at the church down the street. Paul, this is Claude, a...a friend."

Paul stood and extended his hand. "Nice to meet you."

Ignoring his hand, Claude took another puff from his cigarette and looked at Laura. "Thought I would surprise you and meet you here. Guess I did," he said looking meaningful at Paul and blowing a cloud of smoke in his face. "Do you always hold hands with your customers?"

"Claude, really." The exasperation remained in her voice. "Be nice." Laura stood and headed toward the kitchen. "We were just talking. I'll get my purse and meet you in back. Paul, please turn the latch on the door when you leave."

"Eat here often?" asked Claude, blowing another puff of smoke in Paul's direction.

"Sometimes."

"Just remember, she's my gal." With that, he tossed his cigarette in Paul's glass and walked outside. A few moments later he saw Claude roaring off on his Harley motorcycle with Laura, her arms around his waist, hanging on behind him.

Paul sat staring at his half-full glass of Coke containing the remains of the cigarette. Then, drinking the rest of the beverage from the bottle, he slowly made his way outside into the heat of the Ozarks summer, locking the door behind him.

Claude. What a character. Right out of the billboards he had seen on the front of movie theaters showing tough thugs dressed the same way. Paul felt a keen sense of disappointment that Laura had a boyfriend, especially somebody like Claude. He thought he knew a little about her from their brief conversations in the diner and their dinner in the woods. Claude didn't seem her type, but he shrugged. What did he know about her, really? Or what did it matter? His job was to pastor a church, not get involved with the local girls.

The parade started with Mayor Tom Peterson riding down the middle of the street in a white Cadillac, followed by the Bethel Springs High School marching band and drill team. Behind them came a marching troop of soldiers dressed in World War II uniforms. Next came an F-51 Mustang World War II fighter plane riding on a flatbed truck. A waving, smiling man in a pilot's uniform sat in the open cockpit with the inscription under the cockpit that read: "Lt. James Hayes, World War II ace." Behind them came a group of soldiers riding in cars identified as World War I veterans.

More floats and groups passed with people applauding for each one.

After the parade passed where Paul was standing, he grabbed a folding chair from the church and followed the crowd to the city square, chatting with the few people he had met, and introducing himself to those who didn't know who he was.

Finally, he wandered over to where the Spradleys said they would be and sat his chair down beside theirs to eat fried chicken with them and watch the activities at the gazebo behind the library near the center of the square.

While they were eating, Patricia nodded toward his husband. "Tom used to march in this parade years ago until he gave his place to someone else. He's a World War I vet, you know. A fighter pilot."

"Really, I didn't know that." Paul turned to Thomas. "Tell me about it."

The older man smiled and looked down at his feet. "Not much to tell. Near the end of the war, I helped the British and flew SPADS and Sopwith Camels, among other planes."

"He became an ace," added Patricia. "Shot down seven German planes over Germany and France."

"Are you the one who shot down the Red Baron?" asked Paul with a smile.

"Not quite. But it was an adventure. I'm glad it's over. Maybe I'll tell you about it sometime."

In spite of his curiosity, Paul didn't pursue the subject, realizing Thomas didn't want to talk about his time spent in the military.

The night passed quickly. Mayor Tom Peterson gave a short speech. The Veterans' Band played, the ladies' glee club sang, more speeches, more music, ending with fireworks.

After the festivities were over, Paul picked up his folding chair and walked back to church in the darkness.

He had barely sat down to relax for the evening when he heard a knock on the front door. He was surprised to see Laura standing there.

"I'm sorry to come so late at night." Nervously, she adjusted the band holding her pony tail and ran her fingers through her bangs. "But I just had to talk to you."

"Come in." Paul stepped back and held open the door. He could see she was near tears. The compassionate pastor part of him kicked in. "I was just getting ready to have a snack before I went to bed. I'm out of coffee but have some Sanka left. Some people think it's healthier than coffee. Come upstairs. I'll fix you a cup. Have some hot water left over."

"No, really, I shouldn't stay."

"No problem. I wasn't ready for bed yet."

He led the way upstairs and motioned her to sit in the old brown cracked leather couch that had been left by the previous pastor while he fixed her a cup of Sanka and buttered another piece of toast.

She accepted the hot brew and toast while Paul sat on his bed. "I really need to apologize for Claude," she said. "I'm not like him. Not anymore. He's my neighbor. Shortly after my dad left, his father and mother kind of adopted Mom and me and helped us out. His father does repairs on our house when it needs work and does what he can to help out. Claude helps too. When I was younger, his mom watched me sometimes when Mom was at work. A while back we started to date. About the same time he became a rebel, or thought he was. His hero is the actor, James Dean, the rebel in the movies. Claude likes to dress like him and act like him. He saw his movie *Rebel Without a Cause* four or five times at the Roxie Theater downtown. I even watched the movie with him a time or two.

"I went along with that for awhile, but I soon realized that wasn't the way to go. I told Claude to either get right with the Lord or leave me alone. He wouldn't do either. He kept pestering me, saying I belonged to him, that I had better be nice to him or he would come after Mom and me. He would fight any boy who paid attention to me."

She took a sip of Sanka. "Like I said, I want you to know I'm not like Claude anymore. I'm glad I'm going back to school so I can get away from him. But you better watch out for him. He has a temper. If he thinks you like me, who knows what he will do." She took a bite of toast, stood, and set the Sanka and toast on the kitchen table. "I'd better go now." She smiled again. "It wouldn't look good if Claude or anyone else saw me alone with you at the church and in your home so late at night. I really should have waited until morning, I guess, to see you. But I didn't want you to go to sleep thinking I was some kind of... some kind of person like Claude."

Paul followed her down the stairs feeling he should say something. "I know you're not," he said when they reached the main floor.

He touched her hand briefly as they walked down the center aisle between the pews toward the front entrance of the church. "Thank you for coming." Paul faced her and took her hands in his as they stood by the door and looked into her soft brown eyes. "I know that took a lot of courage." He stared at her for a moment, suddenly overcome by a desperate urge to kiss her. The look in her eyes made him realize she would respond, even be eager for a kiss.

Out of the corner of his vision he noticed a man and woman walk by on the sidewalk outside the picture windows. He suddenly realized to his dismay that with the lights on in the hall, anyone walking by outside, or probably even people in cars passing by or across the street, could see in.

Stepping back, he let go of her hands. "Probably you should go," he said, his voice sounding shaky.

Laura took a deep breath. "You're right. I'm sorry. I should go." Without a backward glance she hurried out the door and down the street.

Paul locked the door, then walked up the stairs on rubbery legs. Throwing himself on the bed he covered his face with his hands. "God," he said out loud in a pleading voice. "I'm so confused. What should I do?"

Laura. He barely knew her. But there was something about her that attracted him. What was it? Her looks? Her confident demeanor? The way she smiled at him? He didn't know if it was the noise from Zeb's Bar and Grill or his confused thoughts about Laura that kept him awake long after he usually fell asleep.

CHAPTER 12

Paul had just finished his breakfast of oatmeal, toast and coffee when he heard a knock on the back door of the church facing the alley. Thinking it must be kids playing outside he ignored it. When the knocking continued the second time, he made his way downstairs and opened the door to a young woman. He barely recognized her as the cheerful woman he had seen just a few days earlier. She appeared to be near tears. "May I come in and talk to you?" she asked without any words of greeting.

"Certainly." Paul opened the door for her, his compassionate pastor mode wrinkling his brow. He pointed to the front bench on the left side of the hall. "Please, sit." He took a chair from off the platform and placed it a few feet in front of her and sat down.

"How may I help you?"

"I'm sorry to bother you and I'm embarrassed. Please don't let anyone see me or know I was here. And please don't tell anyone what I am about to tell you."

"What's the problem?" Paul surveyed the young woman, not much older than himself. Pretty, with dark hair hanging down to her shoulders. She was wearing what appeared to be an expensive blue dress with a short, white jacket. "You can be assured I will keep our conversation in confidence if that's what you want."

"Thank you. I'm sure you remember me. I'm Helen Gannon, Pastor Gannon's wife. We talked briefly outside the church with my son Jacob after you met my husband, David, a few days ago."

Paul nodded a little apprehensively, wondering what was coming next.

"I didn't know who to go to. I haven't talked to anyone about this for such a long time. Being a pastor's wife, I can't share private things with very many people, if anybody. But I'm desperate. I know you're young and don't have much experience, but at least you are someone I can talk to."

"I've been told I'm a good listener. Maybe I can help."

"David, my husband." A sob escaped her lips. Pulling up the sleeve of her jacket she showed Paul black and blue marks above her right elbow. "He did this to me last night. I could show you bruises on other parts of my body. He gave me a black eye once, but generally just hurts me in places that can't be seen."

"Why would he do that?" Paul stared at the woman in astonishment. "He's a successful pastor, good church. I thought he had a good marriage with a cute little son."

"Jacob. David controls him too. Spanks him too much. I'm scared for him, too. David is a perfectionist. Everything and everyone has to be perfect. He gets angry at himself if things aren't as he likes them and sometimes takes it out on me or our son. If I make a mistake…" she paused and looked at the floor, a sob escaping her lips. "Last week we had the Franklins over, a church family. I made a cake. When I handed Peter Franklin his cake my foot slipped, the plate tipped over, and the cake ended up in his lap, frosting first. Peter laughed it off and so did David. But when they left he gave such a tongue lashing and pinched my arm until it turned purple. And that night, in the bedroom…"

Paul raised his hand palm out. "I get the picture. I am so sorry for you."

"That's not all. Last night at dinner, in front of Jacob, he raked me over the coals about not serving healthy food: too much fried food, not enough vegetables and fruits.

"He talks about you sometimes. Says you are a greenhorn, wet behind the ears. You are an old-fashioned fundamentalist that is giving modern Christianity a bad name. You are taking Christianity back to the nineteenth century. And he goes on and on sometimes about how you aren't going to last in Bethel Springs or anywhere else. I think he's afraid he might lose members to you. He said almost as a joke, or maybe he was serious, that he wished your church would burn down and blow away.

"Pastor Paul," Helen dabbed at her eyes with a lacy handkerchief from her purse, "I was raised a Baptist. Our pastor preached from the Bible about the cross, that Christ could change our lives through His death and resurrection. He preached about hell and heaven and that we needed to repent and turn from sin and serve Jesus.

"David," she continued, almost with a sneer, "preaches from books—success prosperity, health, happiness, good standing in the community—those are his gods; that's what he preaches about. He looks down on poor people and whoever doesn't see things his way. When I mention preaching about sin and salvation, he says he doesn't want to offend people and drive them away. He wants people to feel good about themselves and the church and not feel condemned and unhappy."

She shook her head. "When I talk to my parents, they don't understand. They think David is just one step down from being divine himself and think I'm exaggerating." She turned to Paul with a pleading look. "I'm sorry to lay this on you. But it all looks so hopeless. I don't know what to do."

Paul's heart was stirred with compassion toward this attractive young woman. No doubt she got married with stars in her eyes and dreams of a beautiful future and a wonderful family. Now, she saw her life, future and family crumbling around her.

Throwing up a quick prayer, Paul cleared his throat. "Nothing is hopeless with the Lord." He tried to give Helen a reassuring smile. "With God all things are possible," he added, quoting a Scripture that popped into his head. Then he stood, deep in thought and put his hands in the pockets of his jeans, walking toward the pulpit where he kept his preaching Bible, leafing through it for a few moments. Helen sat on the front bench, looking at the floor, nervously twisting the handkerchief in her hands.

Finally, he sat back down and handed Helen a piece of paper. "Helen," he said gently, "I could sit here and tell you all I know about how to handle a situation like this and read you a dozen Scriptures. But, instead, here is the name and phone number of Grace Carpenter. She's a professor at my Bible school. She teaches counseling. She is very qualified and I know she can help you. Give her a call. Tell her I asked you to contact her. If you can go see her in Springfield I know she would be happy to talk to you. Or, if you can't go there, I know she would be willing to come here, and you could meet here at our church or somewhere."

"I have a sister who lives in Republic, which is close to Springfield. I go see her quite often. Maybe I can tell David I'm going to see Joyce and fit in a visit with this counselor at the same time."

Paul smiled. "I trust this will be helpful to you. Let me know if I can help in any other way. Now, let's pray," he added. Taking Helen's hands in his, he said a simple prayer that God would change David's heart, that Helen would get good advice from Grace Carpenter, that God would heal their family, and that all things would work together for good to them that love God and are the called according to his purpose.

After the prayer Helen reached over and gave Paul a hug. "Thank you." She smiled and clutched the paper Paul had given her. "For the first time in a long time I have hope. But," she added, turning sober, "again, this is between us, right? If David, or anyone from my church found out I had come here he would kill me. I mean, maybe literally. Or maybe take it out on you."

Paul stood. "Besides Grace Carpenter, I won't tell a soul. No one in my church, not even my mother."

"Thank you." As if suddenly in a hurry Helen went out the back door of the church. A moment later Paul heard the engine of a car start.

He went back upstairs to his apartment for his second cup of coffee. He looked out the window at the stone church on the hill, the steeple pointing toward the clear blue sky. Suddenly, Paul no longer felt envious of the church or its pastor or its people. A stirring of anger toward the pastor filled his heart, followed by a feeling of compassion for Helen and their young son, and a heaviness for the congregation. Weren't they hearing the gospel? Were they being preached heresy? Were they being deceived into thinking they were following God and on their way to heaven when they really weren't?

Slowly sipping his coffee, he meditated on his conversation with Helen. No clear answers came, except he knew that if Helen was able to link up with the Bible school counselor she would be in good hands.

PRESENT DAY   **CHAPTER 13**

The white haired man gently closed his notebook and slipped it back into his portfolio. Then he slowly rose from his park bench, threw the empty soda pop container in the nearest trash can, got back into his car and started it.

For a few minutes he watched the children playing and jumping into the swimming pool, listening to their excited voices and wondered where they had moved the library that had sat on that spot. He kept the windows closed to keep out the heat and turned the air conditioner up a notch, then opened the second can of Root Beer he had purchased and took a sip of the beverage that was no longer cold.

A smile creased his face as he looked out over the town square as the hot afternoon sun hung high in the sky. Some remembrances didn't have to come from his notebook. It may have been fifty years ago, but he still remembered conversations and other memories from back then. Maybe these recollections would help him in his quest to find the origin of the fire. Or maybe not. But he would indulge himself for a few moments anyway. Leaning back in his seat he mentally shut out the noise of the children, closed his eyes, the smile still on his face, and remembered.

1955   **CHAPTER 14**

Patsy Lundquist unlocked the library door of the stone building on the town square at five to nine on Monday morning and turned on the lights. Then she flipped on the overhead fans and opened the windows to make the library as cool as possible for what was going to be another warm day.

Back at her desk she pulled a mirror from her purse, fluffed up her beehive hairdo, examined her face, applied a fresh coat of lipstick and other light makeup, and was ready for her day. While she was logging a stack of returned books piled on her desk back into the system, she had her first customer. Mary Jane Harmon, one grade behind her during their school years, was now a hair dresser at Cherry's Hair Boutique.

"In for more books on hair styling and color," Patsy asked with a smile, "or here for more romance novels?"

"Both." Mary Jane sat on the edge of Patsy's desk in her white rayon pants and pink sleeveless blouse. "I have the day off, just taking a walk before it gets too hot and thought I would catch up on my reading and the latest gossip."

Patsy sat down her work and took a sip of her Pepsi Cola. "How's your church doing with your new pastor?"

"Still moving slowly along. Pastor Paul is an okay preacher. You can tell he's new. But he's passionate about what he preaches. And tells good stories to illustrate his points."

"He's cute too, isn't he?"

"I guess. Someone said he looks like that evangelist Billy somebody."

"We went out to dinner the other night at Riverview Restaurant. I asked him to see if he could help Lamar."

"Competition for Michael?" teased Mary Jane.

Patsy frowned. "I don't know. Michael and I have gone on several dates lately. He's sweet and handsome. I like him a lot. He has an almost new Rolls Royce. His family's rich and he has that pipe dream of making a lot of money with his instant hamburger restaurants." She gave a short laugh. "That will either lead him to being a rich man on his own or to bankruptcy; I'm not sure which. But either way, he has his family business to come back to, so he should do okay."

"Paul lives above a storefront church," cut in Mary Jane. "I'm sure he makes at least ten dollars a week." She laughed. "Stiff competition."

Patsy smiled in return. "Yes, but he's nice and about the kindest, most thoughtful young man I have ever met." She took a sip of her Pepsi. "He's poor now, but he doesn't have to stay that way." She held up the little finger of her right hand and drew a circle around it with her left hand. "Ever since I was in grade school I've known how to wrap boys around my little finger. If I chose to, I bet I can change his income level."

Mary Jane leaned closer. "How do you propose to do that?"

Patsy paused, took another sip of Pepsi, then leaned toward her friend. "Dad employs a lot of people. I bet he would add one more if I asked. He needs a job where he could make more money and still pastor the church.

"Helen Gannon, our pastor's wife, seems happy. She's looked up to in town, well respected. She wears nice clothes, leads women's groups at church, and is current president of the Bethel Springs school PTA and a member of other clubs in town. A great life being married to a pastor. especially if he's as nice and good looking as Paul."

She shook her head. "Mary Jane, I don't know. I'm just babbling. Michael, Paul, or maybe someone else. I don't know." She stood and grabbed a stack of books. "Please don't tell anyone about our conversation. Just thinking out loud."

1955　　CHAPTER 15

Laura Taylor unconsciously tightened the brown band holding her pony tail in place, combed her fingers down through her bangs to straighten them out, then pulled out of the driveway of her home on Valley Drive and turned south toward Cape Fair. It was Sunday morning. The sky was clear and the temperature had not yet risen. A beautiful day to be alive, she had the day off from work and could go to church.

She enjoyed attending services in the small Pentecostal church in Cape Fair when she was home from school and not working at the restaurant. Pastor Brent was a good preacher and she enjoyed worshipping and fellowshipping with the people in the church.

Her thoughts drifted back to her childhood as they often did when she was alone. It was not an easy childhood. Her dad, Hank, worked from the proverbial dawn to dusk as a dirt farmer, raising corn, tomatoes, peas and other farm products on their five acres of land, taking on odd jobs when he could. Two chicken houses her mom and dad operated on the farm helped supplement their diet with eggs plus added extra spending money when her mom was able to sell the eggs to local grocery stores and friends. Twice a year they made a little more money selling a batch of chickens to the chicken processing plant.

When she was ten years old, Katie, her friend from down the street, persuaded Laura to go to church with her on Easter. Laura went that Sunday. A few weeks later she went again and accepted Christ as her Savior in Miss Peggy's junior Sunday school class. From then on she began faithfully attending church whenever she could, even after Katie moved away. Her parents usually took her but only stayed for church when she was performing in a Christmas program or for other special occasions.

When Laura was twelve, one morning, she and her mother woke up and found a scrawled note from her father. He said he was taking a vacation by himself. He left and they never heard from him again.

The family had always lived from day to day. After her dad left, she and her mom, Mildred, couldn't keep up the farm. The next year she leased it out to friends but managed to keep the chicken houses.

When Laura was seventeen her mother fell asleep in bed one night with a cigarette in her hand and started the house on fire. Mildred and Laura escaped unhurt but lost everything. With nowhere else to go, they kept one chicken house operating but sold the chickens from the other one and, with the help of friends, remodeled the second chicken house into a living area with linoleum on the floor and Sheetrock on the walls and ceiling. That's where Laura now called home. One cold water faucet running into the kitchen sink was their only source of water. Baths were taken in a round wash tub with water heated up on their two-burner camp stove. Their only heat source consisted of a wood stove sitting in the central room of the chicken house. Friends built them an outhouse behind their new home.

Laura's dream was to break free from her life of poverty and be able to make it on her own. With that goal in mind, she got a job as a waitress at Martha's Café when she was sixteen and meticulously saved her money. On work days she always left her house early and went to Martha's home, who lived near the diner, to take a hot shower and wash the smell of cigarette smoke out of her hair, a habit her mother couldn't seem to break. She left her work clothes at Martha's to keep them free from the stench in her home.

After graduating from high school she enrolled at Burge School of Nursing in Springfield with plans to become a registered nurse. In September, she would begin her last year at Burge and hopefully graduate with an RN degree in May.

Along with seeking a way out of poverty, she yearned to become part of a loving, Christian family. Occasionally, after church on Sunday mornings, Pastor Brent and his wife, Millie, would invite Laura and others over for Sunday dinner of fried chicken, peas and potatoes, or maybe cornbread and beans. Each time she ate with them she savored the moment when Pastor Brent, Millie, their three children and the guests sitting around the dining room table would hold hands while he led in a table grace. His short but fervent, heartfelt prayer often brought tears to her eyes. Then they would eat their hearty meal and discuss the morning service and whatever else had gone on the last few days. No cigarette smoking, no beer drinking, no swearing or cursing, no harsh words for Millie or other guests or yelling at the kids. Just love, acceptance, good times and lots of laughs. That's the kind of family Laura craved.

Life was moving ahead as she had planned until her long-time neighbor boy, Claude, began taking more than a neighborly liking to Laura. Their families had been neighbors for several years. Claude's parents, Bert and Ruth Ragsdale, were a friendly, helpful couple. Bert had a supervisory position at Lundquist Shoe Factory. When Laura's dad left they stepped in and helped whenever they could, repairing their home when needed, occasionally helping with the chores and sometimes bringing them food.

Claude was a cool cat, funny, aggressive—he lived on the edge. No knight in shining armor had appeared yet in her life, and she was lonely. She had never met anyone like him and was fascinated by his unorthodox lifestyle. When he invited her on a date she set aside the checklist of qualities she was looking for in a man and decided to see what he would offer. His parents were kind, wholesome people—surely Claude was, too.

Their first date was perfect: a picnic dinner by the White River. Other interesting outings followed. He soon gave her his ring to wear around her neck, and she was flattered by his attention.

Then he started to get more aggressive and began to treat her as his property. That's when she told him to back off and leave her alone. He said he would, but didn't follow through on his promise, continuing to demand more and more of her attention.

Laura stayed away from Claude as much as she could. Just one more year and she would graduate. Then she could leave Bethel Springs, find a job in some hospital as a nurse, purchase or rent a nice home, find a good church and make new friends. Hopefully, sometime in the next few years, she would find a godly husband and start a family.

That was her plan and had been for the past several months. Then Pastor Paul came into her restaurant that Sunday morning back in June. He was tall, blond, slim and handsome. The first time she saw him he reminded her of Billy Graham, that young evangelist she had heard about. She remembered seeing his picture and reading in the Springfield newspaper that on Easter Sunday Billy Graham had been in England and preached to the queen. She smiled to herself. Maybe one day Pastor Paul would preach to the Queen of England, maybe the president of the United States, or maybe pastor in a beautiful church building and preach every Sunday to a congregation of a thousand people.

Recorded like a movie picture in her mind was his smile and warm, friendly, gorgeous blue eyes. The first time she saw him, when she waited on him at Martha's Café, she almost broke down in tears when he asked if he could pray for her. No man had ever shown that much interest in her needs.

Then the night of July fourth, she felt her face grow hot at the recollection. How sweet he had been. He had wanted to kiss her; she could tell. She had wanted to be kissed, but it didn't happen.

She needed to forget Paul and move on with her life. He was way out of her league. Besides, if he found out about her past, he wouldn't want to have anything to do with her. She knew that for a fact.

1955 CHAPTER 16

Kate Fuller looked at her watch. Five o'clock on the dot, time to leave the Ben Franklin five and ten cent store where she worked full time during the summer and part time during the school year.

As she walked the five blocks to her house she carried bags in both hands, material she had purchased for the Vacation Bible School they were planning. She had written Paul a letter, and he had agreed to hold a VBS with her in charge. She would drive up early this Sunday to meet with Paul and the VBS committee he had chosen.

The VBS would start at nine thirty Sunday morning, August twenty-first, and go until noon, then have the same hours Monday through Friday with a big finale on Friday night that would, hopefully, bring out many of the children's parents.

During the VBS she was taking the week off and would stay at the home of Frieda and her daughter Jessica. She envisioned spending quality time with Paul. Maybe he would even take her to eat out, just the two of them, hopefully not at Martha's Café. Kate didn't like that waitress, Laura. Was that her name? She still remembered how she looked at Paul the Sunday they ate there, and Paul's non-verbal response.

Paul. Would they ever get married? Was the time getting close he might propose to her? He was already twenty-one, on his own with a career and ministry. A pastor, his dream fulfilled. She was twenty, just the right age. Still a year left in Bible school, but they could work that out.

A pastor's wife: she liked the sound of that. During girls' summer camp when she was thirteen, she felt God called her into the ministry. Since then she had planned for it, prayed about it. Knowing Paul, her neighbor, was also called into the ministry, they both planned together what they would do. Paul would preach to the adults and Kate would play the piano and minister to the children. Since they were both only children, they talked about having a houseful of kids, always an undetermined number.

She wanted to be known as more than a pastor's wife. That title simply meant she happened to be married to a pastor but didn't reflect any of her own individuality or ministry. She also wanted to be called a pastor. She and her husband would co-pastor their church. It would be their ministry together. She didn't want that title just to boost her ego; she wanted people to know she also was called by God to be in the ministry, not just the wife of a minister.

Paul often told her she was attractive, but she didn't believe she was. Short, barely over five feet; thin, too thin. A strong wind would blow her away, her dad often said. When she smiled she knew an unsightly gap showed between her front teeth. No dimples, small nose, weak chin, a plain, forgettable face, except for her round, steel-framed glasses. She wore her auburn hair in a poodle cut with short bangs, a style she hoped made her look taller, and at least somewhat attractive.

Knowing she was not physically attractive gave her an added incentive to work on making her inner life beautiful. She started each day reading her Bible and spending time in prayer. Daily she quoted Psalm 19:14: "Let the words of my mouth, and the meditation of my heart, be acceptable in thy sight, O Lord, my strength, and my redeemer."

She concentrated on the blessings in her life, often naming them one by one, as that hymn they sang in church admonished her to do. She genuinely loved people and did her best to give words of encouragement or wisdom as often as she could. She smiled a lot and people smiled back.

Friendly and outgoing, she had been popular in high school, active on the pep squad and the debate team, always getting good grades.

In Bible school, even though she didn't live on campus, she made friends easily and spent as much time as she could studying in the SUB or visiting with her friends. She was the secretary for the Latin America Missions Prayer Team and vice-president of her class. So far, she had been on the honor roll every semester in Bible school.

Life was good that warm sunny, summer day. Reviewing in her mind her favorite chapter in the Bible, Psalm ninety-one, she believed she was dwelling in the secret place of the most high, and that God would satisfy her with a long life as she worked for Him. She found herself humming the chorus, "I've got the joy, joy, joy, joy down in my heart."

She was excited about getting to see Paul again at his church and getting the VBS organized with his people.

Early Sunday morning Kate and Mary Brunner got in Kate's car and started the drive south to Bethel Springs. They stopped for breakfast in a restaurant at Galena, then kept on driving with their windows down, letting the air cool them down as much as possible.

They discussed their studies, upcoming assignments, and traded stories of campus life at a Bible school. Then they rode on in silence for several minutes winding through the rolling hills and valleys, passing green forests, farmland and occasional houses.

Then Mary spoke up again. "Any more news about you and Paul? Has he proposed yet?"

Kate ran her fingers through her curls and gave a short laugh. "Not yet. Nothing since we talked about it on our last trip. But I think—I hope—that's his plan. It has been, I think, for the past year or two. I figure now that he's on his own and pastoring, he's probably thinking about it more. So am I.

"That's my plan too. That's how I think it will turn out." Her voice got quieter. "Of course, Paul lives in Bethel Springs. Except for this next week I won't see him much until the first of the year when I will start going to his church on Sundays. That waitress in the restaurant seems to be sweet on Paul. Probably other girls are too. And that librarian somebody was telling me about." She shook her head. "Maybe God has someone else for him and someone else for me. I don't know. I guess I will just wait and see; leave it in the Lord's hands."

While she was talking Kate glanced over at Mary who was staring straight ahead out the window, twisting her high school class ring around her finger, round and round and round.

PRESENT DAY   CHAPTER 17

Opening his eyes, the white-haired man looked out the windshield of his car, observing the children in the pool and the buildings surrounding the city square. Oh, the memories. A smile touched his lips again and remained there a few moments. Then his lips firmed and he frowned. Fifty years ago. Where had the years gone?

After talking to Laura and Patsy, his mother, Professor McFee, the church board, and after several days of agonizing prayer and indecision, he had decided to stay and try to overcome the evil that was invading Bethel Springs. Had that been the right decision?

He was successful in many ways and often thought about the programs and ministries he had implemented. But, in spite of the many people he had ministered to and the good memories he had, he considered his three years of pastoring in Bethel Springs a black mark on his career and had tried to block it out of his mind. He was sure everything he started had collapsed when he left.

After the fire he struggled to stay on as pastor of Community Chapel. Most church members remained as supporters and declared his innocence, as did several of the other people in town. Some agitators and others outside his church continued a daily barrage of accusations questioning why the church kept Paul as pastor since he was the arsonist that set fire to the rival church. They demanded he be fired and run out of town. The fire and the accusations about him were even carried by newspapers in other cities of Missouri and into neighboring states.

Finally, after a month of turmoil, with the church attendance dwindling, Paul was called into the Missouri headquarters of his denomination for a meeting. Reverend Orville Cantor and the seven-person board suggested that for the good of the denomination, the people in Bethel Springs, and the kingdom of God, he should voluntary turn in his credentials, and that they were closing down the church.

Tired of struggling with the issue, and realizing he probably wasn't cut out to be a pastor after all, he resigned from the denomination. Leaving Bethel Springs and moving two thousand miles away to Seattle to live with his mother's sister, Aunt Sina, he got a job driving a school bus. His mother sold her home and also moved in with her sister. They began attending Aunt Sina's church, which was affiliated with the Maranatha Pentecostal Union. Shortly after they began attending the church, Paul was asked to be the adult Sunday school teacher. The following year the senior pastor left and Paul was elected to fill his place. After two years of pastoring, he became an appointed world missionary with the denomination and began a new ministry in Bolivia, South

America—many more thousands of miles away.

Bethel Springs was behind him as far as he was concerned. He had left no forwarding address and threw away unopened the letters from people in the area who did manage to find where he lived.

After serving as a missionary for over forty years he had retired just two years ago. In Bolivia he had planted and pastored several churches, most of them much larger than his first church here in Bethel Springs. Mainly he had taught in the Bible school in Cochabamba, raising up new national workers to pastor the growing number of churches in his denomination. He told himself that even though he wasn't qualified to be a pastor in the United States, he had been successful as a foreign missionary.

But, he reflected, the years had been kind to him in many ways. He was still alive and feeling pretty good for a senior citizen of seventy-one. "Besides a little arthritis and high cholesterol, you're fit as a fiddle," his doctor told him at his last checkup in April.

His hair was now snowy white, but he still had most of it. Gained a few pounds but still feeling good and looking relatively fit, he told himself. A few aches and pains but he still walked a mile every morning when he had the time, and he could still do ten pushups, probably more if he really tried.

He was retired but could still travel and preach. Just last month he preached a week's revival for Peter Lovell, a missionary friend in Lima, Peru. Yet, even though retired and back to the scene of his failure, he reassured himself that he still had value to the kingdom of God and to those around him.

But, he reflected, as he stared out the window, he wasn't here to reminisce. He was here to save his grandson's happiness and marriage.

Starting up his car he looked west up the wooded hill. During the winter when the trees were bare, townspeople could clearly see Hope Fellowship Church, the large stone building on the hill with the cross on top of its steeple. During the summer and fall the leaves on trees hid the building from many of the town's residents.

What had the congregation done after the fire? The flames had gutted the roof and interior of the church, but the stone walls of the building were left relatively intact. Were the ruins still there? Had they rebuilt the old church? Had they demolished the structure and replaced it with a new building? Or had they relocated to the south of town, as some had mentioned they had wanted to do, even before the fire. He was on his way to find out.

Leaving the town square he headed down main street for three blocks, then turned right onto West Hill Drive, the road that wound around and up the hill before arriving at the church that sat on the summit.

Fifty years ago the drive had been mainly through woods. A few more houses had been built since then, but mostly the drive was still through trees, many of them overhanging the road. As the population moved south, apparently this part of town had been largely overlooked. Circling around the hill he arrived at the summit and was surprised to see the walls of the old church still standing. Gaping holes in the gray stone walls indicated where the doors and windows had been.

Parking on the obviously unused graveled parking lot, now overgrown in places with grass and shrubs, he got out and pocketed his keys, not bothering to lock the car. Making his way to what used to be the main entrance, he stepped inside, a kaleidoscope of emotions filling his mind.

Smaller than what he had remembered it, he stood at the entrance staring about him. This is where it happened. A fire had destroyed this church, a fire many people think he had set. No official charges, thank the Lord.

But, three years of his life—a total loss. A waste. His work, his prayers, his plans—all in vain. The memory still gnawed at him on a semi-regular basis, even after almost fifty years. Now, it returned in full bloom.

Was leaving town the right course of action? After having been kicked out of his denomination, should he have stayed and started up another independent church and continued the fight against the evil in this town? He didn't know. But what's done was done. Now, his job was to prove his innocence. How could he do that almost fifty years later?

The interior wooden walls that separated the foyer and rooms from the main sanctuary were gone, leaving one big empty roofless structure. He looked up and saw the sky, then noticed the sun hitting the rock walls on the west side. The concrete floor that had been under the carpet was still mostly intact except for several places where shrubs had sprung up through the cracks. A small oak tree stood where the pulpit had been. As he reminisced he heard a quavering feminine voice. "Hello, somebody there?"

Startled, Paul looked toward the voice and noticed a small table behind a shrub. Making his way over, he saw an older woman sitting on a lawn chair, a large Bible in her lap. Two devotional books sat on the square metal outdoor table beside her.

"Hello," Paul answered. "Sorry to startle you." He smiled in what he hoped was in a disarming way, realizing one of his important goals was to not let anyone know who he was. Or to scare people. "I am visiting in town and was driving around and noticed this old structure, so I thought I would have a look. I didn't see you here. My apologies."

"That's okay. You are welcome to join me." Paul looked at the speaker, a frail-looking woman, her face wrinkled with age. Probably in her eighties, she wore a shapeless long-sleeved blue dress with a wide white collar and black, thick-soled shoes. A cane sat on the tile floor beside her. "I live close and often come to my old church to start the day with prayer and reading the Word. Makes me feel closer to God being here." She patted the table. "My son bought this table and chair. The new church is so far away, and I can't drive anymore, so I can't go as often as I would like. But this is a good substitute."

She had attended here when the fire happened, Paul reflected. Could she shed some light about the fire? Maybe if he was subtle enough he could find out information without revealing his identify.

"I notice the stone walls. So this was a church? What happened?" Paul asked as a way of starting the conversation.

"Well." The woman frowned. "About fifty years ago, it was nineteen fifty-eight, in the summer, as I recall. So forty-seven years ago or so. My," she shook her head. "How time flies. The church burned down. Quite an event back then that stirred up the whole town." She paused. "Some say the preacher from the other church started the fire because he was upset with the pastor here, or jealous of the church, or what was being preached, or some such thing. 'Course, I don't believe it. I knew him a little, the pastor from the other church; I think they called it the Community Chapel back then. I don't think he would have burned the church down in spite of the friction between our churches. But," she shook her head, "he left town shortly after that. So I can't say for certain"

Paul raised his eyebrows in surprise. His first day in town and already someone was talking about him—someone had remembered him. "Interesting," he said. "So tell me about that pastor."

"Well, from all I know about him, he was a good man." She closed the Bible and sat it on the table. "Before the fire, long about fifty-six or fifty-seven, when Rodney, my son, was seventeen or so, he got in with the wrong crowd, started to run around with them. He stayed out all night, sometimes. There wasn't the drug problem back then like there is now, but he got into smoking and drinking. Almost killed himself one time driving. He was on his way home about three o'clock in the morning, alone, in the middle of town, when he smashed into a telephone pole. The car started on fire. The pastor from the other church, I forget his name, Peter, Paul, James, something like that, happened to be awake and heard the crash. In his pajamas he ran out and pulled Rodney from the car. Got a few burns doing it, but he got Rodney out and drove him to the hospital. Rodney had broken ribs, cuts and bruises, but besides that he was okay.

"But Pastor Paul, yes, that was his name, took an interest in Rodney. They would meet sometimes for coffee or go for a drive and talk. Apparently they talked about the Lord and life. Rodney started going to his church. We thought about changing churches too, but since my husband was head of this church board and I was an officer in the Ladies' Guild, we kept attending church here. Really, I guess neither my husband nor I wanted to attend a little storefront church. But Rodney enjoyed the church and really turned his life toward the Lord. He stopped smoking and drinking and running around. He went to college, married a beautiful Christian girl. Now, he runs the State Farm insurance company here in town and does pretty well for himself. He and Sarah gave us three beautiful grandchildren."

Paul cleared his throat and unobtrusively wiped his eyes. "Interesting story. I'm sure you're proud of your family."

"Yes I am. We have a daughter and her family that live in Kansas. Two more grandchildren from them. Well, I best be getting back." The woman stood, picked up her books, and reached for her cane.

"Would you like me to drive you?" Paul asked hoping to continue the conversation.

"Well. I suppose so, although I don't live far. But that would help." She laughed. "Can I trust you? You have a kind face, but you're not someone that robs old ladies, are you?"

Paul returned the laugh. "I hope not. After all, I was a pastor once." Then he winced. Why had he said that? He didn't want anyone to know who he was. He figured after fifty years, even if he saw someone who had known him, he had changed so much they wouldn't recognize him. And, probably he wouldn't recognize them either.

"Oh?" the woman stared at him. "Is that why you are so interested in this church?"

Paul gave what he hoped was a casual laugh. "I'm interested in all church buildings, especially their history."

"Where have you pastored?" the woman asked as Paul helped her into the passenger seat of his car.

Paul got in the driver's seat, started the car and steered down the road. "I was a missionary in Latin America. I retired just two years ago."

"Wonderful, I'm sure you had a wonderful ministry. Well, to finish my story about the church, the police and fire marshal never did find if it was Pastor Paul or who had started it. As the years passed most people forgot about it. The insurance money pretty well covered the cost of the fire. They bought land to the south part of town, built their new church there, and life moved on."

"Interesting. That's quite a story."

"Here we are. Over there is my house with the green shutters. By the way," the woman added as Paul helped her out of her car. My name is Mabel,

Mabel Tinsdale." She extended her quavering hand toward Paul. "My Kenneth went to meet the Lord five years ago."

"Nice to meet you," said Paul returning the handshake. My name is," he hesitated. He didn't want to lie, but he didn't want to reveal who he was, either, at least not yet. Especially with the woman having remembered his name. "My name is Andrew," he said, using his middle name. A true statement, he told himself.

"Nice to meet you, Andrew. I'm usually at the old church about nine o'clock every morning when the weather's nice if you want to come by to chat again, or to pray and talk about the Word."

After walking her to her door, Paul drove away, fondly remembering his relationship with Rodney. Pulling Rodney out a burning car had been one of the most traumatic, fearful events he had ever faced. He still shuddered sometimes to think about what may have happened to him. To both of them.

At least I had one success here in Bethel Springs, he told himself, feeling a little better about returning to this town.

His conversation with the woman left a question mark in his mind. Mabel probably knew more than what she had told him this morning. She was grateful to him for how he had helped her son. Would she be willing to give him whatever information she knew if he revealed his identify to her? If so, would she keep who he was a secret? Or, would she tell a friend about him who would tell a friend, and it soon be all over town that the former pastor who had burned down the church was back in town?

After dropping off Mabel, Paul drove back past the burned out church and stopped at the top of the hill at the edge of the gravel parking lot, the town spread out before him. When he lived here there were about five hundred people within the city limits of Bethel Springs, with probably another thousand in the surrounding area. The new part of town had moved south, he noticed, leaving the center of town about the same as when he lived here with the exception of several new buildings that had replaced older structures.

Getting out of the car he walked to the edge of the parking lot and stared down the hill. Then, glancing to the north, he noticed there was still a wide path from the edge of the parking lot down to the bottom of the hill, the trees and underbrush still carefully removed to keep a clear area for the power lines overhead. He remembered during the winter when there was snow the city fathers would often close off Market Street at the bottom of the hill and let kids, and even adults, use inner tubes or sometimes skis to slide down the hill, about a hundred feet in length. He smiled to himself as he remembered that infamous night when he drove his car down that path.

Returning to his car he shut off the engine, opened his car doors to catch the cooling breeze, closed his eyes and, as a silent prayer, asked the Lord what his next step should be. Who, he asked himself again for the thousandth time, would have been responsible for burning down the church?

Sure, their churches had had their differences: some through Paul confronting the pastor about his false doctrine and his lack of addressing the sins around them; some through people leaving Hope Fellowship Church and attending Paul's church; some through cultural differences between the wealthy from this church and the mostly poorer people who attended Paul's church. It had reached a climax when Marvin Kittleman, the biggest lawyer in town, had switched churches, telling his church friends that if they really wanted to go where God was, they needed to attend Community Chapel downtown.

Pastor Gannon had fought back, saying some untruthful and exaggerated statements about Paul and his church from his pulpit.

Paul, after much prayer, and consulting with other ministers and friends, decided to not respond to the charges, at least not from his pulpit. But, the people in town knew what Pastor Gannon was saying and realized Paul must be angry and hurt by the accusations. When the church burned down, fire inspectors had said it was definitely arson; it had been deliberately set. But by whom? Rumors started that Paul had set the fire because he were angry at Hope Fellowship Church and Pastor Gannon. The police interviewed Paul and other church members, but no one was ever arrested or officially accused of starting the fire.

On the other hand, Paul had always wondered if someone from Hope had set up the arson fire to get the insurance money to rebuild elsewhere and had tried to throw the blame on him? Because, he reminded himself, for the past several years before the fire, the town had been moving south. The church on the hill was becoming a farther distance to drive for the new people settling in town. Attendance was starting to drop. But no one had ever voiced this theory as far as Paul knew. Today Mabel had just confirmed that the church had moved south, probably onto more land and, no doubt, had built a larger and more modern building. Should he review the list of church members from that time to see who may have been responsible? Or was it Pastor Gannon himself? Or, Paul had certainly challenged George Hackett over his desire to bring gambling to Bethel Springs. Was it him or one of his cronies? Or Milton Passmore who had bought cheap land around town in anticipation of the building boom when legal gambling became approved? Or he had certainly stirred the anger of big bad Zeb from Zeb's Bar and Grill down the street. Was it him? Or Claude?

As Paul reflected some more as he gazed over Bethel Springs in the morning light, the sun shining in his face from the east, there were other people he also had to consider as to who may have been responsible for the fire.

Returning to his car and taking his worn notebook from his portfolio, he opened it again and began reading, hoping the words on the page and his memories would give him some answers.

1955

CHAPTER 18

Sunday morning, July seventeenth, Paul preached his first hell-fire-and-brimstone message. He had prepared all week by praying and studying. Saturday he had fasted all day and prayerfully went over his message again. He was pleased to see Kate and Mary Brunner in the congregation. He knew they would be praying for him.

When preaching time came, Paul made his way to the pulpit and surveyed the congregation. A lot had changed since he had first preached on Bethel just a few short weeks ago. His congregation had grown a little. He had gotten to know them better. He now knew better their joys, victories, needs and problems. Rather than trying to impress them with his knowledge of Scripture and preaching ability, he now felt a burden for several of these people—his congregation, that needed to hear from the Lord that morning. His confidence was increasing. Maybe he did have the talent and ability to be a pastor, after all.

"My first sermon here a few weeks ago," he began, "was about the namesake of this town, the Bethel in the Bible. We discussed how Jacob had just deceived his brother Esau out of his birthright and had to flee. In Genesis twenty-eight and Genesis thirty-five we read how Jacob named Bethel and how God blessed him in many ways.

"Now let's move forward several hundred years. Jacob has been dead a long time. Israel had become a nation with Saul, David and Solomon as kings. The temple had been built in Jerusalem where the Israelites came and worshipped God.

"After the death of King Solomon, the nation of Israel had a civil war and the nation broke into two factions. In First Kings chapters twelve and thirteen we read where a man by the name of Jeroboam was made king over the part of the nation that did not include Jerusalem. He was afraid if his people went to Jerusalem to worship God, they would begin to serve Solomon's son, King Rehoboam, the king of Judah, instead of him.

"Therefore, Jeroboam went to the town of Bethel and created a worship center there. He told his people they were to come to Bethel, not Jerusalem, to worship. He created golden calves for them to worship instead of the true God. He went so far as to appoint false priests. This was a blatant sin in God's eyes."

After reading several verses from the Bible from those chapters Paul quickly looked out over the congregation, trying to make eye contact with as many as possible.

"I have a question. Are there any golden calves or idols that the people here in Bethel Springs are worshipping today?"

After a long pause he continued: "Bethel Springs has come a long ways from what those Quakers intended the town to be. It is still a wonderful place to live. There are many good people, great businesses and other fine establishments. But, as in every town and city in America, and in most of our hearts, there is sin, or the potential to sin. And there are certain people who profit from sin, who like to entice people into sin and drag them away from God and into worshipping our modern idols that have been placed within our reach.

"An idol is anything that replaces God in our lives or stands in the way of our worshipping God. It could be another person, if that person takes us away from our relationship with God. It might be a hobby, if we spend time and effort on the hobby we should be devoting to God. Some of you are starting to buy television sets. If you are watching television when you should be in church or having a devotional time with the Lord, or watching what you know is against biblical principles, that becomes a god right in your home.

"Are there any establishments here that promote idolatry? Any establishments that would entice people to come and partake of the pleasures of sin? Sin in any form?

"Are there any so-called churches where the preaching of the Bible is pushed to the sidelines and what is preached, instead, is the pursuit of success and financial prosperity? If so, that's also idolatry."

As he spoke he continued to keep brief eye contact with his audience. Most were looking intently at him, some were staring at the floor. He glanced down at Kate and Mary. Kate had a slight smile on her face. Mary had her face buried in her Bible as if re-reading the passages to confirm what Paul was saying.

As he concluded his sermon Paul described God's love and mercy and forgiveness to any who would repent of any idolatry. Then, with Emily coming to the piano to play softly the hymn *Just As I Am*, he made an invitation for anyone to come forward who wanted to repent of their sins and turn their lives over to God.

Out of the corner of his eyes he looked over at Sam Pittman sitting beside his wife Betty, his bowed head, staring at the floor and not moving. Then, over to his left he saw movement. Jimmy Miller, just seventeen, slowly rose to his feet and shuffled forward, stifling sobs as he walked.

Paul motioned for Thomas Spradley to come pray with Jimmy. After waiting a few more moments with Emily playing the hymn of invitation and no one else coming forward, Paul closed the service in prayer.

As Paul was shaking hands with the congregation as they were walking out, Jimmy Miller gave Paul a hug, his eyes still wet with tears. "Sorry for what

I said when you first came, Pastor Paul, that you would run when the going got tough. You are a good man that helped me get back to Jesus." With that he hurried out, his head up, a small smile on his face.

After everyone had left, Paul, along with Kate and Mary, met with the volunteers who were going to help in the VBS. Paul looked at his church members lined up on the two front benches: Fred and Nadine Pittman, Frieda and Jessica Thornton, Thomas and Patricia Spradley, James and Polly Harmon and Emily Miller, a glow on her face after seeing her son come forward for salvation. Good, solid, Christian people who had stayed with the church during its recent problem. They had told Paul they were here to support him and keep the church going forward. Even Frieda. Paul smiled to himself. In spite of her rough exterior and his first impressions of her, she did turn out to be one of the most faithful members.

Kate laid out her plans for the classes, gave assignments, passed out teachers' books and handed out other material to help them prepare for their classes. After about an hour of planning Paul closed in prayer and everyone left.

After the planning meeting Paul took Kate and Mary to Martha's Café for lunch. "I'm excited about the VBS," commented Kate when they had sat down. "I hope it will help grow your church. If you can get the kids coming, their parents will probably follow."

"Are either of you coming for visitation Saturday?" Paul asked. "As I announced this morning, we are meeting Saturday at nine to canvass the town as much as we can. I'm making up some flyers about the VBS we can pass out."

"We'll be here," Kate said. "Mary and I talked about it on the way up. In fact," she added, "I talked to Frieda and her daughter Jessica again this morning. They are still expecting me and seem excited that I'll be staying with them."

Mary added, "I can come Saturday for visitation, but I can't come the week of VBS. I just started working at Dairy Queen and the boss won't let me off."

Paul smiled at her across the table. "No problem. We just appreciate all you are doing. Anybody for dessert? I think I'll have a piece of their apple pie a la mode. Anyone else want anything?"

Kate noted that a waitress named Holly waited on them instead of Laura. She secretly hoped that Laura had quit waitressing and moved out of town.

Before they left Kate opened her trunk and unloaded two boxes of books

Paul's mother had sent, plus some other household items including clothing and a suitcase.

After they left Paul put away the clothes and other items his mother had sent and set up his small bookcase containing his Zane Grey library and other books.

Next, he put the suitcase on his bed and carefully unpacked his thirteen chess sets one by one and examined them. This was his pride and joy, an heirloom left to him from his father that his mother gave him when he graduated from high school.

During the years Paul's father was in the Navy, he traveled to many places in the world. Being a chess enthusiast he purchased chess sets whenever he could. Paul's favorite, and the most valuable chess set, came from India. All the pieces were hand carved from elephant tusks. The king and queen in both colors each had a diamond on their crowns, purported to be from the famous Golconda diamond mines. His next favorite set was purchased in some country in Africa, Paul couldn't remember which one, which featured pieces hand carved from ebony: the robes of the kings and queens and bishops were gold plated. Another hand carved chess set made from the tagua nut, known as vegetable ivory, came from Ecuador. When his father visited Russia he purchased a chess set carved from jade. The other chess sets were not as valuable, yet reminded Paul of the many places around the world his father had visited.

After looking them over, he replaced them in the suitcase and stored it under his bed.

The following Saturday at nine o'clock, twelve people met at the church. Since it had rained the day before and it was cloudy, the temperature was only supposed to get to around eighty degrees, making a relatively cool day for the middle of summer.

Paul had gotten a map of Bethel Springs from Patsy in the library. Splitting the group in couples, he assigned them areas of the town and outlying areas, gave them handbills, prayed with them, and told them to meet back at church at noon. Frieda and Jessica would provide hot dogs and hamburgers for lunch.

Paul assigned Mary to go with Nadine Pittman to the north part of town. He teamed up with Kate as his partner and chose the southeastern part of the town. He had driven through there a few times and noticed the run-down homes. A poorer part of the community, people there needed Christ as much as the wealthier residents. He didn't have any plan to help them yet, but wanted to get a chance to meet some of them.

Paul liked people but always had to force himself to go door to door. He was always a little apprehensive as to who would be behind the doors that opened.

He pulled his car into the driveway of the first house they came to on Valley Drive, a small frame house badly in need of paint with the lawn nearly a foot high. Paul knocked on the door, then stepped back several feet, as he had been taught, to not appear too aggressive. The door was opened by a young woman with two small children standing behind her holding her skirt. "May I help you?" she asked. "If you are salespeople, the answer is 'we don't want any'."

"No, we're not," said Kate. They had agreed if a woman came to the door Kate would do the talking. She gave her invitation to the woman to bring her children to the Vacation Bible School and handed her a brochure.

The woman shook her head and handed back the brochure. "Don't have a car or no way to get there. My husband, Donald, he...he sold the car. So he gots to walk to work now, more'n a mile or so. I gotta walk to the grocery store to buy food now when there's money for food."

"How about if someone came to pick up your kids?" Kate knelt down and reached out her hands to the two little boys behind the mother who stepped further back into the house. "How old are your children?"

"Joshua's four and Chipper is six."

"Perfect ages." Kate turned to Paul. "Could we get someone to pick them up?"

When Paul nodded she turned back to the mother. "My name is Kate. This is Paul, the pastor." She gave the woman a hug. "Nice to meet you and your children. What was your name?"

"Molly. Molly Rice." She smiled for the first time. "I guess that will be okay. You look honest. It will give the kids something to do next week. What time will you be by?"

Paul spoke up, "Have them ready about eight thirty or quarter to nine or so. I'll try to come by to get them or send someone. And," he added. "you are welcome to come to Sunday school tomorrow too."

The next house they came to, Paul knocked on a flimsy, weather-beaten door that was eventually answered by an older man with a cane. Paul introduced himself and invited the man to church who said his name was Michael, and he already attended another church.

They visited about a dozen more houses with various responses.

"One more visit," commented Paul as they got back in the car. "Then we need to get back to be there by noon."

A building sat back almost hidden by trees off to the east as they continued going south on Valley Drive. "A chicken house," observed Kate. I saw several of them on our recent trip to Arkansas. "Probably vacant. In fact, two of them," she observed as another similar structure appeared behind the trees about thirty feet behind the first building.

"Look." Paul pulled off the road and started down a narrow driveway. "Appears this one is occupied. Smoke is coming out of a chimney. There's a small lawn and flowers in front that seem to be kept up." They pulled up and stared for a moment at the long, narrow unpainted wooden structure. There were tire marks in front of the building as if a car often parked there. An outhouse stood behind the building off to the left. Curtains hung in the two windows on either side of the wooden door that had a latch instead of a knob.

Paul looked at Kate and shrugged. "Let's see if someone lives there."

A woman who appeared to be in her fifties answered the door, a smoking cigarette between her index and middle finger. "May I help you?" Her voice was raspy and she coughed twice.

"We are from the Community Chapel in town," spoke up Kate, extending a flyer to the woman. "We are out visiting people in town, inviting their children to a Vacation Bible School we are starting tomorrow morning."

The woman chuckled and threw her cigarette out on the lawn. "My daughter is growed up. She's too old for kids' church."

"We also have church on Sundays and Wednesdays for adults," added Kate, pointing to the schedule on the brochure that the woman had taken. We would love to have you visit us sometime."

The woman shook her head. "My daughter goes to church but I don't. I don't go to church nowhere. Never have. I figure if there's a God I can worship him at home and not have to go to some highfalutin place where everyone goes to show off their clothes and how good they are."

"That's not our church," replied Paul. "We all are just plain folk, just there to worship God and have a good time of fellowship."

The woman turned her head and coughed, not bothering to cover her mouth, then handed back the brochure. "Good luck with your church," she said and closed the door in their faces.

"Why don't you take charge of the luncheon?" suggested Paul as they arrived back at the hall around noon. "You are good at that type of thing." When everyone had returned, Kate seated the group around two old folding tables Paul had brought down from upstairs, while Frieda and Jessica served everyone. After the meal, Kate asked each team to report on how they did. Most mentioned some interest among the people in town. Some met with grumpy people. Nadine and Mary knocked on a door and were met with a rough-looking bearded man holding a shotgun. They decided not to ask him if he had children who wanted to come to the VBS and made a hasty retreat.

But most agreed it had been a profitable morning and were looking forward to the VBS.

That night Paul spent an hour in prayer. Then he sat down at his typewriter to write a letter. "Dear Kate," he began. Then he took out the paper, threw it in his metal trash can by his desk and inserted a new sheet. Too generic. Not intimate enough for a letter of proposal. "Dearest Kate," he began again. Then he jotted down all the reasons why he loved Kate. In the last paragraph he asked her if she would marry him. Taking the paper out of the typewriter he re-read it several times, then slipped it in the top right drawer of his desk. He wanted to ponder what he had written before he put it in an envelope and sealed it.

He was fond of Laura and Patsy. But he didn't know them well. They were distracting him from his ministry. Besides, Pasty already had a guy that liked her. Laura had that weird thug chasing her, and Paul didn't want any trouble with him. And, he knew Kate. She was safe. He felt if they got married it would help his ministry. He was in this small town all by himself, he reminded himself. His nights were lonely. There was no one he could really confide in. Sometime during the VBS, Paul decided, he would give Kate the letter. He realized the normal way to propose was in person. That's what most men did. He felt by proposing in a letter Kate would have a chance to think it over and pray about it before giving him her answer. Yes, that's what he would do.

1955 CHAPTER 19

Paul counted twenty-one children in church by a few minutes after nine on Sunday morning. Paul had picked up Joshua and Chipper, and there was a new family with three children who shyly walked into church about nine-thirty.

After the Sunday morning service Paul invited Kate to join them at Martha's Café for lunch. Laura served them with a smile. "I hear you are having VBS at your church starting tomorrow. My church used to have them when I was a kid. I think they still do. I always enjoyed making the crafts. I hope your VBS goes well."

"You should come see us when you don't have to work," suggested Paul. "You could just come and watch, or you could help. We have some women coming to teach the classes, but we could always use more."

"I'll think about it. Now, what will you have? We're having a special on pork steak with potatoes, gravy, fried okra and apple pie for dessert."

Back at church Paul and several church members busily prepared for the VBS that would start the next day, getting the stories and crafts and other material ready.

After the Sunday night service and everyone had left, Paul walked upstairs to get ready for bed. A wave of lonesomeness washed over him, so he decided to go for a walk. Changing into jeans and a blue nylon shirt, he locked the church door and began walking down the dark street, heading in the familiar direction of Martha's Café, enjoying the cooling night air, looking at the stars and moon, reminding himself how fortunate he was to finally be pastoring a church in a town such as Bethel Springs.

Just after he had walked by Martha's Café that was closed for the night, looking dark and lonely, he was aroused out of his daydreaming by the roar of a motorcycle that pulled up beside him. He looked over and was a little frightened to see the dark form of Claude Ragsdale who stopped the motorcycle, shut it off, and dismounted.

"Out for a walk, preacher man?" he called out taking long, menacing steps as he approached Paul. He took a drag on his cigarette, then threw it at his feet and ground it out with his black leather boot. He was dressed in jackboots, tight jeans, a leather jacket and a wide motorbike belt with a huge silver buckle. His swept back duck tail haircut crowned his head, every hair in place.

Paul took his hands out of his pockets. "Beautiful night for a walk, Claude. Nice night for a ride too, I'm sure."

Claude walked up to Paul and stood within a few inches of his face. Paul could smell the cigarettes and beer on his breath. "You stay away from my Laura, you hear," he growled. "You show up where she works making eyes at her," he nodded toward the restaurant, "and you let her in your church house at the dead of night. Not only that, now you are sweet talkin' her mama. It's going to stop. Right now."

Paul saw it coming and turned his head as he jerked away, but he still caught the wild punch of Claude's clenched fist on the side of his jaw that knocked him back. He fell to the sidewalk on his back, but quickly sat up. Claude stood above him, his fists doubled up. "That was barely a tap. Now, get up and fight like a man, preacher," he called down to him.

Paul sat on the sidewalk looking up at Claude. His jaw felt like it was on fire and he seemed a bit groggy. He had taken a boxing course in high school and gotten an "A," but had never fought in anger, except in the third grade when he fought Billy Thompson to see who would carry Sally Peterson's books home from school. That fight had ended in a wrestling match with no one winning.

Paul thought about getting up and running. He figured he could outrun Claude who was wearing boots. But he knew that would probably only set up another confrontation later. He thought about getting up and fighting Claude, figuring he could, at least, hold his own. But, unless he could give him a decisive beating, he didn't see where that would do any good either.

Instead he stayed on the ground. "You know, Claude," he said in a conversational tone, "you and I could fight it out and smash each other up. But that wouldn't solve any problems. It's really up to Laura, isn't it? She can like any guy she chooses; you, me, anyone, or no one. Right? She doesn't belong to me, you, or anyone else. She's her own person. If you want to really win her over, do it the right way. But fighting me won't solve any problems. By the way, I've never met her mother, so I don't know where you got that idea."

As he talked he could see Claude in the moonlight curl and uncurl his fists as he stood over him, as if trying to decide what to do.

"You know, Claude," he said, deciding to continue the one-sided conversation. "Before you go living this tough act of yours that you will soon learn to regret, think about what you are doing. You can become a rebel like James Dean if you want. But he's an actor. He pretends to be a rebel so he can make a lot of money and be famous. He's in movies where things always turn out like he wants. But that's not real life. In real life rebels don't win. At some point along the way they realize they have rebelled against society, but they haven't made anything of themselves. They grow old and discover they are really losers. Their friends are losers. The life they rebelled against goes on, and they are left behind, angry and bitter.

"But from the little I know about you, and what Laura has said, you are an intelligent person. You have a lot of potential, real leadership qualities. I notice you are stubborn and stick to whatever you are doing. That's a good quality.

"I know that God has his hand on you. He sees potential in you. So do I, believe it or not. I can see you being a great salesman or work your way up to being the head of a company, or maybe a preacher like me. It's happened before. A lot of people from small towns make it big."

When he finished talking Paul stayed seated on the sidewalk, looking up at Claude, ready to stand to his feet in an instant, but trying to appear relaxed and as non-confrontational as possible.

Claude stood staring at Paul for a good ten seconds, continuing to clench and unclench his fists. Then he let go a string of swear words and a vicious kick that caught Paul in his thigh. "This isn't over yet, preacher," he growled. Pulling something out of his pocket he extended his hand toward Paul. With a flick of his finger the cutting edge of a switchblade knife suddenly appeared inches from Paul's face. "I always got this with me, and I know how to use it," he growled. "I can get you with this piece or in more ways than you can imagine." With that he put the knife back in his pocket, got back on his bike, started the engine and roared off into the night.

With a sigh Paul got to his feet and leaned against the side of the building for a few moments to clear his head. His jaw not only hurt but felt wet. He wiped it with his hand and saw blood.

Holding his handkerchief to his jaw he started back toward home. He smiled ruefully in the darkness. Was he being persecuted for righteousness sake, he asked himself, or for foolishness sake?

1955   CHAPTER 20

Monday morning at eight Kate and Jessica showed up at church. After prayer and drinking a cup of Sanka, Paul and the two women started setting up chairs and tables and laying out the materials for the VBS. At eight thirty Paul left to pick up little Joshua and Chipper Rice.

When Paul returned a few minutes to nine, there were already several children and adults at the church in a festive attitude looking forward to the program.

Kate opened the meeting with prayer and a chorus, gave a few instructions, then Kate took the four through six-year-olds to Paul's bedroom upstairs. Jessica worked with the seven through ten-year-olds around the upstairs kitchen table, while Polly Harmon taught the older children in the hall on the main floor. Patricia Spradley and Betty Pittman prepared the Kool-Aid and cookies for the children at snack time in the back of the hall near the platform and floated from class to class helping at needed.

Paul went to Kate's class and sat Joshua on his lap to keep him from fighting with his brother when he heard a creak on the stairs and turned to see Laura. She was coming up from the hall, dressed in her blue waitress uniform, minus the red and white apron.

"Laura." Paul's stage whisper couldn't keep the surprise and pleasure out of his voice. "Nice to have you show up."

Laura looked around the room and saw two boys sitting on Paul's bed, three girls seated on folding chairs around Paul's desk, a boy sitting on the floor by Paul and one on his lap, most of them busy coloring animals on construction paper. At the same time, Kate was trying to keep their attention as she told the Bible story, putting figures on a flannel graph.

Not wanting to disrupt, Laura stood at the top of the stairs watching the proceedings, a smile on her face.

When the story ended a few minutes later, Kate and Paul picked up all the color crayons and papers and passed out a hunk of modeling clay to the children, asking them to create an animal to put in Noah's ark that was sitting on Paul's desk which he had made from a cardboard box.

The children had just started on their project when Patricia came up the stairs. "Pastor Paul," she said, "can you come talk to the teenage class? One of the girls asked the meaning of sanctification. Can you explain it to them?"

"Sure." Paul stood and sat Chipper on the chair. "Stay there, buddy, until Miss Kate says you can get up," he commanded sternly. "When I come back I'm going to ask how well you did. I expect her to tell me you had fun and did a good job. So don't go hitting your brother, okay?"

Then he turned to Laura. "Thanks for coming. You here to observe or help? If you just want to watch, that's great. But if you have a few minutes to help Kate keep the kids in check, that would be great too."

"Sure, no problem." Laura seemed eager to help as she walked over to the two brothers, smiled at them, and asked what animals they would like to make with their modeling clay.

As Paul walked down the stairs he looked toward the front door as he saw it open. He felt his fists double up as he saw Claude Ragsdale burst into the hall; his boots, tight jeans and leather jacket were a sharp contrast to everyone else in the building.

Forgetting about the sanctification question, Paul hurried toward him, his fists doubled up in his pockets, not wanting a confrontation inside the church.

"Where's my girl?" Claude spat out the words too loudly for the size of the building. Chatter from the hall class stopped, and all eyes turned toward this neighborhood bad boy.

Paul's first instinct was to take him by the arm and lead him back outside. But realizing Claude would probably resist and cause a bigger scene, he simply pointed with his chin to the stairs. "She's up there helping with the children."

As Claude stomped up the stairs Paul uttered a quick prayer and held his breath waiting for whatever chaos was coming. A minute later Claude stomped back down the stairs. Giving Paul a dark look he silently walked outside, loudly slamming the door.

Catching his breath again, Paul hurried up the stairs only to find Kate and Laura quietly laughing. "What magic words did you use to get him to leave?" Paul asked.

Laura cleared her throat and attempted to keep a straight face. "When I saw him walk up the stairs and give me his James Dean sneer, my first thought was to get ready for another yelling scene. Thinking fast, before he could say anything, I handed him some modeling clay and told him, 'Claude, thanks for coming.' I pushed Chipper toward him. 'Here, this little boy could use your help. Chipper,' I said, 'meet my friend Claude. He's going to help you make an animal for Noah's ark.'

"Chipper wrapped his arms around Claude's leg and asked him to make him a big elephant. Claude took the modeling clay from Chipper, looked at me, then at Chipper. He threw it down on the floor, shook Chipper loose, and left without another word."

Paul smiled and shook his head. "Good thinking. I'm sure that averted a big scene. But beware, he may be waiting for you when you leave here."

Laura lifted her chin. "In nurses' training we learned some self-defense for handling rough patients. If Claude tries anything, I can take care of myself."

"By the way," asked Kate, "we ran out of Scotch tape. Do you know where we could get another roll?"

"There may be a roll or two in my desk. You might check there," replied Paul as he started back down the stairs.

The rest of the week went by smoothly. Kate and the other women did a magnificent job in handling the children. Laura showed up every day except for Wednesday and helped Kate with her children. Claude didn't return.

By Friday, Paul had the names and addresses of more than forty children who had come to the VBS. The church was almost full on Friday night for the program. During the altar call, seven children and two adults came forward and prayed the sinner's prayer for salvation.

Kate stayed over Saturday and directed the Sunday school on Sunday. A total of forty-two people came for Sunday school and most stayed for the Sunday morning service. This was the best attendance in several years, according to church members.

Mary Brunner drove up for the Sunday morning service, and she and Kate returned to Springfield after the evening service on Sunday night.

After everyone had left and Paul was relaxing in his apartment above the church with a toasted cheese sandwich and cup on Sanka, he reached into the top right drawer of his desk to look over the proposal letter he had written to Kate. He had eaten a few meals with her, but always with others present. They had never been alone as a couple, except during the Saturday visitation. It suddenly dawned on him that the week had gone by and he hadn't given the letter to her.

Then he froze with the paper in his hand. On Monday, Kate had asked for the Scotch tape. He had told her to look for it in the desk. After writing his letter, he had left it face up in the right hand top drawer.

Two rolls of Scotch tape were in the big drawer in the center of the desk. Had the girls started there they would have found the tape and not opened the right side drawer with the letter. But, had one of them opened the top right drawer first, she would have probably seen the letter. If so, had she searched for the tape, ignoring the letter? Or, had whoever opened the drawer read the letter and kept it to herself? Or, had she shared the letter with the other girl? Did both Kate and Laura know the contents of the letter? Or just Kate? Or Laura? Or neither one?

He re-read the letter, folded it in half and stuffed it in the bottom of the drawer. Good grief, he told himself, what have I done? *Do the girls and now my whole world know I wrote a letter of proposal to Kate? Or, does no one know? And, why didn't I give it to Kate? I had all week to do it with several opportunities. And I didn't.*

Why not?

Paul spent some of the next week following up on the newcomers, visiting their homes and getting acquainted with the families and their needs. He discovered many of them were poor. Some of the husbands worked in the chicken processing plant. Others were dirt farmers, barely able to eke out a living. A few worked at the shoe factory and made a modest income. Two of the families he visited slyly admitted making moonshine on the side and Pete Hamilton offering him a jug, which Paul politely refused.

Two of the children, five-year-old Jamie Ashpole and eight-year-old Peter Harper had single mothers, according to what Kate had told him. Thinking it would be awkward for a single man to visit these homes, Paul showed up at Martha's Café on Tuesday morning when he knew Laura would be working. Quietly over breakfast he asked if she could go with him to visit the homes. She agreed and said she could meet him at the restaurant at seven that evening. Knowing she got off earlier than that, Paul wondered why she didn't want him to meet her at her home, but agreed without asking any questions.

The visits went smoothly. Both mothers graciously welcomed Paul and Laura into their homes. Mary Ashpole and Jamie lived a frame house with a sagging roof, badly in need of repair. She was a widow that got some money from the state and babysat to earn a little extra. Sylvia Harper, with little Peter, lived in an old mobile home that sat on the edge of the woods with a dirt driveway and just a small yard. She told Paul she cleaned rooms at the Wayside Motel on Mill Street. She didn't volunteer any information as to what happened to her husband, and he didn't ask.

They left the Harper's about eight thirty. Paul offered to drive Laura home, but she said her car was at the restaurant, so they drove there. It was still open and over a cup of coffee and piece of blueberry pie Paul mentioned how many of the people that came to the VBS were poor. "You'll find many people in this area are poor," Laura said. "For some reason, the richer people in town go to the church on the hill. The poorer people, if they go to church anywhere, go to your church. Unfortunately, some people in that church wouldn't welcome them, so they don't go there."

"We certainly welcome them in our church. I just wish we could help some of them. Any ideas on what we can do to help them?"

They discussed the topic for several minutes without coming up with any answers.

The next day Paul walked to the library in the coolness of the morning to return the books he had checked out and to try to find books on the addiction of gambling. Patsy was alone in the library, standing at her desk, recording returned books. Her black Capri pants and yellow short-sleeve blouse with her blond hair that sat like a halo on her head made Paul's heart skip an extra beat when he saw her. She met him with her usual cheery smile. "I just fixed some coffee. Want some? I have an extra cup I keep washed for guests."

When Paul nodded, she walked over to the coffee pot and poured him a cup. Returning with the beverage she pointed to an empty folding chair by her desk. "It's time for my break. Want to join me for a minute?"

Patsy poured herself a cup of coffee and sat in her swivel chair behind her desk. "Michael was in again yesterday. He told me he was leaving today for California to visit the Kroc brothers. As you know, he has his heart set on opening a hamburger restaurant. If that goes well he will build several of them like they are doing with McDonald's. He should be back in a couple of weeks. Only thing is," she pouted, "I had invited him to attend my twenty-first birthday party on Saturday. My parents are planning a big wingding at our home. And now he's going to miss it."

She paused and looked down at her coffee, swirling it around in her cup. "I think he likes me. He's invited me out on a few dates. But, I don't know now. He's so caught up in his work he barely has time for me. When we are together all he can talk about is hamburgers. What kind of life is that?" She laughed without humor. "How do I know his fancy plan will even work? Who is going to want to eat in a restaurant where all they serve is hamburgers, French fries and milkshakes? What a boring restaurant, even if you can get your food instantly. He may lose the money he's saved and all the thousands of dollars his parents gave him. That would break his heart. And mine," she added more softly. "I thought I had my life—our life all figured out." She shrugged. "Now, I don't know."

"But," she stood and reached for a stack of books on the desk, "I apologize for burdening you with my troubles. I'm sorry."

"Hey, that's okay." Paul was at her side but with an effort refrained from touching her. "I'm sure it will all work out some way. You will be in my prayers—and Michael too—I promise you that."

Patsy brightened as if an idea just occurred to her. "My birthday party. Why don't you come and meet more folks in town, some of the more professional people my family hangs around with."

Paul felt his heart rate go up, then he felt a check. "Oh, I don't know. It might not look good."

"What wouldn't look good? About fifty people or so will be there. What's one more? Just show up Saturday night. Bring your girlfriend Kate: is that her name? Mary Jane told me about her. Anyway, think about it. No gift needed. Just come about seven, if you feel like it."

1955 CHAPTER 21

Dressed in his black suit with white shirt and narrow red tie, Paul felt self-conscious as he stepped through the front door of the spacious Lundquist home. An older man dressed in a tuxedo with long coat tails led him down the hall and to the left into what he called the 'great room.' Paul stared, wondering for a moment if he was on the set of a romance movie. Crystal chandeliers hanging from a high vaulted ceiling held up by white round pillars lit up the huge room that was already filled with men in black suits or tuxedos and women sporting the latest style in dresses, milling about, many with drinks in one hand and a cigarette or plate of pastries in the other. An orchestra of several musicians was tuning up in the far corner.

As Paul stood looking around, trying to bring himself back to reality, and wondering what he should do next, a man and woman approached him. "Good evening," the man greeted Paul with a smile in a cultured voice, extending his right hand. "I'm Daniel Lundquist." He nodded to the woman beside him. "My wife Bertha. We're Patsy's parents. You must be Paul Whitfield. Patsy has told us so much about you."

"Thank you." Paul returned the handshake. "Nice to meet you, Mr. and Mrs. Lundquist. I appreciate the invitation to your daughter's birthday party." He surveyed the couple. Probably in their middle forties, Daniel Lundquist was dressed in a black tuxedo, white shirt and black bow tie. Bertha Lundquist, and older version of her daughter, wore a full-skirted deep blue evening gown that swept down to her ankles. Her permed graying blond hair was topped by a wide brimmed hat, the same color as her dress.

Daniel Lundquist led Paul over to a long table with a white tablecloth filled with pastries and other desserts. "Help yourself to whatever you want to eat." He pointed to the end of the table. "Drinks are down there."

Paul picked up a plate with some pastry he couldn't identify just to have something to hold in his hand and looked around the room again.

Then he saw her, surrounded by friends. Her blond hair was piled in curls on top of her head, exposing her slender neck that was adorned with a pearl necklace. Her yellow evening gown ending just below her knees with matching gloves and high-heeled shoes made her by far the most captivating woman in the room.

As he was staring at her, Stan Manning, the hardware store owner, approached him, a drink in his hand. "Quite a party," he commented to Paul. "Nice to see you here."

"Nice to be here," replied Paul, having to speak loudly to be heard above the blended voices of everyone else in the room. He talked briefly with the hardware store owner.   After milling around the crowd, greeting several people who came to him and introduced themselves, he continued slowly walking around, feeling awkward, yet trying to look like he belonged. Then a middle-aged women in a long black dress went to the stage and clapped her hands and introduced herself as Brenda Page, Patsy's godmother. "Thank you all for coming to honor Patsy as she celebrates twenty-one years today." She called Patsy forward, motioned for her to sit in a chair that resembled a throne and said some complimentary things about her. Then Brenda went to the table loaded with gifts and, one by one, brought them to Patsy. There were oohs and aahs as Patsy held up clothing and other gifts that had been given her. Paul realized he should have purchased her something and hoped she wouldn't notice his oversight with all the other gifts she got.

At the end of the gift opening, someone put on a "Sing Along with Mitch" long play album and the floor cleared for dancing. Paul stepped to the edge of the room and was ready to leave when he felt a hand on his shoulder. He turned to see Patsy, her blue eyes flashing above her dazzling smile. "Paul, thank you so much for coming. This is a special night for me, and I'm glad you came. Come." She took him by the hand. "You can be my first dance."

Paul drew back. "I don't dance. Never have. Well, just once, at my senior prom. But I'm a pastor. I probably shouldn't dance. Might not look good. My church doesn't believe in dancing."

"Oh, come on." Patsy gave another tug. "No one from your church is here. At least, I don't think so. Besides, the Bible talks a lot about dancing." She gave him a pleading look. "Please, just for me. It would mean a lot to me."

"I'm not a good dancer—really, don't know how. Didn't do a good job the one time I tried."

"It's easy." She drew him onto the dance floor. "Move your left foot like this when I move my right foot. Then move your right foot like this. Then just follow me. It's easier than it looks." She put her arm around his shoulder and started pulling him toward the center of the room. He suddenly felt that wild urge he sometimes got as a kid when he did something he knew he shouldn't be doing just because it felt good. Paul followed Patsy, moving his feet as instructed. He stepped on her feet a few times and made several miscues, but before long he got the hang of it and actually enjoyed swaying to the music, holding Patsy's soft body in his arms, looking down at her smiling up at him.

The song ended. The dancers stopped and applauded. "Enjoy that?" she asked. Before he could think of an answer, the music started again. Patsy again drew close to Paul, grasped his hand and placed her hand on his shoulder. "Let's do one more."

At the end of the second dance Paul knew he was enjoying this too much.

He had to get away and leave before he became tempted to stay and dance all night. He backed away from Patsy and cleared his throat. "Thank you for inviting me to your party. I enjoyed it. Happy birthday. Now I've got to go." With what he hoped was a smile, he made his way toward the front door, avoiding eye contact with the other party guests.

Just before he stepped outside he felt a hand on his shoulder. He turned around and was surprised to see the smiling face of Daniel Lundquist. "Thank you again for coming," said the older man. He gripped Paul by his right arm and led him into the hallway beyond the sight of the partygoers. "I just wanted to ask what you think of our daughter Patsy."

Paul felt his face turn warm and he knew he was blushing. "I...I think she's a nice young lady," he sputtered. "When I go into the library to check out books, she is always gracious and friendly."

"I understand you will be going out to dinner with Patsy, and she will be introducing you to our son, Lamar, to try and help him. We appreciate the interest you are taking in our children."

"I trust I can become friends with him. I'm sure he is a fine young man that has a lot of potential if he can find his place in life," responded Paul, glad to get away from talking about Patsy.

Daniel Lundquist added, "I'm sure you know that Michael Champion is sweet on Patsy. He would have been here except he's in California or Chicago or somewhere making hamburgers." He shook his head. "That young man scares me. First, he left a girl at the altar in Kansas City. My daughter doesn't need that to happen to her. Second, that ridiculous obsession he has with starting a restaurant selling only hamburgers. That will only lead him to the poor house, I'm afraid."

He paused, then gave Paul a friendly pat on the arm. "So, I'm glad she likes you, and you get along. I know you don't have much going for you now, but I know you are an honest trustworthy man who has a bright future." With that he turned and disappeared back into the ballroom.

Patsy stared after Paul as he made his way across the room and was surprised to see her father follow Paul out into the hallway and out of sight. She had initiated the dance partially because she liked Paul, but mostly hoping that somehow word would get to Michael and make him jealous. Dancing with Paul had somehow made it hard for her to catch her breath when she was so close to him. His smile, his strong arms, his gentle ways made her feel content and secure. Was she starting to lose her heart to Paul?

Back in his car Paul drove to his parking spot in the alley behind the church, made his way in through the back door, and up to his bedroom. "Dear Lord," he said out loud as got ready for bed, "forgive me. I don't think I should have done what I did. Help no one from church to find out. Or, if they do, that it won't cause a problem." He glanced at the calendar. Today was Saturday, September 30. Tomorrow was Sunday. Would anyone mention it in church?

He then asked himself: *Why did Patsy's father say what he did about Michael? And about him? Was he trying to persuade Paul to get serious with Patsy?*

The thought scared him. At the same time he felt a stirring of excitement run through him. Then, wondering about the implications, he frowned as he lay in the darkness as a cool breeze swept through the two open screened windows. But the more he reviewed the evening: the memories of the dance, being close to Patsy, feeling her arms around him, the more he smiled in the darkness.

1955   CHAPTER 22

He felt like he had been asleep for just a few minutes when he was awakened by pounding on the front door of the church. He looked at his watch. Six o'clock. Who wanted him at this time of the morning? Hurriedly dressing he ran down the stairs, turned on the hall light and made his way to the front of the church.

He opened the door to see Claude standing in the morning dawn, wearing a pair of worn jeans and wrinkled T-shirt, his uncombed hair hanging over his eyes. He was crying.

"What's wrong, my friend?" Feeling instant compassion for this wayward young man, Paul gently took Claude's arm, led him into the church, and closed the door.

Not seeming to mind being in a church, Claude took a red handkerchief from his back pocket and wiped his eyes. "James Dean is dead," he blurted out with a sob.

"What!" You mean the actor? Dead? How?

"Just heard it on the radio. Yesterday, James Dean was driving his Porsche to a sports car racing competition in Salinas, California. Some car hit him head on. Killed him. He's dead. He's gone."

"I'm so sorry." Paul's sadness was not for the dead actor whom he had barely heard of, but he did feel empathy toward Claude, in spite of how this would-be rebel had treated him. "What can I do? Want a cup of coffee? I can make a pot. Do you want to sit down? We can talk."

"Why did God let this happen?" Anger took the place of sorrow. He stared at Paul through bloodshot eyes, his voice rising. "If there is a God and He is a God of love as you preachers claim, and if God can control the universe, why did He let James Dean die?"

"God is a God of love," countered Paul, "and He is all-powerful. But life happens. We don't…"

"James Dean was a good man," Claude interrupted. "He loved children and young people and everybody. He was a help to people like me, someone to follow. He shouldn't have had to die so young. He was only twenty-four."

Putting aside his opinion of how good a role model the actor was, Paul said quietly, "I know you are sorry he died. I feel bad for him, too. But, really, Claude, how will his death affect life here in Bethel Springs? Or your life? Life will go on for all of us just like it was before. You will feel sad for awhile, but you will get over it."

Claude stared at Paul, then looked wildly about him as if he didn't comprehend was Paul was saying.

"Would you like me to pray?" suggested Paul. "Pray for James Dean's family and for all his fans, including you?"

"No!" Claude's reply was almost a moan. Then his voice rose. "I don't even think there is a God. Why waste time praying to someone who doesn't exist."

When that rant was over he ran out of the hall and slammed the door. Paul stared after him feeling empathy, sorrow and surprise as to how much the death of someone Claude didn't even know and would probably never have met, affected him. "Lord," he said conversationally, "open Claude's eyes, and the eyes of all of James Dean's fans to the uncertainty of life, and that the only certainty we have is in You."

After the Sunday morning service Fred Pittman waited until almost everyone had left, then asked if he could speak with Paul alone. Paul told little Chipper and Joshua to wait for him downstairs, that he would be there in a few minutes to take them home. One look at Fred's face told Paul it would not be a friendly chat. Kicking himself for having gone to Patsy's party, and fearful this is what the talk would be about, Paul led him upstairs to his apartment.

Sitting on wooden chairs around the kitchen table, Fred sighed and cleared his throat. "You are doing a good job in many ways here, Paul," he began, "but you have to realize this is a small town and word gets around. I hear you went to a party last night and danced." He raised his eyebrows and looked at Paul. "Is that true?"

Paul looked beyond Fred to a picture on the wall of Jesus surrounded by a flock of sheep. "Patsy Lundquist, the librarian, one day when I was over checking out some books to prepare for my sermons, invited me to her birthday party. She said it would be a good opportunity to meet others in the community. To not hurt her feelings I went. When I got there, she asked me to dance with her. I told her I didn't dance and didn't think I should, but she kept insisting so..."

"So to not hurt her feelings you danced with her? Fred Pittman finished. "Is that it?"

Paul nodded. "I hadn't planned to when I went to the party."

"It just happened?"

Paul nodded again.

Fred Pittman looked down at the table and frowned. "Previous pastors have taught us it's a sin to dance." He looked back up to Paul. "What would you do if you caught one of the young men from this church dancing with a girl who wasn't his wife?"

Paul shrugged, feeling more uncomfortable with each comment. "I haven't thought much about it. The Bible doesn't specifically speak against dancing. In fact, they did a lot of dancing in the Old Testament."

"Dancing with women or dancing to the Lord?"

"Fred, I'm sorry. I know I shouldn't have done that. I promise, at least I will do my best to make sure that doesn't happen again."

Fred Pittman rubbed his nose to hide a slight smile. "I hope this never happens again. But I want you to realize this may not be the end of it. Others might have found out about it too. You need to be careful in what you do in a small town, such as counseling a young woman alone in your apartment late at night. That also needs to stop."

The deacon stood to his feet. "I love you, brother," he said and gave Paul a pat on the back. "But you need to be careful. By the way," he added, "I was talking to my neighbor, Ted Strand, yesterday. He goes to Hope church. He said Pastor Gannon told him that since you are likening our Bethel Springs to the Bethel in the Bible, that you are like the man of God in Bethel who disobeyed God and was eaten by a lion. You might want to watch that pastor," the deacon cautioned. "I don't trust him or some of the leaders in his church."

Paul nodded, remembering that Pastor Gannon had told him the same comment to his face.

Back downstairs he loaded the two little boys in his De Soto to take them home, as he often did on Sundays after church.

Paul was asking them what they had learned in Sunday school when he noticed his car kept trying to steer to the left. Slowing down, he realized the problem and pulled off the road at the end of a gentle curve to the left. "I believe we have a flat tire," he announced. Getting out, he looked at the left front tire. "It's only flat on the bottom," he joked, "but I still need to change it."

As Paul jacked up the front of the car, the two boys got out and began having a sword fight off the side of the road with two sticks they had found. Paul had taken off the flat tire and was putting on the spare when he heard the sound of a car behind him. He turned around to see a black car speeding around the corner, dust flying up behind it. As Paul watched in horror, the vehicle kept coming straight for his car without following the curve in the road.

When the realization came to him that the speeding car was going to hit him unless it rapidly changed course or he got out of the way, with an immediate spike in adrenaline, he jumped to his feet, put both hands on the fender of the car and catapulted himself onto the hood, rolling over and landing in a heap on the ground on the passenger side.

At the same instant he heard the grinding of metal as the other car sideswiped the driver's side of his De Soto and kept driving, disappearing down the road in a roaring cloud of dust.

Paul lay on the ground for several seconds in shock. Then, slowly he moved his arms and legs. Discovering they still worked without too much discomfort, he got shakily to his knees, then to his feet. Looking behind the car he saw the two boys, unharmed, staring at him, their sticks still in their hands.

"Wow," said Chipper in an awed voice. "That car done hit your car and almost got you."

Silently he walked over to the boys and gave them a hug, thankful everyone was all right. Wiping the dirt and grass off his clothing, he walked over to look at the damage to the car. It still appeared drivable, but both doors had sustained huge creases. The left front fender had also been dented. The left side of the front bumper had been torn from the car and was lying on the ground, the right side still attached to the car.

"Get in the car," he told the boys. "I'll finish changing the tire. then I need to tear off the bumper if I can and throw it in the trunk and see if the car still runs."

Several minutes later they were back on the road, Paul a little worse for wear, beginning to feel the bruises from his tumble.

He looked over at the boys beside him. "Do you boys know what persecution is?" When they shrugged he shook his head grimly. "Whatever it is, I think you just saw it."

1955   CHAPTER 23

Early Monday morning Paul took his car to the police station and told Police Chief Robert Ferguson the whole story. Paul could only remember that the car was black and was a late model Buick, but he couldn't be sure. He couldn't give any description of the driver. Ferguson took down his information and said he would check around at garages in the area to see if a car fitting that description had come in for repairs.

Remembering that no one had yet found out who had caused the hit and run that had injured the previous pastor's son, Paul didn't have a lot of confidence the hit and run driver who had run into his car and almost killed him would be found.

Next he drove the car to Elven's Auto Shop. Elven told him he could have the car repaired within a few days.

Thursday evening Patsy picked up Paul up at the church in her pink Cadillac. "Lamar said he would meet us at the restaurant at six o'clock. I guess he didn't want to ride with us and be stuck in the car for the thirty minutes it will take us to get there and back."

Patsy spotted her brother as soon as they entered the Riverview Restaurant, sitting at a round table by a window overlooking the valley with the White River below them.

Patsy introduced Paul to Lamar who returned Paul's solid handshake with a firm handshake of his own. Unlike his sister, Lamar was dark-haired and well built, nearly as tall as Paul, although they looked enough alike to be recognized as brother and sister.

After looking through their menu and making their order, Patsy turned to her brother. "Thanks for coming here to meet Paul. He's agreed to meet with you and see what he can do to help you."

"Whoa." Paul held up his hand. "I'm not a psychiatrist. Just a freshman pastor recently out of Bible school. Let's just say I'm here to be your friend. If we can help each other, great. If not, at least we can become friends. I'm in need of friends in this town outside of my church."

Lamar gave a flicker of a smile. "No lectures on how I should stay in college and make something of my life so I won't become a bum?"

Paul returned the smile. "None of that, I promise. But I will be as honest as I can be with you. Life isn't a matter of doing your own thing. It's a matter of doing the right thing."

Their food came. Paul did his best to try and make Lamar feel comfortable with him. At the end of the meal, Lamar agreed to meet next Thursday with

Paul at a restaurant closer to town.

Back at the church, before getting out of Patsy's car, she reached over and gave him a hug, giving him the full effect of the perfume he had been breathing all evening. He couldn't identify the fragrance, but he liked it. "Thank you for taking the time to meet with my brother. He doesn't like many people, but I think he hit it off with you."

That Friday when Paul was eating breaking at Martha's, Laura told him she was leaving the following day to return to Burge School of Nursing in Springfield to begin her third and final year. "I'll usually be back on weekends and holidays, so I can continue working some," she told Paul as she briefly sat across from him, setting her pot of coffee on the table between them. She smiled. "I will miss serving you. I hope you will keep coming in even when I'm not here. You will find that Holly and Angel are good servers. But," she added pointing her thumb meaningfully to the kitchen door, "they already know I have dibs on you." Then she laughed. "I'm sorry. I didn't mean it that way. I mean," she added somewhat flustered, "that I have dibs on serving you when I'm working."

Paul nodded and returned the laugh, feeling his face get suddenly warm.

After Bible study the following Wednesday night, Paul packed his overnight bag, locked up the church, got in his recently patched up De Soto, and headed for home, arriving at his mother's house in Springfield around midnight. At his last visit he told his mother he was coming to celebrate her birthday which was the next day, so he quietly unlocked the door and went to his room, knowing his mother would expect him for breakfast.

He woke about seven o'clock to sounds of breakfast being made in the kitchen and the smells of bacon and coffee. Dressing in his dungarees and newly-washed blue nylon shirt, he went downstairs and greeted his mother who was already dressed in her green and white striped dress with every strand of her permed graying hair in place.

After a hug and kiss they ate breakfast, catching up on each other's lives over the past few days. Dorothy told her son about some of her experiences at the First National Bank where she was a part-time teller. Paul told his mother that the church was growing and doing better since the VBS.

"Kate came over a couple of days ago," commented Dorothy over their second cup of coffee. "You know she's getting ready to start her last year in Bible school. You've known each other most of your lives, and I know you have talked about marriage. Why don't you get over to see her while you're here. I know she'll be thrilled. I've been telling her about how you are doing in your church. With the church growing, you could use a full-time helpmate. Besides," her mother smiled, "you could use some help in washing and ironing your clothes."

Paul returned the smile as he studied his cup of coffee. "Mother, it's so complicated." He sighed. "I always thought Kate was the one. Maybe she still is..." His voice trailed off. "But..."

"Is there someone else?" His mother's voice sounded a little shrill.

"I don't know. Yes," he added, "there may be." He shook his head. "I don't know. I'm a little confused." He raised his hands palms out. "I don't want to talk about this right now, if you don't mind. But I have something for you." He ran up to his bedroom and came back down with a wrapped package. "Happy birthday. Hope you can use it."

He handed his mother the package that opened to reveal a pair of brown work shoes. "Last time I was here," Paul added, "I noticed the shoes you wore in the garden looked like they were on their last legs...or feet," and he laughed at his own joke, "so I bought you a new pair at Lundquist Shoes. You may or may not know this, but Lundquist Shoes was started by Jeremiah Lundquist before the Civil War. The fourth generation, Daniel Lundquist and his brother Charles, now own the business. There are dozens of stores in the South and Midwest. Daniel and his family live in Bethel Springs. Their daughter, Patsy, works at the town library."

Dorothy raised her eyebrows. "Is she the other girl you are interested in? The one you like more than Kate?"

Paul frowned at his mother's subtle sarcastic tone of voice. "I really don't know how to answer that. I know Patsy, the daughter. She's a nice girl, but I'm not saying she's the one. Besides, she already has a young man in Bethel Springs who likes her. Rich and handsome, way out of my league."

Suddenly, like a flash, an idea hit Paul. Maybe he could help his mother understand his dilemma, or maybe get her advice; he wasn't sure which.

He looked at his watch. "Mother, it's almost ten. I know I said I'd take you out to lunch at Hamby's, but I need to run an errand first. I'll be back shortly."

Laura Taylor looked at her watch as she sat in third period anatomy class at Burge School of Nursing in Springfield. Another hour till lunch. She hadn't slept well the night before. Starting back in school for her last year, she had difficult subjects. Her mother was ill. Thoughts about Paul and Claude floated unbidden into her mind. The more she tried to crowd them out, the more they returned. Claude, how to get him out of her life. How to try and forget Paul. She liked him but knew he would never go beyond liking her as a waitress if he only knew about her past.

As third period ended and Laura walked out of her class, Penny Middleton, the school secretary, was waiting for her. "There's a gentleman in the office to see you," she said. "I think he said his name was Paul something."

A warm feeling came over Laura at the thought that Paul had come to see her. Then panic. What was wrong? Why had he driven all the way up from Bethel Springs just to see her? Tightly clutching her books she hurried down the hall toward the office where she saw Paul standing there, tall, handsome, his blond hair freshly combed. But she saw none of that. "Paul, what's wrong?" she said hurrying over to him. "My mother? Martha? Holly? Angel?"

Paul grasped her free hand and laughed. "Nothing's wrong. I was in the neighborhood, so thought I would stop by and say 'hi'."

"Oh." Laura took a deep breath, then returned the laugh. "I'm glad everything's okay. I mean, I'm glad to see you. Thanks for coming by." Noting that Penny was still standing there staring at them and realizing Paul was still holding her hand, she gently pulled it away.

"I'm sorry to have scared you," Paul said apologetically.

Laura looked over to Penny. "Thanks," she said staring at her for several seconds until Penny took the hint and returned to her desk. Laura glanced at her watch. "I have another class in a couple of minutes, but let's go outside." She led him out the door and to the front lawn where they were alone.

"You drove all the way up here to see me?" she asked, that warm feeling returning, putting all other thoughts behind her.

"Not exactly. Since it's Mother's birthday today, I came to spend the day and celebrate it with her. Then I remembered you were in Springfield too, so thought I would drop by." He paused and looked down at his shoes.

"Thank you for coming to see me," she said prodding him to go on. Wondering if he was hesitating because he wanted to ask her out and wasn't sure what to say, she added, "I have three more classes, but I'm off at three o'clock."

"Good." Paul looked relieved and seemed to have found his voice again. "I just wondered..." he paused again. "I just wondered..." He looked up at the blue sky. "It's a beautiful day. Would you like to go on a picnic with me for dinner? Maybe at Fassnight Park? I can get some chicken and rolls at Hamby's Restaurant or something when I'm there with my mother. Could I pick you up, like at five o'clock?"

Laura felt her heart beat faster. Was Paul really inviting her on a date? Pastor Paul? The handsome man who came into the restaurant that she had dreamed about but thought he was out of her league? The Paul whose marriage proposal letter to Kate she had inadvertently seen?

With a myriad of unanswered questions she looked over to Paul and smiled. "Yes, that sounds like fun."

"Good." Relief was evident in Paul's voice. "Give me your address and I'll be by about five."

The rest of the afternoon dragged by with Laura scarcely paying attention to the class lectures. Why was Paul taking her on a picnic? Was it a date just to have fun and to get to know her better? Or was he going to tell her he was leaving Bethel Springs? Or that he was marrying Kate and couldn't come into the restaurant anymore? Had he found out the truth about her and Claude? Other possibilities came and went through her mind as the day went on.

Arriving back to her apartment a little after three she told her roommate, Patricia Perkins, she had a date for the evening and what should she wear for a picnic. After trying on nearly all the clothes in her closet, she finally decided on a pleated fawn colored skirt with a white blouse. Adjusting her ponytail and combing her bangs three separate times she was finally ready when Paul knocked on the apartment door precisely at five.

Finding an empty picnic table at Fassnight Park, Paul spread out a white tablecloth, then brought out a basket with fried chicken, rolls and salad from Hamby's restaurant, along with plates, glasses and silverware borrowed from his mother and two bottles of Coca Cola.

Over dinner they discussed life back in Bethel Springs and Laura's schooling. After the meal was over and the leftovers and remains of the meal put back in the car, they wandered down to the stream. "When I was little I used to take off my shoes and hunt crawdads with my friends," commented Paul. "Here," Paul sat down and began taking his shoes and socks off. "Want to wade in the stream with me?"

Laura, rather taken aback at Paul's desire to walk barefoot in the water, yet wanting to please him, sat beside him, also removing her shoes and socks. As they stepped into the water, Laura slipped on a rock, and Paul grabbed her hand to keep her from falling. After she steadied herself, still holding her hand, Paul began walking through the water, Laura beside him. After a few moments of stumbling over the rocks, she finally figured out how to walk along the stream and began to enjoy herself, holding hands with the tall, strong, handsome man beside her who obviously now held more than a casual attraction to her.

After walking to the bridge and back to where they had started, they put their socks and shoes back on their wet feet and started back toward the car.

"Why did you invite me on this picnic?" asked Laura when they were almost back to the car.

"Just to get to know you better, and have an enjoyable evening with a friend."

They sat at the same table where they had had their dinner.

"How much do you know about me?" she asked.

"I know you are an attractive young woman, a good waitress and a wonderful Christian. I've appreciated your help with the church in visiting people, your help in the VBS and in other ways."

"Have you ever wondered why I haven't invited you to my home?"

Paul thought for a moment. "Yes, the thought had occurred to me. But it's no big deal."

"It is to me." Laura sighed and looked away from Paul. "Do you remember when you visited that older, sickly woman on Valley Drive who lived in the chicken house?"

"Yes."

"She's my mother. That's where I live. Lived there for the past several years." She looked back at Paul who was staring at her.

"We used to live in an old cabin and raise chickens in two chicken houses. Dirt farmers. Grew corn on our land, potatoes, tomatoes—anything that would grow. Poor. I guess Dad couldn't take it anymore after awhile. One day when I was twelve, he just left and never returned. Never heard from him again although we heard rumors he settled down somewhere in Kentucky.

"Then things got worse, if that were possible. One night Mom went to sleep in bed while smoking a cigarette and set her bed and whole house on fire. We got out okay but it burned the house down. With nowhere else to go we ended up living in one of the chicken houses.

"That's how I was raised. At sixteen, I got a job at Martha's Cafe mainly to save money to go to college. I decided to get my nursing degree to get myself and Mom out of poverty."

"Well, I admire you for what you have made of yourself. You are the best waitress in all of Bethel Springs, and I'm sure you will make a fantastic nurse."

Paul stood to his feet. "Now that our picnic is over, how about if I take you to meet Mother? I told her we might be by tonight."

"Oh, my." She put her hands to her face, shocked at his invitation. "So many surprises in one day." Then her common sense took over. "Why? Why do you want me to meet your mother?"

Paul was at a loss for words for a few seconds. Finally he said, "I don't know. She lives in town not far from where you are staying. You live here during the school year. Just thought you may want to get acquainted."

A few minutes later Laura followed Paul into his boyhood home. "Mother," said Paul to the middle-aged woman that came to the door, "this is

Laura. Laura, this is my mother, Dorothy."

"How do you do?" Dorothy greeted Laura with a slight hug, which Laura returned.

"Nice to meet you, too," replied Laura, noting Dorothy's nervous half smile and forced friendliness.

"Come into the living room," suggested Paul. "I think Mother made some ice tea and a German chocolate cake."

While Dorothy went into the kitchen, Laura followed Paul and sat beside him in a black couch facing a large console radio. A crocheted oval rug sat on the hardwood floor in front of them. The flowered wallpaper gave the small room a homey, intimate feeling. She listened to Paul as he discussed his growing up years in this home. He told his rambling stories, it seemed to Laura, to cover up his nervousness.

After several minutes Paul's mother came back in carrying a tray with two cups of ice tea and two pieces of cake on small plates with forks. She placed the tray on the coffee table in front of the couch and retreated to a wooden rocking chair facing the couch. "So tell me about yourself, Laura," she said, attempting to smile.

"I've lived in Bethel Springs all my life," Laura began as she picked up the fork and plate with the cake. Then she hesitated. She usually didn't tell people about her past or even where she lived now. But she had just told Paul. He would probably tell his mother even if she didn't, so it might as well come from her.

"I was raised poor," she continued. "My parents were dirt farmers and raised chickens. My dad took off when I was twelve, and we never saw him again. After our house burned down several years ago we ended up living in a chicken house, which is where I live now with my mother.

"When I turned sixteen, I started waitressing at a local restaurant so I could earn enough money to go to college and become a nurse. I've just started my third year at Burge and hope to graduate next May.

"I first met Paul in June when he came into the restaurant where I work. He happened to sit in my section when I was on duty. Since then I've attended his church some and helped out in various ways," she finished, suddenly feeling rather proud of what she had made of her young life so far.

"She has been a big help in church," added Paul. She helped in the VBS and helped me in visiting a couple of the single mothers. We are trying to come up with ideas to help some of the people on Valley Drive, one of the poorer sections of town."

"Paul told me that you raised him alone for much of his growing up years too," added Laura, suddenly interested in how Paul's mother had managed to raise such a wonderful son.

At Laura's question, Dorothy looked away and didn't answer for so long that Laura was afraid she had offended her. But finally Dorothy looked back and cleared her throat. "It was a shock to have Bob gone. I'm sure Paul told you how he was killed in World War II. Paul was seven."

Laura looked over at Paul who was looking down at the carpet. "It was harder after that," Dorothy continued. "But Paul was a good boy and with the Lord's help we made it." She smiled at Laura, a genuine smile this time. "More tea?"

After several minutes of casual conversation, Laura turned to Dorothy, then Paul. "Thank you for the tea and cake and visit. But I need to get home. I have lots of homework. I've enjoyed the picnic and seeing Paul's boyhood home and getting to meet you, Mrs. Whitfield."

"Dorothy," said Paul's mother. "You can call me Dorothy. And thank you for your visit. It was nice meeting you too."

On the way to Laura's apartment she turned to Paul. "Thank you so much for the afternoon," she said touching his shoulder briefly. "I appreciate the thoughtfulness of your visit. I had fun at the picnic. I enjoyed meeting your mother." She chuckled. "Even though I think it was a little awkward for all of us. Thank you."

At Laura's apartment, as Paul opened the car door for her, he took her hand as he walked her to her door. Just before reaching the glow of the porch light, in the darkness, she turned to him. "As I told you at the picnic I come from the wrong side of the tracks to most of the people in Bethel Springs. Even for you, I wasn't raised like you. But even after telling you this, and you still wanting me to meet your mother—and taking me back to my apartment like this…" She swallowed a sob. "That means a lot to me. Thank you." Then, still not wanting to commit herself to a kiss she thought Paul might have on his mind, she hurried into her apartment before Paul could say or do anything else.

Back in her apartment she leaned against the closed door, savoring the moment and the feel of Paul's hand in hers, reliving the walk through the stream at the picnic and the other events that took place. She had appreciated Paul taking her to meet his mother, in spite of the awkwardness of the visit. Then she thought about what Paul would think if he knew about that incident in her past, and she sighed as she took off her shoes and damp socks.

Paul slowly made his way back to the car and got in. Only the scent of her perfume lingered in the car. He had enjoyed the afternoon and evening. He was glad he had decided to take Laura to meet his mother. He valued his mother's judgment and wanted her reaction.

Back at his mother's home, she had cleared away the tray from the living room and was waiting for him in the kitchen with another piece of cake and glass of milk.

"Well, what did you think of Laura, Mother?" asked Paul as he sat down and took a bite of the cake.

Dorothy sat down across the kitchen table from him. "She seems to be a nice girl," she said slowly. "I'm sure she will make a great nurse and a good wife and mother to someone. But with what she told us about herself, don't you realize she was raised in a totally different environment, a different world than you were. With her past, with the way she was raised, with how she is living now, she would never fit into our family. Can't you see that, son? She's not for you. I could tell that the minute she started talking about herself. I'm sorry, but that's how I feel."

Next door, Angela Fuller closed the curtain on her windows. "Earnest," she told her husband, "when Kate comes home from her concert, we need to tell her that Paul brought a girl home tonight to meet Dorothy. She stayed for an hour and ten minutes. A tall, pretty girl with dark hair."

1955   CHAPTER 24

Saturday morning, back in Bethel Springs, as Paul was having breakfast of oatmeal and toast, he heard a knock on the door downstairs. Making his way down he was met by Art Atkins, a young man he had met briefly at Elven's Auto Repair where he worked with Sam Pittman. He was holding a clipboard and a pen.

"Good morning, Pastor Paul," he said heartily with a smile. "Beautiful day today in Bethel Springs and in the Ozarks."

"Yes it is," said Paul suddenly wary of the visitor's forced cheerfulness and was waiting to hear what product he was pitching.

"I'm making the rounds today to ask people to sign a petition so we can get enough signatures to put legalized gaming on November's ballot."

"What's gaming?"

The young man cleared his throat and looked down. "That's the new fancy word they are using for gambling."

"Why do you want gambling in town? Don't you realize that will bring in all kinds of undesirable people? Some of our townspeople may even get hooked on gambling and lose their cars, homes, families or worse. Maybe you will."

Going through his memorized script, Art Atkins told Paul how gambling was just a small part, almost a sideline of the new bathhouse, opera house, hotel and other businesses that would be brought into town. The increase of tourist trade would provide jobs for dozens of people. This new venture would improve their standard of living and increase the economy of the whole town and everybody living there.

Paul then asked why not follow through on their other projects but leave gambling out. Art replied that the financial backers wouldn't put up the other buildings without getting the approval to build a gambling casino.

As Art talked, Paul tried to remember all he had learned about gambling. When his visitor stopped for breath, Paul spoke up. "Haven't you read in the Bible about greed? Proverbs chapter 28 says that someone who makes haste to get rich will not go unpunished. Other Scriptures talk about the foolishness of trying to get rich quickly.

"George Washington," Paul added in a flash of remembering what he had heard somewhere, "the father of our country, told his nephew to avoid gambling. He said this vice produces all kinds of evil and will injure morals and health. He told his nephew that few gain from gambling and that many are injured. Thomas Jefferson, our third president, said anyone who gambled should not be eligible to any state office."

Paul talked to the young man for several minutes trying to show him the evils of gambling and all that came with it. As an example he used Hackett House where gambling was already going on.

After the visitor left seemingly unconvinced with Paul's arguments, and with Paul not signing the petition, he closed the door and walked to the altar. "What is going on, Lord?" he said conversationally. "What more should I be doing about this, if anything?"

A conviction grew within him that increased as the day went on. He didn't want to do it, but felt compelled. He hoped it was by the direction of the Lord and not some other feeling.

That night Paul waited until dark, then drove down Mill Road to Hackett House. This time he would not try to sneak around but would go in as a paying customer. As he turned into the driveway, a man dressed in jeans and a white T-shirt got out of a car parked beside the driveway and waved him down. Paul recognized him as one of the men George Hackett had introduced him to several weeks earlier at Martha's Café. As Paul rolled down his window and the man leaned down to look into the car, he wondered if the money collector would recognize him and send him away. "By yourself? If so, two bucks." He reached a beefy hand through the window. Paul opened his wallet and handed him the money. "Enjoy yourself," he said and slapped the top of the car. Paul continued down the driveway and parked beside the other cars, backing in so he could make a quick getaway, if needed. As he got out of his car he noticed the man walked toward the front of the house and went inside.

Making his way up the five concrete steps onto the back porch, he hesitated and looked around, observing the two white pillars holding up the roof over the deck and the slatted white railing that surrounded it. Then, taking a deep breath and whispering a silent prayer, he opened the wooden door painted a fiery red and went inside.

As he stepped into the room that was about half the size of his church auditorium, the first thing he saw was visible smoke in the air coming from the men who were standing in groups, most with a cigarette or cigar in one hand and a bottle of liquor in the other. The sound of their loud voices competing with a hi-fi loudly playing *Cry, Cry, Cry* by Johnny Cash, completed the atmosphere.

Paul stood in the doorway and surveyed the scene, wrinkling his nose at the stench. To his right was a bar lined with men with bottles in front of them, talking or watching a television on the wall almost hidden among the various bottles of liquor. Walking away from the bar to his left he slowly made his way around the room, trying to not draw attention to himself, but looking for anyone he recognized and trying to figure out what all was going on at Hackett House.

From behind a closed door he passed he could hear men laughing and what sounded like a movie being shown. As he kept walking he passed a smoke-filled room with an open door where men were playing cards at four tables. In the next room to his right, men were playing pool at two pool tables with a stack of bills on the edge of each table.

"Wanna smoke or a drink, big boy?" Paul turned to see a young woman approach him through the smoke, holding a wooden tray at her waist held up by a white leather strap around her shoulders. She took a pack of cigarettes and a small bottle from the tray and held it up to him. "What will it be?" About the same age as Paul, she was dressed like a bar maid with long, straight borox blond hair. Her smirk appeared to challenge Paul, and he wondered if she knew who he was.

"I'll have a Coke or Pepsi," he answered with a smile.

"Don't got any of those." She put them back in the tray. The smirk stayed on her face. "Only the real stuff."

"No thanks, then." Paul turned away to continue his tour around the room. He had gone past the bar and almost finished circling the room and was near the door he entered when George Hackett came down the stairs and approached him, a welcoming smile on his face, followed by the man who had taken his money and the other man Paul remembered from that Sunday morning at the restaurant.

"Welcome to Hackett House, preacher," he said loudly, giving Paul a slap on his shoulder. Then he moved up and spoke softly into his ear. "You've been here just walking around, casing the place and looking for your church members. Right?" The smile left his face. "Preacher, unless you're here to join us and have your fun, get out of here right now and don't ever come back." He gripped Paul's arm so hard he almost cried out in pain. He turned to the two men. "Jake, Carl, please escort our friend out the door." Releasing his grip on Paul, he shook his finger in his face. "This is the only fun in this town these men ever get. Let them be. They need this. You try to change what we are doing here and you'll be sorry. Remember, I know where you live. I know your church and some of your members. I know who your friends are. I know how to get back at you. If you think that's a threat, it is."

With that, he pushed Paul toward the two men. They each took an arm and dragged him out the door and across the porch. With another push, they sent him down the stairs. Paul tried to stay on his feet as he went down the steps, but he stumbled and could feel himself falling. Putting his hands in front of him to catch his fall he hit the grass and rolled two or three times before coming to a stop.

Lying on his back with the breath knocked out of him, he held his hands in the air feeling like they were on fire. Finally, fearfully, when his breathing returned to somewhat normal, he moved his fingers and wrists to see if any were broken. He experienced jabs of pain with each movement, but as least they worked, as did his elbows and shoulders.

Slowly rising to his feet he staggered toward his car, noticing the two men were standing on the porch watching him. "Hey, Pete," one of them called out to a man watching from the driveway. "If this creep tries to come back don't let him in. Ya hear?"

Paul's hands were so weak and trembly it took him three tries to get his key in the ignition. The car started with a welcoming roar. With his hands still on fire, Paul managed to put the car in gear and slowly drove out of Hackett House onto the highway.

Arriving home, he drove around to the back of the church in the alley and parked by the back door, as he usually did. As he locked his car and got out he was puzzled to see the back door of the church was open.

Walking inside, he turned on the lights and was horrified to see his church had been vandalized. The pulpit was knocked over on its side and broken. Benches were turned over. Songbooks were torn and lying on the floor. The display of tracts and booklets on a wooden rack near the back of the church was smashed, papers scattered all around. The stove pipe from the oil heater had been torn out of the wall and was crumpled on the floor. It looked like someone had taken a sledge hammer to the piano. The top was smashed in, most of the keys were broken and lay in pieces on the floor.

Paul stared in horror at the sight. Then he looked upstairs. What had they done to his apartment? With still trembling legs and weak hands, he managed to get up the stairs and turn on the light. His bed was turned upside down, his pillow and sheets cut into pieces. His kitchen counter, stove, cabinet, and everything else was in shambles. The bathroom door had been torn off, the sink and toilet smashed. He was surprised with all this destruction there wasn't water spraying everywhere. Most of the books from his small library had been tossed around the room, some with pages torn out. His Bible, given to him by his parents when he was a young boy, was torn in half.

His chess sets? Paul hurried to his bed. He had stored them in a suitcase under his bed. Gone.

He sat in the one chair that had not been smashed and put his head in his hands. Tears came to his eyes. "Why, Lord," he heard himself saying out loud. "Why did this happen? Who did this?"

Had someone from Hackett House known he was going there and did it for spite? Or someone from Zeb's bar? Or some disgruntled church member? Or Laura's boyfriend Claude?

Making his way downstairs, knowing tomorrow was Sunday and people would be arriving in church, he straightened up the hall the best he could. Two hours later he dragged the torn-up mattress from his bed onto the floor, threw two blankets on the box springs with his sleeping bag on top and climbed in. After saying a quick prayer he tried to shut his mind down, and finally drifted off to a fitful sleep.

PRESENT DAY   CHAPTER 25

The white-haired man had struggled over the weekend with a decision. Before coming to Bethel Springs he had promised himself he would not reveal to anyone who he was. He didn't want to experience the negative repercussions he knew he would face if certain people found out his true identity. Granted, most of the people living here when the fire happened were either dead or had moved. That event was now ancient history that few remembered. Still, there was no doubt some here who knew about the fire wouldn't like it if they knew the man accused of setting the fire was back in town. But, he wasn't getting anywhere with finding out who had been responsible for the fire. Should he enlist Mabel's help, or not?

After spending Friday night in a Shell Knob motel room, he had taken the next day to go over his journal again and drive through town to see if it brought back any memories that would help him in his quest.

Along Valley Drive a newer, larger house stood where the Rice family had lived. The chicken house where Laura had lived was replaced with several duplexes on the same property. Many of the other houses were still there, some having been fixed up, some more run down; two of them looked abandoned.

Driving farther south, he noticed a large church had been built on Rocky's old place. He smiled as he recalled his visits with the old man after the encounter he and Laura had with Rocky and his shotgun on their picnic. He remembered the day, several months later, it was a Tuesday, sometime in August of 1956, that Rocky said a simple prayer and committed his life to follow Jesus. Rocky was uncomfortable around people and never did come to church, but he eagerly looked forward to the Tuesday Bible studies Paul taught him while sharing a home cooked meal he always brought with him.

Driving farther to the west, Paul went by the new Hope Fellowship Church sitting on five acres of land; a structure about twice the size as the old stone church, with a playground, soccer field and a large apartment building on the far edge of the property. A beautiful church. This is where Trey and Rachel would get married next month. Maybe.

He wondered again if someone from the church had arranged the burning of the building. That way, the arsonist could kill the two proverbial birds with one stone: blame him, the pastor of the rival church, and get the insurance money to put up a new building.

The day before, he had attended the Sunday service in a little church in Shell Knob where the people were friendly, and the young pastor and his wife had invited him over for lunch after church. Paul declined, afraid he might give himself away as they visited during the meal.

Having prayed some on Saturday, and most of Sunday afternoon and evening, he had arrived at a decision.

Promptly at nine o'clock on Monday morning, Paul parked his Ford Sedan in front of the stone walls of the old church. The sun was bright in a nearly cloudless sky. The fresh breeze stirred up the trees on the hill above the town that helped cool the rising temperature. A red cardinal flew away from its perch on a nearby shrub when he drove up. Paul had considered cardinals one of the most beautiful birds he had ever seen, and always enjoyed catching sight of one when he lived here. It promised to be a beautiful day and Paul felt a rise in optimism. Surely God would help him today, or soon, to solve this decades old mystery and allow his grandson the happiness he deserved.

Dressed in gray slacks and a short-sleeve blue shirt, he got out of his car and made his way into what used to be the sanctuary. As she said she would, Mabel Tinsdale was sitting in her lawn chair, a Bible in her hand, wearing a faded blue dress and a straw hat to keep the sun off her face.

"Good morning." Paul spoke up when he was a ways off to keep from frightening her before he got too close. "I thought if you were here again this morning I would join you."

Mabel looked up. Seeing Paul, she smiled. "Good morning to you, too." She closed her Bible, keeping her finger between the pages to mark her place. "I'm surprised you're here. I thought you would be long gone by now. But nice to see you again. Andrew, was it?" She motioned toward the empty space beside her. "I'm sorry I don't have another chair to offer you. But please join me if you don't mind standing. Or, I suppose you could sit on the table."

"No, that's okay." Paul approached her and leaned back against the table, folding his arms. "I don't plan to stay long. Just wanted to come and chat for a few minutes."

"I'm glad you came. I'm reading right now in Ephesians. I like that book. Encourages me how Paul reminds us that the same power that raised Christ from the dead is dwelling in us also. Would you like to read a chapter or two with me?"

"Yes, I like that book too." Paul had difficulty holding back from going into his preacher mode and expanding on Paul's writing in that book. Instead he said, "Really, I didn't come to join you in devotions. I wanted to talk to you."

"Yes." Mabel stretched out that word, wariness appearing in her eyes. "If you're wanting money or anything like that I can't help you." She struggled to her feet. "Maybe I had better go."

"No, no." Paul held out his hands in front of him. "Please sit down. I just want to ask you a question. Then I'll leave if you want."

"Okay." Mabel settled back in her seat, but her wariness remained.

"Can I tell you a secret?" continued Paul. "A secret I don't want you to tell anyone?"

Mabel shifted uncomfortably in her chair. "I don't know. What is it?"

Paul started his rehearsed speech, hoping it would influence Mabel to help him. "Do you know, or have you heard of Jacob and Susan Gannon? I believe both of them work at the local bank in town."

"Yes, I know them very well. Mr. Gannon is president of First National Bank. My husband and I have banked there for years. Susan also works there. His father, you know, used to pastor this church years ago; I think about the time of the fire."

"Well, my grandson, Trey, is engaged to their daughter, Rachel. Do you know her?"

"Yes, I've seen her around town some. Lovely girl, from all I've heard. I think she went away to some college. Don't know if she's back yet or not."

"Yes, she is a lovely girl. My grandson is head-over-heels in love with her. Their wedding is just a month away. They are planning on getting married at the new Hope Fellowship church, the church built after this one. I think they are planning a honeymoon in Paris, France."

Mabel smiled for the first time. "And they want me to be the flower girl?" she teased.

"Not quite." Paul smiled back. "The wedding has been planned for quite awhile. But something lately cropped up that may cancel the wedding."

"What's that?"

"Me." Paul paused and let Mabel reflect on his answer for a moment.

"You?" Mabel dropped her smile. "Why would you stop the wedding?"

"Because of who I am."

"Didn't you say the young man is your grandson? So you are his grandfather? Am I right?"

"Yes, I am. It's not just because I'm the grandfather. It's because of what they think I did."

"What's that?" Now he had Mabel's interest. "What do they think you did?"

Paul paused again, walking in a circle around the table, looking at the bare stone walls and up at the open sky. "Because..." He paused and looked at Mabel, a surreal feeling coming over him. For the first time in nearly fifty years he was going to say these words. "Because they think I burned down this church."

"What?" The Bible slipped from Mabel's hands and fell unnoticed on the floor.

"They think, Rachel's parents—Jacob and Susan Gannon—think I burned this church down nearly fifty years ago."

Mabel stared at Paul, then looked around at the walls of her old church, then looked back at Paul again. "Why would they think that?" She squinted her eyes, surveying him. "Well, did you?" she demanded. "Are you the one that burned down the church?" She paused, continuing to stare at Paul. Then her eyes widened. "You're him, aren't you?" She pointed a bent arthritic finger at him. "You're Pastor Paul. I can see it now. Older, white hair, but the same eyes, the same voice." She paused again. "Am I right?" she asked quietly.

"Yes." Paul's reply was equally as quiet. "I'm Pastor Paul. Back after fifty years. Not because I want to, but because the Gannons won't let their daughter marry Trey unless I can prove it wasn't me who started the fire."

"Well, did you?" she demanded again. "I didn't think so at the time. But some people think you did. Were you really the one who burned this church down?"

Paul chuckled. "The pastor and his wife were out of town that night so apparently no one could prove who was or wasn't here. After the fire, someone started the rumor that I had been here that night and burned the church down. They claimed I was mad at the Gannons and the church and retaliated by setting fire to the church.

"How do you squelch a rumor like that? The police interviewed me. They interviewed others. They could prove it was arson, but couldn't find who did it. Since no one could find the real culprit, a group of people in town blamed me, a convenient target. As you probably remember, I left town shortly after that, and the denomination closed down the church.

"I moved to the west coast and became a missionary and tried to forget about what happened here. And I would have had it not been for the misfortune—if you want to call it that—of my grandson falling in love at college with the granddaughter of the man who pastored the church at the time it was burned down.

"As I said," Paul continued, "Rachel's parents won't give their blessing on the wedding and have threatened to cancel it unless I can come up with the real arsonist and clear my name."

Paul paused and leaned up against the table again. "I'm telling you this because you said you were attending church here when the fire happened. Did you live in the same house you live in now? If so, did you see anything that night that may have given you a clue as to who had burned down the church? Or, do you know of anyone I could talk to that may be able to help me find the real arsonist? And," he added, "I have told you this in confidence because I need your help. But please, please don't tell anyone who I am. Can you understand why?"

Mabel shook her head. "My, oh my. This is a lot for an old lady like me to take in. First, Pastor Paul, I guess your name is not Andrew. Probably now you just want me to call you Paul. But, yes, I won't tell anyone who you are. Second, my husband and I were home at the time of the fire. You should have seen the fire trucks and police cars. Everybody was up here, it seemed like, cars and people all over. But I don't remember seeing anything unusual before the fire.

"Of course, you did have enemies here at that time who may have set the fire and tried to blame you for it. Pastor Gannon, bless his heart, didn't like you. I don't know if it was because several members had left our congregation and went to your church, or because you preached about his church worshipping idols, or some such thing. Or if he really thought you were a heretic as he claimed, but he did preach against you quite a bit.

"He's gone now, passed away about five years ago. His wife, Helen, is at the Mercy Nursing Home in Cape Fair. She's had dementia for the past year or two. She can't remember much of anything most of the time, so she probably wouldn't be of any help. I can't think of any church members still around that say anything other than they think you started the fire. I doubt if talking to any of them would help. Although it might, I can't say.

"Have you looked into George Hackett from Hackett House?" She pointed a shaking hand toward the south. "A wicked place when you pastored here. You were taking away a lot of his business the last year or so you were here, if I recollect right. Old George—he's gone too—didn't like that, I'm sure. And you helped keep gambling from coming to town. Norman, his son, I don't know anything about him, whether he's dead or alive or where he is, but his daughter, Katie, she's still around here. Works at the mill, I think, but I don't know that for a fact.

"I'm sure you have considered several young thugs we had about town back then, I can't remember their names. But they had it out for you, as I remember. A few might still be around."

"Yes," added Paul. "There was Claude the rebel. We never got along. And Zeb at Zeb's Bar and Grill down the street from our church. And I'm sure there were others."

"I know what I can do," interrupted Mabel. "Rodney, my son. I told you about him. He liked you. You changed his life. If I told him, I believe he might have some answers."

"Oh, I don't know." Paul held up his hand. "I don't know if I want anyone else to know. It only takes one person talking for word to get around in a town like this."

"Rodney can keep a secret, I know he can." Mabel reached down and picked up her Bible. "I'm getting tired and need to rest. Want to drive me home again? Let me ponder our conversation and talk to Rodney. Why don't you come back in a couple of days and I'll see what I can come up with."

Paul wrote down his name and cell phone number on a piece of paper and gave it to Mabel before he dropped her off at her home.

Back at his motel room Paul fixed himself a cup of decaf coffee from one of those little packets in his room, using the coffee maker on the counter.

Then he sat at the round table by the television set, adjusted his glasses, and opened up his notebook again.

The morning after his visit to Hackett House and the vandalism to the hall and his upstairs apartment, the congregation, as they came to church, helped clean the mess the best they could. A generous offering was received to purchase new songbooks and other items that had been destroyed.

Police Chief Robert Ferguson was called in. He took pictures, got fingerprints from the broken door and other places. He interviewed Paul and various church members and took copious notes. When he left he assured Paul he would get to the bottom of the vandalism and apprehend the party or parties that caused the destruction.

Someone donated a used piano to the church they had in their home that was no longer being played. Others donated a used mattress and other household items to Paul to replace what had been destroyed. In a few weeks, life at Community Chapel had returned to normal.

No one ever discovered who the vandal or vandals were, or where his chess sets were, or who had been the driver of the car that apparently had tried to kill Paul.

The church grew slowly. A few people got saved, mostly from Valley Drive. The Everson family with their five children left Hope church and began attending his church. The Foster family followed with their two children. Paul continued his Friday night meetings with Lamar. After a month, they decided to change the meeting time and place from the restaurant on Friday night to a breakfast at the church on Saturday morning and make it a church event for young men.

Paul got up early each Saturday, fixed a big breakfast, brought chairs up from downstairs, placed them around the table in his apartment, and opened the church at eight. The first week just Lamar came. The second week Brad Ferguson showed up, the son of Police Chief Robert Ferguson. In a few weeks so many young men came they had to move the breakfast downstairs and had to borrow a larger table.

In the meetings Paul had a short devotional, had prayer for special needs, then opened the meeting for discussion about any topic the boys wanted to talk about.

In his preaching on Sundays, he occasionally alluded to the idolatry of Bethel in the Bible. Without mentioning names, his congregation knew he was talking about the sinfulness at Hackett House and the counterfeit Christianity being espoused at Hope Fellowship Church.

Nadine Pittman, Fred's wife, and other women from the church and friends of Nadine's, started driving to Hackett House on weekends when it was open. They would stand at the entrance. When a car turned into Hackett House, they would wave signs with Bible verses and other sayings they had printed on poster boards and yell at the men to go home to their families. One of their favorite signs read: "Be sure your sins will find you out." Another sign read: "Gambling: The sure way of getting nothing for something."

Paul drove by Hackett House one Saturday night praying for the men who frequented the place. He remembered George Hackett telling him that Hackett House was the only fun the men could get in Bethel Springs.

That gave him an idea. He set up a meeting with his church board. With their approval, he talked to Mayor Tom Peterson. With his approval, he approached the Rotary Club, an active group of men in the community. Within two months they started a Friday and Saturday night "Fun Night" for families in the large auditorium at city hall. Pool tables and ping pong tables were brought in. Table games and other play equipment were donated. Local restaurants brought in snacks and beverages to sell. Patsy or another woman went in a side room and read to the children most nights. A 16 millimeter projector and screen were donated, and a family movie was shown in another side room every Saturday night.

One by one families started coming and playing games together and visiting with each another until this event became the place to be on weekends. Some husband cut back or stopped entirely their visits to Hackett House or Zeb's Bar and Grill and brought their families to city hall on weekends.

Paul contacted Angela Shell, editor of Bethel Springs Record, and asked if he could start writing devotionals each week. She agreed. Paul's writings were mostly inspirational, but sometimes he brought up the community issues.

Some nights he would grab a few tracts, walk slowly by Zeb's Bar and Grill and hand one or two out to men as they were either walking in or out, and then quickly go around the corner before Zeb saw him.

Paul and the church board discussed ways of helping the poor on Valley Drive. Laura told Paul that on Saturday nights Martha's Café threw away the food they had prepared but hadn't served. She assumed the other two restaurants in town did the same. With Laura's help, board member Thomas

Spradley and his wife Patricia began making the rounds of the restaurants and the grocery stores every Saturday night and picked up whatever food donations they could get. On Sundays the church served a noon meal to the families on Valley Drive at the home of Donald and Molly Rice and followed with a short service. Their little boys, Chipper and Joshua, always enjoyed handing to their neighbors the bread, pastry and other food that had been donated.

When Paul's first year was up, the church members voted to keep him on as pastor. Only two people voted against him. Paul never found out who those people were.

The anti-gambling forces won on the November ballot, fifty-four percent to forty-six percent to keep gambling out of the county. George Hackett and others made no secret about blaming the religious fanatics in Bethel Springs for holding back the growth of the town. They vowed to try again the next year to bring legal gambling to Bethel Springs. Pastor David Gannon from the pulpit sometimes spoke about other so-called Christians that set back Christianity in America by preaching their old-fashioned fundamentalist judgmental views of the Bible.

Then Paul, in his journal, turned to December nineteen fifty-five and his mind went back to that eventful month.

1955 CHAPTER 26

Thursday morning, December first, Paul was just finishing breakfast when he heard a knock on the front door of the hall. Hurrying downstairs he opened the door and was surprised to see Fred Pittman standing there.

"Good morning, my friend," said Paul cheerfully. "Come in. Have some fresh hot coffee I just made. Want some?"

"No, thank you." He had a manila folder in his hand. "Can we talk?"

"Sure." Paul looked at his deacon sharply, suddenly frightened by his somber tone of voice. "Come on upstairs."

Sitting at Paul's dining room table, Fred opened the folder and took out a copy of a bank statement. "Milton Passmore at the bank called me and, as the treasurer from this church, asked me to come see him. I just came from the bank. He said his daughter, Sarah, who works there as a teller, noticed that you took church money from the bank on two separate occasions. He asked me if it was okay for you to do that."

Without looking at Paul he ran his finger down the column. "On Tuesday, July nineteenth, this shows you took out fifty dollars from the church fund. On Wednesday, August third, you took out one hundred dollars." He looked up at Paul. "Is this true? Was there some church expenses you wrote a check for that you forgot to tell me about?"

Paul stared at his deacon. He felt his stomach knot up. Was this another attack from whomever wanted to run him out of town? "I didn't sign any church checks on my own for the church or for personal use. I would remember if I had. That bank statement can't be true." He looked Fred in the eyes. "First," he said, "as you well know, we have it set up with the bank that both you and I have to sign every check. If a check has the signature of just one of us, the bank is not supposed to cash it. So if this is true, which it's not, they were in error. Second," Paul felt his eyes well up with tears, "since I was a little kid my parents have drilled into me that stealing is wrong. I would never steal from anybody, much less the church I pastor. You've got to believe me." He swept his hand around his apartment. If I've absconded with any church money, I've hidden it well. I drive the same old car. Haven't bought any clothes since I've been here, just one new pair of shoes. Look in my refrigerator and freezer. Not much there. Mostly just what the church people bring me plus a little Spam and bologna.

"I get fifty dollars a month from my mother and the Sunday night offerings. That's it. I spend my money on a little food and gas money and that's about it."

Paul stood to his feet. "Let's go to the bank. I want to see those checks I supposedly signed. If someone is forging my signature, I need to find out."

Paul and Fred walked the two blocks to the bank in the frosty December morning, keeping their coats wrapped tightly around them as they faced the cold wind, Fred carrying the bank statement in the manila folder.

"Good morning, Hannah, may we meet with Milton Passmore?" asked Fred to the teller at the first window, an older woman who had waited on Paul in the bank a few times. "It's important."

A few minutes later Hannah told them the bank president would see them now and led them back to his office. Sitting in the two chairs across from his desk, Fred opened the folder. "About the matter you talked to me about, Pastor Paul says he doesn't know anything about the two withdrawals he supposedly made. He reminded me that both of us needed to sign the checks."

Milton Passmore studied the bank statement Fred showed him for a moment. Then he went to his phone and called his daughter Sarah into his office.

Within moments Sarah walked in holding two checks. "Here they are," she said breezily. "Just like I said. A check for fifty dollars dated July nineteenth and a check for one hundred dollars dated August third. These are our own checks because you said you needed the money and didn't know where the bank checkbook was."

"May I see the checks?" Sarah handed them to Paul.

"That's not my signature." Paul pointed to the check. The 'P' in Paul looks pretty close. But the 'A' for my middle initial doesn't look like my signature, nor most of the other letters in 'Whitfield'."

He took a pen out of his pocket and signed his name on a piece of paper he found on Passmore's desk. "See, it's not alike. Look at the other checks I have signed, plus the signature on the application when I opened the bank account."

Milton Passmore examined the checks against Paul's signature. "Looks close to me," he said finally. "Besides, no one writes the signature the same way every time."

"Fred's signature is not on here either," countered Paul. "It should be here."

"But you came in personally," replied Sarah. "I figured you were in a hurry and didn't have time to get Fred's signature."

"Look." Paul stood to his feet. "I do come into the bank quite often to either deposit money or take some out. But it's always personal money from my personal checking account. If it's related to the church, Fred, our treasurer, comes in to handle it. So, I don't know what is going on. I don't know anything about these checks. I don't know why you approached Fred instead of me, if these were supposedly my checks."

He paused and took a deep breath and looked at the bank president's daughter in the eyes. "I believe you know these are bogus checks. I believe you know I didn't come in here and ask for two checks to fill out to take a hundred and fifty dollars from the church account. I suggest you find who did this and get this church money back in the bank before I pass along this information to Police Chief Ferguson." He felt his anger rise. "What are you trying to do? Get me fired from the church so I'll leave town too?"

Without a backward glance he stomped out of the office and out into the street. He hardly noticed the cold wind against his back as he made his way to the church, feeling his heart beating at an accelerated rate during the entire time.

He walked into the hall and made his way up to the altar and stared at the ceiling. "God," he said finally, "I don't know what's going on. But You do. So I commit this whole stupid mess into your hands." He remembered his mother telling him to not call anything "stupid," but he figured this time that word applied. Calming down a little bit, he spent the next few minutes praying a little more coherently.

He was just starting up the stairs to his apartment when he heard the front door open and close and footsteps approach him.

"Paul," Fred Pittman hurried down the aisle. "After you left I had a face-to-face with Milton after his daughter left. He finally agreed she probably had made a mistake and will reimburse the money from the two checks to the church."

"Who actually took out the money?"

Fred shrugged. "I don't know if someone was trying to pull the wool over our eyes and get you in trouble, or what happened. I didn't get that far. Enough to say that things are back to normal and you can forget this ever happened. But," he added, "I would be careful if I were you with your finances and everything else. You mentioned the car that sideswiped you and the church and your apartment being ransacked. It's just like what happened to the last pastor who spoke out against gambling and the other sins in town. I think some people would like to see you gone, too, and they might not be done trying."

1955   CHAPTER 27

Snow was slowly falling when Paul started up his De Soto that early December Monday morning. Normally on a cold morning like this he would have stayed home, sitting by the oil furnace in the hall with an extra cup of Sanka and a Zane Grey book and a warm blanket over his shoulders. But he needed to get to the Rice home before eight o'clock to pick up the pots and other containers and return them to the establishments that had donated the food, so they could be reused as quickly as possible.

Starting his car, he scrapped the ice off his windows and let the heater warm the car for a few minutes. Then he pulled away from the church and made his way carefully through the ice and snow covered streets.

As he approached the Rice home on Valley Drive, he saw a school bus stopped in front of their house, lights flashing, with a car pulled just off the road and several people crowded around something on the side of the road.

With his heart starting to beat faster, Paul stopped behind the bus, left his car running, got out and approached the crowd. What he saw petrified him with fear. Chipper was lying on his back in a graveled ditch, looking like a tattered rag doll. His arms and legs were spread away from his body, his right leg and arm at unnatural angles. A teenage boy and girl, whom Paul recognized as high school students, with their arms around each other, were staring at Chipper, not speaking.

Paul ran up to the crowd. "What happened?" he asked.

A young woman in tears, apparently the school bus driver, nodded to the teenagers. "They were driving too fast for the weather," she said between sobs. "Chipper didn't see the car coming and he got hit as he crossed the road to get on the bus. A neighbor has called for an ambulance," she added.

Paul looked down at the silent figure. He had learned in first aid not to move an accident victim. Staring at the young boy he didn't see any sign of life. Gently clutching his wrist as he had seen doctors and nurses do to him during his doctor visits, he checked Chipper's pulse. No throb against his fingers.

"God," prayed Paul out loud, his eyes open. "Please do a miracle here for my little buddy."

He was interrupted by a wail behind him. "My baby, my baby." Molly came running in her bare feet, hugging her yellow housecoat around her. She knelt down beside Paul and started to pick up her son.

Paul grabbed her arms and pulled her back. "He'll be fine," he lied. "Please go get him a warm blanket," he said more to get her to leave her son alone than for anything else. Shaking with sobs, she shuffled back toward the house.

"I'm so sorry..." began the boy whose name Paul remembered as

Tim. "I thought I could stop in time. But when I saw the little boy run in front of us across the road, I tried to stop but couldn't. The car just slid right into him and sent him flying."

Paul looked at him and his girlfriend, Patty. Tears were running down both of their faces and they looked pale and shaky.

Not wanting to have more victims to deal with, Paul replied, "Don't worry about it now. Just get in the car and wait for the ambulance and police to come."

Looking back down at Chipper he still saw no movement. The boy's face was white, his wrist Paul held was getting colder by the minute. "God," he prayed again in a quiet voice and had to pause because of the sob that rose in his throat.

"Here's a blanket." Swallowing and trying to shake the tears from his eyes, Paul took the quilt Molly had brought and gently laid it over Chipper. "How is he?" Molly quavered, tears running unchecked down her face. She again tried to reach down and pick up her son.

"Let him be," commanded Paul, trying to sound authoritative. "Don't touch him. An ambulance will be here soon." Paul gripped Molly's hand with his right hand and Chipper's with his left. "Let's pray for Chipper, Molly. Pray with me." With that, Paul led in a heartfelt prayer, his eyes still open and alert, his attention shifting between Chipper, his mother, the occupants of the car and the children staring out the window from the bus.

The wail of an ambulance cut into the prayer. Two attendants dressed in white quickly brought out a stretcher and approached the group. With great care they worked on Chipper as he lay on the ground, then gently lifted him onto the stretcher. One attendant, a man in his thirties with a crewcut and glasses, looked into Paul's eyes and gave a quick shake of his head.

"We are praying for a miracle," replied Paul, touching Chipper's face as they put him in the ambulance. By now a police car had come and was talking to the couple in the car. A neighbor lady and her husband were comforting Molly and promised to take care of Joshua while she went to the hospital with Chipper.

Forgetting about his errand for the eating establishments, he followed the ambulance to the hospital.

Paul was forced to remain in the waiting room for nearly an hour before they would let him into Chipper's room. He looked small and helpless in the big hospital bed. Various tubes ran into his body while other machines at his side checked his heartbeat, breathing and other functions. Donald had been called from work. He and Molly were there, silent and pale, holding hands. A nurse and a doctor hovered over Chipper.

When Paul entered, one of the nurses looked up at him. "I am his pastor," spoke up Paul. "How is he?"

The nurse was older, business-like, efficient, in her white uniform and starched white cap. She nodded toward the bed. "We are calling him our miracle boy." She looked to both Paul and his parents. "When they brought him in he wasn't breathing. No heartbeat. No sign of life. We were ready to take him to the morgue when Pam, the other nurse here, thought she saw an eyelid flutter. We checked again and detected a small heartbeat, so we started treatment and he began responding. He's still unconscious, but his heart is beating and he's breathing with the help of oxygen. We don't know the state of his body as of yet, or how this will affect his mind, but at least he's alive."

Donald and Molly walked over to Paul. "Thank you for your prayers, Pastor Paul," said Molly softly, gripping his hand. Her face was red and her eyes were swollen from crying, but she was calmer now. "I could feel God there, and here now. I think he's going to be okay."

Paul smiled and turned to the doctor. "Would you mind if I said another prayer?" When she nodded, Paul gripped Donald and Molly's hands in his, thanked the Lord that Chipper was still alive, and prayed for his complete recovery, and for peace for Donald and Molly and little Joshua at a neighbor's house.

Paul visited Chipper every day while he was in the hospital. His hip, right leg and right arm were broken, and he had suffered broken ribs, internal injuries and bruises all over his body. He was in a coma for two days, then woke up. Each day he got better and by the end of nine days he was able to return home with a cast on his right leg and right arm.

1955   CHAPTER 28

The Sunday night before Christmas was the big night the whole congregation had been working toward for several weeks. Patricia Spradley and Laura had practiced a Christmas play with the children. Emily Miller had worked up a musical presentation from the teens. The adults had worked hard at decorating the church and putting together bags of candy and fruit for the children.

At seven o'clock the hall was almost full of people. Paul could sense the excitement as he noticed the noise level of conversation was higher than it had ever been since he had been there. Just before the service started, he saw his mother walk in with Kate and sit in the next to last row on the right side. His mother had told him she may come, but he was surprised to see Kate with her. He walked back and quickly greeted them.

Promptly at seven Emily went to the piano and played one verse of "Silent Night" to quiet the crowd. But, instead of quieting down, they started to sing along. Then Fred Pittman stood on the platform, now minus the pulpit, with play props behind him, and led in several more Christmas songs.

Next came the children's play. Boys and girls who had been waiting in the alley behind the church came through the back door and began their program. Mary and Joseph came on the platform and asked for a place to stay only to hear the innkeeper beside a cardboard door say there was no room in the inn. They retreated to the stable by the oil stove where Mary picked up a doll hidden on the floor and placed it in a cardboard box covered with straw and a blanket. Several children then came in from the alley dressed in bathrobes as shepherds or wise men and knelt down before the doll in the box.

While they posed there, seven teenagers came down the stairs from Paul's apartment, walked onto the platform, and Emily led them in three Christmas songs.

Parents quietly walked up and took photos of their children with their Kodak box cameras, changing flash bulbs as fast as they could to not miss out on the next activity their children were in.

When the program was over the children and teens sat down in the congregation with their parents and Paul rose to preach. His heart was warmed as he stood before the congregation. His congregation, his flock, his people. His faithful members were there, plus the parents of some of the children who came to Sunday school had come for the first time. As his eyes roved around the congregation, he spotted several people he didn't know. Then, seated in the back row, he was shocked to see Patsy, dressed in a modest yellow dress, her blond hair in a bouffant style.

Then reality hit him. The three young women in his life were present tonight in his church. Lovable Kate. Her conservative beige dress with a festive red scarf for the occasion fit in with the rest of the congregation. Raised in the church and being a committed Christian for as long as she could remember, he knew her relationship with the Lord was as solid as it could be. With Kate at his side they could fulfill all their future dreams and plans. Like a glowing fireplace on a cold night, she made him feel warm and safe and secure. He was glad she had come. She would fit right in with his congregation come January when she could begin coming on Sundays to help in the church on a regular basis. Sitting next to his mother she seemed to fit right in with the family.

Laura sat two rows in front of them, looking especially attractive in her coral red dress with matching jacket and flowing dark hair. She had gotten saved as a child. Mature, practical, personable, he believed she loved the Lord with all her heart. He liked spending time with her; she made him feel good about himself. What would life be with her?

Then Patsy, beautiful, organized, talented Patsy. Life with her would be one exciting day after another, he was sure. He felt she was a believer. He did have some questions about her spiritual commitment, but believed she was growing in her spiritual walk with Christ.

Forcing his thoughts away from the three women he returned his attention to the rest of the congregation. They were looking at him, some with smiles, most with expectations of continuing to enjoy the evening.

"Welcome to our annual Christmas program," began Paul. "Didn't our children and young people do a great job?" Following a round of applause Paul told a few jokes and stories to warm up the crowd, then began his message.

"The Christmas story is about relationships," he began. "Jesus loves us so much He wants to have a close, personal relationship with us. But, how could He as God in heaven relate to us here on earth?

"Maybe some of you have heard the story of the farmer who loved birds. A storm had come bringing rain, hail and high winds. He already had led his cows and other animals into the barn for safety. He wanted to invite the birds to find shelter and safety in the barn, also. But he knew if he went back outside to invite them into the barn, he would just scare the birds away. 'If I could just become a bird,' he told himself, 'then I could communicate with them and lead them to safety.'

"That's why Jesus came to earth. He arrived as a baby so people could get to know Him and feel His love toward them. He grew to adulthood and went about preaching the good news of the kingdom of God. Then, as an ultimate act of love, He took all of our sins upon himself and paid the penalty of death for them on the cross. He rose again from the dead the third day. Then, in a way that's beyond my understanding, through His death and resurrection He gave us victory over sin, death, and provided for us a way to get to heaven.

"Because of Jesus' love and what He did for us, if we invite him into our hearts and lives and ask Him to forgive us of our sins, He will come in and live with us and give us a new life filled with his love and care.

"So," Paul concluded, "for the follower of Jesus, church is not just a place we attend out of habit. No, it's a place we can come to worship Jesus and fellowship with Him and our other brothers and sisters in Christ. Reading the Bible is not just skimming through some unbelievable stories that supposedly happened a long time ago, but it's God's love letter to us, giving us direction and joy and peace in our daily lives. Prayer is not a dry ritual where we repeat phrases we learned as kids, but it's a vital two-way communication with the Person who understands us the most but loves us anyway.

"Let's stand," he added. "If baby Jesus, born in a manger, who now is seated at the right hand of God praying for us, has been speaking to your heart, why don't you come forward and stand with me at the altar. Invite Jesus into your heart as your Lord and Savior. Ask Him to forgive you of your sins and make you a new person. Begin tonight a life of having Jesus as your best Friend who will walk with you every day of your life and on into eternity. Whatever your need is tonight, Christ is the answer."

Emily came to the piano and began playing the hymn: "Just as I am, without one plea, but that Thy blood was shed for me, and that Thou bidd'st me come to Thee, O Lamb of God, I come! I come!"

Paul stepped back a couple of steps, placed his Bible and notes on the floor and closed his eyes. Emily continued playing. Then she started singing. Others in the congregation picked up on the words. Some opened their hymn books, looking for the words. Others sang from memory.

After several moments Paul opened his eyes. Three people stood facing him, among them Sam Pittman. Tears streamed down his face.

Paul looked over the congregation. "Some have come forward to commit or recommit their lives to Jesus. This will be the start of a wonderful life for you standing here. But I believe there are others. Emily, lead us in another verse."

Then Paul stepped back again. A man and wife stood, strangers to Paul, and came forward, hand in hand. He saw another movement and down the aisle came Patsy to stand with the crowd, tears in her eyes.

"Thank you all for coming," Paul said after another pause. "Now, I would invite members of the congregation to come and pray with our friends that are standing here. Fred Pittman came forward and laid his hand on his son Sam. Patricia Spradley went to Patsy and put her arm around her. Others came forward to pray with those at the altar.

After a few moments Paul asked those at the altar, and anyone else in the congregation who wanted to commit their lives to the Lord to repeat a prayer after him. With that, Paul said a simple prayer of commitment to Christ which was repeated by most of the people in the congregation.

1955   CHAPTER 29

The day after the Christmas program Paul made his plans for the holidays. He was tired and needed some time away from his responsibilities. He knew people were busy with holiday preparations and needed time off too, so he cancelled the Wednesday night service before Christmas. Then he asked Fred Pittman and Thomas Spradley to fill in for him the next Sunday and Wednesday. He planned on being back for the watchnight service on Saturday, December thirty-first.

With that in mind, Paul gratefully headed back home for a few days of rest and fellowship with his mother and his other Bible school and Springfield friends.

Surprisingly, there had been no more attacks on him since the incident when he had almost been killed by the hit-and-run driver and his home and the church ransacked. He had checked several times with the chief of police who said they were no closer as to the whereabouts of his chess sets or who had perpetrated the other crimes.

As usual, Christmas Eve was just Dorothy and Paul. Dorothy's only sister lived in Seattle, and they had no other relatives nearby. Paul had brought his guitar and they sang Christmas carols, read the Christmas story from Luke chapter two, then opened their gifts. Paul bought his mother the new winter coat she had hinted she wanted; gray with a fleece-lined collar. Then Dorothy handed Paul a small gift-wrapped box. He tore the paper off and gazed in pleased surprise at what he saw. "Thanks, Mom." Instinctively he reached over and gave her a hug. "I saw one of these in a Sears catalog the other day and thought it would be neat to have one."

"I know you like new gadgets," replied his mother, "and I know you get lonely, so I thought you might enjoy this transistor radio." She pointed to the large console radio standing against the wall. "That wouldn't fit in your car even if I gave it to you, but you can carry your transistor radio around in your hand or set it anywhere. Since it has batteries you don't even have to plug it in. If they have a nearby Christian station you can listen to the Blackwood Brothers, Stuart Hamblen and all those other Christian singers you like. You can probably get a country-western station where you can hear songs by Johnny Cash, Red Foley and others. "

On Christmas Day, they had supper with the Fullers, a tradition the families had established over the years.

Kate's father, Earnest, shook Paul's hand and welcomed him home. Her mother, Angela, gave him a hug. Kate also gave him what Paul felt was a restrained hug.

Paul gratefully filled up on the home cooked meal of turkey, dressing, cranberry sauce, mashed potatoes and gravy with pumpkin pie for dessert.

After dinner, Kate invited Paul to come out to the back deck and look at the full moon. Paul caught their parents exchanging glances as Paul followed Kate outside.

He walked behind her across to the dark deck where she was leaning against the rail looking at the moon. Paul moved beside her, also leaning against the rail. Frost was in the air and Paul's light sweater didn't keep out the cold.

Kate was silent for several moments, and Paul felt himself shivering, not knowing if it was from the cold or from what he felt was coming from Kate.

Finally she spoke. "I've heard good things about Bethel Springs." She turned and looked at Paul beside her in the darkness. "You're doing a great job there as pastor. I always knew you had it in you. You had a wonderful Christmas program."

"Thank you."

"I've been wanting to tell you something for several weeks. I didn't want to write you. I wanted to talk to you in person. Do you remember during VBS this past summer when I was looking for Scotch tape or whatever it was, and you said to look in your desk drawers?"

Paul nodded, fearful of what was coming.

"In my searching, I glanced at a letter in your right drawer and noticed my name on it. Out of curiosity I picked it up and read it. It was your letter of proposal to me. I was so engrossed in the letter I didn't notice Laura. She came over and looked over my shoulder and she saw it too."

She paused, cleared her throat, and looked back up at the moon. Her voice was flat, as if trying to leave out any emotion. "Our parents had our marriage all arranged, didn't they?"

Paul nodded in the darkness. *Idiot, idiot, idiot, what an idiot I am*, he chanted to himself over and over.

"I thought we would get married too. I waited for your proposal, even before the letter. In our dating over the years I think we both expected we would eventually end up getting married. We even discussed it a time or two. I waited and waited." Paul heard a catch in her voice. "But that's okay, it really is. During that time, this time, I've had time to think. And I've been praying, really praying and seeking the Lord about us, about me, about my future, your future, evaluating, trying to see if the Lord had other alternatives."

She paused. Paul didn't interrupt the silence, waiting for her to sort out her thoughts. " And you know what? You didn't give me that letter for whatever reason. I don't know why. But that's okay. You don't owe me anything. You never made a verbal commitment to me. I never made a commitment to you. We are both free to do as we please.

"I observed you a time or two in that restaurant and last Sunday night at your church. I won't mention any names, but I saw how you looked at someone else like you never looked at me." She paused again and was silent. Then abruptly she reached in her purse and brought out a letter which she handed to Paul. "When you are alone, please read this." She reached up her cold hand and caressed his cheek. "I don't regret our relationship. I've learned a lot from you. But now this is good-bye," she said and ran back into the house.

Paul stood frozen for a moment, watching her retreat. Then, realizing it would look bad to their parents if they didn't come back in together, he crammed the letter into his pants pocket and hurried in after her, a smile plastered on his face. "It's cold out there," he said to the three parents silently looking at them as they came in. He faked an exaggerated shiver and vigorously rubbed his hands together to cover the fact that he really was shivering. He made his way over to their fireplace and began warming his hands. "Getting cold. Wouldn't surprise me if it doesn't snow soon." He looked over at Kate who was sitting on the couch by her parents, looking at him with a forced smile.

Back at his mother's home Paul hadn't even taken off his coat when his mother spoke up. "What's with you and Kate? She walked in from the deck like she was ready to cry. You walked in behind her not doing a very good job of masking your feelings."

Paul was never good at deceiving his mother and decided now was not a good time to start. "Sit down, Mother," he said, pointing to the kitchen table. Without asking he opened the refrigerator, took out a bottle of milk and poured a glass for him and his mother. He put the glass in front of her and sat down across from her and took a sip of milk before he continued.

"She gave me a letter," said Paul reaching into his pocket and pulling it out. He glanced at it, silently reading it to himself. After digesting the letter and reading it over again more slowly, he finally spoke up. "Kate said she's been in contact with a long-time Bible school classmate, Gertrude Wallace. Gertrude, along with two other classmates, are planning to start a church somewhere in Maine this summer. I guess Gertrude is from around there. They want Kate to go there to help start a ministry with the children. Anyway, Kate wrote me in her letter that she has accepted the offer to help in pioneering this church. She plans to leave right after she graduates in May."

Dorothy stared at her son, frowning. "But what about you two getting married? Won't that interfere?"

Paul looked back at her mother without answering, letting her figure it out for herself. The frown continued for a few moments. Finally, she spoke up: "Laura, is it Laura? Does she know about Laura? Did you break up with her over Laura? Do you still like her in spite of our conversation about her?"

Paul took another drink of milk. "Mother, I'm confused. Can I tell you what is going on in my mind with you trying to look at it objectively, and not as a mother, or champion of any certain girl?"

The frown disappeared and a smile touched her mother's lips, but there was still concern in her eyes. "I doubt it. But go ahead. I'm listening."

Paul was suddenly glad he had always had an honest relationship with his mother. He had often shared his growing up problems and dilemmas with her. Usually, they had ended their conversations with an agreeable compromise and with him learning another portion of his mother's wisdom and insight.

He took another drink of milk. "For years I know you and the Fullers thought Kate and I would eventually get married. Both Kate and I kind of thought that too. Mother, she's a wonderful girl. She's been a Christian all her life. Called into the ministry. She's attractive, safe. I know what to expect with her."

He paused. "You mentioned Laura. I met her the day after I moved to Bethel Springs. She's a waitress. I brought her here to meet you. I know you said she's not the one for me, and I respect that. But I felt attracted to her. She started helping in church. I like being with her. She's mature, has good ideas. She training to be a nurse, but I know she would do well in the ministry too."

When Paul saw his mother start to speak, he held up his hand. "Then, there's more. Mother, you remember that attractive blond girl that went forward for salvation at the Christmas program?" When his mother nodded he continued, "I've known her for a long time too. She's attractive, a nice girl. Rich and talented. She's the town librarian, a people person. I've gone out with her a time or two. Her father seems to like me."

"Three girls," interjected her mother. "Son, what has become of you?"

Paul felt himself blush. He took another drink of milk to give himself time to come up with an intelligent or witty response. But he had none.

Paul's mother stood and walked over to the fireplace and poked the ashes, trying to stir a flame, after having been neglected while they were away for dinner.

"Son, when I met your daddy, he was not the only one after me." She put down the poker, threw two small pieces of wood on the fire and came back and sat in her chair. "I was quite attractive back then. I came from a good family, had nice clothes and was well liked in school. I went to Central High

School here in Springfield. Your daddy's family had moved to town a couple years earlier and had started attending our church. Your daddy soon had his eye on me, I on him.

"Then there was Chester. Chet they called him, rich man's son and student body president his senior year at Central. On the wrestling team. One of the best. He had his eye on me, too. I thought he was good looking and nice. They both invited me to the senior prom." Dorothy quit speaking and looked out the window with a faraway look in her eyes.

"So who did you go with?" prodded Paul when his mother didn't continue.

"Who do you think? Chet, of course." She laughed. "Worst mistake of my life. He seemed to be a nice guy if you knew him casually, but on a date he turned out to be a real cad. He acted like he owned me, like I was his prize to show off. That was my first and last date with him.

"But your daddy still liked me and eventually invited me out again. That was the start. The rest is history."

Paul chuckled. "Well, Mother, I'm glad you chose Dad."

"I am too." His mother's eyes were shiny with tears. "I miss him so much, even after all these years, but I'm glad I married him. Best years of my life."

They both sat in companionable silence for several moments. Finally, Dorothy spoke up with a mischievous smile on her face. "Son, can you keep a secret?"

Paul smiled back. "Sure."

"You know the president at People's Bank, the other bank here in town, Mr. Perkins?"

"Yes."

"He's Chet. Chester Perkins."

"Really?"

"Yes, still rich and popular. Still a cad from all I hear.

"You know, son," Dorothy added, "I want to tell you something I've kept a secret from you. And I asked Laura to keep it a secret, too. But knowing you had your eye on Laura I thought I would check her out and try to evaluate her impartially as I could as a mother. See if I was wrong about her. I found out how to get in touch with her and invited her over for dinner two or three times."

Paul raised his eyebrows in surprise. "You did?"

"Yes I did?"

"What do you think of her?"

"I think she's a nice girl. Dedicated, hard working, good Christian. Is she for you? I don't know."

She took another sip of milk. "Son, the question is who do you love? You

151

can only love one of them, you know. You can like a lot of girls, be friends with a lot of girls, but you can only love one. Which one of these girls do you love? Laura? That librarian, Patsy, was that her name? If you want Kate, it may take a little time, but I imagine you can have her back. I trust your judgment. I'm sure they are all wonderful girls. Or will someone else appear on the horizon?" She threw up her hands. "Son, it's your decision. I will back whatever decision you make, and I will love whomever you chose." She looked at her watch. "It's late and time for bed."

1955 CHAPTER 30

Thirteen people, the faithful few, showed up at the Watchnight Service on New Year's Eve at Community Chapel. Kate didn't drive down from Springfield, nor did Laura or Patsy show up. Paul led the singing and Emily played the piano. Thomas Spradley preached a short message. Then they broke for a time of eating the desserts the women had brought. Paul had made coffee and Kool-aid and brought it down. After that they had communion. At a few minutes before midnight Paul asked everyone to kneel and to pray out the old year and the new year in, asking for God's direction and help in the coming year.

While all this was going on, the sounds of fireworks could be heard outside as people celebrated the coming of the new year. Strains of music could be heard from Zeb's Bar and Grill next door.

They had just knelt down to pray when the door burst open. "Hey everybody," a frightened voice called into the stillness. "There's a car on fire out here."

Paul froze for just an instant. Then, grabbing the fire extinguisher by the piano he ran toward the front door, followed by the rest of the congregation who had decided that finding whose car was on fire was more important than prayer.

As he ran outside he saw the entire interior of the car parked in front of the church was burning, smoke pouring from a smashed rear window. Paul hurried toward the car, stuck the fire extinguisher through the shattered glass and sprayed the contents onto the blaze, then quickly stepped back, afraid the car might explode, as the fire continued to burn.

He recognized the car as Fred Pittman's 1952 blue Chevrolet Bel Air. "Dear God," he heard his deacon say from behind him, "what will be next?"

That brought the watchnight service to an abrupt end. The church members backed to a safe distance, yet everyone stayed to watch the spectacle unfolding in front of them. Paul stared at the car, the fire reaching ten feet in the air, smoke pouring from the charred interior, wondering if the fire was caused by a bottle rocket gone astray, or if the persecutors, as he called them, had returned.

In the middle of his thoughts he heard a siren and watched the Bethel Springs' fire truck pull up and two men jump out, both of them holding foam sprayers that they shot into the blaze.

It took several minutes to extinguish the fire. Even with the flames gone, the car still emitted a cloud of smoke that surrounded the vehicle, drifted up past the buildings, and spread out so everyone standing anywhere by the car was having difficulty breathing. Some held handkerchiefs to their noses; others walked away from the odor.

Finally, when the smoke was almost all gone, one of the fireman forced open the back door of the car with a crowbar. In his gloved hand he pulled out what appeared to be the skeletal remains of a bottle rocket. Paul recognized him as Terry Fouts, a middle-aged man who worked at Lundquist Shoe Factory. "Kids," he said disgustedly. "Always happens on New Year's Eve and July fourth." He went up to Fred. "Sorry about this, ol' buddy. We'll tow away your car in the morning, if you want. I hope your insurance will pay enough for you to get another one."

Paul drove Fred and Nadine Pittman home. "Someone will pick you up for church tomorrow," he promised. "If there's anything we can do to help, that's why we are here. You know," he added after a pause, "I hope it was just kids whose bottle rocket went astray."

Fred spoke up from the back seat. "You know and I know this wasn't an accident," he said, bitterness in his voice.

The next day the church was about half full, which was a good attendance for January first. Patsy came for the Sunday morning service and sat near the back by herself. Before the service started people stood in groups and discussed the burning car. In his sermon Paul mentioned the bottle rocket that destroyed Fred Pittman's car, saying no one had determined yet who shot the bottle rocket, if it was an accident or done maliciously. Then he referenced where Jesus said if we were followers of Him, we would be persecuted. "I know this will be hard to take, with what has been happening around here lately," Paul added, "but Jesus said in the Sermon on the Mount that we will be blessed when we are persecuted for righteousness' sake and great will be our reward in heaven. But I believe God can use this incident and other incidents we have faced for His honor someway in the here and now."

Paul knew the hit-and-run on little Johnny Meredith was in the minds of the congregation, as well as the sideswiping of Paul's vehicle, and the vandalism done to the church. Trying to sound as positive as possible, he encouraged everyone to focus on the Lord and the fact that He was dealing with the situation in His own way and time. "We just need to stay strong and victorious in the Lord. And we need to pray for our persecutors, according to what Jesus tells us to do."

Then he closed by praying the blessing found in Numbers chapter six, verses twenty-four through twenty-six: "The Lord bless thee, and keep thee: The Lord make his face shine upon thee, and be gracious unto thee; The Lord lift up his countenance upon thee, and give thee peace."

1956   CHAPTER 31

Saturday morning Paul showed up at Martha's Café, hoping that Laura would be home from college and working. He was disappointed to see Holly come out of the swinging black louvered doors with a pot of coffee in her hand.

"Morning, Paul," she said brightly when she saw him and approached his table, filling his cup of coffee without asking, knowing that would be his request. "Disappointed that I'm not Laura?" she asked with a mischievous laugh, fluffing up her hair and twirling slowly around as if she were modeling for him. "I'm pretty too, you know."

"Of course you are. You are beautiful both on the inside and outside, just like Laura." He smiled at her, knowing Holly was teasing, but also noting a seriousness in her tone of voice. "You know," he added, "when the right guy comes along, he's going to win your heart and you will get married and have five kids and live happily ever after. Just you wait and see. That's my prophecy for today."

"Oh, stop it." Holly pushed his shoulder with her free hand. But he saw her eyes light up and a smile touch her lips.

"I'll have the biscuits and gravy," he said changing the subject. "I'm sure they will taste just as good as if Laura served them."

"If you want to see her, she's back in town from Springfield but took the day off to spend it with her mother who is feeling rather poorly."

"Thanks." Paul ate his breakfast wondering if he should try and see Laura. She was ashamed of her home, being a made over chicken house filled with her mother's cigarette smoke. She might not want him to go there. On the other hand, he wanted to see her this weekend and didn't know how else to get in contact with her.

After breakfast he waited until ten o'clock when he figured Laura and her mother would be done with breakfast and up and around and made his way out to their home on Valley Drive.

Parking in front of the remodeled chicken house, he hoped he was doing the right thing as he walked up to the door and knocked. He heard voices and scuffling, then silence. He was ready to knock again when the door opened and the same woman that he remembered from his previous visit opened the door. Her uncombed gray hair surrounded a wrinkled face with a missing front tooth. A shapeless gray dress hung loosely over her bent frame. Smoke from a cigarette wedged between her index and middle finger rose between them.

"Yes? What do you want?" she asked in a raspy voice.

"Hello. My name is Paul Whitfield. I was wondering if Laura is here?"

"Laura," shouted the woman turning her head to be heard inside the house. "Man here to see you."

Paul felt his face redden with embarrassment, and he suddenly decided he wished he wouldn't have come.

The older woman returned into the house closing the door behind her. Paul waited outside for at least a minute wondering if he should leave or stay. Then the door opened again and there stood Laura, a flustered embarrassed look on her face.

"Paul," she said almost accusingly. "Why did you come here?"

"To see you," he replied with a forced smile. "And to see your mother. I heard at Martha's she wasn't feeling well."

Laura hesitated. Her dark hair was combed in the usual pony tail and bangs, but she was wearing a frayed pink housecoat in her bare feet.

"I can leave," offered Paul and started to back away.

"No, that's okay." Reluctantly, she stepped aside and Paul walked into her home.

The windows were cracked open and the smell of cigarette smoke wasn't as bad as Paul had anticipated. As he followed Laura into her home he noticed on the left a sink with a single water faucet on the wall of the first small room they entered. Beside the sink a small stove stood on top of a counter under which he saw three shelves containing pots, pans and other kitchen supplies. To his right in this first room he saw a curtain half pulled back that revealed an unmade bed.

Going into the next room of the home, to the left Paul could see another bed behind another curtained off area. Heat drifted his way from a wood stove that stood in the center of the room. Laura led Paul over to the right where she motioned him to sit on a worn couch covered with a colorful blanket. Her mother parked herself in a rocking chair by a large console radio. Snuffing out her cigarette in an ash tray, she lit another one.

"Can I get you some coffee?" offered Laura. "I made a pot this morning for breakfast. It should still be hot. I know you like yours with a little cream. No charge this time," she added with a smile.

"Yes, please." Paul decided if he had a cup of coffee he could at least politely stay while he drank it.

While Laura was in the kitchen, Paul turned to her mother. "Mrs. Taylor, I understand you've been a little under the weather lately. Anything I can do to help?"

"Mildred. No one calls me Mrs. Taylor no more." She coughed twice, then cleared her throat. "Have a little cold. Must be the weather outside."

Laura brought the coffee and sat it beside Paul on a small round table with a glass top sitting beside the couch. Then she sat stiffly in a wooden chair across from Paul, seeming to have somewhat gotten control of herself and the embarrassment of having him see her in this environment.

Paul talked to the two women, trying to put them at ease, asking about Laura's school and telling stories of his Bible school days. Between her coughing spells, Paul was rather surprised to note that Mildred, once she got over her intimidation of meeting him as a stranger, was friendly and outgoing, even with a sense of humor as she told stories of Laura's childhood.

"Laura has told me a little about you," added Mildred when there was a break in their conversation, a twinkle in her eyes. "Appears you've been making eyes at her."

"Mother," burst out Laura. "I never said that. I just said Paul and I are friends."

"You have a lot of friends," replied her mother, "but you don't talk about them with the same look in your eyes as when you talk about this preacher man."

Paul saw Laura open her mouth to give another reply so he cut in. "You know, my grandparents raised chickens." He stood and walked to the window where he could look out at the chicken house. "They had two chicken houses and a brooder house where they raised pullets until they were old enough to be sold. When we visited them when I was little, my grandmother used to let me gather the eggs from under the nesting hens."

He turned back to the women. "I came to see if both of you wanted to get out of the house and go to some restaurant for dinner. Treat's on me. Laura, do you want to? Mildred, would you like to come too?"

The older woman shook her head. "I don't feel up to going nowhere today. But you two lovebirds go ahead. I can make my own dinner. Have for years."

Paul turned to Laura. "Is that okay with you? Can I pick you up about noon?"

Laura nodded. "Okay. I'll be ready."

"Before I go," Paul said to Mildred, "would you like me to pray for you? I know the Lord can touch your cough and whatever else might be wrong."

The older woman shrugged. "I don't believe as you do. Don't go to church nowhere, but can't hurt, I guess."

Paul walked over to Mildred, gently laid his hand on her shoulder and prayed that God would touch her body and her life and reveal himself to her.

As he walked out he turned to Laura. "See you about noon."

Silently she nodded. Paul thought he saw tears well up in her eyes.

He had barely gotten back to his apartment when he heard a knock on the church door. Going back downstairs he opened the door to a young man that looked like he was still in high school. "I have a note for you from Mr. Lundquist," he said handing Paul a sealed envelope. "I'm to wait for your reply."

A little mystified Paul tore open the envelope and read the note. "Paul, could you come see me at three o'clock today for a short interview?" Signed "Daniel Lundquist."

Paul looked up at the boy. "Do you know what this is about?"

The messenger boy shrugged. "No idea. I'm just the delivery guy."

Paul folded the note and slipped it in his pocket. "Tell him I will be there at three."

1956 CHAPTER 32

Promptly at twelve o'clock noon Paul knocked at Laura's door. She answered almost immediately and went outside, quickly closing the door behind her, almost as if to hide the odor and the atmosphere of her home.

"You look nice today," remarked Paul as he held the door open in his De Soto for Laura. Under her gray knitted cap, her dark hair was combed into a perfect pony tail, her gray car coat covered a chocolate brown dress with vertical white stripes.

Paul closed her door and looked up at the overcast sky, a hint of snow in the air, darker than usual for the middle of the day. Tightening his coat around him to counteract the biting, icy wind, he walked around to his side of the car and got in.

He started the car and turned up the heater as high as it would go. He looked over at Laura still bundled in her coat. "Scarves." Paul held up the end of his dark blue scarf wrapped around his neck. "I remember when I was a little boy I heard Dad say the scarf is the warmest piece of clothing you can wear. It protects your neck and keeps the cold air from going down your chest and back. So," he paused and reached into the back seat and handed her a package brightly wrapped in Christmas paper. "I haven't seen you since Christmas and didn't have a chance to give you a gift. Merry Christmas."

"Thank you." Laura accepted the gift with a smile. One look at her eyes, and Paul could see something was wrong. His mother told him on several occasions that she could read what was going on inside of people by the look in their eyes. Usually she was right. Was it Shakespeare who said, "The eyes are windows to your soul"?

He watched as Laura unwrapped the gift, a knitted red scarf with tassels at both ends. Carefully creasing the paper she placed it in the back seat, then unfolded the scarf and wrapped it twice around her neck.

"Thank you." She reached over and gave Paul a small hug. "My old scarf is in tatters and I don't wear it in public anymore. Just what I needed."

Paul put the car in gear. "Do you like barbecue? If so, I found a new place in Branson. I went through there the other day and saw a restaurant called 'Ben's Barbecue Pit.' It's in an old World War II Quonset hut. The smell was fabulous as I drove by."

"Sounds good." Laura looked over at Paul and gave him a tentative smile.

"What's wrong?" Paul looked over to Laura, a frown on his face. "Your mom, is she okay? You feeling bad? School okay?"

Laura shook her head. "No, really, I'm fine. Just tired."

"Okay." Paul dropped the subject but wasn't satisfied with her answer.

Ben's Barbecue Pit was as good as Paul had hoped. Tender, fall-off-the-bone pork ribs with a tangy, yet somewhat sweet sauce. Hot, toasted French bread, potatoes with spicy pork gravy and two ears of corn. For dessert they had hot apple pie with a scoop of ice cream on top.

Paul had to carry most of the conversation. Laura smiled, responded to his questions, but he could tell she was distracted about something.

The drive home consisted of Paul making small talk about the holiday and the vacation time he had spent in Springfield with his mother and other friends, mostly from Bible school.

When he pulled up in front of her house, snow had just started to fall and Paul had turned on the wipers.

"Paul," began Laura as the car came to a stop. "I want to tell you something."

"Yes." Paul turned off the engine. He could tell by her tone of voice that something was coming he probably wouldn't like.

Looking straight ahead out the windshield she continued. "Paul, I appreciate all the attention you have been giving me the past several months. I like you. I like you a lot. And thank you for making me feel special. I don't know what your future intentions are toward me, but before anything goes further I think there is something you should know about me."

"Yes," Paul said again. He swallowed and felt his heart pick up speed. "I'm listening."

"You've met Claude. I've talked about him. How I went out with him for awhile."

"I remember."

"One time I went out with Claude. We had gone to some party with his friends. I knew I shouldn't have gone with him, but I did. He got drunk. I didn't drink, but he did. Plenty. I told him I wanted to drive home but he wouldn't let me. So he started driving me home, weaving all over the road. It was dark, of course, about midnight. We came around a turn in the road and right in front of us a man was walking on our side of the road. When Claude didn't swerve or even slow down, I realized he was too drunk to respond, so I grabbed the steering wheel and tried to turn away from the man. But it didn't work. Our car hit him. I can still picture it in my mind and feel the jolt of our car.

"Claude didn't even slow down. I yelled at him and hit him and told him to stop, that we needed to help the man. But he kept on driving as if nothing had happened.

"When we got to my house he told me to forget about it, and that if

I ever told anyone he would beat me to within an inch of my life and hurt my mother as well.

"As soon as he left I got in my car and drove to that spot. A police car and ambulance were already there. I saw a man on a stretcher as they were putting him in the ambulance.

"I thought about getting out and telling them what happened, but didn't have the nerve. The next day I found out it was Farmer Lester, we called him, an old man who lived alone not far from where we hit him.

"No one ever found out it was us who killed him. That was about two years ago. But I live in terror that Claude will let it slip in one of his drunken spells or that someone else will find out. I've only told one or two people besides you, but that has weighed on my conscience since then.

"Paul, I was responsible for someone being killed. If I hadn't gone to the party probably Claude wouldn't have gone either. For sure he wouldn't have been on that road driving me home. If I had insisted a little more on driving, Claude might have let me drive, and that poor man would still be alive today. I blame myself. I've asked God over and over to forgive me, but I still feel like a sinner."

Laura opened the door of the car and put one foot on the ground. "Paul, I'm not worthy of you. You're a preacher from a good home that probably never told a lie in all your life. I'm just a poor girl on Valley Drive from the wrong side of the tracks that lives in a chicken house and helped kill someone. For your own good and for the good of your church, you should find someone from the right side of the tracks that is worthy of you and doesn't have a past like mine."

She started to get out of the car but Paul grabbed her left hand. "Laura, may I say something?"

She paused and looked at him, tears in her eyes.

"What happened wasn't your fault. It's on Claude, not on you. I'm sure the Lord has forgiven you for whatever wrong you may have done. You just have to accept it. How about if I say I don't care where you live or what's in your past? God loves you and I love you, Laura. Doesn't that mean anything?"

She stared at him not moving. Still gripping her hand, Paul said again, "I love you, Laura. Do you love me?"

With a slight movement of her head she jerked free, slammed the door and hurried into her house.

Slowly, feeling numb all over, Paul pulled out of her driveway and started down the road. That incident with Claude was certainly traumatic, but didn't she realize it wasn't her fault? Did she mean what she said, that she thought she was unworthy of him because of that incident and because of her background in poverty? Or was there more to it than that? Did she really want to break up with him, or were her emotions causing her to react as she did without really meaning it? When he asked if she loved him, did she nod or shake her head? He wasn't sure.

He asked himself these questions over and over as he slowly drove home on the slippery roads. The windshield wipers rhythmically swept off the snow on the windshield, but not the questions in Paul's mind nor the ache in his heart.

1956   CHAPTER 33

Promptly at three o'clock Paul drove into the blacktopped parking lot of Lundquist Shoes and Boots. The snowfall had paused for the moment, but the brisk air and gray clouds overhead promised of more to come. He carefully walked up the concrete sidewalk on a thin layer of snow, admiring the architecture of the building in front of him, one of the largest and most modern buildings in Bethel Springs. The brick two-story building had an old European look about it. The concrete base about two feet high held a concrete square column on each corner of the building that looked like an obelisk jutting into the sky. Wide windows almost filled the front of the building on the first story. Smaller windows framed in the same gray concrete as the foundation and pillars surrounded the windows on the second story. The flat concrete roof jutted out over the edge of the building. "LUNDQUIST SHOE AND BOOT FACTORY" was stenciled into the gray concrete that stretched the length of the building.

Walking through the large front door also framed with the gray concrete, he was greeted by a receptionist behind a large metal desk, an older woman with a bluish tint in her gray hair. A younger woman sat in a smaller desk near the wall to his right.

"Good afternoon, Reverend Whitfield," she said in a cultured voice. "Mr. Lundquist will be with you in a few minutes. Please have a seat." She indicated a row of leather-bound chairs against the wall by the entrance.

After waiting no more than two minutes, a door opened and Daniel Lundquist walked out. Adjusting the lapels on his obviously tailored gray suit and smoothing his flashy red tie, he extended his hand toward Paul. "Welcome, Paul. Glad you could make it." His presence filled the room. The women paused their work and looked up at him as Paul stood, shook hands, and followed him into his office.

"Have a seat." Daniel Lundquist pointed to a tan leather couch against the wall across from his desk. Rather than returning to his desk, he sat in one of two tan leather chairs matching the couch against the adjoining wall.

"We usually don't work Saturdays, but a few of us came in today to catch up on some work. I'm glad you were free to come see me this afternoon." Lundquist paused and adjusted his tie again. "I've been observing you lately," he began without any preliminary chit chat, "and talked to a few of people who know you. I like what I see." He smiled at Paul, his brown eyes warm and friendly. Paul stared back at the man, feeling pleased at the compliment, yet wondering where this conversation was going.

"I have an opening at the plant. Orville Walker, our chief executive salesman is retiring in a few weeks. He's been with us for twenty years or so. Good man. We are going to miss him. I've been looking for a replacement and thought about you. I would like to offer you his job if you will take it. Pays well." He smiled again. "Probably ten times what you're getting at your church.

"Of course," he added hastily, "you can keep on pastoring. This is just a day job. You could still preach at your church and do whatever a pastor does. With your salary, in fact, you could help your church by starting a building fund. Get away from your little storefront nook and build a larger, better church of your own. As big or bigger than Hope Fellowship Church on the hill."

He paused. "Our business has purchased several homes around our plant with the thought of eventually expanding, if needed. One of the homes, just down the street from here, is vacant. Nice home. Three bedrooms, bathtub in the bathroom, gas furnace. It even has one of those new window air conditioners in the master bedroom, so you could sleep comfortably at night in the summer. If you take this job you could stay in that house rent free, if you choose."

Paul stared at the owner of this successful shoe business. He was offering him a prestigious, high-paying job. Excitement stirred within him. No more meals of Spam or hot dogs. No more hot, sweaty nights in the apartment in the summer or cold nights in the winter. No more counting his pennies to see if he could afford to buy gas the next week. Could this be real, or was there a catch?

"You said," began Paul, "that I could continue pastoring. What exactly would this job entail? How much time would it take? How much would I have to travel? How much time could I give to the church?"

"Walker covers the states of Kansas, Arkansas and Kentucky, taking our shoes to the twenty some stores in those states and checking up on them. One week he's home, the other week he travels. Most trips he leaves one day and comes back the next. Occasionally it's a three-day trip. He's always home on weekends, so you could always preach on Sundays and have most nights and weekends free to work at the church. You would be home most Wednesdays to preach at your church but would be out of town for a few of them. We provide a car so you could scrap your De Soto and drive a nice Ford Fairlane, just a year old. Lots of miles but still in good shape. You can keep it all the time, and drive it on the job and for your pastoring duties."

Paul looked around the office, noting the paintings on the wall of Ozark scenes and the plush furnishings. "You know," began Paul, "I have lived here barely six months. This is my first time in your factory and only the second time I have met you. You must have several dozen people who have worked here for years who are certainly more qualified than I to take on this job. Why are you offering it to me?"

Daniel Lundquist stood to his feet and walked over to the window, looking up at the sky. "Looks like more snow," he commented. "Hope it doesn't last too long."

He stared out the window a few more moments then finally turned around and looked back at Paul. "To answer your question, I like you," he said. "Others tell me you are a likable person. You are dependable, smart and intelligent. The fact that you came here to this small town to try and help a struggling church tells me a lot about your character. You are willing to work and get the job done.

"And," he smiled for the first time, then paused. "I wasn't sure I was going to say this, but I have to be honest. Along with all those reasons I just gave, my only daughter Patsy likes you. That means a lot to me. I love my daughter and want what's best for her."

He paused again, as if trying to decide what else to say. He chuckled. "To be honest, as I told you at Patsy's birthday party, I'm not too fond of Michael Champion who is sweet on Patsy. He already left one girl at the altar, and I don't want him to do that to my Patsy. Plus, his hair-brained scheme of wanting to start restaurants selling only hamburgers scares me. I don't want my Patsy attached to a loser like that. So," he spread his hands and smiled at Paul, "if I hire you, that will let Patsy know in a very real way I'm partial to you.

"I hope I'm not being too blunt." He shrugged and smiled. "Just the way I feel. I'm looking out for the company and my daughter at the same time."

He looked at his watch. "I've got another meeting in five minutes." He held out his hand to Paul who stood to shake it. "I know this is a lot for you to take in. I'm not expecting an answer now. Think about it. Pray about it. Talk to your friends about it. See what Patsy thinks about it. Then let me know. I'll be in touch."

Paul walked out of Lundquist Shoe and Boot Factory as if in a dream. He hardly noticed that the snow had started to fall again. Getting in his car he turned on the wipers and slowly drove home on the streets that were just starting to get slick.

Parking the car behind the church, he went in the back door, first checking the oil tank located just outside the back door to make sure there was enough oil for the next few days. Stomping the snow off his shoes, he took off his coat and warmed his hands over the stove before going upstairs.

Brewing a pot of coffee he took a cup and stood in front of the window facing the street staring at the falling snow.

First, Kate called off their relationship. Then, just a few hours ago, he still felt the pain in Laura's voice that pierced into his heart when she told him she was not worthy of him and that he should stop seeing her.

Now, Patsy's father offers him a high-paying, prestigious job and gave his blessing—his desire—that Paul continue his relationship with Patsy—sweet, exciting, beautiful Patsy. He felt his heart beat faster just picturing her in his mind. He still remembered that suggestive poke in the ribs at Lover's Lookout and other clues as to how their relationship might be.

Finishing his coffee he put his cup in the sink, rinsed it out, and walked back downstairs to stand warming his hands again over the oil heater for a few moments, then walked to the front of the church and looked out the window. Snow continued to fall, painting the sidewalk, street and roofs of the buildings a pale white in the fading sunlight.

Is this what he wanted? He would make more money. They soon may be able to build a church of their own with his additional income. But his church would probably suffer. He would be gone some Wednesday nights. He wouldn't be able to spend as much time in visiting his flock and in sermon preparation. But, didn't most pastors have second jobs in order to make ends meet? What was wrong with that?

He remembered Patsy saying her dad was in favor of gambling in Bethel Springs. Was this offer of a job partially to get him to lay off his criticism of George Hackett and the gambling issue?

And Patsy? Is she really who he wanted to spend the rest of his life with? She had just recommitted her life to the Lord. Was that a sign from the Lord that she was the one? But, did he really love her, or was he just infatuated with her beauty and vivaciousness?

And Michael. Michael said he loved Patsy and had for most of his life. He was working hard at winning Patsy back. He wanted his hamburger restaurants to be a success so he could provide a good life for Patsy. Who was best for Patsy? He or Michael?

Kate. Was she really in his past? Could he get her back again if he felt she was the right one?

Laura. Did she really mean it when she said she didn't want to see him again? Or was she just wanting to shield him from what she felt was best for him? Was her nod saying she did love him?

Mary Brunner. He hadn't thought much about her lately, but she was raised on the mission field. She knew ministry like few people did. Her hair was the color of the sunset. He liked red hair. What about her?

Or was there someone else out there for him he maybe hadn't met yet? Should he hold off on his relationships with everyone for awhile? Or, was it God's will he remain single and unencumbered by marriage? Didn't the apostle Paul talk about that?

Confused and apprehensive about his future, Paul went upstairs, put on his long underwear, two extra blankets, and went to bed. He had that pastors' seminar in a few days. Maybe that would get his mind off his confusion, or maybe he could get some clarity. Either way, he needed his sleep tonight.

1956   CHAPTER 34

The first hour of Paul's drive back from Springfield had been uneventful until the snow started. It had been a snowy winter this year. He had been at a two-day seminar held in Springfield at the First Evangelical Church on the topic of how pastors could use the media in their ministries. C.M. Ward, preacher on the weekly worldwide "Revivaltime" radio program, was the featured speaker. He told the fifty or so pastors in attendance about the potential value to their church of having a radio program in their community and gave tips on how to conduct a radio ministry. Another speaker was Elton Trueblood, well-known author who encouraged the pastors to write for the local newspapers, for magazines, and even to publish books. Television producer Robert Fisher spoke in glowing terms of the importance of getting in on the ground floor of television and movies. "Don't look at Hollywood and television as the devil's tool and the evil eye in your homes," he admonished, "and preach against people attending movies or owning televisions. Rather, look at movies, television, and all media as a way to propagate the gospel to not just one group of people at a time, but to the masses out there who are starting to purchase televisions and who are going to the movies in increasing numbers. Let's take over this part of the entertainment industry for God and not leave it to the devil."

After a stop at Pascall's Jewelry store and a brief visit with his mother, he was on his way.

His notebook filled with scribbled ideas lay on the seat beside him as did a bottle of Coca Cola and a package of fig bars he had purchased on his way home to help him keep awake. When he left Springfield he had looked at his watch and decided he should be home about seven if the weather held. That should be enough time to take a shower and to follow through on his plan for the evening. He smiled as he reviewed the response he hoped to get.

But, as he drove south on Highway 13, the snowfall started. First, occasional small flakes, then larger flakes began to plaster against his windshield in increasing numbers. The wind soon picked up and began blowing snow across the road, making visibility more difficult. *Don't have enough money to stop in a motel*, he told himself, *and don't know anybody around here that will put me up for the night, so I'd best hurry and get home.* He hoped his plan wouldn't be delayed by the snow or anything else.

After driving a little more than an hour in the snow, having to clutch the steering wheel tightly to keep the wind gusts from blowing his car off the road, he neared Bethel Springs a few miles ahead. His tense shoulders started to relax now that he was almost home. Cape Fair was behind him as he made his way in the darkness through farmland with occasional lights showing where families were, no doubt, safe and snug inside, riding out the storm in comfort.

The temperature must be well below freezing, he realized, now that it was dark, and the three or four inches of snow on the road was turning icy. He found it harder and harder to keep his car on the center of the narrow road. The wipers oscillating back and forth across his windshield were beginning to ice up. He could feel the tires occasionally losing their grip on the surface of the road. As a truck approached, Paul moved onto his side of the road as far as he could but found the truck didn't move over into its lane far enough. To keep from sideswiping the truck, Paul moved onto the shoulder as the vehicle blew by, then tried to turn back onto the road after the truck passed. But his tires failed to grip the ice-covered asphalt. His car began sliding off the road and tilted abruptly into a shallow ditch where his car came to a grinding stop. Paul gripped the steering wheel to keep from crashing forward into the windshield and slipping sideways into the passenger seat. His soda pop, fig bars and notebook slid onto the floor beside him.

Holding onto the steering wheel with his left hand, he shut off the engine with his right. Then, taking a deep, quavering breath he examined his body to make sure he was okay in his tilted car. Not finding any damage or sore spots he breathed a prayer of thanksgiving that at least he was okay.

Looking around outside, at first he saw nothing but open fields covered with snow and he wondered how he was going to survive the night in the increasing cold. He was almost out of gas so he couldn't keep his car running and keep his heater going for long. He wasn't sure if anyone else would be out driving at this time of night in this weather who would stop and give him a ride into town. Then he breathed another prayer of thanksgiving because up ahead about a hundred yards on the right he saw a house with lights on. He then realized as he got a better look at it through the falling snow it was the Lundquist home.

Light came through some windows and smoke drifted up from the chimney showing someone was home. He realized his plans for the night would have to be altered. He hoped that Daniel and Bertha, Patsy's parents, would be willing to put him up for the night. He still hadn't answered Lundquist on the job offer yet, so maybe they could discuss that tonight. Maybe Patsy would be there, too, which might make his request to stay the night a little awkward, but with her parents there it should be okay. Early tomorrow he would call Peter Johnson who had a four-wheel drive Dodge Power Wagon with a winch. Hopefully his car wasn't damaged and Peter could pull it out of the ditch and get him home.

Buttoning up his coat and putting on his gloves and stocking cap under his hat he got out, locked the car door, and started shuffling through the snow toward the house, his head down, trying to keep the blowing wet flakes from hitting his face as much as possible.

After trudging through the snow drifts for what seemed like hours, he stepped onto the porch into the brightness of the porch light. Ringing the doorbell he stomped his shoes and brushed his clothing to get as much snow off himself as possible.

The door opened and there stood Patsy in slippers and a yellow housecoat, her blond hair wrapped in a towel. "Paul." She stepped back from the door a look of surprise on her face. "What are you doing here? I mean…" she paused. "What am I saying? Come in. You look frozen." She motioned for Paul to come in, closing the door after him.

"Th-thank you." Paul found it hard to talk as his face was so cold. He pointed outside. "My car. I was driving back from Springfield, almost home, when a truck forced me off the road. My car's in the ditch down the road a ways. Do you think your parents would mind if I spent the night here? Unless your dad wants to drive me home. I don't know how to get the car out of the ditch tonight. Tomorrow, if I can use your phone, I'll call for someone to get my car out."

Patsy's eyebrows went up with another look of surprise. Then she laughed. "My parents? No, my parents won't mind. In fact," she laughed again. "If you stay the night I hope they never find out. They're not here. They're in Atlanta visiting my mom's parents. They should be home in a couple of days."

"Oh, good grief." Paul slapped his forehead and walked toward the door. "I can't stay here with you alone all night. What will your parents think? What will Michael think? Or my church people? Or anyone who finds out?"

Patsy grabbed his arm and pulled him toward the living room where there was a roaring fire in the fireplace. "Come on, be sensible. Don't go back into the cold. Please. You need to stay here. I trust you. I hope you trust me. Besides, no one needs to find out. It will be our secret. And, I've decided that Michael is no longer a part of my life. I've moved on. Here," she pointed toward the white leather couch facing the fire. "Sit. Take off your coat and relax. I'll change back into my clothes and make some hot cocoa. How does that sound?"

Paul groaned inwardly. Why did this have to happen tonight, of all nights? Or any night? Forcing into the back of his mind the ramifications that would occur if anyone found out he was going to spend the night alone with an attractive young woman he was friends with, he took off his coat, hat and gloves, hung them on the coat rack by the door, and moved to the fire where he stood warming his hands.

A few minutes later Patsy returned dressed in jeans and a yellow wool sweater, her hair free of the towel and magically combed back in place, with a tray in her hands containing two steaming mugs and a mound of sugar cookies.

She placed the tray on the glass-covered coffee table and sat on the couch. "Here, sit beside me in front of the warm fire and have some hot cocoa and cookies."

Paul smiled and sat down. "If my mother could only see me now."

"She would trust you, I know." Patsy patted his knee. "Relax. This will always be just between the two of us. Don't worry, everything will be okay. No one will find out. Now let's enjoy the fire. It always seems more cozy on a night like this."

Paul took a sip of cocoa, put the cup back on the tray, and leaned back against the couch closing his eyes. "Long drive," he commented to the ceiling. "First time I've driven so far in the snow like this. No fun. Then to end up in the ditch so close to home."

"At least you got stuck by a home of someone you knew. That was good." She smiled. "Even if was just me." She patted his knee again. "Now just rest for awhile." She got up and went back into the kitchen.

Paul attempted to relax his body, grateful at least he was warm and safe.

Finally he opened his eyes, sat back up, took another sip of cocoa and grabbed a sugar cookie. "Tastes good," he called into the kitchen after eating one and took another one. "Did you bake these?"

Patsy returned to the couch and shook her head. "No, I can't take the credit. Mom did." After a short pause she looked over at Paul. "Do you remember the first time we met at the library, your first day in town?" She laughed, which always reminded Paul of the ringing of chimes. "I wasn't sure what to think of you, how you bumbled your introduction and seemed so nervous. Remember?"

Paul smiled at the recollection. "Yes, I do. I'm afraid I'll never forget that moment."

"You seemed so nervous, yet so cute at the same time. I decided right then and there I liked you. You would make a good addition to our town." She laughed again. "Even if you were a pastor of that church." For several more minutes they reminisced about his visits to the library and the other times they had been together. They could hear the wind outside blowing against the house. Then an eerie scraping noise started at the other end of the house. "That tree," commented Patsy. "Dad needs to have it pruned again. When he lets the branches grow they rub against the house in the wind."

They were silent for several moments, listening to the weather outside, watching the snow falling past the dark windows. Then, after a long pause, she sighed, cleared her throat, got up and stood facing the fire with her back to Paul, suddenly turning serious. "I hadn't planned on telling you this now and in this way, but since we're here I've been wanting to talk to you about something. I've been doing some thinking, deep thinking and praying." She turned around and looked at Paul, a question mark on her face. "Is this a good time to talk? Or would you rather I waited until morning? Or some other time?"

Paul stared at her. Then he swallowed. That 'heart in your throat' expression he had heard others use seemed to apply to him right then. "I...I guess," he shrugged. "I don't know what you want to say. But now is as good a time as any."

She turned back toward the fire, not looking at Paul. "To begin, I want you to know I think you are a wonderful man, very talented and nice. I like you. You have brightened up our town and my life, too. You have encouraged me in many ways and we have become friends. As we just discussed, our first meeting at the library was hilarious. When you left that day your words of encouragement about how important my job was to the people in this small town stuck with me. And our dancing..." She laughed again and pointed toward the great room. "I'm sure you remember our dance at my birthday party."

Then she turned serious and looked toward him with her mesmerizing blue eyes. "And you helped me find God again. You are a good preacher. You're honest and caring. You are good looking, more handsome than that Billy Graham everyone is starting to talk about. You're..."

Paul rose to his feet, sudden fear gripping his heart. "Stop. Please stop." He held up his hand as if he were a traffic cop. "Thank you for these compliments. But before you say any more I want to show you something."

Returning to the coat rack by the front door, he reached into the inner pocket of his coat still dripping melting snow on the hardwood floor and brought out a small velvet box. Returning to Patsy he held up the box. "I want to show you something that may clarify a little how I feel about this night and why I'm embarrassed to be here. For the past several weeks I, too, have been thinking and praying about some major decisions in my life. I just talked to Mother about it again today, and she agrees with my decision and feels good about it." He opened the box and took out a small ring. "I want to show you this."

Patsy glanced at the box, stared at the ring, then looked up to Paul and put her hands to her mouth and screamed. "Paul...Paul. It's beautiful. Thank you, thank you. Oh, my. Thank you." She reached for the ring, held it for an instant, then handed it back to him with trembling fingers. "But no. No I have to say 'no'. I can't. I'm sorry." Tears sprang to her eyes. "I mean, please don't ask. I'm so sorry I led you on. I'm saying it all wrong. I'm so sorry. I'm an idiot." She covered her face with her hands and her body shook with sobs.

Paul froze, instantly realizing Patsy had misread his actions. Quickly, he put the ring back in the box and sat in on the coffee table. "No, Patsy. I'm so sorry." He grabbed her trembling hands and gently pulled them away from her face. "I'm so sorry," he said again. "I'm the idiot. Open your eyes and look at me. I'm so stupid. The ring...the ring. It's not for you. It's not for you."

"Oh." Patsy stepped back from Paul. "It's not?" A look of unbelief crossed her face.

Still holding Patsy's hands Paul stared at her wishing with all his might the proverbial hole in the floor would open up and suck him down into it and transport him safely home—or anywhere, just away from all this. Why did the Lord have him end up here tonight of all nights, anyway? And Patsy. She was staring white-faced at the velvet box. Was her first reaction that she thought he was proposing? Then when she understood he wasn't, did she convey a sense of relief? Or dismay? Had she wanted him to propose to her?

Forcing those thoughts aside, Paul let go of her hands and gave an embarrassed laugh. "I'm so, so sorry I gave you the wrong impression. The ring." He coughed. "The ring is for..." he coughed again, suddenly finding it difficult to continue. "The ring is for... for Laura. For Laura. If ...if she'll take it." He stuck his hands in his pockets, turned from Patsy and looked into the fire. "When I came here to Bethel Springs everyone, myself included, thought Kate and I would get married. That didn't work out as we thought. I met you first here in town, then Laura. You were...are both beautiful on the inside and out. As you said, we've had some good times. Good friends. I trust we will always remain good friends." He gave an attempt to laugh again. "Even after tonight. But you have Michael. Or had. You love him, or I thought you did. Maybe you still do; I don't know. Your life is going in a different direction. I know Laura has that loser friend of hers, Claude. She doesn't even like him. But I love her. I know I do. I guess I have ever since I first saw her at Martha's. Or maybe the infatuation came then and love later. I don't know. I never did understand very well in my psychology class as to how love happens. I think she loves me...at least I hope so. Although," he paused, "the last time I saw her we didn't leave on the best of terms. But I hope she loves me and will say 'yes'." He pointed toward the velvet box. "I picked that up today. I planned to offer it to her tonight at Martha's just before she got off work. He grinned. "Maybe now I should wait another few days to clear the air, should she find out about tonight."

Patsy sighed, then wiped her eyes. "Paul, that's wonderful. Can I give you a hug…as a friend…a hug of congratulations. I'm so happy for you. And Laura." Without waiting for an answer Patsy put her arms around Paul and gave him a gentle squeeze, then backed away. "I'm sorry I misunderstood. Forgive me for being so stupid as to not realize what you were doing.

"I'm glad for Laura. And for you," she added. "You are made for each other. And tonight, what just happened…" She looked at Paul pleadingly. "This is just between you and me, right? Forever."

Wordlessly Paul nodded.

She sat again on the couch and patted the cushion beside her. "Come, sit again, and let me finish my speech you interrupted." When Paul was seated again beside her, he reached for the cocoa and noticed his hand was shaking.

Patsy took a deep breath. "I'm so sorry again I misunderstood. I really am an idiot. My fault. I went on too long. What I was starting to tell you is that I…" again tears filled her eyes and rolled down her cheeks. "What I was starting to tell you," she repeated, "is that I have made up my mind, too. You are a sweet young man, good in every way. Great in every way. Too sweet, too good, too great. And I took advantage of you. I danced with you and in other ways tried to make Michael jealous so he would pay more attention to me and ask me to marry him. I like you and it was fun the times we were together, and maybe I did get to liking our times together too much, but I apologize for taking advantage of you." She looked down at her left hand. "As you can see, what I tried didn't work."

She sighed and reached down to pick up her cup of cocoa. But her fingers trembled so much she put it back. "I wrote Michael a letter. He's in Chicago working at that McDonald's restaurant. I told him we needed to end our relationship. He and I have known each other most of our lives and have been dating off and on for years. I've been thinking for a long time he was going to propose, and we were going to get married and live happily ever after. But then he went to Kansas City and got engaged to another girl and left her at the altar just before the wedding. When he came back he told me he had made a mistake and realized he always loved me. But I don't know if I can trust him now. And the last year or so with his obsession with those hamburger restaurants he wants to start, plus his real job at the pharmacy, we have hardly seen each other. Plus, I don't think Dad likes him.

"So I've made a decision. I just talked to Mom and Dad about it the other day. I'm twenty-one now. I enjoy working at the small library here, but I don't see much of a future here in Bethel Springs. I've decided to move to St. Louis and attend a college there where I can get a degree in library science. Then I should be able to get a job in a larger library and start over somewhere else. Maybe in a bigger city. I can go to a new church where they talk about the Bible like in your church and meet new people.

"Well." She smiled a rather sad smile. "That's my speech. I'm glad I told you. I hope you will understand. I will miss all of you," she added. "You are one of my special friends that I will really miss."

She wiped her eyes and sighed. "It's getting late. Finish your cocoa and cookies while I bring you down a pillow and some blankets. You can sleep here on the couch in front of the fireplace. Bathroom is down the hall on your right. There's lots of wood in the wood box to keep you warm. My bedroom is upstairs. We have an oil furnace which heats up the whole house, so I will stay warm and cozy too. I'll be right back."

As she spoke a gust of wind shrieked through the trees outside, rattling the window panes. Then the lights went out.

"Oh, my." Paul saw Patsy throw up her hands in the dim flickering glow of the fireplace. "That's one bad thing about living so far out. It doesn't take much of a storm for the electricity to go out. I'll grab some candles and couple of flashlights."

A few minutes later the beam of a flashlight came down the stairs with Patsy behind it carrying an armful of bedding. "Here you go. Make up your bed." She handed him the bedding, then went back in the kitchen and returned with two candles in candleholders and a book of matches. "Use these if you want. You can keep the flashlight. If you get hungry or thirsty, feel free to go in the kitchen and get what you want. But don't leave the refrigerator door open too long. I don't know how long the electricity will be off and we want it to stay cool."

After Patsy left, Paul took off his shoes and laid his wallet and watch on the coffee table beside the velvet box and spread out the blankets and pillow on the couch. After putting two more logs on the fire and closing the screen in front of the fireplace Paul climbed in his temporary bed, said a silent prayer and was soon asleep.

What seemed like just a few moments later, he woke up to the sound of someone coming down the stairs. "Sorry to wake you." Patsy came into the flickering light of the fireplace in her yellow housecoat, carrying a pillow and blankets. "I forgot that our oil furnace needs electricity to run and send heat through the house. My bedroom is freezing and I couldn't sleep. It's getting colder by the minute. Would you mind if I curled up in front of the fireplace. I won't bother you."

Paul, now fully awake, sat up on the couch. This was getting too close and personal to his liking. But what could he do? He was a guest. He believed Patsy was telling the truth about being cold. At least he hoped she was.

"You take the couch," offered Paul. "It's more comfortable. I don't mind sleeping on the floor. I've slept on church benches many times. Can't be any worse than that."

Patsy hesitated, standing by the fireplace with her pillow and blankets. "No, that's okay. I'm sure I'll be fine."

Paul grabbed his pillow and blankets off the couch and laid them on the floor. "Don't argue. This is your house. You're the girl. You get the couch."

Laughing, Patsy spread her pillow and blankets on the couch and began to smooth them out. "You're very persuasive. But thank you. I've never had to sleep on the floor before. Wasn't looking forward to it."

After making themselves as comfortable as possible under the circumstances, they told each other their good nights and were soon asleep.

Once, Paul woke up in the night to the sound of wind whistling through the eves. He got up to put another log on the fire. He looked at Patsy on the couch, shadows flickering from the fireplace on her beautiful Michelangelo-like chiseled face. Her tousled golden hair spread on the pillow beside her reminded him of finely spun gold. Her hands clutched the blanket up to her chin, but the rest of the blanket had fallen to the floor. Quietly, Paul moved the blanket back on the couch so it covered her housecoat and feet.

Had he made a mistake? Patsy was so beautiful. So full of life and energy. Life with her would be one exciting day after another, he was sure. But, did he love her? And Laura? Also beautiful. Also exciting. Yes, he had made the right decision.

As he stood there she opened her eyes and looked up at him. A mischievous smile touched her lips as he saw him staring at her in the darkness. "What are you looking at? Aren't you supposed to be asleep?"

He kept staring as if in a trance, still not fully awake himself. "You know," he said after a pause, "I have found the girl of my dreams, if she will have me. With you, one of these days God will put the right man in your life. Go to your college in St. Louis, relax, trust in the Lord, and He will work out whatever is best for you."

Her smile broadened. "Now you sound like a preacher, but thank you. And Laura is a lucky girl. Real lucky. Now quit staring and go back to sleep."

Paul was awakened by a pounding on the front door. He sat up on the floor, noticing his back was stiff and sore. The fire was almost out. He felt cold. The pounding started again.

"Who's that?" Patsy sat up in bed. "What time is it?"

"I don't know. But it's getting light outside. Must be seven o'clock or so."
The pounding continued. "Anyone home?" a voice shouted.

"Oh my goodness. No, it can't be." Patsy got to her feet in her housecoat
and pajamas and nervously ran her fingers through her hair several times.
"Michael! What's he doing here? He's supposed to be in Chicago."

Paul, fully dressed except for his shoes, stood up at once. "Do you want me
to hide? Take the pillow and blankets and run into the garage or something?"

"No. Don't bother. Michael has probably seen your car. He knows my
parents are gone, so he's come to check on me after the storm. What a
nightmare."

Paul smoothed out his hair and stood by the fireplace, a pillow in his hand
as Patsy opened the front door and he heard Michael come in the house. "I
knew your parents were gone. Since the electricity was out at my house, I
figured it was here too. When you didn't answer your phone I came to check
on you. By the way, that looks like Paul's car up the road. Did you know that?"

Patsy came into the living room followed by Michael who stopped when
he saw Paul standing by the fireplace, obviously just having woken up. Then
Michael looked at the blankets on the couch and those by the fireplace. He
turned to Patsy. "I came back to town early to make amends and to see if we
could work something out between us. But," he looked between Paul and
Patsy, "looks like I was too late." Then his voice became harsh. "Looks like
you two got cozy last night."

"Michael." Patsy tugged on Michael's arm. "It's not what you think." She
went on hurriedly, "Thank you for coming back. But I was home alone last
night when Paul came to the door. A truck had run him off the road in the
ice and snow. This was the nearest house. He had nowhere else to spend the
night. We had cocoa and cookies and talked. That was all. Nothing happened,
I promise."

Michael jerked free from Patsy and approached Paul. "A likely story. I did
like you. But I could tell you always had eyes for Patsy. Just waiting for the
right time. Now admit it. This was no accident that you ended up here last
night, conveniently, when her parents were gone, now is it?" He moved closer
to Paul, looking around the room and pointing to the two sets of bedding.
"Did you just move your blankets when you heard me coming?"

Then his eyes fell on the velvet box. "And what's this?" Picking up the box
he opened it. "Aha." His voice became a triumphant shout as he took out the
ring and held it up. "All the evidence I need. You're a conniving liar, that's who
you are. And to think you're a preacher."

"Michael." Patsy voice was a sob. "Please, it's not what you think.

"Right." He stuck the ring in Patsy's face. "Does it fit? Did you say 'yes' last night? Is that what the celebrating here in front of the fireplace was all about?" He put the ring back in the box, snapped it shut and turned to Paul doubling up his fists, clutching the velvet box in his left hand. "What have you DONE." The last word was a shout as he stuck his fists in Paul's face.

"Please." Patsy was sobbing, tears running down her face. "Please. I said 'no.' I mean…I mean, he never asked. I didn't say anything. Michael, listen to me. The ring…the ring is not for me. Paul was just showing it to me. It's for someone else."

"Right." Michael's voice rose again to a shout, dripping with sarcasm. "Everyone is telling lies about last night. But I can see through it. Come on, my friend." He slapped Paul on the face. "Put up your dukes. Let's have it out. NOW." His last word was another shout.

Paul, suddenly realizing he had to respond and do it quickly, threw down the pillow. "Michael," he shouted back, shooting up a quick prayer. He jerked the velvet box from the other man's hand and pushed him toward the couch. "Sit down and listen to me." When Michael resisted he pushed him again, this time harder. "Michael, sit on the couch. Patsy, you too, sit. Hear me out." He walked over to the coffee table in front of the couch, sat the velvet box down, and waited until the pair had sat down. Michael faced him, his arms crossed, his face creased into a frown. Patsy sat close to Michael's right and linked her arm possessively through his.

"Hear me out," Paul repeated, lowering his voice. "Patsy is right. I was driving home last night from Springfield. As you know, it was snowing. The snow turned to ice. A truck forced me off the road. I ended up with this being the closest house. I came here intending to ask Patsy's parents if I could spend the night here until I could get the car out this morning. I didn't know if Patsy was even home.

"When I realized I would have to spend the night here alone with Patsy, I almost decided to spend the night in the car, not wanting to bring reproach on either myself or Patsy if someone should find us here together. But she persuaded me to stay.

"But, Michael, I am a Christian, a believer in Christ. I hope you are too, or at least you should be. I knew God was here last night watching me as He always is with all of us. I knew at some point I would have to answer for everything I did here last night, and whatever I did this morning, and every day. The Bible says that someday, somehow, everything we do in private will be revealed in public. Even though I spent the night alone with an attractive woman, I chose not to do anything I would be ashamed of Patsy's parents knowing, or my mother—or even Laura. Or you.

"Plus, I have a conscience, Michael. I have to live with my conscience every day, every waking moment. I have to go to sleep at night remembering what I did that day. Or last week or last month or ten years ago. Do you think I would have done anything here last night to sear my conscience? To make me roll and toss at night and lose sleep and live my life with regret over some indiscretion or spur-of-the moment thing I may have done?"

Paul's voice rose unconsciously getting into a preaching mode. "Michael, Patsy. I know that someday I will get married. At least I think I will. Someday, I will hopefully have children, maybe grandchildren. Do you think I would want my wife and kids to possibly find out I had crossed the line and dishonored myself by some indiscretion? And dishonored the other person as well.

"Above all of this, do you think I would want to have jeopardized my relationship with God? No, I didn't want to sin against God. I didn't want to have anything stand between me and God. And, I didn't want to have to go to God and ask for forgiveness for anything I might have done last night. So I made sure that didn't happen.

"Michael, you are sitting beside a beautiful young lady, a jewel. A special woman. I like her. I like her a lot. She is a friend of mine. She may have been giving me some of her attention to get you jealous. I may have responded more than I should. I don't know. But she does love you and has for a long time. In spite of her breakup letter to you I believe she still does. I think you love her, except you may have been ignoring her some lately because of your pursuit of money. Don't you see that? Or have you been too blind with your ambition to make more and more money that you have ignored something of greater value than all the money in the world?

"As to the ring. The past few weeks I've been in prayer and in conversation with my mother and others and came to a decision. Yesterday I picked up the ring that I planned to offer to Laura last night. My plans changed. Since I was here and had it, I showed it to Patsy."

Bypassing her reaction to the ring he continued, "Patsy was happy for me. I hope you won't think this too unseemingly, but she did give me a hug of congratulations. That was all. That was the most we ever did. You can ask her."

"Michael." Patsy squeezed his arm. "Michael," she said again. "Everything he said was true. All we did last night was talk. About Laura. The ring…" The ring…" Her eyes glistened with tears. "The ring is for Laura. Michael. The ring is not for me."

Paul backed away from the coffee table, his speech over. Turning his back on the couple he took another log from the wood box, pulled back the screen and threw it on the fire, closing the screen again. Then he stood in front of the fireplace, facing the couple, and waited.

Michael sat staring at the fire for several moments. Then a brief smile touched his face. "Paul, I guess I owe you an apology." He turned to Patsy. "You too. I should have known I could trust you, hon. You too, Paul. You've always been honest and upright, at least to me, and to everyone else I have talked to, even though I haven't always agreed with your theology."

Shaking off Patsy's arm, he stood and extended his hand toward Paul. "I'm sorry. I apologize."

Paul shook his hand looking Michael in the eyes. "Apology accepted."

"You know." Michael pointed to the road outside where the snow had ended and the sun was shining. "I've got a four-wheel drive Chevy pickup at home. I bet I can pull you out."

Two hours later Paul laid on his bed in the upstairs apartment above his church. The electricity had not gone off in this part of town and his room was comfortably warm in spite of the weather outside. As Paul prepared to take a nap, he glanced over at the velvet box on his desk and smiled. He sure blew it last night when he showed it to Patsy. But, he reflected, it confirmed in both of their hearts and minds their desires and intentions. He would go tomorrow and tell Daniel Lundquist he appreciated the job offer but decided not to take it.

Now that his plans for last night didn't work out, when should he propose to Laura? And how? At her home? At the restaurant where they first met? In church? Take her to some romantic spot?

Would she say "yes?" Or would she hold true to what she had told him at their last meeting and refuse him. He hoped and prayed and thought she would say "yes," but he wouldn't know until he actually asked her.

Finally, making a tentative final decision, he closed his eyes and drifted off to sleep.

1956   CHAPTER 35

Paul had it all planned. He hoped. Feeling more nervous than he had felt in a long time, he dressed in his best brown corduroy pants and yellow nylon shirt, made sure his blond hair was combed, his shoes shined, had enough money in his wallet, and started walking the two blocks to Martha's Café, leaving just in time to arrive there by seven thirty, a half hour before Laura got off her shift.

The January air that Saturday night was calm and cold. Snow still lingered in the shady spots that did not get much sun. Stars blanketed the night sky. The crescent moon hung low over the horizon. Only one car passed Paul as he made his way down the concrete sidewalk. He didn't meet any other pedestrians on the deserted streets. Bundled up in his warm wool coat he kept his hands in his pockets, his right hand protectively gripping a little felt box.

Promptly at seven thirty Paul stepped into Martha's Café and walked over to his usual table to the left and sat down, removing his coat and placing it on his chair behind him, making sure the little felt box was within easy reach. Paul counted just seven other people in the diner that Saturday night. He could see Martha through the café doors walking back and forth as she cooked in the kitchen. Laura was the only waitress on duty. Holly and Angel said they wanted to be there but promised to hide in the pantry, out of sight, so Laura wouldn't suspect anything.

Then Laura came out of the kitchen carrying a tray of food for Jeb and Josie Kirby and their two children. Next, she came over to Paul, looking especially radiant tonight. She was even more beautiful tonight than he had ever seen her, decided Paul, in her blue uniform with the red and white checkered apron.

"Hello," she came over to his table with a menu, a tentative smile on her face.

"Surprised to see me here?"

"I'm sorry." Tears sprang to her eyes. She sat across from him in a chair, her voice barely above a whisper. "I am happy to see you, really. I'm sorry for what I told you when I left the car. I was just trying to protect you in what I said, to give you a way out." She smiled tentatively. "Thank you for coming back, if only to eat here again." She squeezed his hand, then stood, her voice back to normal. "What can I offer you to warm you up on this cold night?"

"First, before I order, how's college? Glad you made it home this weekend."

"College is great, but getting harder. Just five more months and I'll be an RN, a genuine registered nurse, the good Lord willing and the creeks don't rise. How's the church and everybody here doing?"

"Doing fine." Paul glanced at the menu. "I'll have the meatloaf dinner with green beans and salad and coffee."

"Coming right up." With that she disappeared into the kitchen.

Paul sat in his chair and nervously waited. Jeb Kirby caught his eye and silently waved. Andrew and Bernice Witherspoon, an older farming couple that Paul had met before in the diner, sat two tables over and briefly discussed the weather with Paul. A younger man that Paul didn't know sat in the corner table on the other side of the room.

Finally, Laura came out with her tray of food. That was the signal. As Paul watched Laura come he saw Martha, Holly and Angel looking at them over the louvered kitchen door. Laura carefully took the food off the tray and sat it in front of him as she had done dozens of times over the past few months. She smiled. "There you are, sir. Enjoy."

Having rehearsed this dozens of time in his mind, Paul almost felt like he was in a dream. "Before you go back to the kitchen," Paul told her looking up at her, his mouth suddenly dry, "I wanted to show you something."

"Okay." Laura sat the tray on the table beside his. "Not real busy tonight. I have a little time."

Paul reached into his coat behind him, taking out the little felt box with his left hand, but keeping it hidden. Then he gripped Laura's left hand in his right hand and knelt on one knee. "Laura," he began and licked his dry lips. "Laura," he said again, "from the first time I saw you here in Martha's Café I knew you were special. Over these past few months I have come to care for you, then to love you. After much thought and prayer, I've decided to ask you if you would do the honor of being my wife." He let go of her hand, produced the felt box, opened it, took out a ring with a small diamond, and extended it to her. "Laura, will you marry me?"

Paul had his eyes on Laura's face as he talked. At first, her face showed a question mark. Then her eyes got big and she sucked in her breath. Then he saw tears glisten in her eyes and her lips quiver slightly.

When he finished speaking, on one knee, with the ring extended, he suddenly realized the diner had gotten quiet. Everyone had stopped talking and their attention was on him and Laura. A car passing outside was the only sound.

Then Laura bit her lip. Tears began running down her cheeks. A slight sob escaped her lips. Then slowly she nodded her head. "Yes," she whispered.

A rush of joy suddenly filled Paul's heart. He wanted the whole world, or at least everyone in the diner, to hear her reply. "What did you say?" he asked.

"Yes," she said in a louder voice. "Yes, I will marry you."

At once applause filled the diner. Martha, Holly and Angel came out of the kitchen and hugged Laura, who by now was crying, trying to choke back her sobs. Bernice and Josie and the two children came over and gave Laura hugs.

Jeb, Andrew and even the stranger walked over and shook Paul's hand and congratulated him, then tried to squeeze in between the women and shake Laura's hand. Then the women ganged up on Paul and gave him hugs.

After a few moments when the hubbub had quieted down a little, Paul came back to Laura and took her hand. Looking at her tear-filled eyes he asked, "How about if we have our first kiss. Here. Now." When Laura nodded he bent down toward her, their lips meeting for the first time. A sweet kiss Paul would remember for the rest of his life.

No one noticed the sound of a motorcycle starting up and roaring off into the night.

1956   CHAPTER 36

It was a simple wedding held on Saturday afternoon, June twenty-third, nineteen fifty-six, just days after Laura had proudly received her coveted RN degree. More chairs had been brought in to Laura's small Pentecostal church in Cape Fair to accommodate the crowd. Laura's pastor, Brent Hawkins, and Professor McFee from Zion Bible School officiated the wedding. Laura helped push her mother down the aisle in her wheelchair as she gave her away to Paul. Paul's mother, looking beautiful and radiant in her new burgundy dress with matching jacket and shoes, had sat beside Mildred during the ceremony.

Tables loaded with food were set up outside on the front lawn of the church where the crowd converged after the ceremony to enjoy the food and listen to Thad, Paul's classmate at Bible school and best man, and Holly, the maid of honor, give their prepared speeches about Paul and Laura and their predictions for long lives, successful ministries, and a houseful of children.

In the late afternoon Paul and Laura finally got in his De Soto where teenagers had painted "Just Married" in the rear and side windows and attached tin cans to the rear bumper. Driving out of the church they turned onto Route 66 going toward St. Louis where Paul had reserved a room at the Booker T. Washington Hotel for an entire week.

They arrived at their destination without incident around midnight, tired from the long day and miles of driving.

The next morning Paul woke up to the light of the sun brightening the curtain covering the window. He opened his eyes, then looked over at the woman lying beside him with tousled hair staring at him.

"Good morning, husband," she said, a bright smile lighting her face.

"Good morning, wife," he replied, a sudden burst of love in his heart for this beautiful woman. His dream had been fulfilled. Laura was now his wife.

They stared into each other's eyes for several moments. Finally, Laura spoke. "Can I ask you something?" she asked.

Paul saw her lips tremble. "Yes you can, my love. Anything."

"I feel so secure lying next to you. A dream come true."

"For me too. You are my dream. Always will be. Forever and ever."

She snuggled up to him and he put his arm around her pulling her close.

"Will you promise me," she asked, her head on his shoulder. She paused and cleared her throat. "Will you promise me," she started again, "that every morning for the rest of our lives you will wake up next to me?"

She sat up and looked into his eyes, a question mark on her face.

He stared back at her, suddenly realizing how important this question was to her. He remembered her telling him several times that her father had abandoned her and her mother when she was twelve. But how was he to answer that? He had no doubt that their marriage would last forever, but with all that happens in a family life, how could he make such a promise and be able to keep it?

When he didn't answer right away he saw tears form in her eyes. Finally, he spoke up. "Laura, my love." He took both her hands in his. "I make you this promise, this solemn vow, that unless one of us is away on a trip, or one of us is sick or indisposed in some way, or one of our children is having a nightmare and needs one of us to sleep with him or her, that every morning for the rest of our lives, it will be my honor and privilege and joy to wake up in the same bed next to you."

The tears in her eyes became a flood down her cheeks. She lay down again, her head on her chest. "Hold me," she said.

Paul wrapped his arms around her soft body and pulled her toward him. "Tighter. Hold me tighter."

During that idyllic week of their honeymoon they visited the Farmers' Market in downtown St. Louis twice, took a riverboat tour on the St. Louis River, visited three of the grand old historic churches, ate out in several restaurants, and just walked the streets of the city, enjoying each other's company, talking and making lifelong plans. Someone had given them a Brownie camera as a wedding gift and Paul took three rolls, most of them of Laura.

On the last morning of their honeymoon, still in his pajamas, Paul opened the hotel door to get the newspaper that was left there each morning. As he picked it up he read these words scrawled across a piece of paper that had been attached to the front page: "Now you have your bride to worry about. Leave Bethel Springs now or your beautiful wife will be sorry she married you."

Paul frowned. He hadn't faced any persecution for several months. The elections were over. The pro-gambling side lost. He hoped whoever was causing him problems had given up or left. But who had done this? Who even knew they were here? They had told only their closest friends where they were going. Had someone followed them?

Burying the newspaper in the trash before Laura saw it, they packed their bags and started back home to Bethel Springs.

Driving west on Route 66 toward Bethel Springs they approached Rolla about noon. Hot day, in the low 90s, according to the weather report on Paul's radio. They had purchased a six pack of Hires Root Beer and a bag of ice to drink on the way back. With the windows rolled down and drinking the soda pop in glasses with lots of ice, they managed the trip in relative comfort.

Pulling into Bob's Southern Diner, Paul parked the car, went around to Laura's side and opened the door for her. He happened to glance up and noticed a black Buick Century Riviera drive into the parking lot and swing around back behind the restaurant. Immediately Paul's mind flashed back to Bethel Springs when the black car had tried to run him down. Was it the same car? Paul had a classmate in Bible school who had a Buick Century. Friends had kidded him about how it looked like the front grill of his car was a smiling face with two teeth protruding on either side.

He shook his head. There were, no doubt, hundreds of black Buicks in Missouri, and maybe the cars he saw weren't even Buicks.

As they walked into the restaurant they felt a refreshing, cooling breeze from a window air conditioner. They splurged on T-bone steaks and French fries with Root Beer floats. "I wish Martha's Café had an air conditioner," Laura commented as she ate her lunch. "It is always so hot in there during the summer. Especially in the kitchen."

After lunch they walked back out into the humid, hot outdoors. Paul again opened Laura's door for her as she got in and closed it after her. He decided right then he was going to do that every time she rode with him. Maybe that was not a part of the marriage vows, but that was one way to cherish his wife. Getting around to his side of the car he started the engine and started to pull onto Route 66. A speeding car unexpectedly came around the corner. Paul slammed on his brakes to stop before he got onto the highway. His brake pedal sank to the floorboard, but the car didn't slow down.

It took an instant for Paul to realize his brakes had failed. Frantically, he swerved the car to the right to get it off the road. He heard the squeal of brakes from the other car, heard Laura's terrified scream, and held his breath waiting for the impact. The car flew past them, just inches away and continued down the road.

Paul kept the car going in a circle in the restaurant parking lot until finally it stopped. He looked over at Laura who was gripping the dashboard as if her life depended on it, her face pale. "What happened?" she asked shakily. "Why didn't you stop? We could have been killed."

"Brakes didn't work." He shook his head. "I had the oil changed and the car lubed just before the trip. I asked Chester to check the car to see if it needed any work done. He said it was in shipshape."

Remembering the car he thought he may have seen and the warning on the newspaper this morning, he felt a tight knot start forming in his stomach. Were the persecutors back again?

"Wait in the car," he told Laura, "I want to check something." Getting out he walked over to where they had been parked. Sure enough, there was an oily liquid that looked like it had been spilled recently. Returning to the car he got out his flashlight and the mirror he had seen Laura use to comb her hair. Getting on his hands and knees he examined the brake lines with his flashlight and mirror and finally spotted a cut in the brake line on the front tire of the driver's side.

Wiping the dirt off his hands onto his pants and throwing the mirror and flashlight in the back seat, he turned to Laura. "Looks like our friends have returned," he said grimly. "They cut our brake line. We could have been killed had I gotten onto the highway and needed to stop suddenly."

Going back in the restaurant he used the phone to call a local garage. Two hours later, using some of the money they had received from their wedding, they were back on Route 66 heading again toward Bethel Springs.

"I'm so sorry I got you into this." Paul looked over at his new wife who was sucking on a cube of ice, sitting near the window to get some of the cooler wind whipping through the open window. "We haven't had a problem for several months. I thought—or at least hoped—whoever was causing the problems had given up or left."

"Their attempt to get gambling on the ballot failed their first try," said Laura after chewing up the ice. "But they are going to try again. You keep talking about it off and on from the pulpit and have mentioned it a couple of times in the weekly columns you write for the newspaper. Plus, you talk about it to people when you have a chance. I guess they still want to get you out of the way."

Paul thought again about the warning on the newspaper he had seen that morning. Should he tell Laura? Maybe not, at least for now. He said instead, "I know what they did to the previous pastor's family." He reached over and stroked her hair. "I don't want to see you hurt by whomever is doing this."

She turned to Paul. "Remember right after we met I took you on that picnic?"

Paul nodded. She laughed. "One reason was I thought you were cute. Mainly, I wanted to warn you what to expect. The fact that you said you felt like the Lord had brought you here and that you were willing to stay and fight the evils in this town—I think that may have been the day I started to fall in love with you."

"I'm sure George Hackett is still not too happy with us. Not only with speaking out about gambling, but I know the weekend events at city hall for families are cutting into his earnings."

"I don't like George. But I think his son, Norman, is just as evil or maybe worse. I don't like his daughter Katie either. She comes to Martha's sometimes with her friends. They're all loud and disrespectful, hardly ever leave a tip.

Neither do Jake and Carl and whoever else works for him. All bad people."

"I've wondered about Milton Passmore, the bank president," added Paul. "I still think he was trying to make me look bad with saying I had taken money from the church for personal use. I can't imagine the bank making a mistake like that. Or maybe it was his daughter Sarah. She could have altered the bank records, too."

"Or Zeb. That annoying bar at the corner. He doesn't like you. I'm sure he and all his drunk friends would like to see you and the church gone from that block.

"Or," she paused, "how about Claude? Always the tough guy, or likes to think he is. Maybe he wants revenge for you having married me."

"Maybe." Paul looked over at Laura. "I know he's caused you a lot of problems. But that's in the past now. You don't have to worry about him anymore. About that night when he ran over that man and killed him, it's up to him to come clean about that."

He shook his head. "Whoever these persecutors are, we will catch them. Or maybe the authorities will. If not, God will in the end. But it will be okay. God is with us. We just need to use wisdom and be careful in all we do."

She moved closer to him until they were touching. "We are in this together, Paul. We are now one. I will be careful, I promise. You be careful, too. Then we need to pray and trust in the Lord to keep us safe and to help us conquer this evil. As you have preached many times, our fight is not with flesh and blood or with the bad guys, it's with the principalities and powers and rulers of darkness: in other words, the devil and his minions. He's the one we have to conquer."

"That's my wife." Paul squeezed her hand, a feeling of pride and gratitude welling up within him. "Love you. Thanks for understanding and for your support."

Late that night Paul pulled up in front of their building. "From now on, let's park our cars in front of the church instead of in the alley," suggested Paul. "Safer that way. Harder for someone to tamper with our cars and not be seen. And let's always check them before we drive off."

Paul opened Laura's door. Clouds covered the moon and most of the stars on this dark night, but a street light on the corner cast enough light for them to see. Down the street loud music blasted out the open windows of Zeb's Bar and Grill. Three men stood in front of the door, the light from the windows illuminated the smoke surrounding their faces from their cigarettes. Their talking and laughter drifted down the street, but Paul and Laura barely noticed.

Taking out his key he opened the front door of the church, reached in and turned on the light that lit up the whole hall. A quick survey showed everything was in order. "Mrs. Whitfield," he said formally, "may I have the honor of carrying you over the threshold of your new home?"

Silently, Laura nodded and put her arm around Paul who picked her up and awkwardly carried her through the door and into the church where he put her down. Then he reached for her hands. "Remember when you came to see me the night of July fourth?" he asked. "As you were leaving, with us standing in this very spot, I wanted to kiss you so badly. I almost did. Did you know that?"

Laura nodded again. "I know. I saw that in you. And I wanted you to. I kept praying, 'Lord, help him to kiss me. Please, please, please'." Tears came to her eyes that she quickly shook away. Then she smiled coyly. "The Lord is going to answer my prayer right now, isn't He?"

Without replying Paul pulled her to him and their lips met in a tender, lingering kiss.

Finally, he backed away, took a deep breath and cleared his throat. "Let's take our luggage upstairs to your new home and close the door before any more flies and mosquitoes come in.

Paul led the way up the stairs carrying two suitcases with a handbag strapped around his shoulders. Laura followed with another suitcase.

At the top of the stairs Paul switched on the light. They both stared. "Holy Cow," was all Paul could think to say.

Laura dropped her suitcase, covered her face with her hands, and burst out crying.

1956 CHAPTER 37

Paul and Laura stared in wonder at the apartment. On the wall facing them a big sign on butcher paper read, "WELCOME HOME PASTOR AND MRS. WHITFIELD." To their right, the kitchen counter was filled with sacks of food. The sink contained more food. Some sacks sat on the floor. Over to their left, their small dining room table was also covered with sacks of food. Several gifts wrapped in wedding paper sat on their bed.

"Wow." Finally Paul got his voice again. "I don't believe this."

Laura dried her eyes with the back of her hands. "Wow is right. Look." She spread her hands out. "Food. Enough for weeks, months." She turned to Paul. "The church people must really love you."

"Love us." He gave her a hug. "They love both of us. An amazing group of people."

"Let's look." Eagerly she walked over to the kitchen counter and began sorting through the food items: cans of beans, corn, green beans, various soups and other vegetables and fruit. There were sacks of flour and sugar, bags of rice and brown beans. One large paper bag contained four boxes of Sugar Corn Pops breakfast cereal she remembered eating as a child.

One large cardboard box on the floor contained lettuce, cabbage and other fresh produce. She opened the refrigerator to store the produce in there only to find it stocked with milk, cream, butter and cottage cheese. She opened the freezer and found it full of steaks, hamburger meat and a package of lamb chops.

Going to the dining room table she found more cans and sacks and packages of food. "I don't know where we're going to store all this," she sighed happily. "But it's a problem I can live with."

Meanwhile, Paul walked over to the bed. Beside the gifts was an envelope separated from the rest of the mail. Opening it, he saw it was a card from Lamar Lundquist. Paul looked at the handwritten note: "Congratulations, Paul, you made the right choice. Patsy is doing well in college in St. Louis. She sends her congratulations too. Will you still be having the Saturday morning breakfasts? Best wishes, Lamar." Tucked inside the card was a hundred dollar bill.

Leafing through the mail Paul spotted a letter from Kate. Turning his back to Laura he opened it. Inside was another card. She had written: "Paul and Laura, Best wishes to both of you on your marriage. A friend always. Kate." Inside the card was a twenty dollar bill.

"Hiding the mail from me?" Laura walked up beside him, a mischievous smile on her lips but seriousness in her voice.

Lost in thought, Paul turned to Laura, startled, thinking she was still going through the food.

"Looking to see what's here." He took a deep breath and cleared his throat to compose himself. He held out the card. "From Kate. Remember her?" He picked up the card he had thrown on the bed. "From Lamar, Patsy's brother."

He threw them back on the bed and took Laura in his arms who looked up at him, a question mark on her face. "Laura, sweetheart," he said, "these girls were in my life, and a few other girls over the years, for a time. But among all of them you are the one who won my heart. The only one. From the moment I proposed, and even before that, you became the only woman in my life. You have my heart and my life and my future. I hope these girls will always be my friends, and yours. But, as I said in my vows, and I meant every word, I have forsaken all others. I will cleave to you, whatever that means. Don't let any worry cross your mind. From now on it's just me and you." He smiled down at her. "Like it or not, you are stuck with me, from now on and forever more. We are husband and wife. Together. And we are going to have a great marriage and be great parents with a houseful of kids that will be an example for everyone who sees us."

Laura sighed contentedly and put her head on Paul's shoulder. He held her tightly and felt a lump form in his throat. *You've taken on quite a chore*, he told himself. *Are you up to it? Never done this before. Taking care of a wife? Quite a responsibility.*

That night when they climbed in bed they realized the church had purchased them a new bedspread, sheets and pillows. A new mattress had replaced the lumpy, sagging-in-the-middle mattress Paul had been sleeping on.

Thirty-three days later, Mildred Taylor, Laura's mother, passed away.

A few weeks before the wedding Mildred finally had agreed to see a doctor. Doctor Carter took x-rays of Mildred's lungs, blood tests, and examined her in other ways. The next day he met with Paul and Laura. He shook his head. "I believe her lungs are full of cancer. Too late for surgery." He gave Laura a bottle of pills. "If she gets uncomfortable give her these. You are a nurse and you know how to care for someone like this. But, unless a miracle happens, she just has a few weeks left."

Paul and Laura spent all the free time they had with Mildred. Laura took some of her vacation days from Bethel Springs Valley Hospital where she had gotten a job, and Paul put off some of his church work to be with his mother-in-law. He prayed with her and made sure she understood that salvation and eternal life came through faith in Christ.

"I'm dying," she said one day to both Paul and Laura as she was lying in her bed that they had moved into the living room of the chicken house. "I know I am. I can feel it. Isn't that what Doc said and what you are whispering about?"

"That's probably true," said Laura, holding her mother's hand.

She laughed, then had a coughing spell. When she could talk again she continued. "I know I've made a mess of my life, Laura. Your daddy leaving was as much my fault as his. I'm so sorry about that. But you turned out okay, didn't you?" She looked up at Laura. "You are beautiful, gorgeous, a good waitress, now a big-time college graduate and nurse." Then she looked at Paul. "And look who you married? A preacher, no less, and a good-looking one to boot." She laughed again. "Guess I didn't do too bad raising you, did I?"

"Mother." Laura bent down and kissed her mother. "You did a wonderful job. You are a good mother. You always loved me and did the best you could for me."

"Now I'm dying. Any day now, I suppose. I do believe, Pastor Paul, the story you tell about mansions in heaven. And Jesus." She touched her chest. "I can feel Him. I know He's there. I talk to Him and He talks to me. Thank you for telling me about Jesus before I go to meet Him."

Mildred Taylor was Paul's first funeral. While in Bible school he bought a book containing funeral sermons and other applicable quotations and Scripture passages. He came up with some ideas from that book and thoughts of his own. The funeral was held at Community Chapel which was filled with people. Burial was at the Bethel Springs Cemetery about a mile out of town.

After the funeral Paul and Laura went through Mildred's meager belongings. Laura kept the afghan her mother had knitted, some of her books, and a few other items. They moved Mildred's dresser up to their apartment over the church. Her clothes was so old they threw them away. Paul called Chester Elden, who had a truck, to haul away to the junk yard most of what was in the house.

They walked through the other chicken house that had not had chickens for the past two years and around the small acreage. "Let's just sell all of this," commented Laura. "Chip Donahue at the Real Estate Office will take care of it for us. With the money we can buy a newer car, a few more things we need, and put the rest of the money in the bank."

Paul nodded. "Sounds okay to me."

1957 CHAPTER 38

The next several months were idyllic for Paul and Laura. The church grew slowly and steadily. Paul continued his Saturday morning breakfasts for the teenage boys and young men. The feeding program and Sunday school at the Rice's home on Sunday afternoon grew under Laura's supervision. The Friday and Saturday family nights at city hall became the most talked about public event each week. Paul kept up his weekly column in *Bethel Springs Record*. Sometimes he got into local politics and mentioned the harm in gambling or some other problem in the community he felt would be helpful to discuss. Usually, however, his columns were inspirational, newsy or humorous.

Paul endeavored to make friends with as many people as he could in town. Police Chief Bob Ferguson finally came around to becoming friends with Paul, mainly because of the change he saw in his seventeen-year-old son Brad since he began attending Paul's Saturday morning breakfasts. Every few months Paul would invite the merchants on his block to his apartment above the church for a potluck dinner. No religion was discussed, just relationship building. Stan and Judy Manning with little Stephanie, who had been born shortly before Paul and Laura's wedding, usually came as did Dolly Knight. After the third event Bull Featherstone finally came with Paula, his Caucasian wife. He always invited Zeb who never showed up. After several months Stan and Judy began attending church and soon accepted Christ as Savior.

Mayor Tom Peterson let Paul know he was a thorn in the communities' side because he was opposed to enriching the citizens through his opposition to gambling.

As much as he tried, Paul was never able to make friends with David Gannon, pastor of Hope Fellowship Church. Occasionally his wife, Helen, would furtively stop by the church and tell Paul and Laura that life at home was not perfect, but better since she was going every few weeks to see Grace Carpenter for counseling at Zion Bible school.

Even though some members from Hope Church had started attending Paul's church, Paul's heart went out to the remaining members. From others he heard how Pastor Gannon continued to preach against the "old-fashioned fundamentalist" views of Paul and his church, and water down the gospel in his preaching so much that his church became no more than a social club with its members thinking they were right with God because they went to church and followed its rules. In Paul's weekly column, without mentioning names, he sometimes wrote about certain heretical views held by Hope Church and gave the correct biblical viewpoint.

Paul continued to hand out tracts one by one to men entering Zeb's Bar and Grill. When Zeb confronted him again, Paul told him this was a free country, that the sidewalk was public property, and that if Zeb tried to stop him he would call Police Chief Ferguson. But, knowing how Zeb could get angry, Paul only occasionally passed out tracts. So far, no drunk from the bar had come to Paul, either to harm him or seeking help.

Hackett House continued to flourish on weekends, although Paul was told the number of men attending was down. There was still talk of bringing the gambling issue back to a vote. Rumor had it that banker Milton Passmore and others were still buying up land around Bethel Springs in the anticipation of building an opera house, bath houses and casino once gambling was approved. Occasionally, Paul saw Claude around town who either sneered at him, gave him a mean look, or avoided him.

Six months after they were married, on a Monday night after Laura got home from her shift at the hospital, they drove the two blocks to Martha's since the winter night was cold and windy. Holly came to their table to wait on them. "How are the newlyweds?" she asked by way of introduction. "Haven't seen you in here much." She turned to Paul. "Apparently your wife is feeding you so well you don't have to come to a restaurant to get good food."

Paul laughed. "You're right," he added, "she is a great cook. But sometimes she needs some time off from cooking, and I need the time off from washing the dishes."

"You need one of those newfangled dishwashers. I hear all you have to do is put in the dirty dishes, press a button and 'presto,' out come clean and dry dishes."

Laura laughed. "Who would want one of those? Costs money and takes up space in your kitchen. Easier just to do it yourself. Only takes a few minutes."

"Speak for yourself," replied Paul good-naturedly. "A fancy dishwasher would save time and keep me from getting dishwasher hands."

Holly laughed. "Better change the subject. What will you have for dinner?"

While they were eating their chicken fried steak and mashed potatoes with corn, Stan and Judy Manning came in with little Stephanie. Immediately the toddler became the center of attention for the few people who had braved the weather to eat at Martha's. Holly brought a high chair for the child and held her for a minute or two, playing with her, before placing her in the seat.

Paul and Laura watched with interest the attention given to their friends' baby. When they turned back to their food, Laura turned to Paul. "Let's have a baby," she whispered.

Eleven months later, on November fifteenth, nineteen fifty-seven, Paul Andrew Whitfield Junior was born in Bethel Springs Valley Hospital.

CHAPTER 39

The white-haired man closed his notebook, stood, and stretched. Then he fixed himself another cup of decaf coffee from the motel coffee maker, looked out the window and all he saw was the past. Picking up the notebook again he scanned a few more pages. He was so busy back then that he had not written much. The few words in his journal brought back a flood of memories but no answers.

With a sigh he put the notebook down and got ready to leave. Time to get back to reality.

Paul drove back to Bethel Springs, going past the State Farm Insurance office, just a block off the square. He thought about stopping and talking to Rodney himself, but decided against it, thinking others might hear the conversation.

He stopped in at the newspaper office still called the *Bethel Springs Record*. "I'm interested in the history of this town," he told the receptionist, a woman in her forties with dark hair and glasses, a Starbucks coffee cup on the desk beside her. "I was just up the hill at that old burned out church. Do you know anything of the history of the church? Why it burned, or how the fire started?"

"The old Hope Fellowship Church? That is ancient history. Must have burned down about fifty years ago." She pointed toward a side room. Our newspapers that old would be in microfiche. Feel free to go back and check out the old issues if you want."

Paul followed her directions and found himself in a room with movable shelves on sliding rails that slid back and forth with a twist of a handle. After looking through several shelves he found the microfiche for 1958. Going to the July newspapers he chose the Wednesday, July sixteenth issue. The first story on the top of the fold was about the fire. Since it happened at night the photo of the fire showed mainly the flames that lit up the sky but didn't have much detail of the church or surrounding area. There was another picture of the gutted church after the fire, taken the next day, and a photo of the church before the fire.

Fire Chief Bruce Evans was quoted as saying the fire was definitely arson. "We found five gallon gas cans in the building, one in each corner of the church, possibly linked together with fuses. Whoever set the fire wanted to make sure the whole church burned to the ground. Of course, the stone walls didn't burn. That's all that's left of the church. At this time we have a person of interest, but no suspects."

The July twenty-third issue showed a photo of Police Captain Robert Ferguson in a news conference. He stated they had interviewed several people who may have been connected to the fire. Witnesses said they had spotted a car near the church around the time of the fire, but couldn't identify it. At this time he had no suspects or motives as to who may have set the fire or why they may have set it.

The next issues contained shorter articles about the fire with no conclusions as to who the arsonist was.

Paul's last day as pastor was Sunday, August tenth. He left town the next day. A short time later he knew his denomination had closed down the church. There was no mention in the *Record* about either of those events.

Looking at the issues over the next several months, Paul saw the articles about the fire grew shorter and less often, and finally stopped, with no answers.

While he was still in the newspaper office Trey called on his cell phone. "Any news, Grandpa?" he asked, hope in his voice. "Have you nailed the arsonist yet?" He laughed. "I know that's asking for too much. Just wondering."

"I'm working at it. Nothing new yet."

"I'm winding up my responsibilities here at Fuller and and hope to leave here early Monday morning to help Rachel and the others get ready for the wedding. That's just a week away. If you haven't found anything by then I want to help. We need to get this taken care of, Grandpa. I want to marry Rachel." The last sentence was almost a cry of desperation.

Paul's heart went out to his grandson. "Trey, as I have said, I'm really trying, and really praying. If the Lord wants this to happen, and I think He does, He'll find a way to help me or help someone find the answer, or change hearts, or do whatever needs to be done. I still believe Jesus when He said, 'Everything is possible for him who believes'."

After leaving the office Paul drove to Cape Fair and looked up the Mercy Nursing Home. If Helen Gannon, the pastor's wife at the time of the fire, had dementia, as Mabel had said, visiting her was probably a long shot. But he had to try.

The nursing home was like most nursing homes; a single story structure with lots of windows, surrounded by lawn and colorful landscaping.

Paul walked through the front door and was immediately hit with an antiseptic odor, also common of most nursing homes. "Is Helen Gannon available?" Paul asked the receptionist sitting in front of a computer in her white uniform at the long counter in front of him. "I'm an old acquaintance from way back passing through town. I know she hasn't been well. But if she's free and able to have company, I thought I would stop in for a few minutes to visit."

"Helen Gannon," the receptionist repeated. She keyed in a few strokes on her computer. "Yes, I think she's finished with her therapy and should be back in her room." Down the hall and on your left. Room eleven.

Paul followed her directions, passing by an older man in a wheelchair who looked at him with a blank expression. He had been in many nursing homes. They all looked the same: hallways with doors leading into rooms occupied by older people living out their last days in an institution. As he came to room eleven a uniformed nurse was just walking out and smiled at him. "Helen Gannon's room?" he asked.

"Yes, the bed on the right."

Paul walked in not sure what he would find. He glanced to his left and saw a woman asleep in a hospital bed, the front half slightly elevated. The older woman snored softly, her gray hair scattered about on the pillow.

On his right another older woman was sitting up on the edge of her hospital bed. He remembered his first visit with Helen Gannon and the few times he had seen her: attractive, in her late twenties with flashing brown eyes and curly jet black hair, tall, slim, sophisticated, always well dressed in the latest fashions.

Age and infirmity had robbed her of most of these features. He would not have recognized her, a shriveled up body wearing a shapeless pink bathrobe, furry slippers on her feet, her thin white hair uncombed, her eyes dull and wandering.

Paul found a vacant chair up against a table, moved it a few feet in front of the woman, and sat down to be at her level. "Helen Gannon?" asked Paul, suddenly wishing he hadn't come.

The woman looked over at him with dull eyes, saying nothing.

"Are you Helen Gannon?"

"What do you want?"

Paul had to strain to understand the faint, quavering voice.

"I'm a friend of your granddaughter, Rachel Gannon." He hadn't met Rachel yet, but he decided he could still call her a friend. "She's getting married in a few days. She's marrying my grandson."

At the mention of her granddaughter, Helen Gannon's eyes lost some of their dullness. "Rachel, yes. Rachel." She wrinkled her forehead as if struggling to remember. "She came to see me today, or maybe yesterday, or maybe last week."

"She is a wonderful girl. My grandson loves her very much." He paused to let that information soak in. Then added, "Do you remember the fire that burned your church many years ago?" he added.

"The fire." Helen Gannon closed her eyes. "Yes, the fire." She opened them again. "I remember. I remember the fire. David said it was a good thing.

197

A good thing. The fire."

"Why would he have said the fire was a good thing?"

"Ask Brice. He would know. David knew. Brice knew. I didn't know, at least at first."

"Brice? Who's Brice?"

"You know." She sounded exasperated. "Deacon Brice. Don't you remember?"

"Oh, him," replied Paul, trying to appease her. "Do you remember Deacon Brice's last name?"

"Brice. Just Brice. Just Brice"

"Okay, right. Brice. Do you remember who started the fire? Who burned down the church?"

"Oh, yes. Everyone said it was Pastor Paul. Pastor Paul burned down the church. That's what Brice said. That's what David said."

"That's what they claim. But do you know who it really was?"

"Ask Brice. He would know."

"Do you know where Brice is now?"

"I don't know. He never comes to see me anymore."

"Try and think who it was who really burned down the church."

Her face lit up. "Ask David. He would know. He should be home by now. Ask him. He knows who really did it." With that, she settled back on the bed, her eyes turning dull again.

Paul asked her other questions but realized her mind was now elsewhere—or nowhere. He paused and looked at her again. She wasn't that old. Probably still in her seventies. Life wasn't fair. She should be home helping plan for her granddaughter's wedding. Why did her mind have to go? Why did she have to spend her golden years like this, just waiting to die?

Suddenly struck with compassion for this unfortunate woman, he asked, "May I pray with you?"

When she didn't respond he grasped her arthritic, bent hands in his, bowed his head, closed his eyes and prayed a quiet, heartfelt pray for Helen Gannon, for her family and for the upcoming wedding.

When he finished the prayer and looked up, he saw tears in her eyes. "You…" Helen paused and shook her head as if trying to awaken a memory. "Your prayer…your prayer reminds me of how Pastor Paul used to pray for me." She paused again, her eyes losing their luster for a moment. Then it returned. "Are you Pastor Paul?"

Paul stared at the older woman. How should he answer her? After a pause he smiled at her. "Yes, I'm Pastor Paul. Good to see you again." He added hopefully. "Now, can you remember who burned down your church?"

She waved her hand in frustration. "Ask Brice. Ask Brice. He would know. He knows."

"Thank you for your time. I will continue to pray for you." Paul gave her a sad smile, then gently hugged the thin, frail woman. "God bless you, Helen."

When he walked out of the room there were tears in his eyes.

CHAPTER 40

Tuesday morning found the white-haired man once again at the skeleton of the old Hope Fellowship Church at nine o'clock sharp.

"Yesterday I went to see Helen Gannon at the nursing home," Paul told Mabel Tinsdale after a few moments of small talk with the older woman who was there again with her Bible and devotional book. "When I mentioned Rachel, her granddaughter, Helen became rational for a few moments. When I mentioned the fire she said, 'Ask Brice.' That's all she said. No last name or who Brice was. Do you know who a Brice might have been back then?"

Mabel placed her Bible on the table. "Brice? I may. There's a Brice Boyles who lives just down the hill a few houses from me. He's getting up in years now, but he used to be a deacon at the church years ago. I think he was attending there when the fire took place. You may want to talk to him. He lives in a two-story white house with a red door. Can't miss it.

"But before you go," Mabel added, "I talked to my son Rodney yesterday. He said of course he remembered you. He just called a few minutes ago and said he has some information for you. He wants to meet you tonight at the community center at seven o'clock. Will you be free then? Do you remember where that is? Could you meet him there?"

Paul nodded. "Sure. But wouldn't it be more private to meet him at his home if he has some information for me?"

Mabel shrugged. "I don't know. That's all he told me."

After visiting a few more minutes Paul took Mabel home and followed her directions to the home of Brice Boyles. He now determined he couldn't go around incognito and hope to get the information he wanted. Whatever the cost, he needed to tell people who he really was, and let people react however they would. That was what he would do.

"Are you Brice Boyles?" Paul stood in front of the open red door he had just knocked at with more fear than he had felt in a long time.

"Yes." replied the older man at the door. A head taller than Paul, dressed in blue shorts and a faded Dallas Cowboys T-shirt and slippers, he was an imposing figure with his long white hair and unkempt beard, still in reasonably good shape for someone his age. Probably a football player in his younger days, decided Paul, and wondered why that ridiculous thought entered his mind at this time. "May I help you?" he added.

Paul nodded. "I'm passing through town. My name is Paul Whitfield. I used to live in town. I was just up to see Mabel Tinsdale and she told me where you lived. May I talk to you for a few minutes?"

"Paul Whitfield?" The man seemed to mull over that name in his mind.

"Paul Whitfield," he repeated. Then his face hardened and he narrowed his eyes. "You mean Pastor Paul? The man who burned down our church?" The man started to close the door in Paul's face.

With an effort he pushed the door back open. "May I talk with you? he asked again, forcing his way into the threshold. "Just for a minute?"

Brice Boyles opened the door and stood glaring at Paul, not two feet away from him. "What do you want?" His voice was almost a growl.

Knowing he had to get it out fast, Paul condensed his talk. "My grandson wants to marry Rachel, Jacob Gannon's daughter. Her parents don't want her to marry my grandson because they think I burned down his father's church. Yesterday, I talked to Helen Gannon in a nursing home. She was rational for a few minutes and said you might know who was responsible for the fire."

Brice Boyles opened the door wider but didn't step back any farther into his house. "Why do you ask me? You started the fire. You were the one who lit a bottle filled with gasoline and threw it through the pastor's office window. It was you who burned down the church."

"Look." Paul didn't step back either. If the other man wasn't going to back away neither was he. Paul looked him in the eye. He took a deep breath. "Look," he repeated. "I know that's not true. You know it's not true. Yes, I did go into the church office. The woman who called me on the phone and said she wanted to meet me in the office wasn't there so I left. But I did hear some noise somewhere in the building as I walked out the door. I know I was set up. Do you know who that person was? Do you know who was responsible for the fire? Was it someone from the church who wanted the insurance money and wanted to blame me for it? Or was it somebody else?"

Brice Boyles glared at Paul. He opened his mouth, then closed it again in a firm line. "I have nothing more to say," he said after a long pause.

"Look," Paul repeated again. "That was almost fifty years ago. I imagine the statute of limitations has long expired by now, so no one will go to jail. I just need to know the truth. Can you help me out so I can help get my grandson married to this girl he loves?"

"All I know is you started the fire. That's what I told the police. That's what everyone in town believes. You must have believed it, too, because you high tailed it out of town after the fire. Now please get out of my house or I will call the police."

With that, he grabbed the door and forcibly closed it in Paul's face. This time Paul backed off, knowing he wouldn't get any more from this man.

Slowly he drove away. He knew by this time tomorrow everyone in Bethel Springs would be buzzing with the news that the church arsonist from long ago that no doubt had become part of community folklore, was back in town.

CHAPTER 41

The white-haired man showed up at the community hall in downtown Bethel Springs promptly at seven o'clock, dressed in gray slacks and a short-sleeved white shirt. He had a hard time finding a parking place because of the number of cars in the parking lot and lining the street. He wondered if some big event was going on somewhere close.

As he walked into the foyer of the community center he heard crowd noises from inside the main room. When he stepped through the door he was shocked to see it almost full of people, some sitting in rows of folding chairs facing the front and more chairs set up against the walls. In front of him on the back wall he noticed a huge banner stretched almost all the way across the room in black letters: "WELCOME BACK PASTOR PAUL." Under the banner was a smaller sign reading: "WE LOVE YOU."

Before he could react to what he had just seen, a young man in a gray suit with a head full of dark hair rapidly approached him. "Welcome, Pastor Paul." He shook Paul's hand. "I'm Benjamin Perkins, pastor of the Church of the Open Door. We've been expecting you. These are all your friends who want to welcome you back." He took him by the arm. "Follow me. Let me introduce you to everyone."

Numbly, not yet grasping what was going on—wondering if he was dreaming and would soon wake up back in his motel room—he allowed the man to lead him onto a small raised platform where he was seated in a folding chair against the wall under the banners.

"Thank you all for coming on such short notice," said his host into a microphone on the front of the stage as the crowd quieted. "Over the years I've heard a lot of good things about Pastor Paul Whitfield and how during his short time here he changed many lives. As you know, he's been out of the country as a missionary in South America for over forty years. When Rod Tinsdale called me and told me Pastor Paul was back in town to help prepare for the wedding of his grandson, Trey, to Rachel Gannon, I thought this would be a good time for some of you to tell him in person what he means to you. So," he paused, "as I already told you a few minutes ago before our guest arrived, I'm going to open up the microphone. If anyone wants to come up and share a few words, feel free to come. After that we can all take as much time as you want eating the snacks that some of you have brought and thanking Pastor Paul in person, according to whatever his schedule is. Who wants to be first?"

Immediately a heavy-set man came to the stage. "Pastor Paul," he said turning to face him, "I'm sure you don't recognize me. I'm Rod Tinsdale. Fifty years ago you pulled me from a burning car and saved my life. Not only that, you helped me get my feet on the ground both spiritually and socially. Today I own and operate the State Farm insurance agency here in town. Seated to my right over there is my wife of thirty-six years, Mary Lou, and two of our three children. Thank you, so much." When he had finished speaking he walked back to Paul and gave him a hug.

Next to the stage was another middle-aged man. "I was a young boy who came to Pastor Paul's church when he first came to Bethel Springs back fifty years ago, in nineteen fifty-five. Pastor Paul may remember me as little Joey Pittman. We had some family problems back then with my dad, as Pastor Paul may remember. But with the Lord's help and his help we got our family straightened out. Both my parents are gone now, but all of us four kids stayed in church and continued serving the Lord, as we are doing today."

A college age young man was next. "My name is George Clute. I have never met Pastor Paul, but I have heard about him from my grandparents. Back when he pastored here he came to my grandparents' home and invited them to church. They came and got saved. Grandpa Clute became a deacon in the church, then my dad became a deacon. Just this past year I was elected a deacon at the church."

Next came Glen Edwards, an older distinguished man dressed in a dark blue suit and red tie. "I was one of the boys who came to Pastor Paul's Saturday morning breakfasts. Best cook in town back then," he said and the crowd laughed. "Pastor Paul led me to the Lord and got me straightened out. After I graduated from high school, I went to Zion Bible School where Paul attended. The school is still there, now called Zion University. For thirty years I was the college campus pastor and just retired two years ago. Many of the students I helped over the years are now pastors and missionaries and work in other ministries or are godly witnesses in their secular jobs. I know I wouldn't have had the opportunity to influence all those students if Pastor Paul hadn't spent time mentoring me when I heeded help."

Several others came up and thanked Paul for his influence on their lives, the lives of a loved one, or someone who had influenced them.

When there was a pause, Benjamin Perkins returned to the microphone. "As Pastor Paul knows, when he left they closed down his church. But, several weeks after that, on the insistence of several church members, the church opened up again in another building in Bethel Springs with a new pastor in our current denomination.

"Pastor Paul may remember Rocky Scranton, an old man who lived by himself in a shack, almost a hermit. Pastor Paul befriended him and led him to the Lord. In the last year or two of his life he finally started coming to church. When he passed away, they found out he had willed his ten acres of land to the church. As you know, we now have a beautiful church building on that location, with plenty of room to expand our ministries.

He paused. "I think we have another speaker," he added, motioning toward the front door. "I was looking for him, hoping he would come. But I see that Jeremiah Rice just walked in. As you all know, he's a world-wide evangelist. This past year he toured Europe in meetings that filled soccer stadiums. I understand that next month he's starting a campaign in Atlanta. I found out he was in Memphis and called him last night. He wasn't sure if he could make it tonight, but here he is. Would you welcome Evangelist Jeremiah Rice."

Coming toward the stage was a tall, slim man with a slight limp. Paul recognized him by his walk, or thought he did. Listening to the speakers coming one by one to the stage had moved him to near tears. At the sight of the next speaker he put his hands over his face to cover the sudden trembling of his lips. Tears formed in his eyes and began to course down his face.

The evangelist walked to the microphone, then turned to Paul. "You have probably heard of me over the years as I have ministered in different parts of the world, although I haven't been to South America yet. But you probably didn't know who I was because you remember me as Chipper Rice. Little Chipper. I guess I got that name because my younger brother couldn't say 'Jeremiah' when he was little, so Dad had him call me 'Chip' or 'Chipper', and the name stuck. And I apologize, Pastor Paul, for not thanking you for all you did for me until now. But I respected what I understood was your desire to put Bethel Springs and everyone connected with it behind you." He turned back toward the audience, paused, and cleared his throat. "I would be dead...I would have died—in fact I think I did die—as a little boy and I would not be here today had it not been for Pastor Paul. Some of you know the story because I have told it around the world. One morning, while I was waiting to get on my school bus, a car driving too fast on an ice covered road came around the corner and hit me. I flew twenty-five feet in the air. Pastor Paul arrived on the scene a few minutes later. When he got to me I wasn't breathing. He laid his hands on me, prayed for me, and kept praying until the ambulance came. Somehow I came back to life. I had a broken hip, leg and arm and various other injuries, but except for a slight limp I'm fine now. First, I thank the Lord. Second, I thank this Lord's faithful servant."

With that, he turned to Paul who stood to accept the hug from his former little church member. As one, the crowd stood and applauded for a good five minutes. Paul sat back in his chair, put his face in his hands and couldn't hold back the tears.

No one observed this, but during the applause a woman and two men quietly left the building.

After three more people spoke, Benjamin Perkins turned to Paul. "Pastor Paul, don't feel any obligation, but would you like to say something?"

Paul stood and walked to the microphone. After a moment of silence he said, "First I want to thank all of you for being here and for the kind words you said about me. When I left here forty-seven years ago with people blaming me for the fire at the other church, and after they closed down my church, I considered my ministry here a failure. A bust. Wasted years. So I tried to forget about Bethel Springs. I didn't open any mail with a Bethel Springs address and told my wife not to either. I threw them all away. He chuckled. "I guess I should have read your mail. I told my mother and others to forget Bethel Springs as well. I felt I had been a failure here.

"When I walked in here and saw the crowd, and then realized you all were here for me, I was shocked, then overwhelmed, then filled with gratitude for all the nice things so many of you said about me. Then humbled. And amazed.

"But you know," Paul held out his hand with his thumb and index finger about two inches apart. "This is how much credit I should be getting for all these accomplishments you have spoken about." Then he stretched out his arms as wide as he could. "This is how much credit the Lord and you should get. None of us would be here if it weren't for Jesus dying on the cross for our sins and for the grace He extended to us when He saved us. Maybe I got some activities started here. Maybe I was able to help some people during my short three years here. But you are the ones who kept all these ministries and efforts and relationships going. You are the ones who make all this continue to happen today. You are the ones who are daily taking up your cross and following the Lord in whatever He is leading you to do.

"As the Bible tells us, some plant seeds. That is certainly needed. I'm thankful I was able to plant a few seeds while I was here. But it takes God to make those seeds grow. It takes people to water and nurture those seeds. A lot of work, sometimes over many years. That's what you have done here. I dare say that many of you are involved in these ministries."

He paused and wiped his eyes. "You know, a thought just struck me as I am standing here. "With all these accolades you are giving me, as undeserved as they are, but which I certainly thank you for, I dare say many of you here tonight feel unappreciated for your efforts. You feel people don't love and appreciate you; that no one recognizes all that you are accomplishing. Or maybe you think you are not really doing much to help others. Yet I would also dare say that you are loved and appreciated more and are accomplishing more than you realize. Maybe starting tomorrow all of us should begin expressing to all of you a little more how much we appreciate you." He pointed to the banners behind him. "Maybe we should give each of you a night like this.

"Anyway," Paul paused and chuckled. "Enough of my preaching. Thank you again. I am overwhelmed. Your kind words have helped remove a dark cloud that's been hovering over my head for the last forty-seven years. Thank you and God bless you."

He remained standing on the platform, hesitating, not sure what would happen next. Slowly, one by one, people came up to him, some to greet him for the first time, others to remind him of memories they had of him when he lived there, and how he had influenced them for the good in some way. Several younger people came up and told him stories of what their parents had told them about Pastor Paul. They thanked Paul, telling him that had it not been for his influence in their parents' lives, the chances are they might not be serving the Lord today. Some recounted stories of the impact Laura had on their lives and asked if she was coming to Bethel Springs for the wedding.

After talking with several people, a petite young woman with short red hair came up to him. "Hello," she said, reaching out to shake his hand. "My name is Rachel. Rachel Gannon, your grandson's fiancée."

Paul stared at the young woman. He could see what attracted Trey to her: bright eyes, intelligent face, attractive.

"Nice to meet you, too." Paul returned the handshake. "I'm glad for Trey. And for you. I'm sure he made a wonderful choice. I hope," he added with a slight smile. "I hope it works out."

"Meet my parents," she added without responding to his comment, indicating a man and woman beside her. "My father, Jacob, my mother, Susan." Paul extended his hand. "Nice to meet you both," he said. Jacob, with a tentative smile, shook hands. Susan briefly shook his hand, avoiding his eyes, her lips in a firm line.

The night wore on. Chips, dip, fruit, coffee, tea, lemonade and other snacks and beverages quickly disappeared from the tables. People began leaving, shaking hands with Paul or giving him a hug as they left. Some asked what his plans were for the future, if he was planning to stay in Bethel Springs. He told them his plans were to return to Seattle. Others, including Jeremiah Rice, set up appointments to meet with him the next day or two.

Finally, Paul felt it was time he left. With another thank you to the host, Benjamin Perkins, and a hug or handshake to everyone else who was left, Paul walked out into the night.

The night had cooled some, but humidity still hung in the air. Stars shone overhead in the clear sky above the street lights. He looked around at the familiar city hall and surrounding area. He shook his head. He always pictured his three years in Bethel Springs as a failure. He couldn't believe what people had said tonight. It was an unbelievable night.

As he got in his car he returned to reality. He still needed to find out who was responsible for the fire. That part hadn't changed.

CHAPTER 42

Monday, June twenty-eighth, just a little over two weeks before the wedding, Trey drove up to Paul's motel room in his late model blue BMW. Now that he no longer needed to remain incognito, over the weekend Paul had moved to a Ramada Inn in Bethel Springs.

Getting his cell phone message that he was arriving in town, Paul met him in the lobby. "I've rented another room for you so we can both have privacy," he said. "Let me help you with your bags and I'll show you where it is."

After Trey was settled in the two walked across the street to the Golden Wok for some Chinese food.

"I hear you had quite a reception the other night," commented Trey after they had ordered their dinner. "I was almost as shocked as you were to see all the good that you had done during the three years you were here. From all you have ever told me about Bethel Springs, I was afraid they were going to run you out of town on the rails and tar and feather you at the same time."

They enjoyed dinner and catching up on the details of each other's lives since they had last seen each other a few months earlier. Back in Paul's hotel room where they had taken a dessert they had purchased from Janet's Pie House next door to the hotel, they settled back in two easy chairs.

"After your amazing reception I spoke again to Rachel's dad and mom and asked if they had changed their minds about not allowing the wedding unless you could prove your innocence. Her dad reluctantly agreed that since you were apparently a hometown hero he would allow the wedding. But her mom," Trey took a bite of his French silk pie and shook his head. "She said it would break her heart if her daughter married the grandson of the arsonist who burned down the church where she was baptized and had sang in the choir for so many years. But, she told Rachel, since her dad had agreed she wouldn't stand in the way. So," Trey wiped his mouth on his napkin, "with reservations from both parents, I guess the wedding is on again, no matter what you find.

"Grandpa," Trey leaned in his seat toward his grandfather. "I heard about the fire from my dad and others. But you have never discussed it with me. Since it's just the two of us, and we are talking about it now, what really happened that night? Can you tell me?"

Paul looked at his grandson, sitting there staring intently at him, a frown on his unlined, handsome face. So young, so much like him at that age. An "awesome" future ahead of him, he reflected, to use the common superlative that people used today.

Trey did have an excellent future in front of him if… There were a lot of "if's" in any young person's uncertain future, full of pitfalls and uncertainties. A right or wrong decision, sometimes having to be made instantaneously, could alter a person's life one way or another. That's what had happened to him.

He realized a part of his God-given responsibility was to pass along to his grandson and whoever else he had influence over the life lessons he had learned. Both the good and, sometimes, the bad.

His gaze drifted above Trey's head and out the window, then over to his portfolio lying on the night table by his bed. With a sigh he walked over and picked it up. Returning to his chair he took out his worn notebook and leafed through it until he came to the page he wanted.

"Trey, when I lived here I kept a journal as I have done off and on over the years. I have never let anyone else except your grandmother read it. But I want you to know what happened that night. What really happened. Something I haven't told anyone, except your grandmother. A secret I have kept for forty-seven years."

He sighed again, feeling his eyes filling with tears. "Trey, I'm the one who lit the match that burned down Hope Fellowship Church that night."

"What?" Trey rose half out of his chair, his mouth remaining open. "Grandpa! You burned down the church?"

"Here." Paul thrust the journal in Trey's hands. "Read this. Read what I wrote about that day. Then we'll talk about it. And I hope you will understand what I did and why I did it."

1958   CHAPTER 43

Since Paul was up before the alarm went off at six o'clock, he shut off the windup clock by his bed so it wouldn't wake up Laura and baby Andy. Quietly he made coffee and started frying eggs and bacon for breakfast.

The odor woke Laura. She came to Paul, gave him a hug and a kiss, then disappeared into the bathroom to take a shower and get ready for her eight to five o'clock shift at Bethel Springs Valley Hospital where she worked as a nurse. When Andy woke up and started crying, Paul changed his diaper and fed him his bottle of milk.

After Laura left for work, Paul played some with Andy, then put him in his play pen so he could put the finishing touches on his sermons for the following day.

About noon he fixed himself two Spam sandwiches and a glass of milk for lunch, fed Andy, then took him next door to the hardware store where Judy had said she could watch him at the same time she took care of little Stephanie. He used the afternoon to visit two of his members in the hospital and check in on Rocky who hadn't been feeling well when he took him lunch on Tuesday. He took Rocky a plate of beans and cornbread, two pieces of apple pie that Laura had baked and some homemade chocolate chip cookies.

Laura got home at five-fifteen. After a few minutes rest she fixed some spaghetti and meatballs and boiled four ears of corn for dinner.

Just as it was getting dark the phone rang. Laura picked it up and talked for a few seconds. "It was a neighbor of Judy's," she told Paul when she hung up, "a girl named Anna. She said she's at Judy's house where, as you remember, they moved a few months ago. Anna said Judy has some baby clothes for Andy. She invited me over to Judy's for a few minutes to give me the clothes. She said Judy would have called, but she was busy feeding Stephanie. Mind if I go? They just live three blocks away. I'll take Andy with me in the stroller so you can study."

"Sure." Paul looked up from his book. Andy will enjoy the walk."

A few minutes after Laura left the phone rang again.

Paul barely got his "hello" in when a woman's tearful voice said, "Pastor Paul, please help me."

"Why, what's the matter?" Paul instantly moved into the pastoral mode.

"I need to talk to you." The voice was raspy, hard to understand.

"What do you need? Do I need to call the police? Are you in some kind of trouble?"

"No, nothing like that. But I'm in big trouble. I need some advice like now. You are wise. I know you can help me."

"If it can wait until morning I would be glad to talk to you at our church before the start of Sunday school. Or you can come to church and we can talk afterward."

"No," the voice was emphatic. "I need to talk now."

"Can you come to the church here? Do you have a car? Or can you walk?"

"No. I walked here to Hope Fellowship Church. I'm in the church office that was left unlocked. But the pastor or no one is here. I need to talk to somebody. Can you please come help me? Now?"

"Sure, I'll be over shortly. My wife just left. She should be back in a few minutes. She can come too."

"No, this is personal. Please. I just need you to come alone. Now."

Paul made it a point of not being alone with a woman without his wife, but this woman seemed desperate so he decided to make an exception. "I'll be there as soon as I can," Paul answered and hung up.

Leaving a note for Laura he drove up the hill to the church. He didn't see any cars there and remembered someone had told him Pastor Gannon and his wife had gone to Nashville for a pastors' conference.

Feeling a little uneasy to be going into the other church with the pastor gone and no one else there, but wanting to help the woman who had called, he turned the handle of the door of the pastor's office which was across the driveway from their home. To his surprise, it opened, and he wondered why Pastor Gannon had been so careless as to leave his office door unlocked.

A light was on in the office, which was to the right of the platform, just off the sanctuary. "Hello," he called when he didn't see anyone. "Someone called me and asked me to meet them here. Are you there?" When no one answered he tried the door leading to the platform and sanctuary but found it locked.

He was getting ready to leave, thinking the woman had misunderstood which church she was at or maybe had already left, when the phone rang. He hesitated. It wasn't his office. It wasn't his church. He shouldn't even be there. But, it might be the woman in distress needing help. After letting it ring several times he picked it up. "Hello."

"Hello, Paul Whitfield?" The voice was a man's, barely above a whisper.

"Yes."

"Do you see some matches on the desk?"

Paul looked at the desk and saw a small book of matches. "Yes, here they are."

"Take out a match, light it and drop it in the wastebasket by the door leading into the sanctuary."

"What?"

"You are going to burn the church down. Yes you are. Tonight." The quiet voice turned gruff.

Paul stood there not believing what he was hearing. Finally, he said, "I don't know who you are and what kind of trick you are trying to play on me, but I'm not going to do what you ask. Good-bye." As he slammed the phone down he thought he heard a woman scream.

Paul stood there, uncertain as to what to do next. Was the woman who had called him in trouble? Was she the one who had screamed? What should he do?

The phone rang again. He picked it up. "Hello," he said again.

"We have your wife, Laura, and your cute baby boy," the whispering voice continued. "You are going to light that match and drop it in the wastebasket. That's all you have to do. We have a fuse running from the wastebasket to cans of gasoline in the rest of the church. It will be over in minutes. But you need to light that match NOW." The last word was almost shouted. "If you don't," the whisper was back in place, "if you don't light that match in one minute we're going to cut off your wife's fingers one by one until you do. Your baby will have to watch that."

"What?" Fear shot through Paul like an electric shock. Had someone abducted his wife and child? No, that wasn't possible. "I don't believe you," he said fearfully, hoping the Lord would forgive him for lying. "You don't have my wife. She went to a friend's house. But if you really do have her, let me talk to her."

The voice laughed. "That phone call was a fake to get her out of the house. There's no Anna. Judy doesn't have any baby clothes. She doesn't even know about the phone call. Fooled you both. We picked up your wife in her yellow Capri pants and blue blouse and your little baby boy in his green stroller right after they left your house. Now, your minute is almost up. Have you lit the match yet? We are watching. I don't see any smoke or flames coming from the church."

"Why do you want to burn down this church? What are you up too? Who is this?"

The answer was a terrified woman's scream, followed by loud crying.

"I'm so sorry," said the whisperer. "My partner got in a hurry and just cut off the little finger of your wife's left hand. If you don't light that match in one more minute her ring finger will be gone with that beautiful diamond ring you gave her. Although we might return the ring. The church has to be destroyed," the quiet voice continued. "It's a wicked church preaching lies, deceiving people and telling them to worship false idols, just like you have been telling everyone. It has to be stopped."

Paul numbly envisioned Laura going through this agony. And Andy? What was going through his little mind? Was he safe? All because he wouldn't light a match. The building was only wood and stone. The church could be rebuilt. But his wife's fingers couldn't be replaced.

"Okay," he shouted into the phone. "I'll do it. Just let her go."

With trembling fingers he struck the match and dropped it into the wastebasket. When the loosely wadded up papers lit on fire Paul heard a thud from somewhere inside the sanctuary. Someone was in there.

Numbly, Paul stared mesmerized at the fire burning up the papers, flames shooting several feet in the air, with smoke drifting toward the ceiling.

The sound of a siren at the bottom of the hill woke him out his reverie. I've been set up, he realized with a sinking feeling in the pit of his stomach. The faces of all the enemies he had made in trying to clean up Bethel Springs and all the other people who didn't like what he was doing flashed before him. One of them, or maybe several of them, must have arranged this whole scenario and called the police ahead of time so they would be here to catch him in the act. Had they really cut off his wife's finger? Or was all that an act by a woman imitating his wife?

He needed to get to Laura to find out. Maybe he should wait for the police to come and tell them about the phone call and have them search for Laura. But, he quickly decided, if he did, they would probably arrest him on the spot and might think he had made up the story. No, he had to try and find Laura first and take care of the fire after that.

As he sprinted toward his car he noticed one of the rear tires was flat. No time to change it now. He got in and started it. He realized with a panic that the only road leading away from the church was going down the hill from where he heard the sound of sirens. The police were on their way. They would stop him, no doubt, and maybe arrest him. If that happened he might never find Laura until it was too late.

The power line path. Just last winter he and Laura and other friends had slid down the hill on inner tubes in the snow to the street below that had been blocked off for that purpose. Could he drive his car down there? Just a few weeks earlier the power company had cleared the underbrush under the power lines, as they did every year. He had to try.

Keeping his lights off, he shot across the parking lot toward the first power pole, slowed down by the flat tire. He looked back at the church. No smoke or flames yet. He hoped his fire would go out and all would be okay again.

Turning his attention to his driving, he started down the hill. Dusk had fallen but he could still see what was in front of him. Going to the right of the first power pole he drove off the graveled parking lot and started down the steep hill, feathering his brakes as he went, so he wouldn't go too fast.

The car bounced through small holes and over several rocks, but they didn't stop him. Down he went, turning his steering wheel desperately back and forth to try and drive straight ahead. He knew if his car turned too far to either the left or right he would crash into trees on either side of the cleared path, hit one of the poles, or the car would roll over. The second pole came toward him at a frightening speed. Seeing there was more room on the left side between the pole and trees lining the path he steered in that direction. At the last second he thought he was going to hit it, but let his breath out as he whizzed passed it unscathed with only inches to spare. One more pole and about fifty feet to go. His car by now, even with feathering the brakes, was flying down the hill at a frightening speed, swinging back and forth like a Yo-Yo on a string.

This last pole at the bottom of the hill was coming toward him too fast and right at him. Giving the steering wheel a desperate turn to the right he closed his eyes getting ready for the impact, shot up an incoherent instant prayer, gritted his teeth and jammed his foot on the brake.

He felt his body fly forward as the car shot across the sidewalk at the bottom of the hill and slam into the pavement on the front tires, his chest smacking against the steering wheel.

Then, miraculously, the car rolled to a stop. Paul opened his eyes. The car was sitting on the street at the bottom of the hill. He looked up the hill from where he had come. A miracle. "Thank you, Lord," he breathed out loud and realized his hands were shaking.

Tentatively, he stepped on the gas pedal, wondering if it would still run, or if he had broken an axle or popped another tire or somehow disabled the car in some way. But it started driving down the road, squeaking and vibrating some, slowed by the flat tire, but still driving. Another miracle. "Thank you, Lord," he said again.

Laura. He needed to find Laura. A phone. Maybe the gas station had a phone. He would call his home first. If Laura didn't answer he would call the police.

Driving three blocks to the Shell gas station where he normally bought gas he pulled in beside the pump. Patrick, the high school boy who worked at the gas station during the summers, came out the door of the station in his uniform. "Hello again, Pastor Paul," he said cheerfully. "A fill up? Gas just went up. It's twenty-three cents a gallon now."

"No, not today. But could you help change my tire. It's gone flat. And do you have a phone? I need to make a quick phone call."

Patrick laughed. "No phone. I've asked the boss several times to install one. He keeps saying he will but hasn't done it yet."

Paul helped Patrick change the tire who waved him off when Paul offered to pay him.

As Paul drove off he looked back up at the church silhouetted against the darkening sky. He thought he saw an orange glow through the windows, but hoped he was wrong.

Laura. His dear, sweet wife. Was she okay? Or had they actually kidnapped her and cut off her finger? He had to find out.

Driving faster than he had ever driven through the streets of Bethel Springs, he hurried back home. Stopping in front of the church, he ran into the hall and up the stairs. "Laura," he shouted. "Are you home?"

At the top of the stairs he spotted his wife mixing something in a kettle on the stove. "Laura." He stifled a sob and ran to her giving her such a tight hug it took her breath away. "Laura, you're okay." He looked in the playpen. Andy lay on his back babbling happily.

His wife pushed him away, frowning. "Of course I'm okay. Why, what's wrong?"

Paul walked to the window overlooking the street and pulled back the curtain. He stood as if in a trance. "Sweetheart." He pulled Laura to where she could see could see flames shooting up above the roof of the church on the hill.

"Oh, my goodness. That's terrible." Laura put her hands to her face. "How could that happen? Dear, do you know what happened? Was this on purpose? Who would do such a thing?"

They watched the scene in silence for several minutes. The night sky was lit up for miles around by the towering orange flame that danced high above the stone walls of the church. They were too far away to see the activity around the building, but Paul was sure that the Bethel Springs fire truck was attempting to put out the fire; the police car and ambulance and other first aid vehicles were probably on the scene as well.

Finally, with a sigh, Paul pulled his wife away from the window and looked her in the eyes. "Laura, honey, I'm the one who lit the match that started the fire. It's my fault that old historic church is burning down."

CHAPTER 44

Trey put down the notebook and faced his grandfather. "Wow, Grandpa. I'm so sorry. I never realized what a burden you have carried all these years. Quite a story. Hard to believe." He paused and looked out the window at the stone walls of the old church. "It's not your fault, you know. I hope you don't blame yourself. I...anyone would have done what you did to protect your loved ones."

Trey paused. "So what did you do...after the fire?"

"Well, we watched the fire for hours, both of us in shock. Laura—your grandmother—at first was angry with me for what I had done. But, after I explained the whole story, she settled down and realized what I had done was to protect her and your father." Paul smiled sadly. "Then she got upset with herself for getting mad at me.

"We had quite a night. Your grandmother went to bed and slept some. I tried to go to sleep but eventually got up, went down to the hall, and spent the rest of the night in prayer. I tried to figure out what to tell the authorities, or anyone, if they questioned me as to where I was or what I was doing at the time the fire started.

"I didn't have long to wait. About seven o'clock the next morning—it was Sunday—there was a knock on the door. I was dressed, back upstairs eating breakfast. Police Captain Robert Ferguson was there. I knew him. His teenage son, Brad, was a part of our Saturday morning breakfast meetings. Brad had been involved in some bad stuff before joining the group, but had committed his life to Christ and had really gotten himself straightened out.

"After much agonizing and praying I had decided to tell him the whole story and let the chips fall where they may—trust in the Lord to take care of me.

"But before I could say anything, Ferguson told me the church had burned down and that someone told him he had seen me throw a Molotov cocktail through the window of the church just before the fire started. I guess you know what a Molotov cocktail is."

Trey nodded. "It's a glass bottle filled with gasoline or something flammable with a wick. You light the wick and throw it. When it hits the target the glass shatters and the gasoline starts a fire."

"Correct. I realized that whoever set me up had made up that story. I decided right then and there I wasn't going to let them win by being sent to jail and having my life and my family and ministry ruined, if I could help it.

"I told the police chief that obviously someone was trying to blame me for the fire to get me in trouble. He knew some of the enemies I had made in my outspokenness about gambling and other issues, and what someone had done to the previous pastor's family and now to me and my church. He asked me several questions which I answered honestly. I told him about my schedule that day, the phone call, what time I had gotten to church, and that I had gone into the unlocked church office. When I didn't see anyone I told him I left. I decided not to tell him about the threat to my wife or the match I had lit until I learned more.

"He wasn't sure what to believe. He told me to go ahead and have church but not to leave town, that he would talk to me again."

"Then what happened?"

"Ferguson wrote down what I told him and said he would check out my story and examine the fire in greater detail with Fire Chief Bruce Evans.

"That morning as people came for Sunday school, of course the main topic of conversation was the fire the night before. Sunday school went on as usual, but I could tell there was an undercurrent of something going on. Then, just before the start of church, Stan Manning, one of the recent converts, came up to me and said it was all around town that I was the one who burned down the church. He repeated the Molotov cocktail story.

"So before I started preaching I addressed the issue. I told the congregation exactly what I had told the police captain. I told them it looked like someone hated me so much that they burned down the other church in town and tried to blame me for it. I discarded the message I had prepared and mentioned how Jesus told us we would be persecuted for righteousness' sake. That people would hate us if we followed Jesus. That we all were facing a battle against spiritual darkness in high places. That just as God uses people to preach the gospel, in the same way the devil uses people for his evil causes.

"Some nodded their heads as I talked. Others just stared at me.

"Attendance was way down that night. The next week some people rallied around me, but a few vocal people made a big issue over it. Ferguson called me into the police station and talked to me again a couple of times. He said Patrick at the gas station backed up my story, that I was there changing the tire when I said I was. He said no one had remembered seeing my car go up or down on West Hill road. He added that, according to his calculation, since the Molotov cocktail would have instantly started the fire, I wouldn't have had the time to throw the Molotov cocktail at the church, drive down the hill, and go all the way around to the gas station. Even though the walls were made of stone, with all the wood and other flammable material inside the church, the fire would have been visible almost instantly.

"Ferguson said after the fire they examined the church and found that someone had placed a five-gallon gasoline can in each corner of the church, probably connected with fuses so a fire starting in one place would start those four gas cans on fire. They also checked the church office and didn't find any broken glass from a bottle where I had supposedly thrown the Molotov cocktail.

"Maybe I was wrong, I don't know. But I never did tell anyone except your mother the real story."

Paul smiled. "Maybe this is semantics, I don't know. Maybe I'm drawing too fine a line here. But I think I'm telling the truth—at least this is what I've been telling myself for forty-seven years—that I didn't burn down the church. Yes, I lit the match that started the wastebasket on fire. But that didn't burn down the church. On its own, the fire would have burned up the paper and died out. But whoever was in the church and set the fuses—he or she or they—were the ones who kept the fire going that I started that burned down the church."

Paul paused and looked at his grandson, a twinkle in his eyes. "I don't know if God intervened that day or not. But shortly after I got home that night, it rained a downpour like we sometimes see in this part of the country. A gully washer. Rained almost all night. I checked the next day and all the tire marks I may have left from my wild ride down the trail had been washed away.

"To make a long story short, as you know, there was a lot of bad publicity about the whole matter. Made the newspapers, even into neighboring states. A black eye on the denomination, on all churches. To try and put this incident behind them, my denomination suggested I resign the church and turn in my ministerial credentials. I don't know if it was the right decision or not, but I did.

"So, we left. The saddest day of my life. I had poured three years of my body, soul, and spirit, and blood, sweat and tears into the church and the town. Your grandmother also. Now, it was gone, I thought. Vanished. Lost. They closed down the church a short time later.

"Your grandmother had no relatives in the area. My mother had a sister who lived by Seattle. She had a big house and invited us to move in with her until I could find another job. My mother sold her house in Springfield and moved with us.

"The rest is history. I left the denomination I had started with and joined the one I hold credentials with now. A part of my heart had always been for the mission field. After pastoring a couple of years in a small town near Seattle we became missionaries and went to Bolivia. The rest you know about."

Paul sighed and patted his notebook. "So here we are."

"So again," Trey persisted. "From all the so-called enemies you made, who would have hated you enough to have set this whole thing up?"

Paul sighed again. "During all these years I wondered who the woman was who called your grandmother saying she was Judy's friend. Was it the same woman who called me saying she wanted to meet me at the church, or a second woman? Who was the woman who screamed? Who was in the church when I lit the match? Who was the man who called me when I was in the church office? Who was watching your grandmother to know when she had left so he could call me?

"I don't know. Of course, I always wondered if someone—or several people from that church set me up to kill two birds with one stone: to get insurance money to build a new church, and to get rid of me.

"Or, George Hackett and his bunch weren't too happy with me. His business had dropped way down the last several months since I'd been talking about his sinful place and had started the family weekends at city hall. Zeb's Bar and Grill had also lost business. Banker Milton Passmore and others were losing money on all the property they had purchased thinking the real estate market would skyrocket when gambling was approved. Your grandmother's old boyfriend, Claude, was still around, with his cronies. I'm sure there were others who didn't like how I was trying to clean up the town.

"It could have been any of those. Or all of them. Or maybe someone who was angry with me for another reason, or someone I had legitimately hurt and didn't realize it. I'm sure I made a lot of mistakes here. I was a rookie preacher. Who knows all the things I did wrong. And still do, for that matter."

He looked over at his grandson. "Do you still want me to keep looking for who did it?"

Trey turned from the window and looked at Paul. "I don't know, Grandpa. I'm confused right now. The wedding is back on. There is still a cloud over our heads, but from the sounds of things I don't know if it will ever be resolved."

The next several days Trey spent most of his time with Rachel and her family preparing for the wedding.

Paul met with old friends and reminisced about the past, all the time doing all he could to uncover, with no success, who was responsible for the fire.

CHAPTER 45

Early one afternoon a late model mauve Toyota Taurus pulled into the hotel where Paul and his grandson were staying. A middle-aged couple got out followed by an older woman. Paul and Trey had been waiting in the lobby and walked out to the car when they saw it pull up.

Paul greeted the older woman with a hug and a kiss. "Sweetheart," he said, "good to see you again." He stepped back and surveyed his wife of nearly fifty years. Still beautiful, slim and ramrod straight after all this time. Still the love of his life. Taking that verse from Proverbs that gray hair is a crown of splendor, she had refused to dye her hair that shone white on her head like new-fallen snow. "I see a month back in Bolivia working as the nurse in the family camps with your daughter-in-law has done you good. You are as gorgeous as ever." He patted his stomach. "But with you not feeding me I think I lost ten pounds."

She kissed him again. "Losing weight will do you good. Maybe I should take off more often," she teased.

Paul turned to the middle-aged man, a younger, taller version of himself, and gave him a hug. "Good to see you again, son. Glad you could make it to your son's wedding."

"I'm glad there will be a wedding," he added. "And Maggie," he turned to the woman beside him who had a warm, friendly face and sparkling green eyes behind her steel-framed glasses, "my favorite daughter-in-law, good to see you too."

With more hugs and greetings, the family took their luggage, went into the hotel and got their rooms.

Paul led Laura into his hotel room. "I missed you," he said, and gave her another hug and kiss. "I told you the story on the phone, but now we can talk in person. An amazing reception they gave me here." He shook his head. "All these years I thought everything we had accomplished had crashed and burned. But," he shrugged, "amazingly it didn't."

Laura smiled. "I knew the good you had done would last. I tried to tell you that, but you wouldn't believe me. Now I'm glad you got to see it. Any closer to finding out who was responsible for starting the fire?"

Paul shook his head. "I've asked around. No clues yet." He smiled. "Maybe I should ask the Hardy Boys or Nancy Drew.

"Rehearsal dinner is tonight," he continued. "Wedding tomorrow. Trey said the parents are okay with the wedding now. But he also added this leaves a cloud over our heads. So," Paul shrugged, "I'm still trying to pursue who was behind it to clear my name and give Rachel's family peace of mind.

Which, really, I'm afraid is a longshot after all these years."

Their discussion was interrupted by a knock on their hotel door. Paul opened the door and stepped back in surprise. His mind went back fifty years to the stone library in the center of town and the most beautiful girl he had ever seen. "Patsy." He stared at her.

"Paul," she answered with a laugh. "Don't be so shocked. Good to see you again." Same smile with a few wrinkles added. Same laugh that reminded him of the ringing of chimes. Same elegantly style hair piled high on her head, now white as snow.

She gave Paul a hug. "Laura," without an invitation she walked passed Paul and gave Laura a hug. "Heard you were in town." She turned back to Paul. "I just got home last night from a trip to Alaska. Heard about you being back in town and your reception. Amazing."

Laura pointed to a black leather chair by the window. "If you have time why don't we visit for a few minutes." She turned to Paul. "How about if you order some sodas from room service. What do you all want to drink?"

The order made, Patsy sat back in her seat and surveyed Paul and Laura. "Who would have thought that we would meet fifty years later. You both long-time missionaries. Paul, you a hero." She laughed again, then turned somber. "Me, a rich widow."

She adjusted her hair and cleared her throat. "To catch you up briefly, I moved to St. Louis to attend college, which you already know. During my first year in college Michael often came to see me and our romance picked up again. Finally, he moved to St. Louis to live near me. He started going to church with me and found faith in Christ that I could tell was real. We got married a few months after that. His Champ Burger restaurants took off big, so my second year I dropped out of college to help him.

"Life was wonderful. We bought a mansion on Table Rock Lake, traveled around the country setting up restaurants. Then we began going around the world to set up restaurants overseas. It was a grand life. Good times. Wonderful memories. Michael became a wonderful Christian and husband and father."

She sighed. "Five years ago he had a heart attack. He survived his first, but didn't the next one a few weeks later. But," she brightened, "we had over forty years of a great marriage. We have three children: Michael Junior, Franklin and Cindy. They are wonderful children, all married, and all working for the company. They gave us eleven grandchildren. We now have over eight hundred restaurants in the United States and a couple hundred overseas. I'm a millionaire several times over. I don't even know how much money I have. The kids now run the company and all I do is spend the money.

"Paul, you would be interested to know that Lamar, my brother, finally decided to do something with his life. He went to college and become a veterinarian. He's had a practice for several years in Kansas City. He never married, but he's living for the Lord and doing well.

"After Michael passed, since my family still owned the home I was raised in, I moved back there. I live there now with my two dogs and Yolanda my maid."

Patsy sat back in her seat, folding her hands in her lap. "That's my story in a nutshell. What have you two been doing since you left Bethel Springs?"

An hour later Patsy left. Laura invited her to the rehearsal dinner that night and Patsy invited Laura to come to her home after the dinner for a cup of tea.

It was nearly nine o'clock when Paul walked out of the rehearsal dinner at city hall into the warm evening air that was just starting to cool down. The dinner had gone well. Filet mignon and baked potato for the main course, with cheese cake topped with strawberries for dessert. The bride and groom had been toasted several times. A PowerPoint presentation had been displayed of their growing up years. Paul tried to be sociable with Rachel's parents who smiled and responded politely but still let him know in unspoken ways they were not happy with him.

Laura had left earlier with Patsy with a promise to be back at the hotel before midnight. Most everyone else had already left by the time Paul got in his car. Putting on his seatbelt he started the engine, then heard a movement behind him and saw the reflection of a face emerge in his rear view mirror. At the same time he felt a sharp object pressed into his ribs between the seats.

"Paul Whitfield?" a female voice said.

Paul swallowed and took a deep breath. What was going on? Was this a joke by someone in the wedding party? Or real? He had heard about carjackings but never thought it would happen to him. Why hadn't he locked his car? Should he get out and run? Or honk the horn and yell for help? But the gun stuck in his back, if it was a gun, might result in his getting shot if he tried any of those things. What should he do? Finally he decided to speak up. "Who are you? What do you want?" His voice sounded shaky, even to him.

"I have a pistol in your back. Unless you want to get shot you won't ask any questions and do as I say." The female voice sounded raspy, like a smoker. "Now, don't roll down your window and yell for help or honk your horn or make any signs to anyone. If you do, I will shoot you, I really will. I will. Now just drive and follow my directions. And don't touch your cell phone if you have one."

Without another word, suddenly feeling lightheaded, Paul backed out of his parking spot. Apparently this was not a carjacking. But what did this person want? "Drive out of the parking lot and go south," the voice said.

As he turned onto the highway and increased his speed, he thought about slamming on his brakes and jumping out of the car, but decided the risk wasn't worth it. He would wait and see what this person wanted.

"Drive to the Hope Fellowship Church," the voice said. "The new one. Not the one you burned down."

An increased jab of fear stopped his breathing for a few moments. Did this have anything to do with that incident in this town that happened almost fifty years ago? "Why should I do that?"

"Just drive. When you get there we'll talk."

Without further comment, with his heart beating wildly, all of his senses alert, trying to figure out how to avoid whatever he thought may be coming, he slowly made his way the three or four miles to the now-familiar church he had driven by several times the last day or two. The parking lot was well lit from floodlights surrounding the area. The church was illuminated with several lights placed in strategic spots in the foliage surrounding the building, except for the front of the church that was shrouded in darkness.

"Drive to the front door of the church and park," commanded the voice behind him.

What was that saying: Dejá vu' all over again? "What do you want me to do?" he asked, fearing he already knew what the woman had in mind.

"The same thing you did fifty years ago. Burn down the Hope Fellowship Church to protect someone you love."

"You can't be serious?" Paul still wondered if this was some sort of cruel joke someone was playing on him.

Paul stopped the car by the darkened front door.

"Get out and stand by the door," the woman said. "We have knocked out the lights so no one can see you. It's too dark."

Paul did as instructed, walking to within a few feet of the double glass doors at the front of the church. Tall bushes lined both sides of the front door against the wall with flowers bordering the sidewalk. In the darkness he couldn't see the color of the flowers.

The woman got out of the back seat and approached Paul, a pistol in her right hand. She then reached into a bag she was holding and took out a bottle which she extended toward Paul. It appeared to be a glass bottle filled with a liquid that smelled like gasoline. A cork on the bottle held a piece of cloth in place. "Take this," she commanded. "A Molotov cocktail. Like the one we told everyone you used last time."

With trembling fingers Paul reached out and took the bottle. "Now take this," the woman said, reaching into her jacket and handing Paul a cigarette lighter, which Paul did with his other hand.

"Now, light the bottle, throw it through the glass door and burn down this church. This time I will make sure you get caught so you will end up in jail, like was supposed to have happened fifty years ago."

Paul glanced over at the highway about fifty feet to his right. He hoped someone in one of the cars passing by would see what was going on and call the police. But the shrubbery and darkness provided an almost perfect hiding place. He turned back to the woman. "Why do you want me to do this? After fifty years. You're crazy."

"Maybe so. But you killed my father," the woman said simply. "Now you are going to pay." Dressed in jeans, a dark shirt, and a shapeless jacket with a hoodie that covered her hair and hid part of her face, the woman holding the pistol appeared to be older, near his age.

"I killed your father? What do you mean?" As Paul drove up here he envisioned several reasons why someone might want to do him harm, but not for this reason.

"Milton Passmore? Remember him from when you lived here before?"

"Yes, of course. The banker." She was standing about six feet away from him in front of the glass door leading into the foyer of the church. As his eyes got more accustomed to the darkness he began to make out some of her features. She appeared to be in her sixties, a leathery face lined by hard living. Rather short, slight of build. Her hand holding the pistol trembled slightly.

"Milton Passmore was my father. He...we...had it all figured out. George Hackett at Hackett House and his family and cronies were making money hand over fist with their gambling house. Dad figured if one could do it we all could, so he and Hackett led the way to get gambling made legal in town. Figuring it would happen, Dad started buying up land around here where he thought the gambling casino, opera house, bathhouses and hotels would be built. He—we—would make a bundle of money selling or leasing that land.

"But you." She spat out the word. "Then you came along with your holier-than-thou preaching. You harassed and harangued everyone who didn't agree with you. Preaching, newspaper articles, inciting the community. Your church people stood in front of Hackett House on weekends with your despicable signs and slogans. You turned people against gambling at Hackett House and everywhere else. People voted it down. We wanted it back on the ballot again, but we had to get rid of you first.

"Dad had hired two crooks from Springfield. They were the ones who scared your previous pastor away by dusting up his little boy. Dad thought it would work with you too. So he had them come back from time to time. One time they punched a hole in your tire and almost ran you down when you went to change it. They blew up your deacon's car in front of the church on New Year's. They almost got you on your honeymoon with cutting your brake lines." She shook her head. "But you were always lucky and didn't scare easily.

"Then Dad came up with the idea he was sure would work. Getting you to burn down the other church in town. Make you look like the bad guy. Then the townspeople would run you out of town. Dad talked to George Hackett who was all for it. He talked to the pastor from the other church. Reverend Gannon wanted you gone, too, and wanted to rebuild the church bigger and in a better location. They worked it out. Gannon and his wife left town so they wouldn't be blamed, then let us in the church where Dad set up the cans of gasoline and fuses.

"That night, after it was all set up, Jake, who worked for Hackett, watched your home and waited until your precious wife, Laura, left with your baby. Then he called me and Dad from the phone booth on the square and told us she had gone. "By the way, I'm the one who called Laura about the baby clothes to get her out of the house. And I called you pretending to be a lady in distress. You fell for my act and came to the church. George Hackett's son, Norman, and I were across the driveway in the church parsonage. When we saw you were in the church he called the cops and told them someone was trying to burn down the church. Then Norman called you and said we had kidnapped your wife and would cut off her fingers if you didn't burn down the church. I'm sure you remember. I screamed and cried and pretended I was her." The woman laughed in her raspy voice. "Pretty good, wasn't I? Convinced you, at least.

"So, like a coward, or maybe because you loved your precious wife and kid so much, you started the trash can on fire, as Norman asked you to. While you were starting the fire I went outside and let the air out of your back tire so you couldn't get back down the hill before the cops came. They would catch you with your car in front of a burning church, or at least partway down the hill. Arsonist. Jail time. Disgrace. With you gone, we could get back to the business of getting the voters to approve bringing gambling to town.

"But that didn't work. The papers in the trash can burned but didn't light the fuse that Dad had set running from the trash can in the office to the cans of gasoline in the sanctuary. So Dad had to light the fuses himself, then hightail out of the church before the cops came. Carl, another employee of Hackett's who was in on it, had dropped us off and left with the car, so none of our cars would be around when the cops showed up. After the fire started we ran in the woods until the cops, firemen and half the town showed up. Then we came out and blended with the crowd.

"But somehow you got away when we were hiding in the woods, even with the flat tire. Apparently the cops or no one else saw you drive away. When you weren't arrested we started the rumor that someone had seen you start the fire with a Molotov cocktail. That wasn't enough to get you arrested, but at least it got you out of town."

"Sarah." Paul interrupted the monologue and pointed his finger at the woman. "You're Sarah, Milton Passmore's daughter, the cashier at the bank."

"That's right."

"But what does all this have to do with killing your father? You got me out of town." Paul pointed to the church and then her gun. "Why this, now? After fifty years?"

"Because, like I said, you killed Dad."

"How? What do you mean? I didn't kill your father. He was fine when I left town."

"That family weekend stunt you started at city hall where half the town started showing up, and those crying women protesting at Hackett House finally worked. About a year after you left, Hackett House shut down and people quit talking about gambling. When the gambling issue was voted down the second time, the cronies who wanted to bring gambling to Bethel Springs left town and went elsewhere. Dad realized he had spent a fortune on land that was almost worthless. He was almost bankrupt with no hopes of getting any of his investments back. He got fired as bank president because of all the other people he had persuaded to also invest in land. The stress finally got to Dad, and he had a stroke a few months later that killed him. It was your fault."

"So this, you are taking this out on me because you blame me for the death of your father?"

"That, and you being welcomed back as a town hero. You were supposed to be in jail for burning down the church. We had it figured out so well. I don't know what we did wrong. But you are not a hero. You have to pay for what you did." She spat on the ground. "Over these years, every time I had thought about you, I got angry. I thought I was getting over it the last few years. But when you came back and everyone in town started gushing about you, it was more than I could take." She spat on the ground again. "So Norman and I, we got married a few years after that, came up with this little scheme. We followed you around town the last few days. We saw your precious wife was back. Why not try the same thing again, we decided. Except this time make it for real."

"What do you mean for real?"

"Take a look." Keeping the pistol pointed at Paul she took out her cell phone and adjusted the contents of the screen with her thumb. Then she showed it to Paul and he felt his whole body turn cold. It was a picture of Laura and Patsy, dressed as he had seen them at the dinner, walking into Patsy's home. Then the woman showed Paul another photo of a man standing in front of the same house holding a similar bottle and cigarette lighter as Paul had.

"Your choice," the woman said. "You light this bottle and throw it all the way through the glass door. That should burn down this wooden church all the way to the ground. No stone walls this time. Burn it all down. Do that, or I will call Norman and tell him to throw his Molotov cocktail into your old girlfriend's house. She and your precious wife might get away or might not. But even if they survive, that grand old house will burn down with all that precious stuff your old girlfriend got from around the world. And it will be your fault."

Paul shook his head in disbelief. "How do you think you can get away with this? Your husband at Patsy's house. You here. People are driving by. Someone will find out you're responsible. You will be the ones that end up in jail."

"No, we both have rental cars from another state. We've changed the license plates. Right now a friend of mine is letting the air out of two of your car tires. This time you won't get away. We will make sure of that.

"Now, enough chit-chat." She pointed toward the Molotov cocktail. "Light the wick and throw the bottle through the glass door into the church. You have one minute. If you don't, I'll call Norman and tell him to throw his bottle into your old girlfriend's house."

Paul held the Molotov cocktail in one hand and the cigarette lighter in the other hand. "This is crazy. You will never get away with this. Don't you see what you've done? You've let your anger that you've held for fifty years get the best of you. Look," Paul turned on his pastoral charm. "Why don't we sit down and talk about it. I realize I did criticize those who wanted to bring gambling to town. And, I'm so sorry that affected your dad's finances and job. I'm so sorry he had his stroke and died. But you've got to learn to forgive or it may affect your health...or your whole life." He spread his hands to include her and the church. "Like what is about to happen now."

"Shut up." The woman's hand shook holding the pistol. "Shut up," she said again, almost in a scream. Paul saw her face screwing up in anger. "Light the wick. You have thirty seconds. If you don't, I'll shoot you and light it myself. I will. I really will."

Paul suddenly felt fear almost choke the breath out of him. He could see this woman meant what she said.

A noise came from behind a bush. "Aren't cell phones wonderful?" Trey walked toward them holding a small instrument in his hand. "Back at city hall I noticed Grandpa getting in his car. Then I saw someone's head pop up from the back seat. Thinking that was strange I followed him." He came and stood beside his grandfather and tapped his cell phone. "When I got here I called 911 and turned on the video. Every word you said and your image is being recorded. I'm sure by now the cops are on their way here and to Patsy's house."

"Why you…" The woman screamed out the words and raised her pistol.

"Grandpa," screamed Trey. As a shot rang out, he pushed Paul to the ground.

CHAPTER 46

Patsy opened the front door of her home, held it open for Laura, went in and locked it behind her. Yolanda hurried in from the kitchen and took Patsy's jacket. "Tea, Miss Patsy?" she asked as she hung it up on the coatrack by the front door. She looked over at Laura. "For your friend, too?"

"Yolanda, this is Laura, an old friend. Laura, this is Yolanda. Please make that two teas, and any pastries you may have."

"Have a seat anywhere." Patsy swept her arm around her enormous living room. Two couches, two recliners, four easy chairs, a large coffee table. The largest screen television Laura had ever seen was attached to the wall above the huge stone fireplace.

Sitting on one of the couches Laura sank down in the softness and relaxed. "Long day," she said with a sigh and laid her head back after a moment. Then she sat back up. "But a good day. I'm glad the flight worked out so our son, his wife and I were able to get back here in time for the wedding. And," she added, "I'm glad there will be a wedding. It will be a gorgeous wedding, I'm sure. Beautiful bride, handsome groom."

"Trey made the right choice," added Patsy, "I've known Rachel ever since I came back five years ago. She's a real peach. Intelligent, hard-working, loves the Lord."

They talked for several more minutes, enjoying the tea and pastries and reminiscing about the past years.

Finally, when there was a pause, Laura spoke up hesitantly. "Patsy?"

"Yes."

"I've got to ask. I hope this won't embarrass you, but is this the fireplace that you and my husband slept in front of the night he showed you my engagement ring?"

"What?" Patsy was so startled her hand shook and a few drops of tea spilled on her blouse.

"I'm sorry. Maybe I shouldn't have asked you. But," Laura paused and her eyes took on a twinkle, "when you've been married to someone for almost fifty years you don't have many secrets. One day, after we'd been married a few years, he told me about that snowy night you spent together."

Patsy, her composure back in place, put down her tea and chuckled. "Is that all he told you? Did he tell you anything else?"

"Yes." Laura smiled back. "Now that the years have passed I'm sure it doesn't seem that traumatic now, but I'm sure it did then." She held up her left hand. "He said he showed you my engagement ring. At first you thought it was for you. That embarrassed him so much. He told me as soon as he said it he realized it had come out wrong."

Patsy took a bite of cookie. "I'm glad that happened," she said solemnly. "That night solidified in my mind and, I think, in his mind that we were going in different directions and that he had made the right choice. And Laura," Patsy leaned over and placed her hand on Laura's arm, "that night I saw how much of a gentleman your husband is. He could have tried to take advantage of me. Maybe he would have succeeded, I don't know. But he went out of his way to let me know his intentions were proper. And when Michael came he gave us such a sweet talk about why he would never take advantage of any situation like that. I heard Michael pass down similar advice to our children. So it must have made an impression on him, too."

Suddenly Patsy noticed red and blue flashing lights outside of her front window. Then more lights and the sounds of cars and voices. Before she could react the doorbell rang. Not waiting for her maid she hurried to the door. Officer Steve Blanchard, a tall, good-looking young man she had seen around town, stood respectfully back, his hat in hand. "Miss Patsy," he began. He pointed to one of the two patrol cars where another officer was pushing a handcuffed man into the back seat. "A little trouble, but all taken care of."

"What happened?"

"We had a report that someone wanted to burn down your home, so we hurried over. Caught him just in time before he did anything. I think it's Norman Hackett. Ma'am, someone said Laura Whitfield came home with you. You might want to tell her that I just heard on the police radio a Paul Whitfield had been shot and was being taken to Valley Hospital. If she's here I can take her there now if she wants me to."

By this time Laura was at the door and heard the officer's last comment. Without another word, Laura and Patsy hurried into the back seat of the patrol car as it sped off, siren blaring, to Bethel Springs Valley Hospital

When they arrived Laura jumped out of the patrol car and without taking time to thank Officer Steve for the ride, she and Patsy rushed through the revolving door. "Where's Paul Whitfield?" Laura shouted at the receptionist, choking back a sob.

Wilma Clay momentarily took the telephone away from her ear and pointed to her right. "He's in ER down to the right."

Hurrying down the hall toward the emergency room they were met by a policeman. "No one is allowed past here, ma'am."

"Benny." Patsy tried to push him aside. "This is Paul Whitfield's wife. I'm his friend. We need to see him. We heard he was shot. Is he still alive? Is he dead?" She couldn't hold back the tears.

"Please be seated ladies," the officer responded calmly, gently leading them to a row of padded chairs against the wall. "Please relax. I'll go check and get back with you. But…please," he held out his hands palms out toward her, "please stay seated. Okay?"

Wordlessly, the women nodded.

Minutes passed. Doctors and nurses walked by and briefly greeted them but offered no information. Patsy got out her cell phone and checked the local news to see if the media had picked up anything about the shooting. Nothing. Laura picked up a People magazine. The celebrities smiling at her in their expensive outfits did nothing to calm her fears. Did Paul being shot have anything to do with Norman Hackett trying to burn down Patsy's house? Were the two incidents connected with the burning down of the stone church nearly fifty years ago? Had Paul's return to Bethel Springs brought back the nightmare?

As Laura was brooding over these thoughts, she glanced up to see Rachel Gannon hurrying down the hallway toward her followed by her parents. Laura and Patsy stood as they approached. Laura spoke up: "Paul's been shot. I guess you know that and that's why you came. Have you heard how he's doing?"

"What?" Rachel's face was red a puffy. "Has Paul been shot too?"

"What do you mean?"

"We got a call from my friend Angela who happened to be in the hospital when they brought Trey in. She recognized him and asked what happened. They told her some woman had shot him. He's in ER now. We rushed down to see how he was."

"My goodness." Laura's eyes filled with tears again. "How awful that Paul and Trey were both shot. And right before your wedding." She gave Rachel a hug. "I'm so sorry."

Just then Officer Benny returned. Rachel ran up to him. "Can I see Trey? How is he? I heard his grandfather was shot, too. How is he doing? Can we see them?"

The policeman shook his head. "What are you talking about?" He surveyed the women and shook his head. "Just one Paul Whitfield was shot. Who's Trey? There's no record of a Trey being shot. Only Paul Whitfield."

Laura and Rachel stared at each other. Wordlessly their eyes held the question: Which one was shot?

"Did you see the man who was brought in?" asked Laura. "Was he young with dark hair? Or older, with white hair?"

"Let me check. Why don't you all sit down. I'll try to sort this out." Officer Benny disappeared through the ER doors.

Laura sat by Rachel and clutched her hand. Rachel's parents sat across the hall from them offering comforting words to both of them.

A few minutes later the ER doors opened and Paul Whitfield stepped out.

"Paul." Laura was up in an instant and in his arms. Then she stepped back. "Where were you shot?"

"I'm fine. I'm fine." He smiled. "It wasn't me." Then he walked over to Rachel. "Trey was shot in the left shoulder. He's being operated on now, but Dr. Beck assured me he'll be fine soon."

"Oh, what a relief." Rachel stood and gave Paul a hug. Then she hugged her parents and Laura.

After a moment Paul spoke up again: "I hear there was a misunderstanding." He gave a brief smile. "My name is Paul Whitfield. Trey's official name is Paul Whitfield the third. We're both Paul Whitfield." He turned to Laura. "I apologize for the anxiety that may have caused you. But, Rachel," he said looking at her, "your man is a hero. When Sarah Passmore pointed her gun at me and pulled the trigger, Trey pushed me away from where the gun was aimed. Instead of the bullet hitting me in the chest as she intended, it caught him in his shoulder. He saved me from being shot and probably saved my life."

The six of them sat in the hallway by the ER doors. Rachel sat by her parents. Paul took her place, sitting by Laura. Quietly Laura took his hand and smiled at him, her tears drying on her face. Patsy sat by Laura taking her other hand.

For what seemed like hours later Dr. Beck emerged through the doors, smiling. He turned to Rachel. "Your young man is going to be okay. His arm will be in a sling, but he should be fit as a fiddle for your wedding."

CHAPTER 47

The wedding was beautiful. Paul and Paul junior—grandfather and father—conducted the ceremony. Paul "Trey" Andrew Whitfield the third kissed his bride, and he and Rachel marched back down the aisle on their way to a new life together.

After the reception held in the gymnasium of the New Hope Fellowship church, with lots of pictures and videos taken, the bride and groom, with his left arm in a sling, rode off together in Trey's BMW to spend the first night of their honeymoon at the Chateau on the Lake in Branson, then on to Paris, France, for a week with plans to tour the Louvre, have dinner in the Eiffel Tower, and spend a night in one of their famous castles.

Andrew and Maggie left immediately after the reception and drove back to Springfield in their rental car so they could catch an early morning flight back to Bolivia. They didn't want to miss the Bible school graduation in Cochabamba, where Andrew was the director.

Paul and Laura were getting ready to leave when Jacob and Susan Gannon approached them. They were dressed as the perfect conventional parents of the bride: the father in a black tuxedo, the mother in a lacy pink gown with matching shoes and purse. "Wonderful wedding," spoke up Paul to break the ice.

"Beautiful bride. Your daughter is gorgeous," added Laura. "We are so proud of Trey. He chose a wonderful woman for his wife."

The Gannons smiled back. "Thank you," said Jacob. "We are proud of our daughter, too. We too think she made a wise choice. And," he added, suddenly looking uncomfortable, "I need to make an apology. I really did think for all these years that you burned down Dad's church out of spite. I was angry with you." He laid his hand on his wife's shoulder. "Susan was angry too, and couldn't believe our only daughter had chosen to marry the grandson of an arsonist." He smiled. "But Trey explained everything. How you were tricked into lighting the match. And, I watched the video Trey made of Sarah Passmore last night in front of the church. She said the fire you set in the trash can went out and that her dad had to start another fire, the actual fire that did burn down the church. So the match you lit didn't have anything to do with burning down the church."

He looked at Paul. "Will you forgive me?"

"Of course." Paul reached over and gave Jacob a hug.

"Please forgive me, too." Susan's eyes were full of tears. "I realize now this anger I've had toward you has hurt me more than you. And it was all for nothing. I've been such an idiot."

Paul enveloped her in another hug. "I understand. You're forgiven too."

Laura spoke up. "It's late. We're all tired. How about if we meet for lunch somewhere tomorrow so we can get better acquainted?"

"Sounds good to me," Jacob agreed. "How about if we pick you up at your hotel around noon?"

Paul recognized the couple who approached them next. "Thad, Kate." He gave each one a hug. "Glad you could make it." Paul had heard some of the details over the years, that after graduation Kate had gone to Maine with her friends and started a church in that state. Classmate Thad Baker visited her on several occasions and finally decided to join them in their endeavors. Shortly after that Thad and Kate had gotten married. "Three wonderful children and eight grandchildren," Kate announced proudly. "All serving the Lord: two of our children and their spouses in the ministry. Our daughter teaches school in New York." She and Thad discussed several of their classmates and what they had done over the years and where they were now. "You may remember Mary Brunner, another one of our classmates," Kate added with a glint of humor in her eyes. "She married Charles Brubaker, another missionary kid from Latin America. They served as missionaries in Uruguay for many years. I think they retired a couple of years ago."

They talked for several more minutes and set up a time to meet the following day.

As soon as Thad and Kate walked away, another older man slowly approached them, walking with a cane. He wore alligator skin cowboy boots, a gray, western tailored suit with a silver belt buckle sporting a black embossed skull and crossbones. Almost bald, the little hair he had left was formed into a short pony tail. "You probably don't recognize me," he said in a voice that brought sudden memories back to Paul, "but I'm sure you remember me." He gave Paul a tentative smile, then looked at Laura quickly, then back to Paul.

He reached out and shook Paul's hand with a firm handshake. "Claude Ragsdale." He laughed without humor and ducked his head down, suddenly embarrassed. "I gave you a hard time back when you lived here. But the words you told me that night when you were sitting on the ground after I had whacked you went round and round in my mind for several years." He looked up at Paul. "Finally, I quit grousing at you and feeling sorry for myself. About the time you left I went to college. I realized the death of James Dean wasn't God's fault and even started going to church. Ended up in Viet Nam during the war. Got a couple of medals. When I got out I started a security firm, believe it or not, protecting homes and businesses and such in Springfield. Retired just four years ago."

He paused and cleared his throat. "Paul, what I said and did to you face to face and what I did behind your back has haunted me over the years. I'm so sorry."

He turned to Laura and forced himself to look at her. "I didn't treat you very well either back in the day. I'm sorry, especially for that one night. The hit and run when I was drunk, and for not stopping to help like you wanted me to do." He cleared his throat and looked away. "Finally, after several years of a guilty conscience and the Lord prodding me, I confessed to running down that poor man. Served some time in jail. But I'm glad I confessed." He looked back at Laura and then Paul. "I don't deserve the forgiveness of either one of you, but I just want to apologize and say I'm sorry. I'm glad you returned so I could do it in person."

He started to turn away when Paul grabbed his arm. "Claude. That was a long time ago. A lot of water has gone under the bridge. We have all matured since then, and the Lord has been good to all of us." He gave Claude a hug. "I forgive you, my friend. I'm glad we are able to clear the air."

Laura reached over and gave him another hug. With tears trickling down her face she said, "I forgive you too, Claude."

They stood for a moment facing each other, tears in all of their eyes.

"Oh, one more thing." Claude took a handkerchief out of his back pocket and wiped his face. "I hope you can forgive me for this too. I got so angry at you one night I waited until you left and came in and trashed the church and your apartment. I didn't see much of anything of value until I looked under your bed and saw your chess sets. I took those, not because I liked chess, but out of spite." He smiled again without humor. "I kept them stored away in my attic all these years. When I heard you were in town I dusted off your old suitcase they were in, and took it to your hotel, leaving a note to give it to you. They're all safe and sound, I assure you."

Later that night, back at the hotel room, Paul opened the suitcase he had gotten from the front desk. Quickly he spread the contents out on his bed and set up all thirteen sets, carefully examining the pieces. "All here and in good shape," he reported happily to Laura. "You know," he added, "we could sell one or two of these sets and take a trip around the world."

"Oh, no." Laura shook her head. "I know you're just joking, but we are keeping these to pass along to Trey and his children. They can sell them if they want to, but these are now valuable family heirlooms that have become another family miracle we can pass down."

The next morning while they were having breakfast, Paul got a call on his cell phone. "Good morning," said the caller. "I hope I didn't wake you up."

"No, we're up and at 'em."

"This is Benjamin Perkins. You may remember me from the other night at city hall. I'm the pastor of the Church of the Open Door. Got your phone number from Trey. Would you and your wife have time today to meet me at the church? We want to give you a tour. This is really the church you pastored, under a different name. And, as we mentioned, it's on the land given to the church by Rocky, that man you won to the Lord."

"Sure, what time?"

As Paul and Laura drove into the parking lot of the Church of the Open Door, Paul couldn't help but contrast the storefront church he pastored fifty years ago with this attractive structure. On the right was an asphalt covered parking lot with yellow lines designating the parking spots with tall light poles interspersed that, no doubt, lit up the area at night. In front of them stood an attractive brick-fronted sanctuary with a white steeple. Adjoining the sanctuary were other facilities that stretched out in both directions.

Paul opened Laura's car door and as they walked into the foyer they were met by Pastor Ben, dressed in jeans and a T-shirt displaying the name of his church.

"Thank you for coming," he said. Paul judged him to be in his early thirties, medium height, medium build, clean shaven face, casual, friendly, curly dark hair. "Before we talk, let me give you a brief tour of the facilities. We built what is now the youth center as the sanctuary about ten years ago, then we built the present sanctuary three years ago." A people person, Paul decided as he surveyed the warm smile on the pastor's face and the sparkle in his eyes as he led them through the sanctuary, gymnasium, youth chapel, classrooms, kitchen and the other rooms in the church.

When they finished the tour they ended up in Pastor Ben's office to the right of the sanctuary. "We have ten acres," he added, as he directed Paul and Laura to a tan colored leather couch. He sat in a padded chair across from them. "This was Rocky's land. Most of it is still in woods, but we have plans eventually to build a retirement center where senior citizens can purchase or rent apartment units. And a few other plans are in the works.

"Anyway, enough chit chat." Pastor Ben settled back in his chair and surveyed the couple in front of him. "I'm sure these past few days have been quite eventful for you." He smiled. "Paul, of course I've heard about you over the years. The fire and all. But I never realized the impact you—and you too, Laura—had on the community and church. I'm impressed as to how much you were able to accomplish in such a short time.

"A few weeks ago I preached a series of sermons on the Bethel in the Bible, which had quite a history over the centuries. As you know, that's where Jacob, when fleeing from his family he had deceived, had his dream of the stairway up to heaven where God told him that he and his descendants would inherit the land. Then you know how several centuries later King Jeroboam erected a temple, set up an image of a golden calf, and established a false religion. A man of God came and tried to stop him, but ended up getting eaten by a lion."

Here Pastor Ben stopped and chuckled. "You were the man of God way back then. You may have been run out of town, but at least you weren't eaten by a lion. But, seriously, because of your efforts and the efforts of those you encouraged, gambling never did come to Bethel Springs. They voted on it two or three times, and it was always defeated, so the proponents of gambling moved on. There is now gambling in St. Louis, Kansas City, Oklahoma, and other places. But not in Bethel Springs. We have you to thank for that."

He paused and cleared his throat. "But that's not why I called you here. For the past year or two the staff and I have considered adding another staff member, a seniors pastor—someone to care for our senior citizens. We have about twenty or twenty five seniors. Some of them, no doubt, attended here when you pastored here. I think one or two of them were saved under your ministry.

"Anyway, we need someone who will teach a seniors Sunday school class, maybe start a small group. Maybe once a week or so take the men, or maybe the women, too, to Martha's Café for breakfast, or some other restaurant for a time of fellowship. Maybe once every few weeks go on an excursion with them to Silver Dollar City or somewhere like that. We have two vans you could use. You could make hospital visits and help meet their needs in other ways. In other words, be a pastor to our seniors in whatever way works out best for them and you.

"I know you are retired," he added, "but this would just be a part-time ministry. Just doing what you are able to do." He smiled, "If you feel up to it, and it if you feel it's the Lord's will, I believe you would be a tremendous help to the seniors and to everyone in our church, and the whole community.

"I know you live in Seattle and have your roots there. If you choose to return there I would certainly understand. However," he spread out his hands to encompass his surroundings, "the people here seem to love you. I'm sure they would welcome you back."

Pastor Ben stood as if to dismiss them. "I'm not expecting you to make a decision right this minute, but think about it and pray about it, and let me know what you decide."

Paul stayed seated for a moment and looked at Laura. Her eyes were wet with tears. He felt a lump form in his throat. "Well," Paul asked, "What do you think, sweetheart?"

She stared at him, a small smile on her face.

"I think I know the answer," Paul answered as he stood. "But we will pray about it and get back with you."

As they drove out of the church parking lot Laura looked over at Paul. "Let's go celebrate at Martha's Café. Unless I miss my guess I think you've already decided to come back. I know I have, if you agree. A great opportunity. A new ministry. Or maybe better said, the return to your first place of ministry."

When Paul nodded, her face lit up with her dimpled smile that still made his heart do flips after almost fifty years. She laid her hand on his shoulder as they drove down the road. "You're not like Jacob, you know, in that you didn't run away from your family because you deceived them. You're not like the man of God who was disobedient and was eaten by a lion.

"You came to Bethel Springs as a young man who answered the call of God. You had some great times and some rough times. But you were obedient and you were faithful through it all. I think that was the key. You came when God said to come. You left when God said your time was up. While you were here you did what God told you to do. Even if you hadn't gotten those accolades the other night, you were not a failure, you were a success here. I've tried to tell you that over the years.

"And," she added with a twinkle in her eyes, "you were obedient to God when He told you whom to marry. Are you still glad you did? I know I certainly am."

Paul leaned over and kissed her on her cheek. "I love you now more than ever. You're the best part of my time in Bethel Springs. You've been faithful to the Lord, too. A wonderful wife and mother and a tremendous asset in our ministry."

They pulled into the parking lot of Martha's Café and stared at the restaurant for just a moment. With the new paint it looked bright and new and fresh in the morning sun. Before they got out of the car Laura took Paul by the hand and looked into his eyes, her smile still in place. "Here we are, ready to begin a new chapter in our lives. Back to the town where it started for you, and back to the place where it happened for us."

Paul looked back at her, returning the smile. "I've been anxious to eat here again, but didn't want to until I could do it with you sitting across the table from me. I find again where that Proverb we like so much does come true."

"Which one is that?"

"The one in chapter three that I memorized as a boy in the King James version: 'Trust in the Lord with all thine heart; and lean not unto thine own understanding. In all thy ways acknowledge him, and he shall direct thy paths'."

"So true." They made their way into Martha's Café and sat at a new round table in approximately the same place where Paul had usually sat fifty years earlier.

A smiling young waitress in blue jeans and a sleeveless white blouse came out of the same swinging door Paul had seen Laura come through so many times before. She placed menus before them, asked what they wanted to drink and said she would be back in a few minutes to take their order.

When she left Laura looked at Paul, a mischievous twinkle in her eyes. "It was here where you kissed me for the first time. Want to try it again, just for old times' sake?"

ABOUT THE AUTHOR

Throughout Owen Wilkie's 45-year career as Assemblies of God pastor turned editor he's written and edited thousands of articles, ads and other writings for dozens of compassion, missions and religious publications. His writings also include family memoirs, books filled with humor and illustrations, biblical commentaries and more. He is the son of missionary parents to Latin America.

His first novel, *Another Mt. Moriah* is available on Amazon.com and Owenwilkie.com.

Owen and his wife, Beverly, live in Battlefield, Missouri, where they raised their two children, Matt and Debbie. Matt and his wife April are parents to Parker and Owen Fisher. Debbie and her husband Scott are parents to Madison, Aidan and Judah. Above even his writings, Owen's faith and family are his greatest joys.

RETURN TO BETHEL SPRINGS

Made in the USA
San Bernardino, CA
03 May 2017